TIMECACHERS

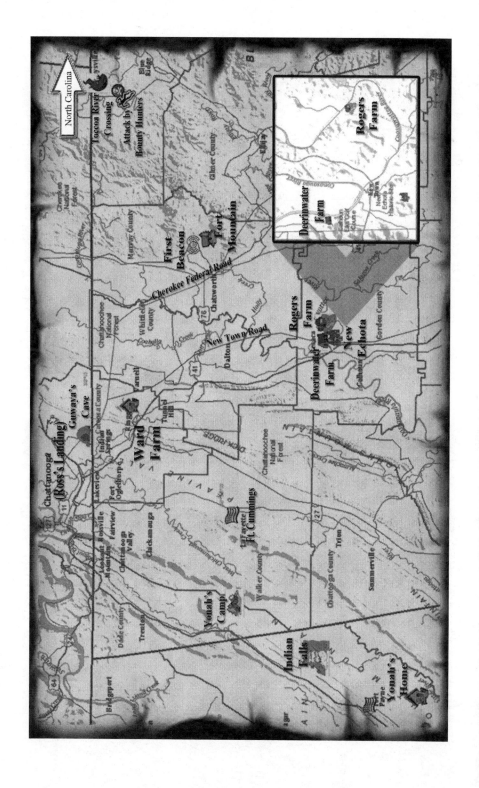

Timecachers

BY
GLENN R. PETRUCCI

Although portions of this novel are derived from real events, all characters and organi-
zations portrayed are products of the author's imagination or are used fictitiously. No
reference to any living person is intended or should be inferred.

Published by ReturnSide, LLC, New Castle, Delaware

ISBN-10: 1466230762
ISBN-13: 978-1466230767
Library of Congress Control Number: 2011915487

For Kathy...

who fills my life with love and my writing with clarity.

Chapter one

Adam shook his head as he looked through the storm door at the rain drenched package. "Crap!" he muttered. "I wish that delivery guy would put the packages under the awning when it's raining." His next thought was that he was probably expecting too much from the sleepy-eyed deliveryman.

Springtime brought frequent rainstorms to Delaware. This year they were a welcome nuisance, a wet promise of warmer weather after a particularly cold winter. And rain was much better than snow.

It was still cold enough outside to form a layer of condensation on the storm door window, the moisture droplets tracing slim, wet tracks in the fog as they dribbled down the glass. Adam used his sleeve to wipe a porthole in the condensation, inspecting the front yard and noticing the thick, pale-green tips of daffodils peeking through the sparse remnants of melting snow; the victors of winter's final battle against the coming of spring. It wouldn't be long before he would have to find time to fire up the lawnmower.

Contrary to the geek stereotype often associated with engineers, Adam Hill led an active lifestyle, was well-groomed, dressed stylishly, and had an athletic build. He didn't consider the pudgy "Dilbert" physique to be a very accurate portrayal of his colleagues. Some of the hardcore gamers who seldom ventured into direct sunlight let themselves become as squishy as gummy bears, but most of the folks in his circle led very active lives and kept in pretty good shape. He believed that staying physically active kept his mind sharp; as much as the mental calisthenics he performed to keep abreast of new technology. Adam spent as much time as he could outdoors—hiking, biking, swimming, and rock-climbing—whatever he could do that would let him replace the glow of his computer monitor with the radiance of sunshine. His preference was for non-competitive activities; while his taller-than-average frame gave him a physical advantage, his easy-going nature could sometimes be a handicap in fiercely competitive sports.

Not that his choice of activities were limited; there were always plenty of invitations to join one outing or another. His swarthy good looks, intelligent conversation, and pleasing mannerisms assured Adam's popularity among his peers. He was more troubled by how often he had to decline their invitations. Finding enough time to spend with his friends was often difficult for the twenty-eight year old business owner.

Covering his head with his shirt, Adam retrieved the soaking wet package and brought it into the house. He wiped away the droplets of water to read the hand-written priority mail label with his name and address, and a return address showing the shipper as *TSO, Inc., Natick, MA.* "At least he brought it to the correct address," Adam conceded. He carried the package to the kitchen, found a handy dishtowel to sop up some of the water, and then used a steak knife to cut through the packing tape. The box hadn't been sitting in the rain long enough to soak through, and the pink Styrofoam peanuts inside appeared to be dry as they spilled out onto the countertop. More peanuts bubbled from the box as he fished out an object about the size of an electric razor. It was wrapped in a pink plastic bag and had the proper ESD cautionary labels required for electrostatic devices.

"They passed the packaging test," he thought. He was always amazed at how many companies failed to use anti-static packing materials to ship electronic devices. "So this is the latest in spaceman navigational devices."

The peculiar phone call came about a week ago. Not that it was unusual for a company he'd never heard of to contact him about testing a new product; most of his business came by word of mouth referrals from development engineers who had used, and appreciated, the service he provided. Adam's company, Overhill Engineering, LLC, specialized in testing microprocessor-based devices, specifically the embedded software that allowed the devices to function. Adam started the company with his former partner, John Overton, a few years ago when the bean-counters at his former employer decided it made good financial sense to eliminate the product test department and have the development engineers perform their own testing. It wasn't long after that misguided pronouncement that the company began having quality issues, especially with the usability of their products. They had learned a hard lesson about the difference between what engineers thought was user friendly and what the typical consumer considered easy to use. The company ultimately had to contract the work back to Adam, paying him a lot more than they used to, benefits notwithstanding.

Having his own company gave him the luxury of choosing which products he wanted to test, and allowed him to offer his services to several other companies. Adam and John had since gone their separate ways, but the business was already established and Adam saw no need to change the company name—a not-very-imaginative combination of their names.

What *was* peculiar about this phone call was the description of the device, and the relatively obscure explanation of its functionality. Adam had received the functional specification the day after he agreed to test the product. Even after his initial scan through the document he wasn't quite sure how to begin the test plan. He was exceptionally technically astute and kept abreast of most emerging technologies, but the covariant space-time operators, infinite-component wave functions, and proper-time Schrödinger equations mentioned in this document went far beyond his understanding of physics.

UAT, User Acceptance Testing, was Overhill Engineering's specialty. The company's principal value-add was having both the technical acumen to understand the complexities of development engineering and still test for LCU. Least Competent User was simply a politically correct term for making sure a highly technical device could be operated by the dumbest person on the planet.

The phone call was from Edward Odan, PhD., president of Time-Space Obversions (TSO), Inc., a greater Boston area engineering company that had been formed by Dr. Odan, in conjunction with MIT's department of physics.

Odan's slight New England accent was just enough to give his voice a scholarly inflection, yet not Bostonian enough to sound haughty or pompous. When Odan spoke, Adam got the feeling he was listening to a college professor, which, in fact, he was.

The company was developing a highly advanced product that promised to be "the next big thing" in handheld navigation devices. "What we are looking for is someone to do the field UAT testing for us," Odan explained. "You see, our engineering group is highly advanced in theory and design, but we need someone with your particular professional and personal background to conduct the user application testing of this product."

"I understand the need for my real-world testing services, but what is it about my personal background that's relevant?" asked Adam.

"Well, for this product we need someone not only familiar with hardware and software testing methodologies, but someone who also has a very diverse aptitude for several types of outdoor adventure activities, you see, including backpacking, orienteering, and rock climbing, as well as survival skills and some practical knowledge of early American history. The background research we conducted on you turned up a good mixture of the types of skills we need for this testing."

Adam thought he'd better carefully scrutinize the personal information he put on his LinkedIn profile from now on. "I'm not sure I understand the need for someone with my outdoors experience, and knowledge of early American history? Do you mean the colonial period?"

"Pre-colonial as well—but don't concern yourself with that at this point. Your historical knowledge could be helpful in analyzing certain peculiar reactions of the device. Your team will be required to conduct most of your testing in remote, rugged, terrestrial areas—wilderness areas in the Southeast to be precise." Odan cleared his throat and changed the subject.

"I'd like to send you the functional specifications to look over and a non-disclosure agreement. I can promise you that this will offer you one of the most unique testing experiences of your career. The details of the test plan will be up to you, but you will need to set aside one full week of testing time in addition to the test plan development. One week of exclusive testing time, and a team of three to four resources with skills similar and complementary to your own. You may choose your own team of course, but they must clear our background check. I can offer you generous compensation--triple your usual fee, in fact, plus reimbursement for any expenses you incur."

Money wasn't the only consideration, although Adam had to admit that such a lucrative contract was attractive, and the timing for access to his best engineers was perfect. He could afford to be selective about the jobs he took, having managed his finances well enough to cover his own basic living expenses for quite a while, but he had been promising his contractors there would be new work coming along for them soon. At present, he was the only fulltime employee of his company. Several of the engineers who contracted to him had inquired about fulltime positions, and he hoped that someday he could offer them permanent jobs.

His extracurricular activities were enjoyable, but they didn't do much to grow his company. He had promised himself at the onset of this venture that it would not become an obsession; he would be selective about which jobs to take and leave plenty of time to enjoy life. He soon discovered that keeping a viable business proved to be more time-consuming than he imagined. Perhaps this opportunity with Dr. Edward Odan of TSO Devices, Inc. would allow him to do a little of both, and give his company the financial boost it needed to hire a few fulltime employees. The project was different than others his company had done, requiring the testing to be performed outside of a laboratory environment, yet it was well within his area of expertise. It certainly promised to be a fun and interesting project!

Chapter two

*A*dam returned Dr. Odan's call the same day he received the functional specification. He had already signed and faxed back the non-disclosure to TSO, Inc., but he needed a follow up for additional details and clarification of their expectations. "The theory, at least what I can understand of it, is fascinating," Adam said into the receiver. "Using the stellar emissions from space to determine navigational positioning is ingenious, Dr. Odan," he stated.

"Call me Ed, please—and the fundamental design is not all that novel," Odan replied. "Man has used stars for determining his position on the planet since the ancient Greeks, and probably even before that. The ingenuity was designing a device that could receive the signals sent out by those heavenly bodies. Our primary 'value-add' for this technology is employing a new discovery, my discovery, of how those star emissions can be received by a micro device. Until now, radio telescopes of tremendous size were required to 'listen' to the stars. By receiving the star signals and syncing them to the time-constant frequency of another heavenly body like a pulsar, we can determine our exact location anywhere on the planet without the need of a supporting satellite system like NAVSTAR or Galileo that global positioning systems use. The technology is basically the same, except we don't need satellites; we use the stars." Odan paused a moment to let Adam absorb the significance of his last statement.

Not getting a response, he elaborated. "One of the weaknesses of the satellite GPS systems is that you can often lose the satellite signals, especially in remote areas and under heavy cover where you really need it the most. The stars are everywhere, always available, and the emissions strong enough so that is not a problem with this device, you see." Another slight pause, then, "In fact, we've also discovered some interesting anomalies that may actually enhance the unit's functionality."

"Anomalies?" asked Adam. The word set off his internal alarm. He'd been doing testing long enough to know that usually meant serious design obstacles, and dealt with enough marketing types who tried to turn bugs into features.

"Not to worry," Ed replied. "Nothing has been discovered that would impede development. The schedule is still on track."

Adam was still skeptical, but he set aside his concern for now and moved on. "How far along in the development phase are you? You sent me a functional spec; have you completed a design specification?"

"We have a working prototype. Of course, the anomalies I mentioned are not part of the original design features. They turned up in our initial design testing. The necessity, at least in part, for engaging you to perform UAT testing is due to those anomalous discoveries."

"Meaningful test results require testing to the design standards," Adam pointed out. "I assume you want me to test the accuracy of your device against a traditional GPS receiver, but I'll need some sort of parameters to determine if you are in range of your design goals."

"Your assumption is only partially correct. We have already verified the accuracy of the positioning, and the testing you will be doing for us will take you beyond the range of the current GPS receivers," Ed answered.

Adam knew that modern GPSr's could receive from multiple satellites, and the ground-based WAAS stations improved the reliability of the system where signals were weak. Some were also augmented by land-based cellphone towers. Most of the receivers, even the consumer hand-held and automobile models, were pretty dependable. Finding places to test without GPS coverage would be a challenge.

"Let me clarify our testing needs further to you. We aren't looking for you to do a typical software or product testing project." Ed said. "More a field alpha-test if you will. It will be most helpful to us to have someone with your background in usability testing to provide feedback in an actual field environment."

"I see," said Adam haltingly, "but I'm pretty sure I won't be able to arrange access to a spacecraft…"

"Of course not," Ed laughed. "We only need your inputs for the land-based navigation, so all of your testing will be earthbound. For your testing parameters we will provide you with a basic testing scenario for you to execute. The scenario will have specific goals for you to accomplish using the device to guide your team. You will determine the details of how to carry out the scenario in your test plan. Since you will be using new technology, your plan will need to be flexible, and allow for impromptu adjustment of your testing strategy. The test results I am most interested in are the experiences you and your team encounter during the testing, you see, not so much the functionality and performance of the device itself. Therefore, it will be essential that you keep extensive notes of the scenario execution."

"We always provide well-documented test results," Adam replied, sounding a bit defensive. Alice Delvecci would be an ideal engineer for this project, he thought. While he enjoyed writing the proposals and test plans, when it came to the tedious recording of every minute detail of test results, no one was better than Alice. She would tirelessly document every step of an executed test procedure and each variation of device response through multiple regression tests. Adam was a good documenter when he had to be, but to him the redundant recording of test results was as mind-numbing as mowing the lawn.

"Undeniably," said Ed. "In fact, your company has produced exemplary test results reports which I have examined in our background search. For this testing project, I should warn you that your engineers will likely have to resort to somewhat more manual note-taking than usual."

Adam had already considered that possibility, since they would be testing in remote areas. However, something in Odan's voice gave him the impression that it was going to be even more challenging than he expected.

"Ed, I'm getting the feeling that the functionality of this device and the details of the anomalies are something we need to discuss in more depth. I admit that the project is intriguing, and I am most definitely interested, but I don't believe it will benefit either of us if I'm not adequately prepared to test your device. Since you already have a prototype, I assume you will want me to begin my testing soon. I still have to put together a test plan and select the most appropriate of my engineering resources for the team."

"Fair enough, Adam. You will need to prepare and select your personnel quite carefully for this project, although it may require a somewhat different approach than your usual evaluation. You will have to consider physical skills as well as technical aptitude. You will also need a team that can react quickly to unplanned events and stay composed when put into unfamiliar situations.

"As for the device's functionality, let me begin with a quick refresher of the evolution of navigational technology.

"As you are no doubt aware, celestial navigation and dead reckoning techniques have been in use for centuries. By dividing the earth using lines equally spaced running parallel to the equator, and then again with lines running at right angles to the equator, we devise a grid system known as latitude and longitude. If a navigator can determine his latitude and longitude, you see, he will know exactly where on the planet he is.

"By using Polaris, the North Star, determining latitude in the northern hemisphere is a simple matter of measuring the angle of the horizon to the North Star. That is because Polaris appears to be a stationary star that never varies more than one degree from the celestial North Pole. So Polaris is directly overhead at the North Pole, and directly on the horizon at the equator. The basic function of a sextant is to measure that angle. If a navigator measures the angle of the North Star and finds it to be ten degrees from the horizon, then he knows he is somewhere on a circle around the earth at ten degrees of geographic north latitude. When the angle is thirty-three degrees of difference to the horizon he is at north latitude thirty-three, and so on. It gets a little more complicated if you are in the southern hemisphere. Because Polaris is not visible there, the navigator must use the Southern Cross, or Crux, to calculate latitude, but the concept is basically the same. You can see that many things can cause issues using this method, since the stars are only visible at night and clouds can block your view, but it worked well when the conditions were right. Eventually other methods of determining latitude were discovered that could be used in the daytime.

"Now then, longitude was quite a different navigational problem. The lines of longitude are not equally spaced due to the curvature of the earth, you see. The closer you are to the poles, the closer the lines of longitude become. Coupled with the fact that the earth is always rotating, finding your longitude becomes quite complicated, especially if you are also in motion, such as in a sailing ship. Early navigators like Columbus had to rely on both celestial navigation and dead reckoning. Dead reckoning, in very simple terms, is using one or more fixed objects whose positions you know to determine where you are. For example, you can find your way back to your car in the mall parking lot if you take note of the number on the pole where you parked, as long as you can see the pole. A navigator can expand on this concept by taking a fix on his position, and keeping track of the speed and time he has been traveling. Using these techniques nautical navigators could get a fairly accurate idea of where they were longitudinally, but you can imagine the difficulties of determining your speed in a sailing ship on the open sea and going for days without site of any landmarks.

"Calculating longitude is what makes accurate time measurement necessary. The longitude of a point can be determined by calculating the time difference between the time at the location of the point and another known time, such as Greenwich, England, the location of zero degrees longitude. Since there are twenty-four hours in a day and 360 degrees in a circle, the sun moves across the sky fifteen degrees every hour. So if the time the navigator is in is three hours ahead of Greenwich, then that person is able to determine he is near forty-five degrees longitude (3 hours × 15° per hour = 45°) by observing the position of the sun.

"For many years, having an accurate source of time on board a ship was a major problem. Because the clocks at that time worked by using a pendulum, it was impossible to install a clock on a pitching and rolling ship. The invention of the chronometer solved the problem of ships having an accurate source of time measurement, making an accurate determination of longitude aboard ship possible. If the sun was at its zenith (directly overhead) and your chronometer said the time was three o'clock, you knew the time was three hours earlier at your present location.

"So far I have been discussing a geodetic, or earth-based navigational system. When we plot a point such as a star or planet in space from the earth, we have to extend the coordinate system to include the celestial sphere. If you imagine space as a hollow sphere with earth at its center, we can still map out points on the inside of that sphere using a coordinate system. Celestial latitude lines are called declination, and longitude becomes right ascension. We also have to take the distance from earth into consideration, which is done using Astronomical Units.

"Now then, imagine the complexities of astronomical navigation for space travel, considering the multi-dimensional aspect of ship movement through space and time. With so many moving planets, gravitational forces, and the expanding universe, an astronomical navigator has many variables to keep track of. Technically, he is pretty much back in the time of Columbus. Now imagine how significant a device that is not dependent on man-made satellites would be to a space traveler. A device that can receive signals from the stars and planets themselves!

"We began this development project hoping that the final result would culminate in just such a device. We had in fact, already discovered the ground-breaking micro-technology needed to intercept the transmissions from the stars, but our early work was confounded by the same issue that plagued the early nautical navigators—time measurement. When measuring speed and distance of objects in motion, the point from which the measurement is taken is critical. You may have heard of a phenomenon known as time dilation?"

"Something to do with Einstein's Theory of Relativity about how a clock runs slower when it is moving," Adam answered. "Isn't that just a theory, though? I thought that the effect was pretty insignificant."

"On the contrary, Adam, it is most significant. Even our current Global Positioning Systems must account for time dilation by constantly making adjustments to the satellite's onboard clocks so they match the clocks here on earth. If they did not, in fact, the most accurate a GPS receiver could get would be more than fifty feet from any particular point."

"I'm not sure I understand that," said Adam. "Doesn't the calculation just involve the amount of time it takes the signal to get from the satellite to the receiver? Not much time at the speed of light."

"You also have to consider the objects frame of reference to each other. Even though many navigational satellites are geostationary, they are still moving through space, as is the earth and the navigator. The motion of all those objects must be taken into account. Imagine measuring the amount of time it takes a beam of light to travel between two mirrors. We know the speed of light and the distance between the mirrors, so figuring out the time of travel is simple. If you were to place the two mirrors on railroad cars parallel to each other and traveling at the same speed, your measurement when taken from one of the moving cars would be the same as it was when the mirrors were stationary. However, if you were to measure from a non-moving location your result would be different. The beam of light, relative to you, would have traveled farther in the same amount of time, you see, because you would have observed the forward motion of the beam as the trains moved forward. This is known as the Lorentz transformations, which has to do with how the coordinates of moving objects slide through space.

"Earth navigational time is calculated easily enough even taking time dilation into account, but in space time no longer follows our earthly rules. Other factors such as gravitational time dilation come into play, and the curvature of space hampers the calculation of space-time just as the curvature of the earth hampered the calculation of longitude. Due to the Lorentz transformations, our calculations required the use of advanced physics techniques such as extended Lagrangian and Hamiltonian methods that treat time as a transformable coordinate, rather than as the universal time parameter of traditional Newtonian physics. In celestial navigation, you see, time is allowed to transform, so the Lorentz transformation of special relativity must be considered in the equations. Put simply, the algorithms hardcoded into this device involve some very complex formulas.

"We also required a selectable reference for time synchronization. During the course of searching for solutions to our time measurement issues, we determined that it was possible to alter the time-grid system of the device by syncing its 'internal clock' if you will, on a selectable celestial body, much like one would change the coordinate system in a conventional hand-held GPS receiver. The selectable time-source could be a neutron star such as a pulsar or black hole whose radio emissions reflect the heartbeat of their galaxy. These neutron star emissions would accommodate the space navigator who must transverse the intergalactic time boundaries by clocking at the appropriate frequencies. In fact, when we began testing the device using the alternate time-grid systems, we also began to record the anomalies I mentioned previously.

"When a person is earthbound his internal clock is synced with earth-time, his frame of reference, so that time appears to pass the same way, more or less, for each person. In space, the human clock will be relative to the particular time system that the person is in since that becomes his new frame of time reference. However, when the device is synced to an alternate time source by an earth-bound individual, the disparity between the two frequencies causes a time-variant field to be generated. The field becomes a sort of 'bulge' in the time fabric, through which the individual can now navigate. Furthermore, this 'time-bulge' appears to emit a signal of its own. We made enhancements to the receiver logic in the device to decode the bulge signals, which appear to be 'beacons' indicating a path to particular places and times where ripples in the time-fabric appear. The device is able to track on the beacons, using them much like a traditional GPS receiver would use a waypoint to plot a route to a particular set of coordinates."

Adam was beginning to doubt his qualifications for this testing project. Complex physics was beyond his expertise, and he wondered if Odan was under some misapprehension about his credentials. Still, he was intrigued by the project and held back from expressing his reservations for the moment. It certainly wouldn't be the first time he had tested a device that employed technology that stretched his knowledge. It wasn't necessary to have a complete understanding of how a device is engineered to be able to effectively test it. In fact, sometimes it was a benefit to be a little fuzzy about the design elements. He prodded Odan for more details. "Just where would following one of these beacons lead you?"

"Well, that is one of the things we would like you to find out, Adam. We have been able to determine that the source of the signals are from the disparity between the two time frequencies, but not exactly what is causing them, or if they really mean anything at all. We are looking for feedback strictly as an end-user, you see. From your testing, we would like to learn several things. Actual field performance as a handheld navigation device is foremost. We are also looking for input about the device's ease of use and dependability under actual field conditions. By plotting to one of the time beacons, you will also provide us with feedback about those particular anomalies. That part of your testing may be the most nebulous, since we don't really know if the anomalies have any importance at all, or if there is anything for you to observe about them. Basically, we are asking you to go to one of the anomalies and see if there is anything there.

"The initial scenario we have devised will require you to follow a time beacon with a particularly strong signal. The beacon is located in the southeastern U.S., somewhere in northwestern Georgia, so your team will need to begin field testing the LANav from there."

"LANav?" asked Adam.

"Lorentz-Astrophysical Navigation," Ed replied.

"Wow. I guess you folks don't have a marketing department yet, eh Doc?"

Chapter three

ost days Alice Delvecci just grabbed a sandwich from the cafeteria and worked through her lunch, but today she was looking forward to getting out of the office for a while. She was well-known for having a healthy appetite, and her friends always asked her how she could eat so much and keep her trim figure. She usually answered with a shrug, which was easier than explaining her routine of rigorous exercise and program of nutritional balance. It annoyed her to be asked questions that should be common sense, but kept her irritation to herself—at least most of the time. It seldom happened, but anyone who had experienced one of Alice's temper flares and the rage she was capable of projecting through her piercing blue eyes had no desire to repeat the experience. Usually her temperament was softly feminine, with only a hint of the intensity she held in reserve; a subtle reminder to those who may be foolish enough to push her too far.

At work, she always conducted herself professionally. She was pleasant and approachable to her coworkers, cheerfully accepting assignments and graciously offering clever input when required. She consciously avoided being over friendly, avoiding the inevitable attention of the office womanizers wanting only to flirt with a young, attractive blonde.

Alice twisted a strand of her hair as she considered her conversation with Adam earlier that morning. He called to let her know the LANav device had arrived, and to ask if she could break away for lunch to take a look. Her current assignment at OSI, Inc. was nearing completion, so she was happy when he requested her to work on a new project. Alice wasn't quite sure what to make of Adam's project. Testing a navigational device was fine enough, but one that received signals from the stars and planets was a bit over the top. Adam convinced her that the new project would not only be well-paid, but fun, and the season was perfect for an outdoor project. Software test engineering seldom presented an opportunity to see more than the walls of a cubicle. If nothing else, the projects she worked on for Adam were enjoyable; everyone got along well, and the easygoing and informal yet professional attitude of the teams he put together suited her. She could always count on Adam for interesting work and the other team members usually provided plenty of amusement.

Alice had been working as an employee at OSI, Inc. along with Adam, when the decision was made to eliminate the software testing department. Since then OSI had given both of them plenty of contract work paying much more than they would have earned as employees, plus the opportunity to work on projects for other companies as well.

The only member of the original testing group still working as a permanent employee of OSI was Dana Natsu. Dana was a wiry Asian-American who had an abundance of energy and a penchant for corporate politics. He was not as technically astute as the rest of the group, and functioned as the project manager for the software quality department. When the company decided to eliminate the software quality assurance engineers, they kept Dana in place to coordinate the testing schedules for the development engineers and the contractors. When the group was internal, things ran pretty smoothly. Dana's primary function was to attend the meetings with management and relay the progress of the testing activities. He also maintained the schedule, which was usually dictated by management and seldom reflected an accurate assessment of task times. Dana Natsu was notorious for always accepting whatever tasks and timelines management set in place, whether they were achievable or not, earning him the nickname "Nutso" among the test engineers. Dana wasn't incompetent, although he tended to be obsequious and naïve. He was often the object of ridicule by the engineers, even though most of the time he wasn't aware of it. Actually, the team appreciated that Dana preferred dealing with management, keeping them free for more constructive work, even if they would never admit it. Dana was now the company's liaison to outside contractors such as Alice and Adam.

Alice stared through her own reflection in the large glass windows of the lobby, where she sat waiting for Adam, watching the yellow forsythias shed crystal water drops onto the shiny, still-wet blacktop. The streaks of golden sunlight filtering through the receding clouds had brightened the day considerably. The rain had finally passed, lasting just long enough to wash away the last few remnants of dirty snow piles the plows had shoved into the corners of the parking lot. Her contemplation of the corporate landscaping was abruptly interrupted as Adam's GMC Yukon splashed into the circular drop-off spot at the building entrance. Stirred from her thoughts, she rose, tossed her long, blonde hair over her shoulder, and pushed through the immense glass doors of the opulent entrance vestibule. In spite of the bright sun, the temperature was barely in the low fifties. The crisp, fresh air felt refreshing after hours in the recycled air of OSI.

"How are things in the corporate world?" Adam asked through the smoothly descending car window.

"Stifling, as usual," she replied.

"Has Nutso scheduled your breaks out of existence? You're not going to catch a ration from him for not working through lunch, are you?"

"Since when does he have a clue about how long it takes to do anything? Anyway, he's off this afternoon to go on a geocaching outing with his buddies. Two carloads of camo-clad pseudo-geeks following their GPSr's from one light post to the next for twelve hours."

"Yeah," Adam chuckled, "racing each other to be first to find a Tupperware container. At least you should have a productive afternoon without Nutso around to interrupt. I know you are anxious to finish off this project."

"Right now I'd like to finish off a sandwich. Let's grab some chow while you show me this space compass gizmo."

"That's the plan. Tom and Sal are meeting us later at Poet's," Adam said. "We can get something there."

"Poet's is fine with me. I'm not picky, especially when you're buying," she said with a grin. Alice hopped in to the passenger seat, her jeans whispering as they slid across the leather upholstery. The light, fragrant scent of her perfume pleasantly comingled with the familiar electronic smell Adam's vehicle always seemed to have.

Adam steered the Yukon in the direction of Dead Poets, a popular lunch spot for the corporate crowd. It was already past the usual lunch hour, so there were plenty of open parking spots when they pulled into Poets. Adam grabbed the pink electrostatic bag containing the LANav and some documents as they headed in. Upon entering, they caught the eye of the waitress who gave them a quick wave and motioned for them to take any one of the several open tables.

Dead Poets restaurant had previously been a greasy little place called Mom's Luncheonette until Delaware's corporate-friendly taxes enticed many large financial and pharmaceutical companies to move their headquarters to the state. When folks began flocking to Delaware for the jobs, the name was upgraded along with the décor and menu to be more attractive to the professional crowd. The place's claim to fame was that it served many of the cast and crew of the movie "Dead Poets Society" which was filmed in the area back in the late eighties. The stainless steel and red vinyl seat covers were gone, replaced with heavily polyurethaned yellow oak tables, polyester seat covers, and ceiling fans, along with strategically placed movie photos of Robin Williams, Ethan Hawke, and Peter Weir. The diner was well-lit and served delicious food, so it managed to avoid the fate of the many small local establishments put out of business by the fast food mega-chains that cropped up.

They slid into a nearby booth, and the waitress quickly appeared with menus in hand. "Hi, guys. Do you need a menu or do you know what you want?" She recognized them as regulars, but didn't know their names. Delaware folks tend to have a friendly, southern manner, but not so annoyingly friendly as to intrude into each other's personal business. They declined the menus, ordering from memory, and let her know that two more would be joining them.

"So let me see this thing before Sal gets here and breaks it," Alice said.

Adam removed the TSO LANav from its protective bag and slid it across the table for Alice to examine. Until today, no one on the team except Adam had gotten any hands-on time with the LANav. Adam was convinced he had selected the right group for the project, but only Alice had definitely committed so far. He hoped to get a solid confirmation from the other two engineers at this meeting.

The device measured about three inches by five inches, was nearly two inches thick and enclosed in a brushed aluminum case. There was an LCD screen that occupied nearly three-quarters of the unit's face, and the top edge of the device extended at a thirty degree angle into a glass-covered triangular wedge, adding another inch to its dimensions. Just above the LCD screen was a small, round indentation, with holes like the speaker on a cell phone, and a small round hole near the bottom. The bottom edge had a small sliding door, covering what appeared to be a micro-USB connector, and the back of the case had another round array of holes, about the size of a quarter. On the left-hand side there was a single button.

Alice noted the thickness of the device and its hefty weight. "Not exactly streamline, is it? No mistaking it for an iPad."

"Probably ten times the circuitry of a pad computer. Multi-layered, of course."

"What sort of power source? Double-A batteries?"

"That glass wedge extending from the top is a solar cell that charges an ultra-capacitive barium-titanate based battery. It's supposed to be able to out-perform traditional batteries by a factor of ten. The wedge also houses the antenna circuitry. For all the bleeding-edge technology TSO has packed into it, it's amazingly small."

Alice shrugged acquiescence but continued with her critical examination. "Only one button—the power switch? Does the documentation give us more detail about the user interface?"

"A little, but the LCD screen is a touch screen, so the functionality will be controlled by the software and the LCD will indicate where to touch, depending on the current application the device is running. And yes, the button is a power switch, or more accurately a stand-by switch, since the device is always on. The button just enables the touch screen and turns on the backlight. There's a USB connector on the bottom, but that's only for inputting maps and waypoints, and updating the firmware," Adam explained. "It may be redundant, since it has its own proprietary communication protocols built-in. Firmware upgrades, waypoints, and overlay maps can be sent to the unit directly from TSO. In a terrestrial application, or anywhere you can access a communications satellite, it has sat-phone capabilities for voice and data, which is the reason for the speaker and microphone. You can even do SMS text messaging."

Alice snickered. "Handy. So astronauts can text each other while they're flying between planets, huh? I can imagine the messages—OMG IM N SPACE RU2? Seriously, this unit looks like it's permanently sealed. I take it we aren't going to be doing any quality testing of the components or serviceability?"

"No, we aren't. We are doing field user application testing only, and recording our user experiences. Ed Odan supplied the testing scenario and wants some feedback on what might be causing the anomalies they've noticed, but other than that it's all dumb-user testing. The technology is just barely beyond theory, so many of the components are proprietary. No established standards to test against."

"Usually that's pretty boring stuff, just doing the UAT part. Since you took the job, I assume it's not going to be typical end-user testing."

"It's certainly going to be different than any other testing we've ever done. I already mentioned to you that we'll be working in remote areas of the country; as you know, the scenario requires us to travel to Georgia. We're going to be the first ever to use this device. It has the potential to replace nearly every current form of electronic navigation. This could be an opportunity to be part of something history-making, not to mention the marketing value it will give our testing services."

"Now you're starting to sound like our old pal John Overton." Alice smirked, anticipating Adam's reaction to her jibe.

He rose to the bait. "Don't even go there. John would take on any project we could do for a buck. I'd like to grow the company for the benefit of us all, but there are limits. You know my philosophy is to offer a quality service that we can expect to charge for accordingly. I think this contract will give us the credibility to begin testing for more of the emerging technology companies, getting more interesting assignments rather than just testing to see if the next MP3 player is easy enough for junior to use. More of the stuff you, I, and the others really want to spend our time doing."

"I'm all for that," Alice agreed. "It would be great to only work on the things we enjoy. Not sure if that's possible, but it sounds great. It also suits me to be working outside for a while. Traipsing around in the mountains of Georgia instead of sitting in some cubicle or my home office sounds wonderful, almost more like a vacation."

"Don't expect to get off too easy, Alice. I'm with you as far as enjoying working outdoors, but this customer wants very detailed notes on our user experience, and I'm counting on you to put all our documentation together for them into a professional report. Can you imagine if they got a look at Sal's notes? 'Tried it; broke it. Went hiking and used a compass instead.'"

"Ha! That's Sal alright. Don't worry; I'm used to translating Sal-speak into a professional report."

The food orders arrived, and Adam and Alice discussed the challenges of conducting their testing in remote locations. Being without power for over a week would mean that they would have to resort to manual note taking and transcribe them when they returned. They were also both going to have to break out their camping gear, which needed to be checked out after being stored away for the winter. They were discussing whether or not they would need to pack any cold weather gear for this time of year in Georgia when they heard Sal's voice boom at them as he and Tom entered the restaurant. "Greetings, fellow space-travelers! When do we blast-off for Appalachian galaxy?"

Adam chuckled. "More like the Chattahoochee constellation."

Chapter four

*S*alvador Lolliman was a wiry, energetic, and talkative engineering technician. A native of Camden, New Jersey, he conformed to the stereotype of a loud, crass, and short-tempered Jersey urbanite. His short stature, barely five foot five, and a receding hairline thirty years beyond his twenty-three years, caused Sal to endure more than his share of harassment which he learned to counter by preemptive attack. He had the aggressiveness of a Boston Terrier, the tiny canine who shows no fear even when confronting dogs several times his size. Sal would say anything to anyone. To him, tact and political correctness were unknown concepts. Fortunately, no matter how many inappropriate or off-color jokes he told, or how many times he flew into a rage at someone for no good reason, he could project enough positive energy to power a healthy amount of charisma. Sal had an extremely sharp mind, and could quickly comprehend even some of the most complex technology. Regrettably, he was not a details man, losing interest with mundane tasks, which prevented him from becoming a truly exceptional engineer. Nevertheless, Adam recognized his agile mind had a lot to offer the team, and his exuberant personality was contagious to the others in the group, including Adam. Things never got boring when Sal was around, whether he was ripping off lousy jokes or ripping off some poor guy's head for disagreeing with him.

Tom Woody was almost the exact opposite. He epitomized single-mindedness, and would endlessly analyze the details of a project until no facet remained unexplored, with the stoic resolve of a spider relentlessly reweaving its web each day. Smalltalk did not come as easily to Tom; he was a thinker, a southern gentleman, a modern Thomas Jefferson. He usually sat quietly through engineering meetings, tapping his briar pipe in contemplation until he was asked for details about whatever project he was currently working on. Everyone who knew Tom knew not to do that unless they were prepared to spend hours listening to a highly technical monologue, eloquently articulated in his dulcet, Virginia voice.

Tom had spent many years as a software engineer until he became disgruntled with what he called the "assembly line" conditions that programmers now worked under. He decided his talents would be better put to use fleshing out software bugs than cranking out code. Adam knew Tom's engineering talents were more than adequate for this project. He also knew Tom was an accomplished backpacker and rock climber, had a keen interest in American history, and had even had a few papers published on several historical topics. It didn't surprise Adam that Tom's background got such a positive reaction from Ed Odan.

As they slid into the booth, Sal winked at the waitress and barked his order. "Cuppa Joe. Black, extra sweet, Sugar."

"Anything for you, hon?" she asked Tom.

"Just water, thank you, ma'am."

Once the greetings were exchanged and everyone had a chance to get a good look at the LANav, Adam began to ease into discussing the device's capabilities. Initially, he downplayed the anomalies, certain that Tom and Sal would insist on hearing more about them. For now though, he did not want the conversation to get sidetracked by their curiosity. Both Tom and Sal had tentatively committed to being part of the project and he did not want them needlessly doubting their decision. Everyone in the team was senior enough to realize that checking out undocumented functionality went way beyond the scope of a typical testing scenario. It amounted to research, and the team would know that the demands put on them could be excessive. As professionals, they had to be aware of the work requirements before committing to a project. It was important for independent contractors to budget their time to make a decent living. On the other hand, they were all highly interested in breakthrough technology, and Adam hoped that the innovation of this device would stimulate their curiosity enough to compensate for the additional workload.

Adam began, "The standard part of this testing will be a field test of the device's functionality, so we will begin by conducting a set of navigational exercises and record how well, or how badly, the TSO LANav performs. In this case, our testing script is to perform end user activities that require us to plot a course to preselected landmarks in the national forest. We will also use a traditional GPSr, compass, and topographical maps to compare our actual location to the LANav. Once we are on site, we will select a few additional locations where our GPSr's don't perform very well and see if the LANav will work. Finding the GPSr dead spots should be easy in that part of the country with so much overhead foliage in early spring. Since we only have one device, we will do all the testing as a group, but we will have to split up to scout out the GPSr dead zones. Tom, you are probably the best orienteer of the group, so we will use your expertise to plot out some points using compass and topographic maps."

Adam paused, carefully choosing the words he would use to bring up the subject of the LANav's anomalies. "I briefly mentioned the stray signals that Dr. Odan wants us to evaluate. After the standard testing is completed, we will begin to conduct some research into these anomaly beacons. This part is not scripted, since we don't really know what to expect." No one objected, but all three team members shot Adam questioning stares, expecting him to elaborate.

"I know you all are dying to know more about these beacons," Adam said, "but there really isn't a whole lot more to tell you. Ed has asked that we investigate following one of the anomalous beacons and give him a report on what we find, and how the device reacts while tracking the beacon."

"Just what may I ask is he expecting us to find?" Tom asked. His cottony, Virginia accent had a trace of suspicion.

Adam had anticipated Tom's reaction. If anyone was going to question this part of the testing, it would be Tom. "I'm not sure he has any particular expectations. They made a few modifications to enhance the device's ability to track them, but the anomalies could be nothing more than some kind of static or noise."

"Certainly they wouldn't have committed engineering resources to add the functionality to track these beacons without some idea of what they are." He was aware of the budget constraints most engineering groups must work within. It was very unlikely the designers had not considered what the return on their investment would be.

"You're right, Tom, but keep in mind that most of the developers on this project are used to working in an academic environment rather than a commercial one, so they might more readily agree to development work that has no apparent commercial application. They're used to the freedom of conducting pure research. Their curiosity was piqued enough for Dr. Odan to commit resources to the additional development effort."

"What the heck would appeal to a bunch of egghead academic dudes from MIT?" asked Sal. "Is it going to lead us to a cornucopia of pocket protectors?" He winced when Alice gave him a kick under the table. "Ow! Hey, knock it off, woman; that hurt!"

Adam ignored the disruption and continued. "Odan said they suspected that the beacons may be caused by some sort of disturbance that occurred at some time. He wanted some of the testing team members to be knowledgeable in the geology and history of the area. Could be magnetic materials were unearthed by mining activity or something along those lines. Once we follow the beacon, we'll know what's there, and maybe we can determine what is so special about the spot."

Tom stroked his close-cropped beard as he processed Adam's statement. "Hmm, now why couldn't they just plot out the origin of the beacon using topographical maps or satellite imagery to see what's there?"

"They have, and came up with nothing that would account for the anomalies. And apparently the beacons are not just a single point, but a series of points. There is a strong, initial point, followed by a series of weaker, branching beacons, almost like a child's 'follow the numbers' drawing. Maybe 'point two' in the drawing will become stronger once we get to point one so we can follow the numbers."

"Dang," said Sal, "and wind up with a picture of the Easter Bunny? Or better yet, a map to the girl's shower room at MIT! Awesome! My dreams come true!"

"Aw, how cute. I didn't know you still believed in the Easter Bunny, Sal," Alice goaded.

"I'm talkin' honeys, not bunnies, funny girl."

"Anyway," Adam tried to get back to a serious discussion. "Ed simply wants us to follow the beacons as far as possible and provide him with some feedback about what we encounter. Most likely a dead end, but I'm looking forward to the back-country hiking and climbing in the mountains of Georgia, so even a dead end won't be a total loss. At least not as far as I'm concerned."

"Hang on just a darn minute, dude," said Sal. "Part of the testing is going to be using a hand-held navigation device and following it to some point to discover what's there? This is starting to sound a lot like geocaching. I don't know how excited I can get about testing a new device for the kiddie-cachers to use for finding a box of McToys in the woods."

They were all familiar with the geocaching game. The basic concept of the game is that someone hides a box of stuff in the woods somewhere, publishes the coordinates on the web, and the "players" use a GPSr to try to find it. The box is usually a metal, weather-tight, army-surplus ammunition can with a log book inside for the finders to record their visit and also may contain a few items to trade. The boxes are placed in somewhat hard-to-reach places so that finding them presents a challenge—either a long hike or climb to get to the spot. Avid hikers and climbers would usually have a GPSr with them, so geocaching can add some extra fun to a long hike. In the beginning the geocaching community was small, and finding the cache was done clandestinely so others wouldn't find and remove the boxes, not knowing what they were there for. As the price of hand-held GPS receivers declined, making them affordable to more people, geocaching caught on as a popular game for novice hikers, kids, and a fun family activity. Also, the commercialization of the game by some web developers changed it from an activity for hardcore outdoor enthusiasts to a hide-and-seek pastime for the masses. This was good business for the GPSr manufacturers and web developers, but the plethora of geocaches diminished the appeal of geocaching to the more athletic outdoorsman. Nowadays most caches were hidden in easy-to-get-to spots in a tiny container like a film can or pill bottle, and a typical cache hiding place today was under the skirting of a lamp post in a shopping center parking lot. There were still some challenging caches being placed, but the objective of most new cachers was to find as many caches as possible. The website encouraged this by posting the number of cache finds each person had, so the higher the number, the more status they acquired. The result was an excess of easily found caches and lots of geocachers driving around trying to log as many caches as possible.

"If it were a geocaching test, I'd be talking to Nutso Dana, not you guys," Adam replied.

"Bunch of nitwits wandering around mall parking lots looking for an Altoids® tin," Sal said. "Most of 'em couldn't find their butts with both hands and an anatomy chart."

Sal knew that Dana was still very much into geocaching, almost to the point of obsession. He and Dana had a competitive relationship, and they never missed an opportunity to take a shot at each other. Before the shakeup at OSI, the two often geocached together, although it seemed they spent more time arguing than caching. He and Dana remained friends, but clashed constantly, and Sal was usually vocal about his disagreements with Dana.

Sal was still the most active geocacher of the team, whether he admitted it or not, although he had much less time for the game now that he worked as a contractor. Sal and Dana still got together for the occasional caching trip, but that didn't prevent Sal from criticizing Dana's obsession with the hobby. Sal's opinion was that a serious geocacher should only do challenging caches, while Dana did them all, challenging or not. The disparity of style provided fresh quarrelling material, which comprised the essence of their relationship.

"I seem to recall you doing quite a bit of geocaching yourself, Sal," said Alice.

"Yeah, but the ones I did took a little bit of intelligence to find."

"Good thing they only took a little bit," Alice countered.

"In a way, part of the testing is a little like geocaching," Adam said, before Sal had a chance to come back with a rejoinder. "We don't know exactly where following the beacon will lead. Maybe to nothing at all, but I'm certain we aren't going to be led to an ammo can or a lamp post. As far as we know, the beacons are not coming from any manmade source. We may be taken to a natural phenomenon of some sort."

"Awesome, dude. Or maybe ancient geocaches placed by aliens centuries ago," said Sal.

"More likely," said Tom, "the anomalies are caused by an aberration in the time reference that the device uses for synchronization. My guess is that there will be nothing physical for us to find."

Adam agreed with Tom's opinion. Still, his natural curiosity made him anxious to find out what was causing the anomalies, even if it was improbable that they would find anything of significance. Just as with geocaching, the prospect of finding a unique prize encouraged people to dig through the ammo box, regardless of how many times they had been disappointed by finding nothing worthwhile.

Once again Adam brought the conversation back to business. "You guys are on board for this project, correct?" he asked Tom and Sal, getting nods of agreement from both. "Great! I have the preliminary test plan completed, which I will email to Alice today to go over and add in any extra details. Alice, if you will finish that up and email the final document out to the entire team for review, we should be set to go. I'll reserve the tickets for all of us leaving one week from today from Philly International to Atlanta, Georgia. From there, we'll rent an SUV large enough to carry all of us and our gear and head out to Chattahoochee National Forest. That's where we'll be executing the test scripts, so I'd suggest you all spend some time on Google Earth to familiarize yourself with the area. I have hardcopies of the topographic maps of the area and everything else we need for traditional orienteering. You should bring along your own handheld GPS receiver, too. I've made copies of the TSO LANav documentation for each of you to look over. We can get together once again before we leave if necessary, but I believe we can handle everything through email and over the phone."

Adam was happy to have their commitment and relieved that no one expressed any serious doubts about the project. He would spend the rest of the week getting ready for the trip and scrutinizing the final test plans. He wrapped up the meeting, settled the check, and headed for the Yukon with Alice to drive her back to OSI. As they were heading out the door, he could hear Sal in the background, singing his best Alan Jackson "Way down yonder in Chattahoochee…"

Chapter five

I f they had not been so busy preparing for their trip, the team would have observed the dramatic changes brought on by the warming weather. The stark branches of the bare trees had burst with pear-green buds, and vibrant yellow blossoms of daffodils and forsythias transformed the grey winter landscape to a colorful springtime setting. Delicately slender blades of grass sprouted on the lawns that had been mostly dry and hay-brown only a week before.

Adam always enjoyed the spring metamorphosis. This year it had passed him by mostly unnoticed. The hectic preparations for the trip to Georgia made the week pass quickly, and he was feeling the pressure of the rapidly approaching start date. He was usually unruffled about executing a test plan, but this scenario was different from any other project they had ever done before. His anxiety was compounded by the fact that they would be conducting the testing remotely, and he was determined not to overlook anything. If this project ran smoothly, it could potentially open doors to many new business opportunities for him and his team.

He made adjustments to their packing list as he discussed the project in detail with his team. They were beginning to realize the complex logistics of the project. Even Sal, whose first concern was if he could check a case of beer as baggage, took on a more thoughtful tone with several relevant suggestions.

Adam felt much less overwhelmed once Alice took on the task of consolidating everyone's packing list into a single inventory, ensuring nothing would be duplicated or forgotten. Tom recorded the measurements of all the equipment and personal belongings so they would know exactly how much cargo space was required. Adam was proud of the team he had assembled. He was certain he had selected the best resources for the project. They might appear to be overly fun-loving and high-spirited to some, but Adam knew that each could be counted on when they were needed the most.

The equipment was gathered at Tom Woody's house for him to finish the measurements and finalize the packing. The others would only have to bring their personal gear in a single carry-on to the airport. Everyone had been traveling long enough to know it would make check-in smoother by shipping all their gear as cargo and only bringing a small carry-on with them.

Adam and Tom arranged for the local airport shuttle service to carry them and all the gear, while Alice and Sal would be meeting them at the Philly terminal. They dropped off the bulky ruggedized packing crates with the air cargo handlers, and had just entered the security queue to get to the gate when Alice and Sal arrived. They heard their familiar voices echoing over the constant drone of airport background noise as they approached the queue.

"I do believe the other two members of our team have arrived," said Tom, nodding his head in the direction of Alice's reverberating voice.

"I told you we had plenty of time to get here, Sal. You did NOT need to drive like you were at Dover Speedway. Those poor folks you cut off are probably still shaking!" Alice's voice echoed through the terminal as they approached.

"Serves them right. They were poking along in the left lane. Besides, those dudes were from out of state. Somewhere down south. Why the heck is it every car I see with southern plates is poking along in the fast lane? Don't they know what a passing lane is for down there?"

"Oh, hush. Just because they were from out-of-state didn't mean you had to cut them off. How would you like it if they treated you like that when you were driving in their state, just because you have New Jersey plates?"

"What the heck would I be doing in the south? Buying a cow? If I need beef I'll order it from a menu!"

"For heaven's sake, it's impossible to hold a rational conversation with you. I should have driven myself, anyway. I knew the ride was going to be like something from Grand Theft Auto. Honestly, I don't know why I agreed to let you drive me here."

"Because you're too cheap to pay the parking fee, that's why," he answered.

Adam and Tom shared a smile, knowing what a hair-raising adventure being Sal's passenger could be. They also knew that in spite of the aggressive driving habits, riding with Sal was a lot safer than riding with most people. At least he was an attentive driver.

"Hi guys," Adam said. "You can relax now. You made it safely and in plenty of time."

At the gate, Adam, Tom, and Alice passed through the airport security check without difficulty. Sal, as usual, was another matter. "What the hell do you mean I can't take my gel shoe inserts?" Sal was yelling into the indifferent face of the TSA agent. "What do you think I'm going to do? Whip one out mid-flight and bitch-slap my way into the cockpit?"

"Sal," Adam interceded before things got out of hand. "Just give him the inserts. I know you have at least a couple more pairs packed with your gear."

"Sorry," Adam murmured to the security person as Sal pulled the inserts from his shoes and threw them on the floor. The team headed off in the direction of their gate before security could reconsider letting Sal through.

"You know that jerk just wants them for his own fat feet," Sal muttered.

Alice rolled her eyes. "Good grief, Sal, don't be stupid. That guy was twice your size. I'm sure the last thing he wants is your smelly little shoe inserts. They'd hardly fit him."

"I don't believe it was personal, Sal. He's just doing his job," said Tom. "His duty is to inspect everyone for items containing a liquid or gel like that; it could be an explosive. They mustn't allow anything through that could be inflammable or hazardous, you know."

"They let *him* through," Alice smirked.

"I don't know why they made me take off my shoes anyway," Sal complained. "They didn't make any of you take off your shoes. I bet all of you guys have those gel inserts, too. That TSA dude was discriminating against me."

"Discriminating? Don't you think it might have something to do with the way you are dressed?" asked Adam.

"Dude! What's wrong with the way I'm dressed?" asked Sal, stretching out his arms with a flourish.

Adam looked at him wide-eyed. "Arctic camouflage cargo pants, a Che Guevara tee-shirt, and a baseball cap that says 'Viva la Revolucion!'? And you are surprised they made you take your shoes off? I'm surprised they didn't just shoot you."

"All perfectly acceptable urban wear. It's discriminatory to pick me just because of the clothes I'm wearing."

"My gosh, I hope you brought something a little less urban to wear in the mountains of Georgia," said Alice, "or one of them good ol' boys down there just might pick you for something a little more invasive. You know how to call a pig, boy?"

"I'm not worried about them yahoos," said Sal, although the flash of alarm in his eyes revealed that he might be more apprehensive than he was letting on.

They reached the gate and found seats without much difficulty. It was early for the weekend travelers, so the airport crowd was still pretty light and the gate had only an average amount of activity. As they took their seats, they noticed the gate attendant talking on the phone. She quickly glanced at Sal, gave a grim nod, and spoke softly to someone on the other end of the line.

"Great," thought Adam, "now we're all on the security watch list."

The rest of the flight was uneventful, although the air attendants asked Sal several times if "everything was OK." Adam suspected they were more interested in the safety of the other passengers than they were about Sal's comfort. Eventually they became convinced he was no longer a threat risk and put their efforts into ignoring him for the rest of the flight.

Departing the plane, the sauna-like humidity in Atlanta felt like walking into a steam room. Adam's clothes were drenched with sweat within ten minutes of leaving the Atlanta airport. He hadn't expected such a drastic weather change, and was relieved to be in the cool air conditioned air of the airport shuttle as they headed to the car rental place to pick up the vehicle Dr. Odan had reserved for them.

Their gear was to be delivered directly to the rental agency, and would hopefully be there by the time they arrived. Traffic around the airport in Atlanta was heavy as usual, allowing the team a little more time to enjoy the air conditioning. Fortunately, their testing would be conducted in the higher elevation of the Chattahoochee National Forest, where the cooler, less humid mountain air would make hauling their gear and executing the testing tasks more pleasant.

Adam had hiked in the Appalachian Mountains many times, and had done several legs of the Appalachian Trail, although he never had been to this particular part of the Appalachians, or the Blue Ridge, as the range was called here. The AT came through the Chattahoochee further to the east, the trailhead just below Springer Mountain. A little further to the north, in Tennessee and North Carolina, the range became the Great Smokey Mountains. Adam and the others had hiked in Smokey Mountain National Park and they were anxious to visit it again. There would be no time on this trip, though. This time of year the Smokey Mountains were crowded with tourists taking in the spring blossoming along the well-kept trails of the park, so they would be headed to the more isolated trails of north Georgia. They would be heading out route 575, across the Etowah River in Cherokee county, and eventually on up to East Ellijay where they would enter the Chattahoochee National Forest. It was only about ninety miles from the airport to the entrance to Chattahoochee, about a two hour drive, depending upon the traffic. Atlanta always had heavy traffic, even compared to Philadelphia. Once they were beyond the beltway, the congestion would dissipate and the driving would be more pleasant.

Adam had made reservations at a small hotel in Ellijay. It would still be daylight by the time they arrived, but there wouldn't be enough time to unload and set up their base camp today.

As the shuttle van pulled into the car rental lot, Adam was relieved to see the crates with their gear stacked next to the office door. They piled out of the van and back into the Atlanta humidity, placing their carry-on bags next to the rest of the cargo. The lot-boy approached the group and asked Adam, "Ya'll the Adam Hill party?"

"We be all of them, and it ain't no party," quipped Sal. Alice gave Sal a jab in the ribs.

"Yes, that's us," Adam said quickly.

"I'll bring your vehicle right up. A Dr. Odan called to reserve one of our big ol' trucks for ya, so if ya'll be so kind as to step in the office and sign off on the paperwork, ya'll can be on your way," the lot-boy said as he headed off to get the SUV.

Adam said, "I'll take care of the paperwork while you guys start loading up."

"Can't do it. The dude said 'ya'll come to the office', so that means we all have to come with you," said Sal.

"Give it a rest, Sal," Adam sighed. "All the cargo is here, ready to go. In Philly, we'd be lucky if half of it wasn't stolen by now. Load up; I'll be right back."

The rental agency provided a Chevrolet Suburban, which had even more room for passengers and cargo than Adam's Yukon. He quickly took care of the paperwork, and the team was loaded up and on their way with a smile and a hat tip from the lot-boy. The big SUV effortlessly accommodated the team and all the gear as they smoothly rolled out of the parking lot and north onto the Atlanta beltway.

Chapter six

The little hotel in Ellijay worked out perfectly. They had made good time driving up from the airport, and now they could relax and get a good night's sleep after a long traveling day. Adam and Tom spent some time making sure all the gear was intact, while Alice disappeared into her room to organize her notes and devise a format for logging their testing results. Her plan was to keep all the records on her notebook computer while at the base camp, but switch to hardcopy notes in the field. It wasn't so uncommon for her to keep track of her notes on paper, and she often used pen and paper even in a lab environment. Not only did she find it more convenient to record her notes this way, it also served as a backup to the data that was eventually entered into the computer.

Sal planned to take a dip in the hotel pool, but was disappointed when he was told that it had not yet been opened for the season. To everyone's relief, he didn't make a ruckus about it.

It cooled off considerably as evening set in now that they were closer to the mountains. The fresh, chilly air stirred their appetites, and they decided to drive to town to check out the local eateries. While in town, Sal convinced the team to stop at the outfitter shop so he could get a replacement pair of shoe inserts. Adam wanted to stop by the outfitter's place anyway. He had made several calls to the store while making arrangements for this trip, and they had been exceptionally helpful with providing the information about trails in the area, what they could expect for weather, terrain, and in locating spots that could offer navigational challenges. Adam did much of his shopping online, but he liked to patronize local merchants whenever he could. Owning his own business had given him a different perspective; it wasn't just about finding the best price.

The shop was well-stocked with reasonably priced hiking and back-packing equipment, so everyone found something of interest to browse.

While the rest of the team was preoccupied, Adam asked a weary looking cashier for James Adair, the store manager/owner who had spoken with him on the phone. The phlegmatic cashier's attire was disheveled, as if she had just returned from a quick nap in the stockroom. Adam noticed her nametag read "Daisy-Lynn" and grimaced at the thought of Sal's comments sure to come.

She responded with an alarmed grunt, which Adam interpreted as concern that he was going to complain about something. He felt obligated to add, "I wanted to thank him for all his help on the phone." The cashier's eyes, which never actually looked at Adam, returned to their previous uninterested glaze as she pointed toward the rear of the store.

Following Daisy-Lynn's gesture, Adam discovered a man who was energetically refilling a display of daypacks. He turned and smiled with a broad grin as Adam approached. He was about the same age as Adam, dressed in well-worn cargo jeans, a faded olive-drab tee-shirt, hiking boots, and sported a bushy, straw-colored beard and a long ponytail stretching midway down his back.

"Did Daisy-Lynn get you taken care of?" he asked Adam.

"If you're James Adair she did," Adam replied.

"That's me. You must be Adam Hill. I recognize your voice from our phone conversations. I was hoping you'd stop in and say hello while you were visiting our part of the country." More quietly he said, "Don't let Daisy-Lynn put you off. She's not much for socializing, but she's dependable. Most folks down this way will talk your ear off. Were you able to get all the information you needed for your project?"

Adam usually did not share any information about his projects outside of the testing team, as he was typically under a non-disclosure agreement. Since this project was to be conducted entirely in the field, it was impossible not to give a few folks a general idea of what they were doing. If he were too closed-mouthed, people tended to be suspicious and assumed you were up to no good. In this case, Adam just said that they were doing consumer product testing of a new type of GPS receiver. It was pretty close to the truth, and people could accept that he couldn't tell them too much about a new product that the company wasn't ready to announce yet.

"Yes, between you and the ranger in Blue Ridge I was able to plan out our trip very well. You were most helpful, which is one of the reasons I wanted to drop in and say thanks," Adam answered. "We'll be stopping by the ranger station in the morning to pick up the backpacking permits."

"Glad ya'll came in; we're happy to help," James said with a huge grin through his bushy beard. "I know you said you would be testing some new GPS receiver, but are you folks carrying a radio or anything along in case of an emergency? There's not much cell phone coverage where you are going, but that's the type of location you were looking for, you said."

"The device we are testing has some communication abilities, but I don't like to depend on a prototype device in a critical situation. In addition to our cell phones, Tom, one of my engineers, has a Personal Locator Device that can send out an emergency beacon if we need to."

"That's about the best way to go, since those things work just about anywhere. You just don't want to push that button unless you really need to, though, with the cost of sending out a rescue helicopter these days."

"You're right about that. Hopefully it's something we'll never use. It does give us some peace of mind in case of a life-threatening situation," Adam replied.

"Yep, best way to handle emergencies is to avoid 'em in the first place!" laughed James.

"You folks have a pretty good gig going," James continued, "getting to test out new toys before they're available to anyone else. Sounds like a really fun job!"

"The job can be fun, but it's not always so exciting," said Adam, "I was just thinking how nice it would be to have a little place like this. Has to be better than working for someone else, and you get to check out some fun new sporting stuff too. Have you owned the store long?"

"I've only owned this place for about five years, but I've been in the retail business all my life. I worked for my father in his store since I was a kid. He had a general store just outside town. When he passed, I sold the place and bought this one. I guess it's in my blood. We Adairs' have run businesses around here for generations. Apparently I had a great-grandfather that ran a trading post down near Calhoun back in the Indian days. A bit of a notorious character from what I've heard."

"I guess most of us have a few of those in our lineage. This seems like a fantastic location for an outfitter shop. I'd guess that the rural location is a lot less hectic than it is in Atlanta."

"We have a good business, but it's not always so peaceful. The outfitter part of the business can be a lot of fun. I enjoy taking folks out on backpacking trips, but sometimes you get some real jerks that want to tell you how to do things. You have to wonder why they bothered to hire an outfitter if they already had all the answers!"

"Sounds like some of the managers I used to work for. Guess you have to take the good with the bad with anything. I'm looking forward to retirement when I only have to answer to myself."

"Good luck with that. I figure with the way the economy is going these days, I might be able to retire at around age 120," James chuckled.

"You could be right," Adam agreed. "Tell you what, when we get to that age we'll get together and see how far we can hike into the Chattahoochee with our walkers!"

"You're on," James laughed. "For now though I guess we both need to get back to work. It was great to meet you. Ya'll stay safe, have a good time, and good luck with your project."

"Thanks, I'm sure we will. We really appreciate all your help, James."

"Glad to be of service, Adam. Stop in anytime!"

Chapter seven

The hotel offered a free sunrise breakfast, so they agreed to meet in the lounge at first light to get an early start to the national forest. First stop was the Blue Ridge ranger station, where they purchased the required backcountry permits and a fishing license for Adam. Adam sensed that the ranger was skeptical about issuing the backpacking permits to a group of software testers, especially since he was vague about the areas where they would be hiking. The area where they were planning to do most of the testing was near the Cohutta Wilderness Area, which is inside of the Chattahoochee National Park. They would also be close to the Tennessee border and the Cherokee National Park. Adam allayed the ranger's concerns with some pleasant conversation about their previous backpacking trips.

The Cohutta district ranger was patient and willing to be flexible with the permits, persuaded that they were capable backpackers and would be testing out a new type of GPS receiver. She issued the permits, and stressed the importance of keeping her advised of their progress and of any change of plans. She was pleasant but firm when it came to issuing backcountry permits, understandably serious about verifying the hikers had proper experience and common sense before allowing them to spend a week hiking in the backcountry. Adam appreciated the concern for their safety, and understood that the ranger wanted to avoid mounting searches for lost hikers in her jurisdiction. Undoubtedly she had rescued plenty of folks claiming to be expert hikers who had underestimated the immensity of the forest or failed to take the simple precautions necessary to avoid an embarrassing disaster.

While the team was looking forward to backpacking, it was possible the permits would not be needed. In fact, they were not planning on an extended backpacking trip for the initial testing. Rather, they intended on camping at a few primitive tent sites, most of which could be driven to in the SUV. From these sites, they could day-hike or do a single night trip to the areas they had preselected. Once the standard testing scenarios were completed, they would begin following the anomaly beacons. For that part of the exercise, they planned to drive as close to the first beacon as they could get, then hike, carrying only what they needed and leaving the rest behind in the Suburban. Depending upon what they discovered when they reached the first beacon, they would return to the SUV and either retrieve their gear to continue following subsequent beacons, or conclude the testing.

For the first day of testing, they would be taking a relatively short trail, about an eleven mile round trip, known as the Mountaintown Creek trail. It was not a heavily used trail, but it was well marked, and they were able to download an accurate set of GPS coordinates for several points along the trail that had been posted by previous hikers. The downloaded way-points would let them test the LANav against their regular GPS receivers.

From Blue Ridge, they looped around a few country roads to reach Old Route 2, where they could pick up a forest road to a parking spot at the trailhead. The trail was about a six mile hike along Mountaintown Creek, a small trout stream that ran through a mountain gorge. It would be an easy, pleasant hike for them to get started, and there were roads at both ends of the gorge.

Tom had studied the area using satellite maps, and noted the steep terrain on both sides of the creek could offer a challenge to GPS reception. James Adair, the outfitter, had hiked the trail often and confirmed there were many spots along the creek that were tough for the receivers to pick up a satellite signal. James also acknowledged that it was a beautiful spot for a hike in the spring; a noteworthy benefit in Adam's opinion.

The big Suburban crunched to a stop at the tiny pull-off next to the trailhead. A small trail marker was clearly visible from the road, although later in the season, as the vegetation flourished, it would be much more difficult to see.

They had risen early, and with only a single cup of coffee, most of the ride was spent dozing or silently contemplating the testing scenario they would soon be executing. Sal made a few cracks about hearing banjo music and chiding Tom with some off-color remarks about hillbilly inbreeding, which Tom ignored. When Sal looked in Alice's direction, one stabbing glance from her fierce azure eyes was all it took for him to reconsider whatever taunt he intended to cast her way.

They would be taking only daypacks, large enough to carry everything they needed for a single night camping. They brought along two small tents, but if the weather stayed as it was there would be little need for them; their mid-weight sleeping bags would keep them warm enough for a night under the stars. It was already late morning by the time they arrived, after making the stop at Blue Ridge and finding their way along the unfamiliar back roads to the trailhead.

With the vehicle securely off the road, the team disembarked the barge-sized SUV, grabbed their gear, and spent a few moments taking in the quiet majesty of the forest before setting off down the white blazed trail. Each person had their own handheld GPS receiver, and they all habitually punched in a waypoint, marking the location of the vehicle. Adam slipped the TSO LANav from the protective belt-clipped case he had fashioned. He switched it on, and keyed in the selection for TERRESTRIAL NAVIGATION MODE. A secondary screen displayed immediately, and he punched the STORE PRESENT LOCATION soft-key on the menu. The unit responded with a soft confirmation chirp and he slipped the device back into its case.

Adam worried that the magnificent surroundings would make it difficult to stick to business, and then a moment later remembered that one of his reasons for taking this project was to have a little fun while they worked. He got into his walking pace, relishing the familiar comfort of his sturdy hiking boots as he made his way along the trail's uneven terrain. The damp, fragrant forest worked its magic, easing his mind into the serenity his feet had already found. The tranquility of the woodland trail enveloped the members of the team and each fell into their own meditative stride, a Zen-like nirvana which can only be reached by hikers traversing a glorious mountain trail.

They continued quietly along the trail for about a half-mile until they reached their first stream crossing. It was an easy spot to cross, with conveniently placed flat-topped rocks for stepping stones. At the other side of the stream, Tom checked his GPSr, comparing their current location with a list of waypoints he loaded in before they began the hike. They had been gently descending into the gorge as they walked, gradually curving around the higher mountain to their right.

"We are now at the first waypoint that I marked on the trail map," said Tom, "where the stream crosses the trail for the first time. The mountain on our right is Rich Knob, which according to the topographical map is close to 3400 feet high. My GPS receiver indicates we are down to about 2700 feet now. We can begin our tests here, and bushwhack our way up the southern end of Rich Knob to the waypoints I set up in my receiver. As we continue south, we will descend back to the creek and pick up the trail again in about a half-mile."

"Let's get to it then," said Adam. "If we complete this first series of testing on schedule, we will be at the end of the trail by early afternoon and can setup a camping spot for the evening. This stream feeds a pond further south, and our outfitter friend James said the creek has plenty of native trout. I packed a fold-up fishing rod. With a little luck we can dine on trout tonight instead of freeze-dried backpacking food.

"We all know the scenarios, but just to refresh—this first set of tests will confirm basic usability and the accuracy of the LANav by comparing it to the GPS receivers. The LANav has all the features of a standard GPSr, so we will begin with some simple exercises. Usability is one of the major concerns to TSO, and the scenarios today will put the unit through its paces as if it were a regular GPS receiver. Geocaching makes use of a few basic GPS functions, so we'll make today's testing interesting by playing a sort of makeshift geocaching game, only we're going to use flags instead of ammo cans."

"Dang, dude! No searching for swag to trade?" Sal joked. "You mean I carried all these Happy Meal toys Nutso gave me for nothing?" Swag was a term geocachers used to refer to the trade items they placed in ammo cans, which in urban caches was mostly junk, such as small toys and other useless baubles.

Adam ignored him and continued. "Tom, you have the Trimble® reference series GPS receiver and Sal is probably the fastest walker, so you two go ahead and mark out a few waypoints and place the flags. Radio me the coordinates as you place the flags, and Alice and I will follow from a different direction and check accuracy. Pick some spots that have a weak satellite signal so we can see if the TSO LANav has any difficulty at those places."

After a quick radio check, Tom and Sal left the trail and climbed up the slope of the mountain, while Alice and Adam headed a little further down the trail to begin bushwhacking up to the peak. It was still early spring and the foliage had not yet become overgrown enough to make off-trail hiking difficult. They picked a spot to ascend about an eighth of a mile south of where they left Tom and Sal. Within a few minutes Tom radioed the coordinates of the first flag, and Adam entered them into the LANav using the touch screen and activated the GOTO function. The device immediately displayed a topographic map indicating the area where he had set waypoints, their present position, and a dotted line indicating the path they had taken. Alongside the map, there were several soft keys for zooming and repositioning the map's viewpoint. One key was labeled SAT-MAP. When Adam pressed it, the view changed from a topographical map to a satellite image of the area.

"It has unbelievable resolution on these satellite maps," Adam said, showing the screen to Alice. "I can zoom in close enough that I can almost see individual trees. Wow! I can see our SUV! I thought real-time imaging was restricted to military use only."

"Cool!" said Alice, "can you zoom in to my house and make sure I remembered to close all the windows?"

"You can check that out later," he replied. "Just don't let Sal see you or he'll be trying to zoom in on all kinds of things he shouldn't."

They followed the LANav to each point that Tom and Sal set, which guided them to within a foot of every flag. A few of the flags were placed in positions that would not allow them to take a direct path, requiring them to navigate around impassable areas of brush or boulders. By switching back and forth between the topo and satellite map views Adam was able to determine the most obstruction-free way to reach each flag. As they continued up the mountain, Alice took meticulous notes on the testing results, but for the most part the LANav functioned flawlessly, never seeming to lose a signal even though their GPS receivers had done so several times. After the first three flags, Alice took over the testing to contribute her feedback on usability. She found that the device was capable of displaying a hybrid map that combined the satellite view with the topographic map, so they no longer had to switch back and forth between display modes. Alice also discovered a PLOT BEST ROUTE function, which automatically calculated an optimum route for them to take to reach a waypoint, avoiding obstacles in their path without taking detours or backtracking. She found that when this function was enabled, a blinking arrow appeared on the LCD map guiding her along the calculated route. If she deviated from the suggested path, the unit would beep, letting her know she was off course, and offer to recalculate her route.

"I don't know yet how well the LANav will perform in space, but it's a hiker's dream come true, and geocachers would love it—no thinking required, just follow the arrow!" said Alice.

"I never asked Dr. Odan what the retail price on the unit was going to be, but I'd guess it to be beyond the pocketbook of the average geocacher," said Adam. "They might have to wait a while for a consumer version. Maybe they'll just license out the technology to other manufacturers."

Adam radioed Tom and Sal to let them know they would meet up at the next flag, where together they would descend back down to Mountaintown Creek trail. When they arrived, they took a few moments to discuss the performance of the TSO LANav and how the test report would read.

Alice said, "We encountered zero failures, and so far for terrestrial navigation the LANav has proven to be more accurate than even our reference instrument. So far, it's the most flawlessly performing prototype device I've ever tested. There are a couple usability issues I can comment on, like adjusting the menu structure to make primary functions more accessible, but that's a minor issue. Especially considering that we are able to use the device effectively without a user manual. For such a sophisticated device, it is amazingly intuitive. If it continues to perform as well as it has, the final report is going to read more like a glowing review than a test report."

"This morning's testing certainly has been impressive," replied Adam. "Remember, we are testing independently. We're not being rated on the number of issues we find, so there is no pressure to find problems if there really aren't any. We've all been in the position where we felt we had to find problems to justify our jobs. Dr. Odan assured me he is expecting an honest evaluation, not nitpicking just for the sake of finding problems. I'm sure he'll be thrilled if our report shows that his product is perfect, but we've only just begun, so there is lots of functionality still to explore. I also believe that as a researcher he is most anxious for the results of our anomaly beacon testing since that will give him data on something entirely new and unexplored.

"I'll be checking in with him later today to give him a progress report. For now, let's head back to the main trail and scope out our campsite for tonight."

Tom and Sal convinced Adam to set a few flags for them to find, both wanting to get some hands on time with the LANav. Adam and Alice headed off in the direction of the trail, planting flags for them along the way. By the time they all met again at the creek trail, both Sal and Tom were beaming with enthusiasm about all the possible applications the device had, Tom envisioning the military and law enforcement applications and Sal contemplating the treasure-hunting possibilities.

The day quickly progressed toward late afternoon. The temperature was unseasonably warm even within the deep shadows of the forest valley. As the sun climbed higher, the trail was flooded with intense beams of stippled sunshine as it filtered through the newly sprouted leaves of the treetops. Pollen bursting from the budding trees, suspended in the air and illuminated by dappled shafts of light, sparkled all around them like floating embers from a campfire. It was a springtime only event; in a few weeks the treetop canopy would flourish and the trail would be in shadows for nearly the entire day. The team basked in the glorious surroundings, reinvigorating them all after the long, snowy Delaware winter. The deeper they ventured into the forest, the further they drifted from the stress-filled urban life, as their souls embraced the warming sunshine, the fresh air, and the placid sounds of Georgia's Chattahoochee forest.

The team advanced southerly along Mountaintown Creek Trail as they continued to execute the first day of testing. They maneuvered through several more stream crossings and were treated to a few small waterfalls along the way. About four miles from the trailhead, they came across a natural swimming hole formed by the large boulders in the creek. Although the day's temperature reached nearly eighty degrees, the creek water was still icy cold; too cold for a swim but inviting enough for a quick stop to dangle tired feet in the frigid water while they munched down a few protein bars for lunch. The total length of the trail was only about six miles of descending terrain, but the side trip up and down Rich Knob added about four extra miles of climbing and bushwhacking; a decent workout for their winter-softened muscles.

Between splashes and mouthfuls of protein bars, Tom and Sal continued to laud the capabilities of the LANav. It had performed flawlessly throughout the day's testing, impressing the entire team with its capabilities.

Alice nodded toward Tom and Sal. "You might have to look for some more objective testers. These guys are usually critical of everything we test. Good heavens, this LANav has them acting like they can't wait to head up the TSO marketing department!"

"I think it's just the "new toy" syndrome. We're all prone to get more excited about a new product that works really well; especially one that we think would be a fun or useful item for ourselves. When you think about it though, we really haven't seen any earth-shattering new technology yet. Yeah, the TSO LANav seems to be a tremendous improvement on our current geo-positioning tools—and I'm not trying to understate that achievement—but those types of technology improvements are typical, even expected, by our tech-loving society. The high-res SAT map overlays are really great, and so is the route finding software, but it's actually the improvements in all the supporting technology, like satellite imagery and communications, that make it possible."

"You make it sound like no big deal," she answered. "I thought you were looking at testing this product to be a breakthrough that would open new possibilities for us as a testing group?"

"And I still think that—absolutely. It's just that I don't think we've really seen much of the breakthrough stuff so far. All of the testing we'll be doing for the next few days will be dealing with terrestrial navigation and communications, so all we are going to see are enhancements to existing technology. Since we don't have the capabilities to test in outer space, I'm hoping that the beacon tests will give us the chance to see some really exciting new technology."

"In other words, the beacon tests better turn out to be something more than just a dead-end. Otherwise we have a great time testing in the beautiful Chattahoochee National Forest, but all we've added to our testing repertoire is a cool new geocaching toy."

"It's still a cutting-edge device, so the project definitely enhances our resume, but yes, the beacon testing is what could take our company to the next level."

"Then might I suggest we move the beacon test up on the schedule?" said Tom.

"This is coming from the most by-the-book engineer of our group?" asked Adam. "I would have thought you of all people would argue for sticking to the defined plan."

"Usually that would be a correct statement. However, in this case we are actually doing more research than testing. If the beacon anomalies are such a big unknown, we should investigate them as soon as we are comfortable using the LANav. The outcome of the beacon tests could make a big difference in how we proceed with UAT testing, since it could possibly change the entire target market of the device. If it turns out that following the TSO LANav to an anomaly leads us to some new source of energy, an alternate universe, or who knows what, its ability to be used as a navigation device becomes just an interesting secondary function. If there is a possibility that this device has that kind of potential, all the other testing could be moot."

"That's a good point; and a valid argument," said Adam. "It's also a good reason why I'm glad we have a former design engineer on our team. What do you guys think?" he asked Alice and Sal.

"Dude, I'm all for it," replied Sal. "Whatever we can do so this little adventure will get us closer to working full-time as an independent testing company would be awesome as far as I'm concerned. I was hoping this gizmo was going to lead us to the lost Incan treasure, so none of us would have to work at all anymore. Then I could spend the rest of the week playing World of Warcraft."

"Hopefully you're not counting on that too much, Sal," said Alice. "We're a little too far north for Incan treasure. I'm in agreement that we should move the beacon testing forward, as long as the client is amenable to it."

"In that case," said Adam, "I'll discuss it with Dr. Odan this evening. I'm pretty sure he'll agree, since he seemed to be most interested in that part of the testing anyway. In fact, I almost got the feeling that that was the only part he actually cared much about. I just chalked that up to his creative nature, but perhaps he's had some dreams of the potential for his device like Tom and Sal mentioned. Not that I think he expects to be led to lost treasures. The astronomical navigation technology he has developed is certainly ground breaking, but he may need to wait until our space travel capabilities advance before the usefulness can be appreciated. He may be hoping for another facet of his invention to provide a more immediate contribution to mankind."

Chapter eight

The languid mood of the morning had been completely eradicated by the exhilarating hike and the outstanding test results. Reaching the end of the trail, they emerged into a small meadow-like clearing with enough room for three or four tent sites. The sites were primitive, offering no more than a flat spot of ground and a stone fire-ring. There were no other campers present, and it did not appear as if the site had been used so far this season. They saw no evidence of recent campfires, and the tent sites all had new grass that had not yet been flattened by tents or sleeping bags.

There was still plenty of daylight, but as the shadows lengthened they could feel the chill that the night would bring. They dug out light jackets and sweatshirts from their packs, placing them where they would be easily accessible in the dark. The cloudless sky revealed no sign of rain, so they each tossed a sleeping bag on the spot of their choice and pitched a single tent to store the gear. Camp setup complete, the four companions quietly commenced their individual activities, enjoying the peaceful serenity of their surroundings.

Adam grabbed his fishing rod and headed back in the direction they came. The stream continued on southward, but he had spotted a few pools along the way that looked ideal for trout. He was anxious to call Dr. Odan and discuss the test schedule changes with him; though for now that could wait. A freshly caught trout was the perfect camp dinner after a long hike, and right now his priority was to catch a few.

Alice worked on her field notes, rewriting when needed and entering what she had so far into her notebook computer. Normally she scanned in her handwritten notes, but today's testing hadn't required much more than five pages, so it was quick enough just to type them in. She had already given some consideration to documenting the beacon testing, expecting that it would require a more free form style than she was used to. Typically, her documentation consisted of a description of the test and the results. Whenever there were failures, she included the steps necessary to repeat the problem.

She was still a little unsure of how to document the beacon testing. It seemed to be more of an analysis of function, requiring detailed documentation of the entire procedure. She didn't even consider it testing as there was no chance of failure if they didn't know what the expected output was supposed to be. As a disciplined tester, the lack of a structured format troubled her, but it also intrigued her to be part of the early stages of development of a product for a change. She could understand why Adam was so eager for this project; she also hoped that it would lead to more projects for the team. She would like nothing better than to work full-time for Overhill Engineering. It was not her nature to accept change lightly, especially career changes, but her job at OSI had lost much of its appeal since she had become a contractor. The job no longer provided the satisfaction it once did. In some ways she envied Sal, who seemed to roll along easily accepting everything that came his way. Not that she would ever consider telling him she admired anything about him. Sal was a good friend and she had a high regard for him, but Alice knew him well enough to keep those feelings to herself.

It wasn't Sal's nature to sit still for very long. After tossing his pack and sleeping bag into a heap, he volunteered to collect firewood for their campfire. He began piling kindling and logs next to the fire ring, breaking the longer branches into smaller lengths by stomping on them with his foot. When he was done, there would be enough wood not only for them but for the next several campers—if he didn't injure himself breaking logs.

While Sal gathered firewood, Tom performed a cursory examination of the equipment, making sure everything functioned as it should and was stowed away for the night. When he finished he planned to check out the area to the south of the campsite. He knew from looking over the satellite maps that there were one or two farms in the area, and that the stream eventually emptied into a small pond before reaching the road at the southern end of the trail. Tom felt secure spending the night at the campsite, but it was his habit to inspect the surrounding area of any wilderness campsite before darkness set in. His night's sleep would be more restful if he familiarized himself with the surroundings while there was still plenty of light. He found the tiny, overgrown trail leading southward to the pond, and began walking.

Tom was more at home in a mountain forest than any of the others. His family had deep roots in the Blue Ridge Mountains of central Virginia, where he spent his childhood years until leaving to attend college at the University of Pennsylvania. His parents lived in a small town on the outskirts of Charlottesville, Virginia, and he returned home often to visit them and the other members of his family who still lived in the area. Growing up in rural Virginia, he had plenty of opportunity to spend time in the woods enjoying outdoor activities like hunting, hiking, camping, and fishing.

Tom was just over six feet tall, with steel gray eyes, sandy hair, and a trim, close-cropped beard. He had a slight but athletic frame, with tough, sinewy muscles that gave him more strength than his features revealed. At thirty-nine, he was ten years older than the other members of the team, but had more stamina than any of them.

He carried his briar pipe everywhere. He smoked only on occasion, and this evening's solitary constitutional was the perfect opportunity. He joked that he sometimes used the pipe as a prop, to give him a wise, contemplative look whenever someone asked him a question he had no ready answer for. At work, his pipe gave him the look of an astute senior engineer. In the forest, dressed in jeans, flannel shirt, and wide-brimmed hat, he looked much like a country gentleman out for a stroll on his mountain estate.

While he was in high school, Tom expected he would attend the University of Virginia where his older brother and most of his friends had gone. UVA had a great engineering school, and even though they specialized in medical studies the school had provided accomplished engineers in many fields, and an engineering degree from UVA would open many doors for him. It was by chance that an online friend invited him for a visit to the Philadelphia area and to check out UPenn before making his final decision to attend UVA. Tom found that despite his dislike for the congested feeling of the Philly area, he was attracted by all that the area had to offer; not only the cultural urban amenities and close proximity to other metro areas, but the historical significance of the city and its structures fascinated him. Virginia had an intriguing history with its battlefields and presidential homes, and Philly gave him a similar thrill walking the streets of the town where the founding fathers had met to plan the beginnings of our great country. He loved wandering about the city inspecting its many magnificent granite buildings and spending time in the museums and libraries, looking through old photos, etchings, and drawings depicting the city from pre-colonial times to the present. He was soon convinced that UPenn could offer a great degree program as well as diversify his education with the culture and history that the area had to offer.

His folks were a little disappointed that he selected a college outside of his home state, but they understood his reasoning and supported his decision. Fitting in with the Philadelphia crowd was never an issue. The teachers and students were from all over the country, and the majority of the locals were a lot friendlier that he'd been led to believe. He had to admit they were more accepting than many of the folks in his own hometown, who tended to be provincial and sometimes untrusting of anyone not from the area. It also helped that he was well-spoken, and his slight Virginia accent gave his voice a friendly and refined quality-- a sharp contrast to the south Philly slur. His country charm and easygoing nature was pleasing enough, especially when combined with his southern old-school manners.

After his graduation, Tom was recruited by MBNA, formerly a large financial institution headquartered in Delaware, home to many corporations due to their business-friendly tax structure. MBNA was primarily a credit card company, and they were particularly interested in implementing web services for their customers—an innovative offering at the time. Tom was one of the few people local to the area who had expertise in secure financial transactions over the internet, and MBNA had the resources to make an offer very hard to refuse for someone right out of college. Taking the job at MBNA allowed Tom to move to New Castle, Delaware, a tiny, well-preserved colonial town that suited his historical interests and was a four hour drive from Charlottesville. While the job was financially rewarding, Tom began to feel disenchanted with the company as they made more and more demands on his personal time. He felt that the management had little regard for the personal well-being of their employees, and was concerned by the numerous accusations of shady dealings and questionable ethics against some of the corporate officers. He eventually left MBNA to work for the OSI software quality department, where he met the rest of the team. His background in software development made him especially valuable as a test engineer. He was offered a position in development engineering when OSI eliminated their software testing department, but he declined, opting to try his luck as a freelance contractor instead.

Tom watched as the setting sun streaked the sky with orange and red as he walked quietly along the trail. He snapped his vest closed as he felt the chill of the evening mountain air slowly spill down into the tiny valley. Darkness would come more quickly here than at the higher elevations, and he knew he would not have time to walk all the way to the pond and make it back to the campsite before nightfall. He enjoyed his solitary walks, and was accustomed to walking alone in the nighttime woods under the light of the moon and stars. He knew the others would be concerned if he did not return while it was still light, so he reversed course, heading back toward the campsite.

Tom had read the documentation and listened to Adam's explanations of the technology behind the LANav, and shared his excitement about testing something so new and unique, but he could not shake the feeling that there was something mysterious about this project. There seemed to be something that just didn't fit; out of kilter, like an image drawn with slightly mismatched proportions. He wondered what information was being withheld from them. He couldn't understand the reasoning behind selecting an independent group, such as they were, to do the type of research they were about to do. Usually a company with potentially ground-breaking technology wanted to keep it closely guarded, not farm out the research to an independent testing company. Perhaps they already knew what the beacons were, but hoped a fresh set of minds could figure out a marketable use for them. Or, perhaps they had already discounted the anomalies as meaningless but used them as an enticement to Adam. He shrugged off his uneasiness; he was being paid to conduct a test, not question the motives, and at least he was getting outdoors for a few days in a gorgeous wilderness area.

Tom's archeological and anthropological pastimes included the study of American Indian culture and exploring ruins from the colonial and pre-colonial periods. Tom had American Indian ancestors on both sides of his family, but his attempts to uncover his genealogy any further back than his grandparents were thwarted by a lack of records for that part of his family tree. It was almost as if those members of his family didn't want to be traced. He didn't harbor any false hope that he would ever learn much more about his own family's descendants, but learning some facts about the American Indian way of life in this part of the country gave him a tiny feeling of connection with those mysterious ancestors. He knew there were a few Indian ruins nearby, and hoped he would get a chance to investigate them. It would make the trip to Georgia worthwhile for him, even if the LANav proved to be less groundbreaking than everyone hoped.

Tom returned to the campsite just as Adam was preparing to contact Dr. Odan.

"Oh, yes, I agree completely with your team's recommendation," Ed Odan's voice replied through the earpiece of the LANav. They were well outside of any cell phone service area, but the LANav's satellite commu- nications were working flawlessly. "In fact, the other engineers here at TSO are anxious to discover the meaning of the beacons, but the investors are most eager to learn if the effectiveness of our device is improved in any way, you see."

"In that case," answered Adam, "we will spend the rest of the evening preparing to start the beacon research in the morning. As you know, our plan for this part of the project is to simply follow the LANav to the first beacon and record our findings. After we observe the location of the first beacon, we can make a decision about how to proceed. If warranted, we'll return to the site prepared to backpack in with enough supplies to last several days in the backcountry. We know there are additional beacons further on, possibly on a projected path, and we'll follow them to gather as much data as possible. We are likely to be hiking in some difficult terrain, requiring some strenuous and tiring effort, which is one reason why I originally scheduled this part of the testing last. When we return, we will complete the rest of the standard testing. Judging by how well the LANav has performed so far, completing the standard tests should not be too exhausting."

"Your plan indeed sounds most acceptable," said Odan. "Thank you for the update, Adam. The exemplary performance of the LANav is most gratifying. Please report the additional findings to me after you have made your observations at the first beacon, before you begin your backpacking journey. We're all looking forward to your report, you see, and would like updates from each of the subsequent beacons. Oh yes, be sure to enjoy yourselves, and for goodness sake, please make the safety of your team a priority."

Chapter nine

The testing team was excited about the next phase of the project. They had done field testing of products before, but nothing had given them the opportunity for such an adventure. They all loved outdoor activities, and could hardly believe they were actually getting paid to have so much fun. Their voices and gestures were infused with excitement as they discussed the details of tomorrow's tasks. Even Tom, normally staid and unemotional, was animated with anticipation.

Their exhilarated mood mellowed during the preparation of the evening's campfire dinner, as the fatigue of the day's hiking in the Cohutta Wilderness Area set in. They brought along standard freeze dried backpacking rations, but only as a standby whenever "real" food was not available. Adam's fishing yielded three decent-size native trout for them to share, which Tom offered to prepare using some of the pepper-weed seeds and other wild herbs he found on his solo hike. While Sal built the fire, Alice put together a salad from the tender spring dandelions, clover leaves, Day Lilly shoots, and wild onions and garlic she had gathered. She had a knack for food preparation, especially when it came to putting flavors together using native plants. She was adept at edible plant identification, and enjoyed researching the botanical specimens of each new area she visited. Her love of botany and cooking provided her companions with many gastronomic treats on their camping trips. She had no qualms about a woman doing the bulk of the food preparation; it was something she enjoyed and did not consider her gender to be relevant. She occasionally imparted the chore to one of the others, usually enjoying the variety of culinary style. Tom was pretty good at putting together a tasty meal, while Adam's concoctions ranged anywhere between delightful and disaster, and Sal's idea of meal prep was pretty much limited to ordering from a menu.

They were ravenous after their long hike in the fresh air, and the smell of the roasting trout had them drooling. While preparing the meal, their talk turned to reminiscing about past hiking and backpacking adventures they had shared, and how they wished all their projects could be like this one. All conversation ceased once they began eating, focusing their concentration on the delicious meal.

Dinner and cleanup were concluded quickly, and they unanimously agreed that dinner was the best they ever had. They had already completed as much preparation for tomorrow's work as they could, and were anxious to kick back and enjoy the quiet evening at the campsite.

Appetites slaked, they sat staring into the glowing red embers of the campfire, nibbling on a dessert of trail mix, watching the indigo sky transform to a black and silver star field. Stars filled the heavens without the artificial lights of a nearby city to obscure them, while the waxing gibbous moon softly illuminated their campsite with a gentle glow. They listened to the evening melody of the forest transform into a nighttime song, the slosh and gurgle of the stream combined with frogs, insects, and other creatures, all competing for a leading part in the symphony. They spoke in low, quiet voices as they discussed tomorrow's journey.

"In the morning," said Adam, "we'll hike back out to the trailhead and take the SUV to Fort Mountain State Park, just east of Chatsworth. The state park will be a good place to leave the SUV for a few days. It looks like we can reach the first beacon by starting out on the Gahuti trail, a fairly well-used backcountry trail that has a trailhead at the state park."

"How far off the trail is the first beacon?" Alice asked.

"The Gahuti trail is about an eight mile loop around the state park, but we will only take it for a short distance before picking up another trail that leads to a stone wall Indian ruin near the top of Fort Mountain. From the ruins, we'll go off the trail for only about a half-mile to the beacon. Looking at the SAT maps, there doesn't appear to be any trails closer to the beacon. It's in a ravine on the northeast side of the mountain. I expect that last half-mile to be pretty rugged."

"Dude, when I looked at the maps I saw a couple roads that looked pretty close to the beacon. Wouldn't it be better to start hiking from one of those roads?" asked Sal.

"You're right, there are a couple of roads, but remember we have the mountains to deal with," Adam said. "By starting from the state park, we can drive most of the way up the mountain and not have such a drastic climb as we would if we started from one of the other roads. We also avoid private property, and the state park gives us a good place to park the SUV."

"We'll also get to investigate the ruins by going to the park," said Tom.

"Yeah, I'd like to check those out, too," said Sal. "Hey, here's one for ya—why was the archeologist depressed? Because his career was in ruins!" Sal heard the groans of the others as he dodged a piece of trail mix Alice threw at him.

"Oh, my, on that note, I'm going to bed," Alice said as she stood up and brushed the dirt from the seat of her cargo pants.

"Sleep tight," said Sal, "but watch out for bears. You know they always go for the babes first," he said, attempting to frighten her out of a few minutes sleep.

"I'm not worried," she replied. "You're the one sleeping next to the spot where Tom cleaned the fish."

The team turned in for the night, sharing a furtive smile as Sal tried to inconspicuously reposition his sleeping bag.

Chapter ten

T he crunch of gravel beneath the Suburban's tires at the Fort Mountain
    State Park parking area roused the team from their quiet ruminations
about the day ahead. They made good time to the state park by taking a
couple of back roads, courtesy of the LANav's superb mapping capabilities, and at the same time checked off a few additional test suites that they
had planned for automobile navigation. Many commercial GPS receivers
failed to keep up with a moving vehicle when the maps were extensively
detailed, but the TSO LANav's computer handled the quickly scrolling
maps flawlessly.

They had risen at dawn, broke camp, and made quick work of the
five mile hike back to the trailhead, then enjoyed a quiet ride through
the Chattahoochee forest to Fort Mountain, anticipating the excitement
of the day. It was a pleasant surprise to find that the state had installed
roads even deeper into the park, and they would be able to reach the
stone wall ruins, now less than half a mile from the parking lot. Even
better, they would have more time to explore the ruins since they could
reach the first beacon location quicker than they had planned. The chilled
mountain air, not yet warmed by the early morning sun, filled their lungs,
invigorating them with enthusiasm. Stretching as they exited the vehicle,
they decided to leave their equipment behind until they had a chance to
explore the ruins, and only take a few items necessary for a short hike.
They would hike out to the first beacon after they examined the stone
wall, and return to the vehicle if additional backpacking or climbing
equipment was required.

"Hey man, why not just take all our junk now?" asked Sal. "Save us
a hike back to the SUV."

"We could," Adam answered, "but I thought it would be better to get a look at the area around the first beacon. Plus, we want to spend some time checking out the ruins; better to do that without all the heavy gear."

It was still early morning, so there were not yet many visitors and the parking area was nearly empty. A sign reading "stone wall" pointed them to a well-kept paved path leading north. Not more than a few hundred feet along the trail was an overlook with a breathtaking view of the mountains of the Cohutta Wilderness Area, where they had spent the previous night. The morning sunshine illuminated the bright, spring-green fields and budding treetops below. Adjacent to the forest they could see a quilted collage of recently tilled and planted fields of the farms in the valley. The sky was clear and bright-blue. The few high, fluffy clouds cast steam-gray, shadows meandering across the landscape, and a maze of crisscrossing mining and fire roads further added to the patchwork effect.

As they reveled in the view, they noticed a few more cars in the parking lot; mountain bikers who were unloading and preparing to head out on the trail. Fort Mountain State Park is a popular mountain biking spot, having miles of challenging bike trails with plenty of rocks, boulders, red clay, and steep climbs. Their envy of the bikers was evident as they watched them unpack; this park would be an awesome biking adventure! Delaware, being mostly flat, had a few hilly single track bike trails, but reaching challenging mountain biking terrain almost always meant going out-of-state. Adam had considered bringing their bikes along to use on the trails that allowed bikes. He knew that there would be times that they would be hiking in the back country where bikes would not be practical, and so decided against the idea. Looking at the view from the overlook almost made him regret that decision, and he made a note on his mental to-do list to schedule a return trip with the bikes. The bikers rolled past them as they made their way to the ruins of the stone wall, just a short ride from the first overlook.

"Man, what an awesome day for a ride," said Sal.

"Yes, indeed," Tom agreed, "but it's a good day to explore the ruins and take a hike, too. I'd be willing to wager that any one of the bikers would jump at the chance to give up their ride today for some hands-on time with the LANav."

"You think so, dude?" asked Sal. "Hey, Adam, do you mind if I make a deal with one of these cats? His bike for the day in exchange for some LANav fun time?"

"Not if you don't mind my giving him your pay to go with it," Adam answered.

"On second thought," said Sal, "I better not let you chumps go without me. You probably won't be able to do without my highly developed technical skills."

"We could definitely do without your highly developed ego," said Alice with a wink to Tom and Adam.

They descended the overlook platform and followed the path to the stone wall. There was an informational sign about the wall giving the dimensions and some background theories about its origins. The 855 foot long structure ran east-west along the highest point of the mountain, and had a number of shallow depressions spaced about thirty feet apart. In a few places the wall's height reached nearly six feet, but on average was only about two or three feet high. In other places the wall was no more than a pile of rubble.

"The sign has several different stories about how the wall came to be here," said Tom. "Actually, they really don't have any idea what it was for, or when it was built for that matter. The most accepted theory is that it was built by woodland Indians around 500 BC as a fortification. I've even heard one suggestion that it wasn't constructed at all, but just a natural formation of hard rocks that were left by erosion."

"Looks more like Fred Flintstone's backyard fence to me," said Sal. "Hey, Wilma, fetch me a Bronto-burger, pronto!" he said to Alice.

"You'd be better off with some Flintstone Vitamins. You look more like Barney than Fred," Alice said.

"Hey, that's cool," Sal chirped. "I always thought Betty was a pretty hot number. Yabba-dabba-do!"

"Oh, hush. You obviously have the maturity of Pebbles," Alice sighed.

The sun warmed the air as it rose higher in the sky, and the radiated heat from the rock wall added to the increasing warmth as they scrabbled around it, discussing a few more serious ideas about the significance of the structure. They concluded that the most logical purpose of the wall would have been for defense. Whatever the real use may have been, the construction had taken a tremendous effort by someone. An 855 foot span of thousands of rocks would have taken even a large group of laborers many weeks to put in place.

They followed the path northerly for a few hundred yards past the wall to a more recent structure; a stone fire-tower. The fire tower had been built in the 1930's on the highest point of the mountain by the Civilian Conservation Corp, and provided the rangers an ideal vantage point to watch for fire outbreaks in the entire park and much of the surrounding forest. There was a set of wooden stairs leading to the access door of the tower. The team only glanced inside one of the lower openings as they walked past, choosing instead to head for an overlook just northwest of the tower. This second overlook afforded a panoramic view down the western slope of the mountain and the adjoining countryside north of the park boundary.

Looking to the left from the overlook, they could see the streets and buildings of Chatsworth and the smaller surrounding communities far below. Directly ahead and to the north, the looming mountain peaks of the Cohutta Wilderness area were visible through the thin Georgia haze. They watched as several hawks, floating in the gradually warming air, hunted for a mid-morning snack as they drifted over the treetops. Several smaller birds, too far away to recognize, darted between the gliding hawks. Beyond the mountaintops, about fifteen miles further north, was Tennessee.

"Sure don't have views like this back in Delaware," said Adam, his voice breaking the spell of the glorious view. "I'd like to stand here enjoying it, but if you're all done gazing we need to get down to work."

Adam retrieved the LANav from his belt pack and adjusted its settings to show the location of the anomalies. As he faced north from the overlook, the LANav indicated that the beacon was almost directly to his right and less than half a mile from their present location. He consulted with Tom, who had brought along a topographical map, and together they traced a line that would give them the most accessible route to their target.

"To reach the beacon from here," Adam began, "we'll need to hike easterly for only about a half-mile. The heading to the beacon is at about seventy degrees, but there are two ravines between us and it. The first is the little gulley you can see from here, just to the right. The beacon is actually inside the second little valley. Our best approach is going to be to walk along the mountaintop until we reach the second gulley, and then head down. Tom will plot our route along the map, but we will try to rely on the LANav's maps as much as possible. He'll plot our course on the map, just in case the LANav has a problem. The first beacon is so close we won't need any other navigation equipment.

"I don't believe that the terrain is rough enough to need climbing gear, but we can assess that when we reach the point where we have to descend. It's a short hike, so we can return to the vehicle for equipment if we think we need it. Everyone ready?"

The three responded positively, with even more enthusiasm than Adam expected. They were finally getting a chance to find out exactly what, if anything, was causing the mysterious anomalies. While they all hoped to discover that the source of the anomalies had some exciting significance, even if the beacons turned out to be a disappointment, it would still be a fun day.

The lure of the warm spring day was attracting many park visitors who were anxious to get outdoors after a long winter season. There were now several more people exploring the fire tower than when they first passed it. Most of the people were at the tower or the overlook, taking in the views or exploring the stone wall. Adam preferred not to attract attention. He waited until they reached a point along the trail where no one was around, and then led them onto a deer path that headed in the right direction.

None of them were strangers to bushwhacking through the backcountry; even when geocaching they usually ended up trudging at least a few hundred yards through the brush to reach their destination. The foliage was sparse enough to make their way through, following the deer paths along mountaintop ridge when they could. There was a slight descent as they passed through the first valley, followed by a steeper climb as they crested the second ridge. They had only traveled about a third of a mile from the overlook, but making their way through the brush and climbing the last ridge was taxing enough to encourage a short stop to catch their breath.

Pausing at a tiny clearing, the group took seats on a large boulder. They were now at a higher elevation than they had been at the overlook. Through the trees to the northeast they had a view of Grassy Mountain and Beaver Mountain, and the newly tilled fields in the valley spreading between them. They could also see the ravine that held the location of the first beacon.

"The beacon is approximately 600 feet down there," said Tom, pointing down into the ravine.

"It doesn't look as if we will need climbing equipment," said Alice, "but we'll have to take it slowly. From here, it looks like there are a lot of loose rocks. It's not too steep, and there is plenty of vegetation to hang onto."

"You guys hang here for a few more minutes," Sal said. "I'll hike a little further down the ridge and check out a good place to make our way down."

No one argued against taking in the view for a while longer, and the quick-gaited Sal could probably scamper along the ridge faster than any of them. While they waited, Tom stood on top of the boulder and surveyed the gulley. He noted that it was a typical runoff area; a tiny valley formed by years of erosion from snow melts. It was a closed valley, meaning that

the bottom end of it was blocked by another mountain, forming an isolated fishbowl-like area. This was the sort of terrain that would normally
form a small lake if there were a stream running into the valley, but Tom
saw no stream and the valley floor appeared dry.

"Not much down there to observe except rocks and trees," said Tom.

"Not even a shimmering portal to another dimension?" Alice asked
with a chuckle.

"If there's a portal down there, it's disguised as a rhododendron," he
laughed.

"Are you sure?" asked Adam. "I think I can see one of those old British police boxes down there."

"Riiight," both Tom and Alice laughed.

"And which particular time lord is manning the TARDIS?" Alice
asked.

"None other than the original Dr. Who, William Hartnell, of course,"
Adam replied.

They were laughing and joking about other outrageous possibilities
that could be causing the beacon when Sal returned. He wiped the sweat
from his forehead with his sleeve and plopped down on the boulder.
"I'm glad you dudes can sit around yucking it up while I'm out busting
my hump. I've got good news and okay news. The good news is that it
doesn't look too tough getting down into the gulley. The okay news is
that it doesn't much matter which way we go, so we might as well start
down from right here."

"Then you lead the way," Adam said, handing the LANav to Sal, "and
watch out for Daleks."

"For what?" asked Sal.

"Never mind. Just go slow and carefully," said Adam.

"I'm on it, dude. Just start whimpering if you can't keep up," replied
Sal.

They picked their way slowly downward, feet sideways to keep from
slipping on the moist ground, and using the trees to hang on to as they
descended. With the decreasing sunlight in the recesses of the gulley,
the stout oak and pine trees gave way to shade-loving varieties of willow,
chestnuts, and gums. Other than the increasing claustrophobia as the
sides of the gorge narrowed, blocking more and more of their view, there
seemed to be nothing to indicate the area was different than any other
part of the park.

It took them less than twenty minutes to reach the point where the
slope began to level off into the flat bottom area of the small valley. They

felt a significant temperature drop; it would take at least another hour for the sun to be high enough to warm the bowl-shaped valley, and last night's cold air still settled at the bottom.

Sal consulted the LANav. "The beacon indicator on this doohickey is hopping around like a jump dancer, but it looks like we're within two to three hundred feet of it," he said. "It's somewhere in the bottom of this valley, whatever 'it' is."

"Just to be thorough," said Adam, "let's split up and cover the valley bottom from two directions. Sal and I will walk clockwise and spiral in toward the center. Tom and Alice, you guys do the same thing going counter-clockwise. Since the LANav is not giving us a pinpoint location, let's do a careful search of the whole area and note anything that appears to be out of the ordinary. This valley is pretty small, so we should be able to cover the entire thing in an hour or so. Alice, please make some notes of the general description of the area you search, and I'll do the same. If we find anything of interest, we can take some photos when we come back with our gear."

As they began circling, getting closer to the center of the valley, Alice noted that although the ground was wet, it wasn't as muddy as she might expect for a closed valley such as this. Apparently there was adequate drainage for the runoff that made it into this gorge. The trees thinned further, and the foliage of the bottomland consisted of mature Georgia-native plants, such as yellowroot and witch-hazel, as well as other woody varieties of brush that typically do well in wet, rocky soil.

"I feel like Lewis and Clark, documenting the flora and fauna of the Louisiana Purchase," said Alice.

"Their route started a little further north, but I understand your meaning," answered Tom. "This little gorge is quite interesting, though. Not quite as awesome as the Corps of Discovery's adventures, but interesting. I observed that there is a lot more native flora down here, as if the invasive species haven't gotten a foothold yet."

"Not exactly the kind of 'anomaly' that you'd think would cause a blip on a navigational device," said Alice, "but yes, it's an intriguing plant distribution. I suppose TSO can tailor their marketing appropriately. Introducing the TSO LANav, perfect for space-travelers and botanists..." She stopped suddenly mid-sentence. "Oh, my goodness!" Alice cried, nearly dropping her notebook at the startling site before her.

She stared into the eyes of a horse, tethered to a willow, so close to her face that she had nearly walked into it. The horse stared back and made a snickering sound.

"It's a horse," Tom said.

"No kidding, Sherlock." Alice shot back. "What's a horse doing down here?"

"It's not unusual around here," Tom answered. "There are a lot of farms nearby, and plenty of riding trails throughout the park and wilderness area. There are also a few equine camps close by. The real question is—where's the rider?"

"He is right behind you," came the reply, startling them both.

Tom and Alice spun around to face the owner of the voice. Alice was unable to stifle a gasp, causing the horse to jerk its head with a start.

"Easy, *soquili*," said the stranger, stepping past Tom and Alice and stroking the horse's withers. "Excuse me, I did not mean to startle you, miss," he said to Alice.

Alice held up her hand and shook her head to indicate all was well.

The man who spoke was about the same height as Tom, with long black hair, braided and pulled into a bun on the back of his head. He had a deeply tanned, ruddy complexion. His dark and penetrating brown eyes were soft and open, lending his face a friendly countenance, though the eyes had an undertone of intensity, revealing the potential to turn fierce under different circumstances.

He continued, addressing both Tom and Alice. "My name is John Carter. I have observed you two and your friends coming into the valley. This is a good place to search for herbs and medicinal plants, is it not?" He held out his hand for them to shake.

"Pleased to meet you," said Tom and Alice, each shaking his hand and giving him their name.

"Medicinal plants? No, not really," said Alice. "I was just making some notes about any sort of vegetation or other interesting features of this valley we came across."

"Are you gold hunters?" John asked, his eyes flashing a hint of fierceness.

"Gold? Certainly not!" Tom answered. "We are evaluating the performance of some new equipment and enjoying public land."

"Public land? Many have paid a heavy price for this 'public' land," John said with the fierceness in his eyes intensifying.

Tom wasn't sure what to make of this guy, why he seemed to be questioning what they were doing, or why it was even any of his business. Was John a park ranger? He wasn't wearing a uniform. His clothes were very heavily worn and a bit old-fashioned, although well fitting. He had no badge or insignia to indicate he was a park representative, although he presented an air of authority rather than one of harassment. Regardless, Tom decided it was best not to provoke him. "We are aware there is a fee, and have already taken care of that," Tom replied.

A questioning look came into John Carter's eyes, and he was about to respond, but his eyes suddenly flashed past Tom and Alice, into the woods, just before they heard the sounds of Adam and Sal approaching.

"Hey, space travelers, are you guys over there?" they heard Sal yelling as he crashed through the woods.

"Over here," Tom yelled back.

"I think this part of the test is a bust," Adam was saying as he approached. "We haven't come across much of…" he stopped speaking when he was close enough to see John.

"Adam, this is Mr. John Carter," Tom said. "We were just getting acquainted."

Sal strolled up behind Adam. "Whoa, is that a freakin' horse?"

"No," answered Carter, shaking hands with Adam and Sal. "He is just a plain horse. How do you do?"

"It's a pleasure to meet you," said Adam, sending Sal an admonishing "cool it" glance. "Please excuse me and Sal for being surprised. We were doing some exploring in this small gulley, and didn't expect to find anyone else here."

"You surprised me as well when you began climbing down, so I kept quiet and out of sight to observe you for a while. When your colleagues discovered my horse, I felt I should announce my presence," said John. Any trace of annoyance, if it had ever existed, had vanished from John Carter's tone as he continued to speak to the group.

"I am returning from a journey and my horse began to show signs of irritation and swelling in his fetlock," John said, pointing to the horse's bandaged front leg. "I may have over-stressed him, as I am anxious to return home to bring the news of my trip to my people. I was aware of this secluded area where I could rest him, and also find tassel flower, willow and chamomile to treat him. I made camp here yesterday and prepared a poultice for him. I was just about to remove it when I heard your approach."

He squatted and began to remove the bandage on the horse's fetlock, revealing a soggy, green clump of vegetation. "Yes, it looks as if the poultice has done its job, so I may resume my journey. I will walk alongside him for a while until he is fully recovered."

"I think we are about finished here also," said Adam. "We still need to compare notes, but it seems that our explorations this morning have been unproductive and disappointing. We may have to content ourselves just with enjoying the scenery today."

"A worthy undertaking. Although, one never fully realizes the remunerations of a journey until it has been completed," John answered. "The day is still young. Perhaps the benefits of your explorations are yet to come. As for me, I must gather my few belongings, climb the slope out of this valley, and continue my own journey. Good luck to you in your endeavors," he said as he led the horse away from the group.

"And to you in yours, sir," Tom replied as the others nodded their goodbye and moved off in the direction where they entered the valley.

"Man, what an oddball," said Sal as soon as John was out of earshot. "I could have sworn I heard banjo music back there."

"C'mon, Sal," said Alice. "You think anyone without a Jersey accent is a hick."

"Yeah, what's your point?" replied Sal.

"He seemed a bit assertive at first," said Tom, "but I think he was okay. He had a strange way of speaking for a Georgian, I thought, and a couple of his statements were somewhat odd. Just before you walked up he asked if we were searching for gold."

"Gold? Odd for sure," said Sal. "What was with that 'my people' crap?"

"He sounded like he was a Native American," Adam said. "His accent was more northern than southern. Maybe he's on vacation, or part of some reenactment group, trying to stay in character."

"Sure, dude," said Sal. "My people do lunch with your people. We find gold. Take home to Great White North. Buy much beer and bacon," Sal quipped, drawing laughter from the others.

"Seriously," said Tom, "I don't know what he was getting at with that 'gold' comment either. It's not like it would do anyone any good to find gold in a state park. He certainly is an interesting character. I believe your guess is correct, Adam, that he was Native American. And I'd bet that you're right about the vacation part, too. His 'people' are probably just the folks he came here to ride horses with."

"We can ponder the mystery of John Carter later," said Adam. "Let's consider our own mystery for a while. Alice, did you guys discover anything that might account for the anomaly beacon?"

"John Carter and his horse was the most interesting thing we came across," Alice answered. "Other than that, all we noticed that there were more native plants down here. Not really that exciting, since the local equestrian community already seems to know that."

"I'm afraid this is going to be quite a letdown for Dr. Odan," Tom added. "He seemed to be certain that the LANav was indicating something a little more spectacular than a good place to find medicinal herbs. Has the readout changed at all?"

Adam glanced at the LANav. "Hmm, now the beacon is indicating a point back in the direction we came from, back near the stone wall area," Adam said.

"It's trying to tell us to get our butts back there and ride bikes," said Sal.

"Most likely it's telling us there is nothing to the anomalies. My guess is some kind of electronic interference, or maybe even a cosmic interference, but certainly nothing we can physically see," said Tom.

"If that's the case," said Adam, "we better break the news to Odan so they can begin working on a way to filter out the anomalies. I'm sure he'll be disappointed, but they still have made a significant breakthrough with this navigational device. TSO definitely has an incredible product to bring to market."

There was still a few more days of testing to perform, but there was no denying that the discouraging beacon testing had dampened everyone's mood. Even Tom, who had been the most skeptical, could not hide his disappointment. They had all allowed themselves to fantasize that the beacons would lead them to an amazing new adventure, but now they all felt a bit foolish for letting their imaginations override their common sense.

As they approached the point where the slope of the valley floor began to rise back up to the rim, they heard Sal whisper, "Dude, don't look now, but here comes Squanto again."

They turned to see John Carter approaching from behind with his horse in tow. Raising his hand in greeting, John said, "Hello, again, friends. It looks as if our paths may run together for a little longer. If you are walking toward the old ruins, may we keep each other company along the way?"

"That's where we are headed, and of course, please join us," said Adam. Tom and Alice smiled and nodded in agreement, and Sal just rolled his eyes, although John did not seem to notice.

Climbing up the steep, muddy slope took much more effort than coming down. They took a zigzag path, switching back and forth up the slope to make the ascent less arduous. John Carter ascended the mountainside with effortless grace, although his horse showed some strain and still favored his injured leg.

"Do you care to share the reason for your explorations?" John asked Adam as they climbed.

Adam would not normally divulge details of their testing to a stranger, but he felt pretty confident that John Carter was in no way a competitive threat to TSO. He struck Adam as a person who was at ease in the forest, and nothing indicated that he was the least bit high tech. As far as Adam could tell, John was not even carrying a GPS.

"I can tell you a little about it," Adam answered. "We are test engineers, and we do contract work for companies that have a new product they hope to sell. We provide them with feedback about how their devices perform as well as suggestions for improvements, which they use to determine if it is ready to sell. Because these are new devices, the companies are secretive about them until they are announced, so we are usually under a non-disclosure agreement that prevents us from talking about them, but I can tell you that today we are working with a device that will assist with navigation. That's why we are out here in the forest, to see how well the product performs."

It seems," John replied, "that the makers would want very many people to know about their invention, so all could contribute to its improvement for the benefit of everyone."

"In an ideal world, that would make sense. But in the real world of cutthroat competition they need to keep secrets."

"It must be a very valuable invention indeed," John said with a shocked look, "if people are willing to cut each other's throats for it."

"Er, yeah, I guess so," Adam answered, not sure if John was putting him on or not. He thought he should change the subject. "How about yourself? What brought you into the forest? You mentioned returning from a trip?"

"Yes, it was necessary for me to travel to Tennessee for a meeting with my friend to discuss the grave situation that faces us. As you know, we are not permitted to conduct our meetings in Georgia, so I had to travel to him hoping to get some good news that he has made progress in Washington, DC. There is, unfortunately, no progress, and I must carry bad news back to my people and help them prepare for the worst."

Adam shook his head as if he hadn't heard John correctly, trying to determine if he was being put on. "Now I have more questions than before, John. What do you mean you're not allowed to conduct meetings? Who are 'your people'? You aren't engaged in some sort of illegal activity, are you?" Adam regretted asking that question almost before he asked it.

John hesitated, looking gravely at Adam as if he were assessing his veracity. "Are you not from Georgia?"

"No, we are from Delaware," Adam answered, once again failing to bite back information he wasn't sure he should provide. John hadn't answered the question. Who was this guy, he wondered? Some sort of Native American crime boss?

"I see. I believe there are only a few tribes remaining in your state. My people are *Ani-yunwiya*, the Principal People, also called Tsalagi. You probably know us as Cherokee. I am of mixed blood, as both my parents were, but being Tsalagi involves much more than just bloodlines.

"You come from far away, but surely you have heard of Georgia's plan to enforce their illegal treaty, and that they have made it against the law for Cherokee to hold any political or organizational gatherings?" John looked questioningly at Adam.

Adam was now completely convinced the man was delusional. He glanced behind him at the others, quiet due to the exertion of climbing although the incredulous look in their eyes clearly communicated that they had been listening. Tom, who appeared ready to speak, was stopped short by a quick shake of the head from Adam. Alice shot them both a questioning look, while Sal just rolled his eyes toward the treetops and began humming "*One Toke Over the Line*."

Adam tried to continue the conversation as nonchalantly as he could. "Cherokee, you say? There are quite a few people back home who have Native American ancestry, but you're right, there are not very many tribes. I know there are Lenape, and Nanticoke downstate, but I don't believe there has been a reservation in Delaware for many years.

"But, uh, I believe you are mistaken about the Cherokee not being allowed to have meetings," Adam said nervously, not sure how much he should contradict this fellow. "I'm pretty sure there are federal laws, not to mention a little thing called the Constitution that protects your rights to do so."

"Those laws work for the white people," John explained, "but the Cherokee nation is sovereign, and the laws do not apply. We are not granted any rights by the U.S. Constitution. Even though the Supreme Court ruled that the state of Georgia has no jurisdiction over us, the president has said that the federal government does not have the resources to protect us from the state."

"The President of the United States said he couldn't protect you from *Georgia*?" It was inconceivable to Adam that this man actually believed that.

"Yes," John answered evenly. "When Justice Marshall ruled the Georgia treaty illegal, your president told him he would have to enforce his ruling himself. That was some years ago, and we have since made many efforts to persuade the legislatures to reconsider."

"Justice Marshall hasn't been…" Tom began.

Adam interrupted Tom before he could finish. "That's very interesting, John. We wish you the best of luck getting that straightened out."

Tom looked annoyed at the interruption, but Adam would apologize to him later. He knew Tom was about to mention the fact that Supreme Court Justice Marshall, a Johnson administration appointee, hadn't been making any rulings lately, especially since he passed away in 1993. He couldn't tell if John was pulling his leg or simply delusional, but he didn't want to say anything that might get the man aggravated. They would soon be back to the top of the mountain, and would be close to the developed part of the state park soon. There they could part ways with John and leave him to his fantasies. He changed the subject by asking John if his horse was doing OK.

Tom seemed to catch on, and Alice also tried to keep the conversation more subtle by chatting with John about his horse and the medicinal herbs. Sal didn't appear to be the least bit interested in either topic of conversation and walked ahead for a better view, hoping to catch a glimpse of the mountain bikers.

Sal was looking out over the landscape when the rest of the group caught up to him. "What is it, Siesta time in Georgia? I haven't seen a single biker on the trails from here." Adam, Tom, and Alice joined Sal at the overlook, leaving John to check the horse's mending leg.

"You're right," said Alice, "I can't see a soul on the trails from here. It's mid-day on a beautiful spring afternoon; you would think the park would be filled with hikers and bikers."

"Does the view seem a little different? I was pretty sure you could see more of the roads from here," said Adam.

"There's probably some park event going on down by the stone wall," said Tom. "Let's get back there and check it out."

"Yeah, and we can ditch Wacko Squanto," said Sal, keeping his voice low enough so John could not overhear. "He's enough to drive anyone loopy."

"I can understand your concern," said Alice, "you're already within walking distance of loopy."

Sal responded with a snort.

John Carter caught up with them, and they continued walking southwestward along the trail, without speaking. Adam did not want to discuss the disappointing LANav testing with John present, nor did he want to get him started on his offbeat stories about Indians and the president. John seemed to enjoy walking along in silence anyway.

The silence was short-lived, however. Tom suddenly stopped in his tracks and said, "Why haven't we passed the fire tower yet?"

"Dang, we must have missed it," said Sal.

"Missed it? How could we possibly have missed it? You could easily see it from the trail and the overlook," Tom replied.

As Tom spoke those words, he realized that they also had not yet seen the overlook platform. He retrieved the printed map he had brought along, trying to determine if they had somehow gone in the wrong direction.

"We probably already walked passed it," said Adam. "We must have been talking and just didn't see it. What other explanation could there be? I verified our direction with the LANav, and we should be nearly to the stone wall.

"It's been a long and disappointing morning for us. Let's get back to the parking area, see John on his way, and knock off for a few hours to enjoy the remainder of the afternoon. We just need to call Ed first and give him the bad news. Look! We're nearly there; I can see the stone wall just up ahead."

As they approached the wall, their confusion only grew deeper. They asked each other questions they had no answer for. Where was the asphalt path along the wall? Wasn't there a sign posted here? Where are all the park visitors? The wall itself appeared to be more overgrown and unkempt, yet a little less dilapidated than it had been not more than a few hours earlier.

Tom and Sal sprinted off in the direction of the parking lot, while Adam and Alice walked along the wall looking for something that might explain the inconsistencies in its appearance. Not more than a few minutes later, Tom and Sal returned.

Tom was ghostly white. "Gone," he said.

"What's gone?" Alice asked.

"Everything!" he answered hollowly. "Paths, signs, parking lot. No sign of our SUV."

Sal said nothing, just nodded his head at Adam's questioning look. Dumbfounded, they sat on the wall exchanging glances of exasperation, looking from one to another, not speaking.

Adam finally said, "Let's get a grip here. There *must* be a logical explanation for this! Could we have possibly returned to a different section of the wall ruin? A section that has been kept free of the touristy stuff?"

Four sets of inquiring eyes turned toward John Carter, who had been silently watching them become increasingly agitated. He sympathized with their obvious distress, even if he didn't understand the cause. The wall was an ancient place with many strange spirits, but he had never seen the spirits create this kind of anguish in anyone before. He looked at them and shrugged.

"Not many tourists visit our nation's lands," he offered, wishing he could say something more helpful. "The stone wall has been here, in ruins as you see it, for many years before my time. There is much speculation about its origin. There are nearly as many stories as there are rocks in the wall."

"Your nation's lands? Not many visitors?" Adam said. "What do you mean? This is a state park that gets thousands of visitors!"

"This land is part of the Cherokee Nation," John answered. "You said you were testing a navigation device. Did you not know you are within the boundaries of the Cherokee Nation? It's kind of big to miss."

"Are you saying that this is some sort of reservation? This is a state park!" Adam said. He was getting frustrated by this man's idiotic ranting. "Tom, is it possible that we returned to a different part of the park?"

Tom shook his head. "I don't believe that could be possible."

"I do not know what this reservation is you are looking for," said John. "What is left of our nation is over twelve thousand square miles. I admit I have not been to all of it, but I am very familiar with this area, and I am pretty sure there are no parks around here."

"Are you trying to tell me that the Cherokees own this land? It's a state park. It belongs to Georgia," said Adam.

"That is what Georgia and President Jackson have said, but over sixteen thousand Cherokee have been trying to convince them otherwise. That has been the reason for my journey to Red Clay. I was hoping to return with more positive news about our leader, John Ross, and his most recent trip to Washington City," John said.

"President Jackson!" Adam said. "Jackson hasn't been the president for a long time!"

"Yes, I am aware he had been replaced by Mr. Van Buren. Chief Ross hoped that he would be more amenable to our plight. He made another appeal to your congress, but his attempt was again in vain. The new president seemed willing to give us additional time, but Governor Gilmer argued against it, and the issue was once again tabled. I am now on my way to the old capitol, New Echota, to relay this unfortunate news to the Cherokee who still reside there," John replied sadly.

"Adam," said Tom, "this man is delusional. He's talking about a president from the 1800's, and if I remember my history correctly, things that occurred prior to the Cherokee removal. I suppose the 'Justice Marshall' he was referring to before was John Marshall, not Thurgood Marshall! This is the 21st century, not the 1800's. We need to stop wasting time talking to him and figure out where we are."

"I appreciate that you are distressed, Tom," said John Carter, "but I am hardly the one who is delusional. I am not the one who is lost, and believes himself to be in the wrong century. You are in the lands of the Cherokee Nation, and the date is May of 1838."

Chapter eleven

U ntil now, Adam considered himself to be competent to handle most management situations. He was generally fair, level-headed, and decisive. He was experienced and had attended some of the best management seminars that were currently available. But nothing had prepared him for this situation; he felt inadequate and ineffectual. Somehow he must have missed the lecture on suddenly finding yourself and your team transported back in time.

He knew he was soon going to have to figure it out. After John's last statement, his three team members were looking at him, silently waiting for him to give them an answer. He considered his options. Should he make a joke? Did anyone take this seriously? Was he dreaming? He thought that the latter possibility was the most likely. In that case, it really didn't matter what he said, since all would be well as soon as he woke up. Maybe if he concentrated really hard on waking up… Nope, didn't seem to do the trick. No, Adam thought, definitely not a dream.

"Well?" he heard Alice ask him. He smiled stupidly at her.

"None of you are taking this seriously, are you?" said Tom. "I'm certainly not about to believe this is 1838 just because Squanto here says so."

Interesting, Adam thought. Tom seems to be showing signs of hostility. He thought that would more likely come from Sal. On the contrary, Sal was quietly sitting on the stone wall, looking somewhat muddled, perhaps even a little frightened. Definitely a look he never saw Sal have before. Alice was still looking at him, waiting for an answer. Did she seriously expect him to have one? Her cold stare told him that yes, she did.

"Ahem," Adam said. Good start, he thought. Always start with 'ahem' when you don't have a clue what to say. He wished he had a pipe like Tom so he could give the impression of pondering the situation for a while. Since he didn't have a pipe, he figured he needed to give them a little more though. "Does anyone have any suggestions?" he asked. Yeah, that was good, throw it back on them. Use the old Socratic approach.

"You don't have a clue, do you?" said Alice.

Not exactly the reaction he was hoping for. Obviously he wasn't going to bluff his way out of this. "No, for once I'm afraid I don't," he answered sheepishly.

"The LANav has satellite communications. How about calling someone on it?" Alice suggested.

"Good idea," said Adam, wishing he'd thought of that himself. They had left their cell phones behind along with most of the other gear in the SUV, since they only got spotty reception at best. The LANav had been more dependable in the remote areas. He quickly dismissed the idea of calling Dr. Odan. It would be bad enough to call his employer to tell him they were lost. He could just imagine the response he'd get if he asked what year it was. He fished the business card he had picked up at the outfitter's store from his pocket. "I'll give James Adair a call. He knows this area as well as anyone. I bet he knows all about some special event going on today. He'll probably have a good laugh at my expense, but at least the mystery will be cleared up." He retrieved the LANav from his belt pack and set it to "sat-phone" mode. "Uh-oh, that's funny."

"I can't imagine anything that could strike you as funny about this. Now what seems to be the issue?" asked Tom in an irritable tone none of them were used to hearing from him.

"It says NO SATELLITES. I'm sure we had coverage all through this area before."

"Perhaps they didn't pay the bill," Tom said sarcastically.

"More likely it's just a temporary service interruption," Adam answered.

"May I make a suggestion?" asked John Carter.

"Sure. Absolutely. By all means," said Adam, more than happy to let him take focus for a while.

"I know I am a stranger to you, and you all must be in great disharmony because of this upsetting situation. But if you are unable to continue with the plans you had made, perhaps it would be helpful to journey with me for a little while, so that you once again may become oriented. It may be that an explanation can be found along my path, since yours has become, uh, confused."

"That seems as good a suggestion as anything I could come up with," said Adam. "Maybe we'll see a landmark we recognize, or maybe the communication system will come back on line. What do you guys think?"

"You've got to be kidding," said Tom. "You don't actually believe we've time-traveled to the 1800's do you? I think we need to go our own way and figure out our way back to the parking lot."

Adam was beginning to regain his composure. He realized that making sense of this bizarre situation was going to take a level head and strong leadership. His engineers were professionals, but right now they were stressed and prone to rash decisions. He needed to maintain a calm, confident manner despite his own anxiety.

"How confident are you we can do that?" asked Adam. "A few minutes ago you were certain we hadn't taken a wrong turn. I'm not saying I believe we fell into an H. G. Wells novel, but at the moment I don't have a reasonable explanation to offer either. We haven't seen a soul other than John since we left the valley, so I'm not sure it's a good idea to separate from the only other person who may know his way around this area. At least walking in the direction of the New Echota historic site we'll reach civilization before long."

"That's a valid point," said Alice. "But how about consulting the navigational features of the LANav? Is it giving us any other indication of where we might be?"

"I checked it while Sal and Tom were off looking for the parking lot and it indicated that we are in the same spot along the stone wall that we were when we arrived," Adam said. "The beacon indicator is now showing a new anomaly location about twenty miles to the southwest. That's the direction John is going anyway, so we may as well walk along with him toward the second beacon."

"Awesome plan, dude!" said Sal, suddenly coming to life. "Let's follow that freakin' thing to another beacon!" He jumped up and started pacing along the wall.

"For heaven's sake, Sal, calm down. Do you have another suggestion?" said Alice.

"No. I don't know. I guess it makes sense to follow Squanto for a while. Let's just get the hell out of here. Then I'll calm down. Dude, this is seriously creeping me out."

"For once we agree on something," answered Alice. "I don't know what's going on either, but I'm all for getting out of this wilderness area."

"New Echota, where I am going, is in the direction that your device is telling you to go, so it seems your choice is clear," said John Carter. "In any case, I must be on my way to reach the town before nightfall. You are welcome to come with me if you wish." With that, John began leading his horse along the trail.

"Tom?" Adam asked.

"If the rest of you want to follow him, I'll play along. At least until we reach the highway, or to get somewhere with satellite coverage," Tom answered grumpily. "Either way, it will put an end to this foolishness."

The team followed John Carter, plodding along the faintly defined trail, lost in their thoughts as they tried to make sense of what was happening. John moved rapidly, although he had slowed his usual pace to make it easier for them to keep up. He tried not to be annoyed by the tension the group was feeling, reminding himself that he was not the true target of their exasperation, even if they considered him to be. While he did not understand much of their talk about the strange device, or the disorienting effect it seemed to have had on them, he hoped he could find some way to ease their discomfort. He motioned to Adam to walk along side of him so they could talk.

"If you were able to tell me more about your mission and device, maybe I could offer you some thoughts about what is happening. You said you were under an obligation not to reveal its secrets, but I believe anyone would agree that the circumstances are extenuating."

"I suppose that could be helpful," Adam replied hesitantly. "I'm still limited in how much I can say. I gave my word in a signed agreement."

"Of course, I understand you must honor your word, signed agreement or not. "But consider this; if I am correct and the year truly is 1838, then in theory you have not yet entered into an agreement. If, however, your friend is correct and I am just a 'delusional Indian' anything you told me would be safe, since no one would listen to someone who is delusional."

"A logical argument, I guess, but I certainly wouldn't want to try to justify breaking a confidentiality agreement by claiming I was time-traveling. On the other hand, you don't strike me as a corporate spy, so I guess under the circumstances it would be okay to discuss some of the project with you, as long as we don't get into the technical details of the device. What is it you would like to know?"

"You have said that you were testing a new navigation device. Where was it intending to lead you?"

"We weren't sure exactly," said Adam. "It was indicating a place down in the small valley where we first met you. We were investigating to see what might be there. We did a thorough search, but found nothing of interest."

"Perhaps it was leading you to me, since you found me there," John offered.

"I hardly think it was leading us to you."

"You are probably right," said John. "I am not very interesting. I bet it was leading you to my horse. He is much more interesting than I am."

"Now you're pulling my leg, aren't you? No, it doesn't really work that way, John. The device doesn't lead you to people or animals, only to fixed positions on the earth."

"But Adam, you said that it was indicating something new, a thing that you didn't know would be there. In that case, how do you know it wasn't taking you to my horse?"

"For one thing, it has been indicating the place in the valley for several weeks, and you and your horse were only there for one night."

"I see. I have been planning my journey for many weeks, but the stop in the valley was a last minute necessity when my horse became injured." He paused a moment to consider. "Are you able to tell me how your device is able to lead you to these places?"

"Well, simply stated, it uses information from the stars and planets to determine location, and can calculate how to reach a destination by using that information," Adam explained.

"Wonderful!" That is exactly the way the Cherokee have navigated for many years. It is good to hear that the whites are beginning to catch up. We also use the landmarks to find our way. You should recommend that to the makers of the device."

"Uh, okay, sure. But I don't think you get the idea of this device. You see, it can read the information from the heavens and guide you without your having to know anything about navigation. And all you need is this small device," he said, showing John the LANav.

John eyed the LANav with guarded curiosity. He considered what Adam told him and reached his own conclusion. "I think I still prefer our way, though," he said. "I carry all the information inside my head, so I don't have to worry about misplacing a device and losing my way. Of course I could lose my head, but then it won't matter if I am lost. Still, I can see how it would be convenient for the white men who get lost easily. Much easier than taking an Indian with you everywhere," he said with a wry smile.

Adam looked at him curiously until he realized the Indian was mocking him. "I guess I deserve that for talking down to you. I wasn't sure how much technology someone from 1838 would understand."

"We've been finding our way around for quite a while. I have never seen a device such as the one you have. I can understand how it may be useful, though I have never needed to find something that I did not know what it was until I got there."

"That's not really the purpose of the device. Its true function is to guide us to where we want to go. Our current technology uses man-made satellites— platforms in the sky—positioned around the globe to broadcast location information to a receiver that can be carried easily by a traveler. The difference with this device is that it doesn't have to rely on the satellites for information, it receives transmissions directly from the stars," Adam explained.

John rubbed his fingers over his chin as he thought it over. "It seems a reasonable explanation, then, that since the stars have been here for a great number of years, and will be here for a great many more, that they could send you information about other times and places as well."

"Are you suggesting that the stars and planets have a memory? Surely they could only provide location information for the present time.

"Not necessarily. Consider our own planet. We can excavate below its surface to retrieve information about what things were like many years ago. Archeologists and geologists have done this to determine the lifestyles of early civilizations and the formation of the earth. Does it not stand to reason that the other planets would also contain similar historical infor-mation? Not only information about their own formation, but especially of our history. They have been watching over us for such a long time!"

"It's an interesting theory, but it doesn't explain how we were moved through time, if that is really what happened."

"I don't understand how you can have 'platforms in the sky' either, but I do not doubt your word that you have them."

"But why bring us here and now, of all the possible times in history?" Adam asked.

"Don't know," he shrugged. "But it seems as though you are going to find out."

Alice, Tom, and Sal had been listening intently to the conversation. Tom was showing outward signs of irritation that Adam could possibly be taking any of John's suggestions seriously. He was an engineer, and was not going to be easily convinced that they had somehow managed to circumvent the laws of time and physics just by walking into a secluded valley. He was anxious to get to the highway, looking forward to seeing a passing semi put an end to this time travel nonsense. He thought they should have reached it by now, but the up and down hiking through the mountains made it hard to judge exactly how far they had walked. He glanced over Adam's shoulder at the LANav. The topology on the screen looked familiar, yet different somehow, and it appeared that they still had a ways to go to reach the highway. He also noticed the SAT phone icon with a line through it, indicating there was still no coverage. He scowled, his mood made even worse.

Sal did not know what to think. He was completely out of his element, trudging along, lost in the Georgia wilderness. It wasn't the wilderness that was the problem; he'd spent plenty of time hiking in remote places. It was the "lost" part that was new to him. He couldn't recall ever having been lost in his life. Yes, there were times when he had been unsure of his exact location, but he had never been truly lost. Disappearing landmarks were just not possible, and the crazy Indian dude talking about being in the 1800's was making things exponentially worse. When he got out of this mess, he was going to demand some extra hazardous duty pay.

Alice was shaken, although not so much panicked as intrigued. Her natural curiosity kept her mind focused on figuring out a solution to this puzzle. She could not comprehend how they came to be lost. She certainly wasn't about to accept the idea that they had traveled to the past. She was fascinated by John's hypothesis, as impossible as it was. John was definitely an interesting character. If they were going to be hiking together for a while, she wanted to find out more about him. Maybe she could catch him off-guard and prod him to say something to prove he wasn't from the nineteenth century. "John, I hope this doesn't sound offensive, but you seem to be pretty well educated for a Cherokee Indian from the 1800's," she said.

"I am not offended, Alice. I was fortunate enough that my family could afford to send me to one of the white people's schools in Tennessee after I attended the Cherokee school in New Echota. Many of my friends were not so lucky. They did not receive much formal education at all, at least in the ways of the whites, and only know our Tsalagi traditions and language. It was in school where I met and became good friends with Allen Ross, the son of our Principal Chief John Ross. I am in fact returning from a visit with Allen and his father in Red Clay, Tennessee."

Alice continued her questioning. "You said you were returning with bad news, didn't you John? What sort of bad news?"

"Part of the reason of my trip was to learn the outcome of Chief Ross's most recent efforts to preserve the right to remain on our lands. The Cherokee elected John Ross—the Cherokee call him Guwisguwi—ten years ago, even though he is only part Cherokee. He was raised with an understanding of Cherokee culture and also has much knowledge of

Washington politics. In spite of all his knowledge and efforts, he was not able to persuade a reversal of the previous rulings."

"How will that affect the Cherokee living here in Georgia?" she asked.

"Georgia is planning to remove all Indians from its lands and relocate them west of the Mississippi river. In 1802, the U.S. government promised the state of Georgia that it would extinguish all claims to Indian lands within its borders in exchange for Georgia relinquishing its territorial claims west of the Mississippi. A provision of that agreement was that the Indian claims were to be settled peacefully and reasonably. As more settlers came to Georgia, they became more anxious to acquire Cherokee land. Once gold was discovered within the Cherokee nation, the pressure to take the land by force became overwhelming. The 'reasonable and peaceful' provision is now being ignored. When Chief Ross returned from his previous trip to Washington, he found that his house and lands had been taken from him and given away in a land lottery, leaving him homeless."

"My gosh!" said Alice. "Is there no way for him to contest that? He must have something in writing showing that he is the legal owner."

"His own property is not his immediate concern. Having been unable to persuade the government to prevent Georgia from seizing our land, we will all soon be facing the same situation. This is the news that I must bring to New Echota."

"How is it possible that they can just kick all the Indians out of Georgia? They want to take away land you have owned for generations?" said Alice.

John nodded solemnly. "For many years there have been disagreements between Indian and white settlers, as I am sure you know. There have been many treaties between the Cherokee and the whites. The Hopewell treaty in 1785 detailed specific terms for preventing the encroachment of our lands, but those terms were ignored. All of the subsequent treaties have been broken as more white settlers encroach upon the Cherokee Nation lands, so it comes as no surprise to most of my people that another agreement has been broken.

"The Cherokee Nation has been strongly encouraged to change our way of life, to adopt much of the white culture, in order to live amicably. We have altered many of our traditions. Most now run farms as the whites do, instead of hunters and food growers as we had been for generations. The newly formed Cherokee government is modeled after the United States government. Many have accepted the Christian religion, and a large percentage of Cherokee can read and write our language. Chief Ross hoped that these efforts would lead to harmony between our people, even proposed a Cherokee state to become part of the United States, but has been rejected at every attempt.

"There is also disagreement about our course of action from within. Some feel that we have no choice except to give up our homelands and move to the west. They believe that is the only way we can continue to exist as a nation. Some have already migrated west, and a small group claiming to represent the entire nation has entered into a treaty with the whites, agreeing to give up our lands in exchange for a token payment and the promise of land in the western Indian Territory. Called the Treaty of New Echota, our Principle Chief John Ross, in his most recent appeal to Washington City, carried a petition signed by nearly sixteen thousand Cherokee people to dispute the legality of the New Echota treaty. Chief Ross was joined by one of your great speakers, Ralph W. Emerson, to present the petition to the new president, Mr. Van Buren. I have already told you of the disappointing outcome of his appeal."

"That's so horrible! How could another group," asked Alice, "agree to a treaty without the consent of the Principle Chief?"

"Our chiefs are not like your president," John explained. "He is not the 'boss' of his tribe; he is more like a counselor who offers his wisdom when decisions have to be made. The people are free to discuss, modify, or even ignore his advice. The chief does not have to approve the decision. Each village has its own chiefs; some who counsel in times of war, and others who counsel in times of peace. Not having a central governing body led to confusion between our cultures. We restructured our government to model the white man's government, in an attempt to become more compatible. We still retain a very democratic system, however."

"But our government is a democracy," said Alice.

"Actually, it is not," said John. "The United States government is a constitutional republic. While it has democratic elements, it is a nation of laws. The Constitution and Bill of Rights guide the democratic process, and a system of checks and balances within each branch of your government help to prevent the majority from overruling the rights of the minority, and preserve the rights of the individual states."

"Of course, you are right," admitted Alice. "I guess my error is the result of living in a large country and being pretty much isolated from the rest of the world. Many of us tend to take our country's principles of government for granted."

Tom moved up alongside Alice and John. He was clearly agitated. "Speaking of being isolated, we should have come to a town, or at least crossed several roads by now. I don't know what this game is, but I'd like some answers. John, I've heard enough about Indians; what exactly is going on?" Tom demanded.

Before John could answer, they emerged from the forest onto a well-rutted dirt road about forty feet wide that stretched into the distance, around a bend to the north and into the horizon to the south.

John pointed to the road. "Tom, this is the Cherokee Federal Road. Along this part of the road there are no farms, but in many places the road has attracted a number of settlements, by both Cherokee and illegally by whites. There are no other roads to cross for many more miles, until we get much closer to New Echota."

"This is nothing more than an old fire road," Tom snapped back. "I don't know how, but somehow you are deceiving us about the direction we're heading in."

"I have no reason to deceive you, Tom. Does not your device show you are heading in the correct direction? I gather that you are an experienced woodsman. Does not the position of the mountains and the sun in the sky indicate your position to you?"

"Well, yes, it does," Tom answered hesitantly, "but it's certainly not believable to me that we have time-traveled to 1838. Why do you accept that so easily?"

"Is it more believable to you that I am somehow controlling the movement of the sun in the sky?" John answered patiently. "It is strange for me as well, since I have never met anyone from a future time before. But if you tell me it is so, I will accept it, as I have no reason to disbelieve you. It is well known that the Tsalagi have a different notion of time than the whites. A typical view of time is along a linear scale, one thing happening after another. An Indian, though, considers time to be more random, sort of like a bouncing ball. Our mythology illustrates this better than I can explain it, but things happen when they happen, not in any particular order."

Tom offered no reply, looking at John Carter with distrust. The man had some valid arguments, but he wasn't about to believe that they had traveled in time.

John suddenly looked toward the road and said, "Please, my friends, let us step back into the cover of the woods behind us. I hear the approach of a wagon, and have no way to know if they may behave badly toward us. It would be best if we remained hidden until they passed."

"Now we're getting somewhere. It's probably some hikers or campers," Tom said. "I think we should flag them down."

"I would not recommend that. Please," John pleaded, "at least remain hidden until we can see them. If you recognize them as friendly, you can then show yourselves."

They moved back into the trees, Tom going along reluctantly. By now, everyone could hear the sound of approaching hoof beats, pounding heavily along the dirt road.

"Just sounds like horseback riders to me," said Tom.

John shot him an indulgent but stern glance, placing his index finger to his lips. Tom scowled, but complied.

All their attention was drawn to the road. Approaching at a fast clip from the south was a team of four horses pulling a wooden, uncovered, Conestoga-style wagon. Two men wearing military uniforms were driving the wagon, and inside were about a dozen more men. Most of the men were wearing uniforms not recognizable as any branch of service the team had seen before, and the uniform color varied. Most were bearded and ragged, and all were armed with what appeared to be large caliber rifles. The wagon passed quickly, leaving a cloud of red dust behind. For a moment, no one moved. They continued to stare at the receding dust trail, as John said, "I believe it is safe now. It was just a single company of Georgia Militia, most likely heading to the tavern at the old Vann place."

They stood slowly, brushing the dust from themselves, glancing at each other in disbelief. Tom looked bewildered as he struggled to come up with a reasonable explanation. "Maybe it's a reenactment," he said, not sounding very confident.

"A reenactment?" Adam said. "Do you suppose part of the reenactment involves removing the state park or the major highways we should have crossed by now?"

"I don't know what to think anymore," Tom blurted. "This is all going way beyond anything I can understand."

"Let's not panic," Adam said as calmly as he could. "I suggest we keep following John, and keep an open mind for now. Tom, you're one of the brightest engineers I know, so if anyone can figure out what's going on, you can. Hiking along with John can't hurt, and may help to clear our minds so we can evaluate what has happened."

Tom looked at him slack-jawed and shook his head.

"I guess," Alice offered, "we don't really have much choice but to go along with it, do we Tom? Our only other choice is to just sit here in the woods. If there's some devious purpose I'm sure we'll find out soon enough. Let's see what New Echota is like. You wanted to visit there anyway."

"I wasn't planning to walk. And I sure as heck wasn't expecting to participate in some sort of historical reenactment!" he said, clinging to his feeble notion.

"Chill, dude," said Sal. "Maybe we'll get there in time for a powwow," he joked nervously. "In a couple hours we'll all be banging on drums and dancing around a campfire. That'd be awesome; like a native American rock festival." The team chuckled tentatively. For once Sal's wisecracking and bad jokes were a welcome bit of normalcy.

"Sorry," said John in all seriousness. "Not likely to be a powwow, but I am sure there will be nourishment available."

"I can handle some nourishment about now," Sal said, "and a nice cozy tipi to take a nap in." Even in this extraordinary situation, eating and sleeping were a priority for Sal.

"I am afraid not once again, Sal," said John. "You are thinking of the wrong Indians. Tipis are used by Plains Indians. We live in houses."

They crossed the road and continued southwest, in the direction of New Echota. John explained that there were no major roads until they reached the New Town Road, but the going would be easy. It was mostly flat, level terrain and open trails. "My detour to the valley of the stone wall made my journey longer, but I felt that my horse needed the rest and medicinal herbs there. I hoped it would be a place I could camp safely and undiscovered."

"Undiscovered by whom?" Adam asked.

"The Georgia State Militia have been very aggressive to any Cherokee they suspect to be involved in organizational activities. There are also many gold prospectors and settlers who believe they are entitled to their lottery land. It is best for me to avoid just about everyone during these times, which is why I remained concealed when I first saw your group in the valley. My horse is not very good at hiding in the woods, though."

"I guess he is kind of big to hide behind a tree," said Adam.

"I must be candid with you, Adam. There is an element of risk for you and your companions in traveling along with me. Our group is probably too large to be harassed by prospectors or settlers, but the militia will not hesitate. They will aggressively question us if we encounter them, and there have been occasions where they have imprisoned whites whom they suspect as being sympathetic to Cherokees."

"I suppose we might find it difficult to prove who we are, especially if this is really 1838 and we show them identification from more than 150 years in the future," Adam said.

"Yes, if you have such documentation, I would recommend keeping it well concealed," John suggested.

"Whadaya mean, Squanto?" said Sal, "Won't I need my driver's license to buy some firewater in town?" The others cringed at Sal's political incorrectness, but they were happy he was beginning to act like his old self. Alice started to rebuke him with one of her expected comebacks, but John Carter began speaking first.

"The Cherokee have tried to regulate the sale of whiskey for the last few years," he said, "but it has been a contentious issue with the whites. I do not believe you need a special license to buy alcohol if that is your wish. You would need one to sell it. The sale of firewater as you call it has been a widespread and debilitating problem among the Cherokee, so I recommend you avoiding it."

"Uh, okay," Sal said. "I was only joking, dude."

"If I had been drinking," said Tom, "it might make this situation more understandable."

John made no further comment. His stern expression showed he did not take the subject lightly.

They hiked for nearly four hours, and Tom estimated they had traveled about eleven miles. He used the LANav to confirm his approximation, which indicated they had hiked eleven point eight. The others seemed reluctant to use the LANav, feeling a bit spooked by the device and believing it to be somehow responsible for their predicament. Tom logically determined that if it was the LANav that got them into this situation, whatever the situation was, it was likely to hold the solution for getting them out. He could no longer deny that they had somehow been transported to a place other than where they began this hike. There was no way they could travel this far in the direction they were going without seeing some sign of civilization. He had not seen a paved road, any sort of vehicle, or any other person for that matter. There had, however, been several other indications of human presence. The trail they were following, while not a well maintained park service trail, showed obvious signs of use as a footpath, and there were blazes on trees at each branch. They had also passed at least two areas where trees had been cut and removed. The cuts were old, and the people who did the cutting were long gone. A healthy creek flowed alongside the trail for a good part of their journey, and wherever they needed to cross rocks and logs were arranged to provide makeshift stepping stones and bridges.

He did not see any undeniable proof that they were no longer in the twenty-first century. As he walked, he ran through every "what-if" scenario he could think of that might explain what happened to them. Nothing made any sense to his ordered mind. After four hours of unsuccessful reasoning, he was beginning to conclude that time-travel was about as good an explanation as anything else. He decided that in order for him to continue to contemplate what had happened to them, and to productively work on a solution, he was going to at least accept the possibility of time-travel. As outrageously illogical as that theory was, it offered the most reasonable answers.

The others had also been pondering their situation. They had all reached some level of acceptance, regardless of how much it went against the scientific aspect of their personalities. There was little choice. As Alice said, they could either accept their situation and keep walking or sit in denial in the middle of the forest. They were still too much in shock to openly discuss a plan of action to get back to their own time. If they tried, at this point it would only lead to more frustration. They left it unspoken for now, but all four were aware of the most frightening piece of the puzzle; with no concept of how they got here, there was no possibility of planning a return.

Cresting a small hill, they saw a break in the endless expanse of forest, revealing cultivated fields in the distance. Haze from the midday sun shimmered over the furrows in a recently plowed field. John stopped and pointed in the direction of the fields. "Those fields belong to the farm of Benjamin Rogers. We will be at the farmhouse in an hour or less, and we will stop there for rest and refreshment before going on to New Echota. The Rogers' have been my good friends for many years, so it is a safe place to stop."

"Refreshment sounds great to me," said Adam, the others nodding agreement. "All this fresh air and exercise is wearing me out."

"We have several miles to go before we reach New Echota," said John, "but we have time for a short stop at the Rogers farm. It will be good to see Benjamin and his family again. I only wish I had better news for them." With his horse in tow and the team following, he led the way toward the farm.

Adam indicated he wanted the others to stay back some distance from John so they could talk in private. Once John was far enough away to be out of earshot, he said, "At least at this farm there will be other people to talk to. I'd like to hear what they have to say about John's story. They'll either think he's crazy or we are. I'm not sure one is any better than the other. I've been thinking, though. Have any of you considered what it means if we really are somehow in 1838, and on the Cherokee Nation in Georgia?"

"Yes, I have," Tom answered. "I assume you mean on top of the bizarre assertion that we have walked back in time more than 150 years and do not know how we got here or have any clue how to get back. Other than those insignificant details, the particular timeframe is quite troubling. It is not exactly the time I'd pick to visit this part of Georgia."

"No, me either. Does this mean you are accepting that we are actually in 1838?" Adam asked.

"Certainly not! I am willing to consider it for the purpose of our discussion, since I lack any better explanation. In any case, if I were thinking clearly when John told us his story earlier I would have remembered the history of this period. He told us this was May of 1838."

"Oh my goodness," Alice gasped. "If this is May of 1838 that means…" A look of horror appeared on her face.

"Exactly," said Adam.

"Means what exactly?" asked Sal. "What's the big deal about Georgia in May, 1838? I would have paid more attention in history class if I knew I was going to be testing a freakin' time machine."

"This month, in May, 1838," Adam explained, "the state of Georgia enforced the Indian Removal Act. The militia forcibly removed every Cherokee from the state. They were taken from their homes, removed from the land that had been given to them by treaty with the U.S. government. Thousands of American Indians were made to give up their ancestral homeland and relocate, on a forced exodus to Oklahoma territory."

"It was called the Trail of Tears," said Tom, "which led to the deaths

of over 4000 Cherokee."

Chapter twelve

The forest path gave way to cultivated land with long, recently plowed furrows and fields that were already flourishing with unending lines of tiny green sprouts. They passed regiments of evenly spaced peach trees, standing like soldiers at attention, presenting their stout, knobbed branches laden with pink buds. A lone black man, working a horse-drawn plow in one of the adjacent fields, paid no heed to the passing group of hikers, nor did John make an attempt to communicate with him. He continued his trek toward a cluster of buildings, an enormous barn, a substantial, well-kept farmhouse, and several smaller outbuildings of various shape and function. As they approached the barn, John let loose three loud, sharp cries. Noticing the team's startled reaction, John explained that it was a courtesy to let folks know when you were approaching. Alice wondered why he hadn't done that for the man they saw plowing.

On hearing his cries, two mixed-breed dogs ran toward them from the barn, barking vociferously. A short, stocky man wearing high-waist trousers with suspenders, linen shirt, muddy brogans, and a well-worn straw hat emerged from the barn. Aside from the two braids of black hair dangling below his hat, he had the appearance of a typical farmer, or what the team assumed a typical Georgia farmer would look like. The man turned in the direction of the barking dogs, and quietly murmured something to them. The dogs immediately ceased their barking. They continued trotting toward John and the group, now at a friendlier pace. The man in the straw hat smiled broadly and raised his right hand to shoulder height in a salute of welcome to John Carter, who returned the gesture.

"*Osiyo*, John Carter," the man said.

"*Osiyo*, Benjamin Rogers. *To-hi-tsu?*" John replied.

"*T'o-si-gwu*, I am fine, *ni-na?*" said Benjamin.

"*Os-di*, I am good, although I wish my news were better," said John, "but first I would like you to meet my fellow travelers. They are from the future."

"The future?" Benjamin said, "I am happy to hear there is going to be one! From the look on your face, John, I wasn't so sure."

"I carry news that is indeed distressing," said John, "but it must wait until I tell you the names of my friends. This is Adam Hill, Tom Woody, Sal Lolliman, and Alice Delvecci."

Benjamin heartily shook hands with each of them, making the briefest of eye contact and smiling warmly, projecting a sincere welcome.

"*Tsi-lu-gi*," Benjamin said. "Welcome to the Roger's family farm. We have never had visitors from the future here before. I am anxious to hear the story behind John's most intriguing introduction; much more anxious than I am to hear his bad news. First, I must provide you all with food and drink. It is a beautiful day for traveling, but you all look very weary. John, stable your horse here in the barn, and let us talk while we walk to the house and inform Catherine of your arrival."

Adam hoped to speak with Benjamin to get more information about where they were, but the farmer had clearly stated his intention to talk to John first. He held his questions for the moment and listened to the two men talk. It seemed to him that neither seemed to be in much of a hurry to get to the point.

They began by discussing the planting season and how much work there was to do on the farm at this time of the year. Next, John talked about his horse, how his detour led to the meeting of Adam and the team, and made mention that he brought them along since they seemed to have been led out of their "normal place" by a new invention they were testing. Benjamin indicated that he understood, and that John had done the right thing to bring them along. They had no further conversation about Adam and the others, and to Adam's relief, said nothing to indicate any collusion between them to concoct a story.

They spent several minutes discussing John's horse, which seemed to be recovering well from its injury. Benjamin offered to have a look at the progress of the recovery anyway. Considering the gravity of the news John needed to convey, Adam thought John and Benjamin were doing their best to avoid the subject entirely. When the discussion finally turned to John's news, the primary reason he made a nearly 100 mile journey, the tone of the conversation seemed dispassionate and matter-of-fact.

"So it seems that in spite of John Ross' efforts to appeal to the new president," said Benjamin, "we are expected to uphold the illegal treaty of Major Ridge."

John sighed. "So it seems. The petition against the New Echota treaty contained nearly 16,000 Cherokee signatures. Yet the treaty was still ratified by a single vote. The political party of former President Jackson, the Democrats, overwhelmingly supports his position against us. They still hold much power among their legislature. Appeals that were made by some of the greatest white speakers, including Henry Clay, Daniel Webster, and David Crockett, have gone unheard."

"John Ross must have a plan to proceed on our behalf, and you will carry the details of that plan to the others in New Echota."

"There is some indication that the new president Van Buren, who is of the Whig party and sympathetic to our cause, may be willing to give us more time before allowing Georgia to forcibly carry out the treaty. It is not likely to be much time, or acceptable to the Georgia governor. John Ross will continue to do all he can to work on our behalf in Washington City. He holds great concern that the state of Georgia will begin to act even more violently toward us if we have not vacated our lands here before the deadline of May 26th. Even so, he is adamant against giving in to removal. I continue to hope for his success, but it may also be prudent to begin some preparation to remove to the western Indian Territory in the event of his failure."

"My heart feels pity for you, John Carter; if that is the message you must deliver to New Echota. I have known you long and well, but even I cannot begin to understand how to move my entire family and farm nearly a thousand miles westward at the beginning of planting season." The conversation between the two men ended, contemplating the gloomy despair of each other's words.

Adam, Alice, Sal, and Tom exchanged glances in wordless astonishment. It was abundantly clear that there would not be any clarification coming from Benjamin. They heard the conversation; there was no need to further question the man. He would only confirm John Carter's story. Whether they were willing to believe it or not, both of these men were convinced it was May, 1838. The team had little choice other than to accept the possibility that this was real. These folks were preparing for one of the most horrific and shameful events in the history of the United States, the Georgia Indian Removal. And the team was going to have to live through it with them.

Chapter thirteen

*C*atherine Rogers stood on the wrap-around porch of the farmhouse, watching them approach. She was dressed in a sturdy cotton frock, practical and homespun, protected by a white apron which was decorated with a rainbow of stains. Her long, straight black hair hung nearly to her waist, framing her broad smile, the most arresting feature of her round, sanguine face.

The farmhouse was constructed of whole logs, notched and interlocked at the corners, log cabin style, with a roof put together from bark shingles and covered in so much moss it looked like sod. The house was no cabin; it was an expansive, well-made structure, a homestead befitting a successful and profitable farm. The wide porch encircled the entire house, complete with rocking chairs and benches adorning the front of the house. Along the sides were various agricultural apparatus, all well used and most were clearly homemade. Next to Catherine were a few more wooden chairs, a table with a washbasin, water bucket, and ladle, and two large wooden barrels. Four steps led up to the porch. Next to the steps was another barrel, this one open and full to the top with rainwater.

"Need to set a few more places at the table, Silvey," Catherine yelled through the open door to the kitchen. A woman's black face momentarily appeared in the doorway and gave the visitors an indifferent glance, mumbled something inaudible and then disappeared back into the kitchen.

"You are all just in time," Catherine beamed at the group, as if five strangers showing up for a meal was a common occurrence. "'*Siyo*, John Carter. I see you have brought us a few strong backs to help during the planting moon."

"Catherine, *osiyo*." said John Carter, returning the smile. "They will no doubt help with the chores, but I am afraid first they will need thirsts quenched, stomachs filled, and spirits mended."

"Hungry, weary, and disheartened, eh? Sounds no different than most of the creatures who visit our farm these days," she replied. Her smile did not falter. "No matter; you are all welcome here to mend your souls and fill your bellies."

"Catherine," Benjamin said, "John tells me these folks are from the future and are traveling with him to New Echota. We do not get many visitors from the future, so I am hoping they can tell us some new and interesting stories." He smiled and winked at John.

"You have little time for listening to storytelling, Benjamin Rogers, with the planting time upon us," Catherine replied. She was still smiling, but her dark brown eyes revealed enough sternness to convey a serious message to Benjamin, who looked slightly cowed. He made no reply.

John introduced the team to Catherine. Her stern look vanished and her ubiquitous smile radiated to each of them.

"We're very grateful for your hospitality, Mrs. Rogers," said Adam. "It's been an extremely strange and trying day for us, to say the least. We started out this morning on a very short trip and wound up, well, somewhere we never expected to be. I guess that's what John meant by our spirits needing to be mended."

"It is not so unusual to not know where you are going until you get there," said Catherine. "The trick is to know how to make the most of what you find. Please help yourselves to some cool water and come inside to have something to eat."

While they passed around ladles full of water, Benjamin filled the wash basin with water from the rain barrel. He set it back on the table and washed his face and hands using a large cake of soap and drying with a towel hanging over the back of one of the chairs, then followed Catherine into the kitchen. John also washed, using the same basin of water, dried his face, and gestured with an open hand at the wash basin to Adam before turning and following Benjamin into the house.

Adam turned to his three colleagues and said, "What should we do?"

"You're asking us?" Tom retorted. "You are in charge of this project. What are your orders?"

"Hold on, Tom." Adam held out his hands, palms up, in a gesture of surrender. "I'm just as frustrated as you are. This situation has gone way beyond a testing project. Way beyond anything I could even imagine. I accept the responsibility of putting us in this situation, but I freely admit all of this is more than I can deal with alone. I need help from all of you."

"Jeez, dude," said Sal. "I was really hoping you were going to tell us this was some kind of elaborate gag you were pulling on us."

Adam shook his head. "Hardly. If it's a gag, it stopped being funny long ago."

Tom continued to glare at Adam. It was extremely unsettling for him to be in a situation he did not understand, and he wanted someone to blame for it.

Alice sensed the standoff. She was also frustrated, but now was not the time for conflict. It would take logic and cool-headed thinking to solve this dilemma. "My goodness, fellas, arguing about what we should do isn't going to help anything. Adam's right, we all have to work together to figure this out. Tom, you are one of the most capable engineers I know. We need your support."

Tom shot her a look of bewilderment. "My support? What do you expect me to do, invent a time-machine to get us home?"

"Of course not. I'm not suggesting anything of the kind. What I am suggesting is that you put that brilliant mind of yours to good use. Listen, you've had to think outside the box on occasion, to come up with a solution to an engineering problem no one else thought of. Why not do that now?"

"Just what are you proposing?"

"Use the facts at hand. Here we are with two men who believe this is 1838. Something has happened to change the terrain—things aren't where they are supposed to be. I know it's farfetched, but why don't we assume, for the moment, that time-travel is a possibility. At least until we can prove otherwise."

Tom shook his head. "I can't understand the benefit in doing that."

"I can," said Adam. "Alice is suggesting we look at this scientifically. We accept the facts as offered unless we can prove them to be false. By doing so, we may be able to find unique solutions to our unique problem."

"I'm not sure I completely agree with your approach, but I understand the logic." Tom paused, considering their suggestion. "I will attempt to put aside my suspicions of deception and only deal with facts as they are presented. Skeptically, mind you."

Adam looked relieved. "Skeptically, agreed. In that case, let us accept these kind folks hospitality and get something to eat."

"Now there's something I can agree with," said Sal. "We shall follow your lead, my leader.

Adam copied the wash up procedure of the two men, finding the cool, soapy water a welcome relief, leaving behind a basin full of grey, sudsy water with a substantial amount of trail dust sediment at the bottom. He slung the towel over his forearm with a flourish, extended it to Alice, bowed slightly, and said, "Next!"

Alice grimaced at the filthy water in the washbasin and flashed Adam an expression of disgust. Adam simply smiled and shrugged, continuing to hold out his arm with the towel draped over it like the washroom attendant in a five-star hotel.

Tom sensed her reluctance and impatiently sidestepped between them. He grabbed the washbasin, and flung the contents over the edge of the porch. He then refilled it from the rain barrel and set it back on the table. "There's plenty of rain water in the barrel. Just get some more when you need it. Doesn't take much out of the box thinking to figure that out," he said matter-of-factly, giving Alice a good-natured wink.

Alice took the damp towel from Adam, who bowed again, turned, and entered the farmhouse. She splashed the chilly water on her face, delighting in the soft, almost silky feel of the hard rainwater. She lathered up with the bar of soap, which appeared to be homemade and harsh, but did an exemplary job of removing the trail grime. She felt more refreshed than she had since morning, and wished she had time to wash out her tangled and gritty hair. She decided a quick wash-up was good enough for now, as the mouthwatering aroma wafting through the door was doing a splendid job of reminding her how long it had been since she'd eaten. She handed the towel to Tom who did a quick wash and dry. He turned, flung the towel onto Sal's shoulder, and then moved aside. Sal grabbed the basin and replaced the water with fresh from the rain barrel, causing Tom and Alice to give him a sideways glance and a snort.

"What?" said Sal as he washed, "It had girl cooties in it."

"Oh for heaven's sake," said Alice. "You act like a third-grader. If I were you, I'd be more worried about the cooties on some of those skanks I've seen you with."

Shaking his head and laughing loudly, Tom said, "Come on, guys, let's eat!"

The farmhouse kitchen had a huge, sturdy, rectangular table set in the center of the room. One entire wall of the kitchen was a stone cooking hearth, with half a dozen pots of various sizes hanging from iron hooks, and on two stone shelves built into the hearth were several more pans and cooking utensils. The hearth was level with the kitchen floor, which was made from flat stones and warmed by the fire. A low, three-legged stool stood next to the hearth. There was a single large cupboard on an adjacent wall which held a few mixing bowls, pitchers, and another bucket of water. A few more shelves affixed to the walls held an assortment of tins, plates, and a number of other kitchen tools. A churn stood in one corner, next to a small bench and several straw brooms leaned against the wall.

The table was laden with enough food to feed twice the number of people who were seated around it on the wooden benches. In addition to Benjamin, Catherine, and the five travelers, a young boy and girl were seated at the table. The black woman was busily shuffling plates, bowls, and platters of food.

Alice inspected the selection of food that had been prepared for them, which to her looked like a tremendous assortment of leftovers from several meals. There were two large platters of roasted meat. A partially carved haunch of dark, stringy meat—deer meat she assumed— was making its way around the table. On the second platter was a mixture of smaller pieces of light brown meat with chunks of yellow potatoes. She could see a platter of fried trout, and another with fried eggs. There were also at least six bowls containing vegetables, soups and stews, and one enormous basket full of cornbread.

She started with the meat and potato platter, and passed it along to Sal sitting next to her. She picked up a bowl of scrambled eggs mixed with green onions, and took a large helping before passing it on. She was passed two more bowls, one with hominy and bacon and another with fat, greasy-looking green beans, took a spoonful from each, and then grabbed a large piece of cornbread from the basket. She hefted the heavy pitcher of milk and poured some for herself into a tin cup. The milk was slightly cool, not ice cold the way she liked it. It tasted sweet, thick, and rich like drinking melted ice cream. She tried a few bites of the meat and potato main dish.

"My goodness this is delicious," she said to Catherine, indicating the meat and vegetable mixture. "The vegetables taste like yams, and the meat is tender and flavorful. Is it pork?"

"I am pleased you like it, Alice," said Catherine. "No, it is not pork. It is *gv-li* and yams."

Alice nodded as she took another mouthful. "Guh-tlee… what kind of meat is that?"

"Raccoon and yams," said John, "one of Catherine's specialties."

"Raccoon?" she said, pausing her eating and looking doubtfully at the remainder of the meat. "Oh, my. Dear me, uh…"

"What's wrong, Alice?" said Sal, greatly amused at her discomposure. "'Coon got your tongue?" he snickered.

"Actually, it is very delicious," said Adam, coming to Alice's rescue and taking a second helping. "It's something new for us to try."

"Something new for sure, man. Can't say I've ever had raccoon before," said Sal.

"You never had *gv-li* and yams before?" said the young boy sitting across from Sal. It was inconceivable to him that someone had never had the meal before. "Did you just hatch from an egg?" he said, giggling along with the little girl sitting next to him.

"Billy," said Catherine with a stern look at the boy. "Please remember how to speak to guests," she said. The youngster stopped giggling and hastily lowered his eyes. Catherine looked embarrassingly at Benjamin, and Billy knew he would be reminded of his impertinence privately later. It was not customary for a Cherokee parent to admonish a child in front of others. "Please excuse my ill-mannered children, Billy and Sally," she said, introducing them to the group.

"Oh, I think Billy has a point," said Alice. "Sometimes I think Sal was just hatched from an egg, too," she said, wrinkling her nose at Sally, making her giggle again.

The Rogers family members projected the warm and hospitable atmosphere of a loving family to their guests, an atmosphere that felt natural and sincere. The conversation grew lighthearted as the group became comfortable with each other, and the delicious food and cheery talk helped relieve the team's anxiety, at least for the moment. Adam commented to Benjamin that he admired the well-built and sturdy construction of the house and asked him if they had lived in it very long.

"This farmhouse is only about fifty years old, and was built by Catherine's father with the help of some of his clan," Benjamin answered. "John Carter's father also helped. Our families have had close ties for many years, and I have known John all my life. The land of the farm was owned in common by the Cherokee nation, but has been farmed by my mother's family, her clan, for generations. Catherine is *Anitsisqua*, or Bird clan, as is John Carter."

"How many Cherokee clans are there?" asked Adam.

"There are seven; Paint, Wild Potato, Wolf, Deer, Bird, Blue, and Longhair. Children become members of their mother's clan, so Billy and Sally are also Bird clan. People of the same clan cannot marry, because they are like brothers and sisters. John is Catherine's clan brother, and uncle to my children."

"Do the clan names have any significance?" asked Adam.

"Yes," said Benjamin. "Historically, the names of the clans reflected the special skills of the members. My clan, Deer, for example, was known for being especially fast runners and good hunters. As a child, I was a very fast runner," he said humbly. The Wolf clan is the largest clan, and they have produced many chiefs and strong warriors."

"No doubt that would be my clan," said Sal.

"Oh, really. He said they were warriors, not inferiors," Alice chuckled.

"You're so funny you must be from the Clown clan," he smirked.

Tom, who had more agricultural knowledge than the others, asked Benjamin about the operation of the farm, and the sort of crops and livestock they raised. Benjamin explained that they were very proud to have one of the most successful farms in the valley, and while it was not the largest, they had been doing quite well for the last several years. He told them that in addition to growing peaches and cotton, their main crops, they also grew corn, beans, and a variety of other vegetables for their own table. He also had a small patch of fine Georgia tobacco, as nearly every farm did. They raised a few horses, and had a small flock of sheep, a few hogs, and a couple of dairy cows.

Tom remarked that it must be a lot of hard work for their small family. He asked if the black lady and man they had seen along the way were hired hands.

"We are fortunate enough to own Isaac and Silvey, our two slaves," Benjamin answered.

"Slaves?" Tom exclaimed. There was a look of shock on all four of the team's faces.

"Yes," answered Benjamin. "I see you are surprised that we have done so well to be able to afford such a luxury. But as you say, this farm would require much more labor than we ourselves could provide. Harvesting the cotton is an especially heavy workload. In the past, we have borrowed additional slaves from neighboring farms at harvest time, but the owners of many of the larger, more affluent farms have been leaving to move west. Joe Vann, who had one of the largest farms in the area, abandoned his plantation and moved to the western territory several years ago. A few others who could afford it followed, but most of the 'regular' folks are still here."

John Carter licked a dribble of grease from his fingers. "If the Georgians have their way none of us will be here for this year's harvest."

Benjamin grunted. "After all our people have done to take on the white ways and become a thriving community, I don't see how they will be allowed to make us leave."

"You know the greed that comes from the gold. They have already made laws to forbid any Cherokee from digging for gold on his own land, and have conducted a land lottery giving others title to all of our land.

The fields you are planting now may be harvested by a white family after you have been driven away."

"What would you have me do, John Carter?" Benjamin said testily. "Squat on my heels until they come? Or pack up and go to Indian Territory and beg a settlement from the Ridge group?"

"I do understand the predicament, Benjamin Rogers, but it may be prudent for you to spend part of your time gathering the possessions you would take with you if you are forced to go."

"I'm afraid I don't know a lot about farms," said Alice, "especially a nineteenth century one, but this place and your family seem to be pretty typical of what I would imagine one to be like. No different than any farm family of this period, and probably very similar to my own ancestors. If the land has been yours for generations, what right does anyone have to make you leave it?"

"The claimed right," John Carter answered, "is that they are white and we are Cherokee."

Chapter fourteen

W hen the meal was over the three women, Catherine, her daughter Sally, and the slave Silvey began to clean up the kitchen and table. They made no comment, but the three women flashed an expectant glance at Alice. It wasn't that she minded lending a hand with chores; it was more that she had not even begun to accept the reality of time travel, let alone considered what was going to be expected of her in this century. She jumped up and began helping with the cleanup, following directions from Sally, who was delighted to have someone to be in charge of. Sal, clearly amused by Alice's role of domestic woman, winked at her, elevated his nose and said, "Woman, you may clear my place now."

Alice walked over to Sal, leaned over to pick up the few bowls and plates in front of him, and whispered something inaudible in his ear. Sal turned bright red and made no further comments.

"Gentlemen," said Benjamin, "if you would care to join me on the front porch, we can talk a bit and let the women get on with their chores."

"A fine idea," agreed John.

The room filled with the sound of chair legs scraping against the floor as they exited the kitchen and headed to the front porch. The house faced east, so the porch was already shaded from the afternoon sun, with enough chairs and rockers for everyone to get comfortable after the big meal. John and Benjamin extracted smoking pipes, and noticing Tom's briarwood Benjamin offered him a bowl full of his homegrown tobacco. As they were lighting up, Silvey arrived with a tray of hot, steaming coffee for the five men. The coffee was very strong and full of grounds, but hot and good.

They sat quietly enjoying the coffee and tobacco, with full stomachs and a warm Georgia breeze adding to the euphoria, when Benjamin finally broke the silence. "You are planning to continue to New Echota today?" he asked John Carter.

John nodded. "I am. My horse has recovered enough to ride, but I will continue to walk since the others have no horses."

"I wonder then," Benjamin said, glancing at Adam, "if our guests would consider staying on here at my farm for a few days. You will be hard pressed to reach New Echota by this evening if you are walking. I could bring them with me in my wagon when I come to town for supplies and for our meeting. They are welcome to stay, and I can always use some extra hands here at planting time."

"I don't have a problem staying here for a day or so," Adam replied.

"Hey, me neither," said Sal, "I've had about all the walking I need for one day anyhow."

"Hold on just a minute," said Tom. After the meal his disposition had been mellowed by the coffee, tobacco, and a full stomach. Now it took on a concerned intensity. "I'm happy to stay and help, especially after the fine meal we just received, but what about our situation? Remember, I still find it incredible that everyone we met here today believes we are in 1838. I admit that something inconceivable has happened to us. I don't know what exactly. Even if I agree to accept time-travel, shouldn't we be working on finding our way home?"

"Yes, we should," Adam replied. He didn't want Tom becoming aggravated again. He decided to appeal to Tom's practical side. "What environment would you find more appropriate to working on a solution? As I see it, we have three choices. We can go with John to an unknown town, take off by ourselves into the woods, or stay here at this quiet and friendly farm, where we can calmly assess our situation. I think staying here is our best choice. Do you disagree?"

"No, when you put it like that, I suppose it makes sense," Tom admitted. "I hadn't looked at it from that perspective. Staying here does have some advantages."

Adam was glad the composure had returned to Tom's voice. "Yep, there are definitely advantages," he said, patting his belly. "And there are probably less distractions here than in town." Tom and Sal nodded their agreement.

"Of course we need to get Alice's opinion before we decide," Adam added for John and Benjamin's benefit. "We include Alice in all decision making. A lot of progress has been made on women's rights since the 1800's."

"That doesn't sound like progress for the women," said John. "Now they just tell us what they want and we do it," he said to everyone's laughter.

"Yeah, we can get Alice's input as soon as she's done with her 'women's work,'" said Sal.

"What was that, hon?" said Alice coming through the door behind him.

"Oh, uh, nothing. I mean, we really need your expert input on a decision, as a woman that is. Because we value you as an equal, you know," he said to the snickers of the other men.

"Uh-huh," she said, lancing Sal with all the fierceness her eyes could project. "Well, I heard the question," she said, "and staying here sounds fine to me. Of course it will be less distracting here. And who knows? After a good night's sleep we might find out this was all just a dream."

"If that is your decision, then," said John, "I will be getting on my way immediately. If I might suggest something, though, while you are considering your plans?"

"Of course, John," said Adam. "What's your suggestion?"

"You should consider the possibility that you have been brought here for a purpose. I know that many whites consider our traditional ways full of superstition, but even the Christian religions teach that most things happen for a reason. You may want to focus your considerations on what those reasons might be. If you can determine that, your path may become much clearer, perhaps guiding you back to your home."

"What possible reason would there be for us to be here?" asked Tom.

"I cannot begin to guess the ways of the power that brought you here," John replied. "But consider; you have come from a future time and have knowledge of what awaits us in the coming weeks; or at least one version of the things that will occur. It is possible that you were sent to provide guidance to us in this time of crisis. It may also be possible that you are to be shown something about your own past. Perhaps both are possible. One clue is the device you carry which brought you here."

"What do you mean? "What do you know about this device?" Adam asked, holding up the LANav.

"I know nothing of it, Adam, except that on it is written 'TSO LANav.'"

"Yes, the company that makes it is TSO, Inc. and they call the device a LANav."

"In Cherokee, *tso-la-nv* is a phonetic pronunciation for a word meaning 'window'. Perhaps it provides a window we can see through from our respective sides, giving us a glimpse into the future or past that would normally be blocked by the wall of time. The way dreams can sometimes do. If that is the case, it will be up to you to determine how to use the vision that the device is providing."

Chapter fifteen

The four team members and Benjamin's family, including the two dogs, came to the barn to see John off. Benjamin gave John's horse an expert check-up and declared him sound. Everyone said their goodbyes to John with a handshake, and hugs from Catherine and Sally. John calculated that on horseback he would easily reach town before sundown, so he could track down the council and deliver his news as soon as he arrived. Benjamin wished him luck with that chore. He repeated his promise to meet him in New Echota, and to bring the team along. "I will try not to work them too hard with farm chores in the meantime."

Once John was on his way, Benjamin said he and Billy would head to the field where Isaac was working to let him get some supper. He told the visitors to feel free to explore the farm, and he would meet them back at the barn in two hours. He and Billy needed to care for the horses before dark, and they would explain the work that they needed help with tomorrow.

Benjamin and Billy headed off to the fields, while Catherine and Sally returned to the farmhouse, telling the visitors that they would see to their accommodations, giving the four a chance to talk over the events of the day in private.

"I wish I had something enlightening to say." Adam began. "Unfortunately our situation is outrageously bizarre. I'm just as baffled as you guys. Telling you that we need to make the best of the situation seems lame, but I think that's about all we can do for now. I take full responsibility, and I'm really sorry that I got you all into this mess, but I had no idea…"

"Of course not," said Alice, "how could you?" The others nodded their agreement.

"I understand how you're feeling, Adam," said Tom. "I did not intend to imply that you were responsible for this situation. Perhaps for now making the best of it is about all we can do. I remain skeptical, but with all the overwhelming evidence to the contrary, I'd be a fool not to at least entertain the hypothesis that we are in a different time period. The only other reasonable explanations I have come up with so far are that I am dreaming or this is some sort of mass hypnosis, and both are very unlikely. As you suggested, if I accept that we have time-traveled, I can make a more serious effort to use logic rather than emotions to make decisions. From a purely intellectual standpoint, while I would have liked to have known in advance what I was getting into, as I'm sure you all would, I can't help but experience the excitement of discovery, a new adventure, and exploration of a breakthrough in science."

"That's fine for you, Mr. Spock," said Sal. "Hey, I don't hold you responsible either, Adam, but unless we can find our way home, a fat lot of good any new scientific breakthrough is going to be. Being the first person to walk on Mars would be awesome, as long as you can get back to tell someone about it!"

"Yes, for once I agree with Sal," said Alice. "I think our first priority should be finding a way to get home. Visiting another time is cool, and I realize you had no way to foresee this happening, Adam, but I don't want to spend the rest of my life here."

"I don't disagree that that should be our top priority," said Tom. "All I'm saying is that since we are here, we should at least make the most of the opportunity we've been given. It seems to me that the only possibility of return is with the LANav. If it brought us here for a reason, let's find out what it is, complete the task, and hope it leads us back home. I may have to accept that we have time-traveled, but I'm not going to accept that we are here permanently."

"So what then, dude? Do we just follow the bouncing beacons and hope it takes us home? Is that our big plan?" asked Sal.

"Do you have another suggestion?" asked Adam. "Did you happen to get a copy of a manual that shows how to work the LANav time machine that the rest of us didn't? Look, Tom has a good point. We are at the mercy of a device that is using some kind of technology none of us can understand. Probably no one back home understands it either. If we get home, or rather when we get home, we're certainly going to have an interesting test report to give to Dr. Odan."

"The good news is," said Tom, "the LANav is still functioning. I expect the communication functions don't work because there were no communication satellites in 1838. It can still navigate using the stars and planets, and it seems to be indicating progressive beacons. It could be that it is showing us the path we need to take. It is a navigation device after all. Adam, you said the beacon was at our current location right now. We're planning to stay here for a day or two anyway. Maybe it will show another beacon by then."

"Yeah, okay, I guess you're right," said Sal. "There's no choice other than for us to play along with this Native American time-window whatever gizmo. But I'll tell ya what; when we get back, IF we get back, I'm going to go see this Dr. Odan dude and break a couple of HIS windows."

"Sure, Sal. Just try not to break anything else before we get back," said Alice, "especially the LANav, or I'll be breaking more than your windows. Adam, keep that thing away from him!"

Adam was relieved to hear Alice and Sal sniping at each other; at least they were keeping their sense of humor through this ordeal. There was another concern beside their own dilemma weighing on his mind, and he decided now was as good a time as any to bring it up.

"No question that getting back home is our primary concern," Adam said, "but I've been thinking about what John said, and I wonder if he doesn't have a valid point."

"Yo, man, what are you saying?" asked Sal. "That we're part of some sort of mythical Indian wet-dream?"

"No," Adam answered, "and I don't think that's really what he meant either. Think about it, though. To us, all of this is history. We know what is going to happen to the Cherokee in the next few weeks. Or we know as much as our history books have told us and what we can remember about the incident."

"My heavens, do you think there is something we can do to change the outcome?" asked Alice. "Is that something we should even consider? Tom, you've studied more physics than the rest of us. Wouldn't that cause a time paradox or something?"

"Who knows," Tom shrugged. "Like I said, we're on new ground here. But it is an interesting subject, and it's something that's been discussed in detail before. I'm sure you've had a college professor who presented you with a question like, 'If you could go back in time and kill Hitler...' To prevent a war and save lives, would you do it? Should you do it? What other problem would it cause?"

"I believe the question is," said Adam, "since we know what is going to happen, can we NOT do anything? Just our being here could theoretically cause a time paradox. I think we have to let our consciences guide us, and let the universe take care of itself. It isn't as if we TRIED to come here and meddle with history; we were brought here, and apparently can't leave unless we follow the path of beacons the LANav is guiding us along. I believe our safest course of action is to react as we would normally— and give help when help is required. Maybe we need to think of this as a crazy time-traveling puzzle multi-cache, where we have to complete some objective at each point along the way."

"No way, dude. You think this is like geocaching? Timecaching, I suppose?" Sal snorted.

They were all familiar with the variations of geocaches, some requiring several stops, and others containing puzzles to be solved, so Adam hoped it would be an example they could relate to.

"Chill out, Sal," said Alice, "I understand your comparison, Adam. But how much do we really know about what happened here in 1838? It's been a while since my last American history class, and I don't really remember that this event was discussed in great detail."

"Yeah," Sal agreed, "I remember the Trail of Tears mentioned, and that it involved a long march by the Indians and that a lot of them died, but not much more. What the heck are we supposed to do about it?"

"Try being a little less cold-hearted for one thing," said Alice.

"Hey, I'm not trying to sound cold-hearted, Alice," he replied sincerely. "But get real. There are only the four of us and thousands of Cherokees. It sounds like they've already gone to extreme lengths to try and prevent this from happening. Even though we know it's going to happen, there ain't gonna be much we can do to prevent it."

"You may be right," said Adam. "It could be helpful for us to go over what we can remember about this period of time. Maybe in going over the details something we can do to help will present itself. My memory of the history is sketchy, but here's what I remember: Back in the 1600's, the Cherokee ruled most of what is now the southeastern United States. Initial contact with Europeans was with the Spanish explorers and later with colonial settlers as they began to inhabit the country. In the beginning, the Cherokee were friendly with the whites, but as they began to encroach upon their lands, it obviously led to wars. The Cherokee outnumbered whites for a while, but their numbers were greatly diminished by disease, specifically smallpox brought by the whites, and the number of settlers continued to increase. Seeking to put an end to the turmoil and encroachment on their lands, the Cherokee, as well as other tribes, agreed to a series of treaties that successively reduced their lands, but promised to stop the encroachment. One treaty in 1785 called the Treaty of Hopewell, between the Cherokee and the U.S. promised to end any further invasions, but the treaty was pretty much ignored by the U.S., and white settlers continued to move into Cherokee lands. In 1791, another treaty, the Treaty of Holston, contained a guarantee from George Washington himself that the Cherokee lands would never again be invaded by settlers. It even required non-Cherokee to obtain a passport before they could enter Cherokee lands. Tom, do you remember why that treaty was broken?"

"I know that by that time," Tom said, "many of the Cherokee were pretty darn skeptical of any promises made by the whites. They called treaties Talking Leaves, which implied that the leaves withered and died when they were of no further use to the whites. I think there was hope that that wouldn't be the case with the Treaty of Holston, since it was signed by George Washington.

"I remember that one of the problems came about because of a promise from Thomas Jefferson to the state of Georgia that all Cherokee in that state would be given land and assisted in moving west to Indian Territory. I guess they didn't count on the Cherokees being a little reluctant to do that since they would have to give up lands they lived on for centuries. Who would of thought?" he said sarcastically.

"I believe the problem was exacerbated," Adam continued, "by the discovery of gold in Georgia. I guess that explains John's asking us if we were gold prospectors when we first met. After the gold discovery, Georgia was even more anxious to get rid of the Cherokee, and began passing laws to prevent them from looking for gold, even on their own land, and to keep them from organizing to contest the removal. The pressure on the Cherokee to cede even more land was immense and there were many incidences of violence. Another setback for the Cherokee was the election of the Democrat, Andrew Jackson, an expansionist president who demanded they give up more of their land to settlers. Over two million acres I believe."

Tom added, "There was also another treaty, called the Treaty of New Echota. This is the treaty they are contending with now, which John referred to as illegal. The Treaty of New Echota gave up all the last remaining lands of the Cherokee and agreed to move them west to Indian Territory, nearly 1000 miles away, in what is now Oklahoma. That treaty was signed by only a small group of Cherokee leaders who felt that the only option left for them was to give in and go west. Most of the Cherokee did not agree, and wanted to keep their ancestral lands. This led to some of the events John was talking about—many futile attempts to nullify that treaty."

"So where do we fit in?" asked Alice. "If anything, what you've said only goes to prove Sal's point. There is very little we can do to help prevent this from happening."

"Maybe the goal isn't to prevent it," said Adam. "In a few weeks, Georgia will begin to forcefully gather up the Cherokee people, remove them from their homes and herd them into forts, where they will wait to be marched to Indian Territory. Right up to the end, many of the Cherokee families refused to believe that they would be forced from their homes. Maybe the best way we can help would be to simply become part of their daily lives."

"That could be very dangerous," said Tom. "The Georgia militia is not going to look very kindly on anyone consorting with the Cherokee. Our intentions could also be misinterpreted by the Cherokee if it appears we are encouraging them to leave. I bet they've just about had their fill of white people encouraging them to pack up and leave, and sick of hearing that it's their only option. Imagine how you would feel."

Alice was not one to ignore the mistreatment of anyone. "We'll have to tread carefully, but of course we have to help. We have the dubious advantage of knowing what's going to happen, but they don't. It will take patience and tact," she said, with a sideways glance at Sal. "My gosh, if I can do anything to help avoid some of the Cherokee suffering, I'm going to do it. And the militia can just watch out for me."

"Yeah," said Sal. "Those Georgia boys haven't seen anything until they've tangled with a dude from Jersey."

"Easy, guys," said Adam. "Remember, we're talking about trained Georgia militia, not a bunch of coeds from Georgia State. Plus, the Georgians feel they are entitled to the land, and have been waiting many years for the feds to fulfill the promises they have made. The state has already conducted a lottery and awarded land to some of them. They believe the law is on their side, and that the Cherokee should abide by the Treaty of New Echota, signed by their representatives. Georgia is just following the example set by what others have done in the past. You know all those places in New Jersey that have Native American names?"

"Sure, man," said Sal. "They got those names from the Indians that used to live there."

"Well what do you think happened to the Indians? There are a few small communities, but most were pushed out, either forcefully or their land was purchased for next to nothing. Back in the 1600's, the idea of land ownership was something most of the Indians had no concept of, and the European settlers didn't hesitate to take advantage of them."

"So," Tom said, "If I may get back to the point, now that we've refreshed our memories about the history of this event, our plan is to do what we can to help those who will let us. Help them how, exactly? Encourage them to give up everything they own, be held in a military stockade, and then force marched over 800 miles? Anyone else think they might not consider that helpful?"

"No, that's not the sort of help I had in mind. We might just let them tell us how best to help. You know, with the day to day stuff for a while. Once we understand their situation and needs a little better, we could possibly save lives and help make this tragedy less painful for a few of them. Getting involved in their hard lives will be challenging, and certainly dangerous undertaking," said Adam, "but it could be the most important thing any of us has ever done. Are you guys up for it?"

Everyone nodded.

"Of course we'll try," said Tom. "But I've got a troublesome feeling we're going to need more help from these folks than we're going to be able to give them."

Chapter sixteen

That evening Benjamin and Billy showed the team around the stables. The Rogers had about a dozen horses, and each evening they were brought into the stables for the night and groomed. The grooming chore was usually delegated to Billy and Sally, who were thrilled to have the team help them out. Alice found that she enjoyed grooming the animals; it calmed and relaxed her, and the horses certainly seemed to enjoy it. She never considered herself an animal person, but she never had spent much time around horses before.

Benjamin explained that most of the horses were for riding, but they also had a team used for plowing. He told them that in his father's time they used oxen to plow. In those days they used wooden plows that required strong, robust animals to break through the rocky Georgia soil. Nowadays he used cast iron plows, which cut the ground better and were easy enough for horses to pull.

By the time they were finished with the horses it was nearly dark. They headed back to the farmhouse, and Benjamin told them he'd like the three men to help him finish up the planting tomorrow, and that Catherine could use Alice's help with some of her chores. Noting Alice's look of disappointment at being assigned as a domestic, Benjamin explained that Catherine usually performed double-duty, both the household chores and helping in the fields afterwards, so she needed help even more than he did.

Catherine had prepared sleeping arrangements for them all. The farmhouse had three bedrooms. Catherine, Sally and Alice would stay in the main bedroom and the five men would share the children's rooms.

They were gathered in the farmhouse living room. Catherine explained to the group that it was customary in their family to tell a story in the evening before bedtime, and asked if they would like to participate. She said that tonight it was her turn to tell the story of how the world was created. Afterward, if they wished, one of their guests could share a story with them.

She began by saying that at one time, everything in this world was covered with water. But there were two other worlds, one above and one below the water. The one above was the sky-vault, made of rock, where all the creatures on this earth once lived. Below the water was another world where the seasons were backwards and everything was chaotic. Because so many creatures lived on the sky-vault above the water, it became crowded, so the creatures sent *Dayunisi*, a water beetle, down to the water to see if there was any place down there to live. He dove under the water, and was down a long time, but he finally came up with some mud. He spread the mud around so it could form land, but it took a long time to dry. The animals were anxious, so they sent some bird out to keep checking on the mud to see if it was dry enough yet for them to use. They finally sent the Great Buzzard who flew all around checking the mud to make sure it was dry. In the places where the mud was still soft, the Great Buzzard's wings hit the ground and that is what formed the mountains and valleys in Georgia that the Cherokee call home and love so much.

When Catherine asked the visitors if they had a story they wanted to share, Adam offered to tell them a different story of creation, of Adam and Eve, but the two children said they had heard that story many times in school. They liked that story, and didn't mind hearing it again, but didn't they know a new story, being from the future and all?

Alice said that she knew a story that they probably hadn't heard before. It was sort of a silly story, one that her father used to tell her. She heard it so often that she thought she could remember it still. It was a story about a beaver, she said, and it was called *Basil, The Builder Beaver*. Sal just rolled his eyes, but the Rogers family all said they would like to hear a story about a beaver. She began:

> *By the banks of the Pinchynose, if one cared to look*
> *Lived a beaver named Basil, who made his home in that brook.*
> *For in the Pinchynose River, right out in the flow,*
> *Basil, the builder beaver had built his chateau.*
>
> *It was made with great logs, piled high and real sturdy,*
> *But even better than that— it looked kind of purdy!*
> *That's how he had earned the last name of builder,*
> *For the house he had built was a thing to bewilder.*

One day he was making some repairs to the house,
When next to the shore he spied Milton the mouse.
"Hello there," said Milton, as Basil tapped on his wall,
"Can I come for a visit? I won't take much room, I'm really quite
small.

"Why, sure," answered Basil, without stopping his work,
He bade him come on, and gave him a shirk.
Milton jumped at the offer, and ran in the house,
"You'll like me a lot, and I'll be as quiet as a mouse.

It wasn't long after, Basil noticed a squirrel,
Who stood on the bank, crying, "Hi, there, I'm Earl.
"That place you have built seems a great place to live,
"I just hope it doesn't leak like a sieve."

The squirrel that was Earl dashed straight in the house,
Not even asking, like Milton the mouse.
Basil just shrugged, he was way too busy,
To let one little squirrel put him into a tizzy.

In less than an hour, along came Will Weasel,
Who ploughed through the door like he was running on diesel.
"I like having company," the builder beaver said.
"Make yourselves right at home, just stay out of my bed."

At first, the Rogers looked bewildered by Alice's story, never having heard anything quite like it. She continued the tale of more and more animals coming to live in Basil the Beaver's home. She told the story animatedly, using a different voice for each animal, and soon both children were laughing every time she mentioned Milton the Mouse or Earl the Squirrel. By the time she got to Fonzie the Fox, Catherine, Benjamin, and even Adam, Tom, and Sal where laughing as hysterically as the children.

Alice's voice became somber as she described Basil's growing anxiety from the overload of freeloaders taking up residency in his house:

There were so many critters, and so much room they were taking,
All the walls started bulging, and creaking, and shaking!
No one seemed to notice, when poor Basil did say,
"I could use a little help," but they all answered, "No way!"

Basil kept right on working, dragging trees from the land,
But he was starting to think things were getting out of hand.

The faster he worked, the more shaky things got,
With so many creatures, his home was going to pot.

Her expression turned even more intense and her voice became grave as Basil's house began to collapse. She narrated the story perfectly; everyone was on the edge of their seat when it looked as if all the animals might drown:

When all of a sudden, and as quick as a flash,
Basil's home flew apart, with a great watery splash.
All the creatures went tumbling, every one of them wet,
And Basil was tempted to say, "That's what you get!"

Finally she came to the part where the animals learned their lesson and offered to help Basil rebuild:

They gathered 'round Basil to say they were sorry,
But Basil just smiled and said, "Hey, not to worry."
"I'll build me another, it's what I do best,
Then you can visit in pairs, and leave out the rest!"

They offered to help him rebuild his abode,
But he told them, "No, thank you" 'cause he already knowed
He'd teach them to build using wood, dirt, and stone,
So that they could all have a place of their own.

Everyone cheered and clapped, relieved that the beaver was okay and the squatters got what they deserved. They were impressed that Basil would now set limits on his visitors, yet be gracious enough to teach them how to build their own houses. They all clapped again at the end and thanked Alice for telling such a wonderful story.

"Good job," Adam whispered to her. "Was that Dr. Seuss?"

"No, I'm sure it was just something my dad made up," she said. "He was good at making up stories and I always enjoyed it when he told them to me."

Benjamin thanked her again for the great story. He suggested that they should all be getting to bed, as the day would start early tomorrow, before sunrise, and they should get plenty of rest while they could.

Chapter seventeen

In the morning, Alice, who so far was going along with the role of a nineteenth century female, was wakened by the other women earlier than the men to help with the preparation of breakfast. Her storytelling from the previous night had elevated her to the clear favorite of the visitors, and all through breakfast Sally and Billy performed impressions of Basil the Beaver and the other animals. After the men headed off to the fields, Alice and Sally continued the impersonations as they did kitchen chores, to the amusement of both Catherine and Silvey.

The morning dew on the ankle-high grass soaked their pant legs as the men cut across the fields. Benjamin teamed Adam and Sal with Isaac and Billy, instructing them to go to the fields and continue the corn planting. He explained that although corn wasn't one of his major crops, he planted twenty acres of it for livestock feed. He asked Tom to come with him to the barn to help with a few chores.

Tom gaped at the cavernous barn as the huge doors creaked open. During this time of year the barn stood mostly empty. Benjamin assured him it would be filled to capacity at harvest time, when piles of cotton bales would occupy every empty corner, waiting to be transported to market. The attached silos, he said, would be filled with the corn from the field that Isaac and the others were planting.

One section of the barn was loaded with farm equipment. Tom recognized most of the farm implements, antique versions of machines that had long since been automated. The bulk of the space was taken up by equipment used for processing cotton. A smaller, separate section of the barn was allocated to the peach crop. Benjamin explained that while it was more costly and a lot more work to have both cotton and peaches, he believed that it gave his family some insurance against having a particularly bad year with a single crop. He said that at the time he made that decision, slave labor was much easier to come by, and mentioned the Vann Plantation at one time had over 100 slaves. This year he wasn't sure how they would handle the harvest. "Rich Joe" Vann had been forced out of his house three years ago when Georgia held the land lottery, and many of the other more prosperous farms had gone the same route, heading west to get a jump on claiming land there.

Tom hesitated to tell Benjamin that he wasn't going to have to worry about a harvest this year. History taught him that by fall, there would be no Cherokees left in Georgia. The crops would be harvested, but not by the Roger family. He wished he could tell Benjamin to forget about the crop and put his efforts into preparing to move his family to the western territory, but he knew he would sound like another white person trying to convince him to leave. Another white man telling him his situation was hopeless and his only choice was to pack up and leave. No; better to help with the farm chores and keep his suggestions to himself for now. He didn't think Benjamin would listen to him anyway.

"I can read your thoughts in your eyes, Tom Woody," said Benjamin as he continued to show him around the barn. "You believe it is foolishness to continue with planting if we are to be run off our land."

"It's not that I think it's foolish, Benjamin. I can understand your strong feelings for wanting to continue to work your farm as long as you can. I've known families who continued to work their farms even though they were facing inevitable foreclosure because they were not able to make mortgage payments. They continued to hope they could find a way to make it work. It's just that I know what's going to happen. Your future is my history, and I would like to be able to give you the benefit of the things I know will happen."

Benjamin considered this for a moment. "I believe that you only know of one possible future. It is my opinion that there are endless possibilities, so it would be wrong for me to adjust my actions to fit only your version of the future."

"But if I know something bad is going to happen, wouldn't it be unwise not to take precautions to prevent it?"

"That would imply that there can only be one possible future, wouldn't it? Suppose you knew that that wooden beam," Benjamin said, pointing to one of the barn supports overhead, "was going to fall on my head and kill me. If you warned me and I avoided the falling beam and was not killed, then your version of the future would no longer be true."

"That's what we call a time paradox. The classic example being that if you traveled back in time and murdered yourself as a baby, you would have never existed, and therefore could not have traveled back to murder yourself in the first place."

"Which supports my opinion that there is more than one possible future," Benjamin said, convinced his logic was flawless.

Tom was amazed that Benjamin had grasped the concept so easily. "That's pretty clever thinking for a farmer, Benjamin," he said with a grin.

"Just logical. But logic also tells me that I must also prepare for your version of the future. Perhaps I will have my family begin to prepare some items in case we have to move. It will be difficult to find the time, with all the other chores this time of year. We will not be able to pack the things we need for everyday use, but there are some things we could set aside."

"Just keep in mind, sir," Tom warned, "if it is my version of the future that is played out, you won't be given an opportunity to take much with you."

Benjamin responded with a shrug of his shoulders. He led Tom to the storage place of a wagon type farm implement, hoisted the tongue, and began to pull the wagon toward the barn door. Tom lent a hand getting the wagon into a position where Benjamin could hitch up a horse to it. He threw two shovels into the wagon, and led the horse toward the stables. "We need to get this filled and spread on the last field before Isaac can begin plowing."

The back of the wagon was fitted with a cylindrical set of tines running from one side of the wagon to the other, which rotated as the back wheels turned. If Tom hadn't recognized the wagon as a manure spreader, the odor would have given it away. When they reached the stables, Benjamin grabbed the two shovels, handed one to Tom, and began shoveling manure into the wagon. "Pile it toward the front," he instructed, "and when we get to the field, all you have to do is stand in the wagon and use your shovel to push the manure against the tines to spread it on the field." Tom tried not to think of what would happen if he lost his balance and fell against the tines. He supposed that niceties like a tilting wagon bed or an emergency release to disengage the spreader were yet to be considered.

Out in the fields, Isaac handed Adam and Sal each a seed planter and a cloth bag full of corn seed to carry over their shoulder. The seed planters were about four feet long and not much more than a stick with a wedge-shaped foot piece. Isaac showed Adam and Sal the process of corn planting, using the planter and pressing down with his foot to make a hole, dropping in a single kernel from the cloth sack and covering it with dirt using his foot, then repeating the process about a foot further down the row. The procedure was simple enough, but looking out across a field of about twenty acres, they could see it would be a long, tedious chore.

"Man, we'll be here all day!" Sal complained to Isaac.

"Yes, suh," he replied. "This day and a few mo' like 'em." He reached into the bag of supplies he had brought along from the barn, retrieved two battered straw hats, handed them to Sal and Adam, and headed off to the field he was planning to plow.

"Don't worry, the women will come out later on and take over the planting, so you will be able to help with the real work," said Billy. He turned and ran after Isaac. "Unless you would rather do women's work," he yelled back over his shoulder.

"Smartass little Indian," Sal mumbled as he jammed the corn planter into the next hole.

Chapter eighteen

*B*reakfast was barely cleaned up when Catherine began making plans for the evening meal. She sent Alice and Sally to the smokehouse for meat, and reminded Sally to stop along the way and "tend the kraut." As they headed out the kitchen door, Sally stopped and sat down on the edge of the porch next to the rain barrel, pulled off her shoes, and dipped rainwater from the barrel to scrub her feet. Alice watched her curiously. "Oh, my, is it a Cherokee custom to wash your feet before you go to the smokehouse? Should I wash mine, too?"

"No, silly, stop teasing me. You heard mother tell me to tend the kraut. You wouldn't want me to do it with dirty feet, would you?" Sally said.

"Oh, no, of course not," Alice said hesitantly, completely not getting the correlation between kraut and dirty feet. She watched as Sally went over to one of the large oak barrels on the porch and pulled off the wooden lid, revealing a nearly full barrel of sauerkraut.

Sally scooped some salt from a sack under the table, mixed it into a partial bucket of water and poured it into the kraut barrel. Then she climbed onto the table, held out her hand to Alice and said, "Hold my hand, please."

When Alice took her hand, to her amazement Sally stepped off the table and into the kraut barrel, stomping up and down in the briny water. "It is harder to do this in the summertime," said Sally, "because my feet get so dirty from walking around barefoot and I have to spend more time scrubbing them. If I have been wearing shoes, I barely have to wash them at all!"

"Great," said Alice. "If I have any sauerkraut, I'll know what that extra special taste is."

"This barrel isn't ripe yet," Sally said. "The one over by the door is from last year. That one has got the kraut that's ready to eat."

When Sally said she was done, Alice lifted her from the barrel and replaced the top. Sally rinsed her feet and put her shoes back on, took Alice by the hand again and led her down the path to the smokehouse. The smokehouse was a tall, sturdy wooden shed, with a small covered opening at the top. There were hooks for hanging meat under the eaves, and from one end of the shed a beam with a rope and hook held a field dressed deer, hanging about ten feet in the air. "That's the deer father and Billy brought home yesterday," Sally said. "They let it hang overnight, but Silvey will be here later to quarter it and pack it in salt. It will be too warm to let it hang all day."

Inside the smokehouse there were more wooden barrels, sacks of salt, and a few dozen hunks of meat hanging from the roof. In the center, directly under the roof vent, was a fire pit. At the moment there was no fire; most of the time the smokehouse served as a meat storage locker. Alice recalled that preserving meat without refrigeration would mean cutting the meat into chunks, packing them into the salt barrels to cure, and then hanging the pieces over a slow smoldering fire. Once smoked, the meat could be kept hanging for well over a year. Sally pointed to a hanging piece of cured pork that her mother would want to prepare for the evening meal. Alice carefully removed the heavy haunch, and dropped it into a cloth sack that Sally brought along.

The two farm dogs had finally roused themselves and were waiting at the door as they left the smokehouse. They pranced around eagerly, blocking the way, hoping for a chance at a dropped piece of meat. Sally tossed them a couple of scraps, and then firmly shooed them away. She tightly closed the smokehouse door, and Alice heaved the sack of meat over her shoulder to keep the dogs away from it. They wolfed down the scraps and closely followed Alice back to the house, running underfoot so that she had to be careful not to trip and fall over them. The dogs paid little attention to Alice's meek commands to "shoo" and "get away now." Sally simply picked up a large stick and whacked one of them across the rump, and sternly told them to "git." The struck dog let out a yelp and they both backed away, keeping their distance from Alice's feet—and Sally's stick.

Safely delivering the pork to Catherine, Alice could see that the two women had been busy preparing the rest of the meal and already had several pots hanging in the fire. Silvey was out on the porch, using a long, heavy pole to crush corn in a large bowl carved into a hollowed-out stump.

"We let the corn soak in lye water until the skins slip off, then grind the corn into meal with the *kanona* for making the bread," Catherine explained. "We also use the hominy mush to make a drink called *gahno-*

hayna, which we serve to our visitors. Later, we will take out some corn bread and a few slices of the leftover breakfast bacon to the men for lunch. It will be getting warmer by then, and they will want us to help with the planting."

"I don't suppose they will come in to help prepare the meals?" Alice asked.

"No, of course not. Is it tradition where you come from for the men to prepare the meals?"

"Sometimes they do, but many people go out to eat at a restaurant."

"A resta…?" Catherine struggled with the word.

"Like an inn or a tavern. A place where you can go and order your food. They prepare it and serve it to you. All you have to do is eat it."

"Oh, yes. I have heard that there are such fancy places in the towns where the white people live. But, if you don't have to prepare your meals, that must leave much idle time for the people. I wonder if that would make them become lazy."

"I suppose it could, but most of us seem to find other things to fill up the day," Alice said, thinking about how many times she had complained about not having enough time to get her work done.

For the rest of the morning, Alice mostly worked in the kitchen with Sally, cutting up meat and vegetables for the evening meal. She took a turn at the *kanona* so Silvey could go take care of the deer, listening to Catherine describe recipes for the traditional Cherokee meals they made as she pounded the corn. She told Alice that the majority of the meals they made now were "white people's food," but there were several Cherokee meals they still enjoyed. She liked making the Cherokee recipes because it reminded her of her childhood and her mother's cooking.

"Some of our friends will only eat food prepared in the traditional Cherokee style. They believe it is important to keep those things as part of their life. I believe that also, but our family has also tried to adopt many of the white people's traditions too. We hope that by doing so it will ease tensions between our two cultures, and will help us become more accepting of each other."

Catherine knew that some of the Cherokee felt that holding on to their traditions was the only way they would be able to keep their homeland safe from more intrusion. It polarized the people between those who were committed traditionalists and those who were more accepting of the white ways. There were times when she felt the traditionalists were right. It seemed to make little difference to the whites no matter how much they changed; they would never accept the Cherokee as equals.

Catherine intentionally assigned several tasks for Alice and Sally to do together. Even though they were far apart in age, she knew that Sally longed to have a younger woman around, and had often told her mother she wished she had a sister. It could get lonely for a seven year old girl on the farm. She and her brother were close, but it was not the same as having a sister to work, play, and share secrets with. Billy was nearly ten, and had begun spending more time with his father, working on the farm and accompanying him on hunting and fishing trips. That was a good thing, she knew, but it made for many lonely days of playing alone for Sally. Catherine was grateful that Alice didn't seem to mind Sally following her about, and seemed to enjoy spending time with her.

By noontime, Catherine had prepared a basket of cornbread and some slabs of bacon, along with a jug of peach cider, to take to the men for lunch. She sent Alice and Sally to fill buckets of drinking water from the spring to replenish the supply for the house and to take to the fields. Once they had gathered everything together, each of the four women grabbed a basket, jug, or bucket and headed off to the fields.

They met up with Benjamin and Tom by a large oak tree, which had just begun re-sprouting its leaves. Several sawn logs were under the tree to use for seats and tables. The women placed the baskets of food on the logs, and the two men wasted no time digging in.

Catherine wrapped a small bundle of food and gave it to Silvey to bring to Isaac, who was still out in the cornfield. It was not customary for slaves to eat with their masters. The practice of slavery repulsed Alice, but she tried to understand that it was acceptable to the people of this time. She thought it was best to leave her thoughts about slavery unspoken for the moment.

"Oh, my goodness, you really stink!" said Alice as Tom walked by her. "What on earth have you been doing?"

"Don't ask," he answered. "Just be glad you got to work at the house."

"I had a great time working with Sally, and she certainly smells a lot better than you two," she said, winking at the little girl who giggled and held her nose.

As they began eating, they heard Sal's voice from across the field, "Hey dudes, save some grub for us!"

Adam, Sal, and Billy jogged up to the tree and rummaged through the baskets of food. "Well at least you three smell a little better than Tom. Nice hats," Alice said to Sal and Adam, who were still wearing the straw hats Isaac had given them. Sal removed his hat with a flourish and bowed deeply.

"You look like one of those Italian hot dog vendors down at the Jersey shore," Alice said.

"Today I'm a Cherokee corn planter from Georgia," he said, "and I'm about fed up with it. Four hours of dig the hole, drop in the seed, and cover it up, is about all I can take."

"That is good," said Benjamin, "because when we are through eating, the women will take over the planting, and you and Adam will join in our work."

"Now you get to be a Georgia shit-shoveler," Tom whispered to Sal.

After a quick lunch, the women headed to the cornfield and the men joined Benjamin in fertilizing the field. Isaac soon arrived with the plow to begin turning over the soil, and Benjamin teamed Sal with him to lead the horses. He could see that Sal was clearly going to do more complaining than manure spreading. He sent Billy off to the farmhouse to work on his studies. Billy protested, but quieted quickly after receiving a stern glance from his father.

"I have him attend one of the mission schools near New Echota when he can, but it is hard to do without him on the farm this time of year. It is my wish that he become well educated in both Cherokee and white man's knowledge, learning both cultures as John Carter has done. John had several brothers and his family could afford more slaves, so it was possible for him to spend more time at school," he said to Adam.

"Getting an education is important, even in the world we come from, Benjamin," said Adam, as he tossed another shovel full of manure. "He is a very bright boy, and there have been many very successful men through history who were educated at home. I'm sure if he works hard at his studies he will do well."

"I believe that his education will be important for his acceptance into the white man's world."

"Unfortunately, there is greed and bigotry within people of all cultures. Education helps, but doesn't eliminate it. There are plenty of well-educated men who let those bad qualities guide their actions. The best you can hope for is that between a good education and your fine example, your children will learn to recognize both the good and bad qualities in all those they meet, and know how to deal with it appropriately."

"That is very well said, Adam. Spoken like a wise Cherokee. Perhaps you have some Indian blood in you."

"Doesn't everyone have an Indian princess in their family tree somewhere?" Adam said with a grin. "I think by the time I'm done with this job, people might think I'm part skunk! Phew, what a stench!"

"Ah, my friend, a farmer comes to recognize that smell as the sweet smell of home. If he is away from his home, and smells a field that has been freshly manured, it reminds him of his own fields."

"It reminds me of a few places in Jersey," said Sal, overhearing the comment as he passed by leading the plow horses.

"Then you are fortunate," Benjamin shouted back, "to come from a place with such rich, fertile soil!"

They worked through the afternoon, enjoying the warmth of the Georgia sunshine. The weather couldn't have been more perfect, warm enough to be comfortable, scant humidity, and a gentle breeze blowing across the fields that kept them cool and helped dispel the smell of the manure. The sky was layered with color; pale turquoise with fluffy white cloud puffs that drifted between the mountaintops in the distance. Below the clouds the sky became a deep azure blue, accented by an emerging pink streak as the sun made its way toward the western horizon. The fanning spring-green treetops tenderly cradled the sky, their brown trunks like supporting pillars from Mother Earth below.

Benjamin enjoyed listening to Tom and Adam talk about the place they were from. He did not comprehend all the details of their discussion, and understood even less of Sal's comments. It was clear they were already beginning to long for their homeland. He knew John Carter had been right when he asked Benjamin to act as host to them for a while. John felt that a day or two on the farm would give them time to adjust to their situation before they were overwhelmed by the frenzy of activity sure to occur when he arrived at New Echota. John was wise to suggest that the idea appear to come from Benjamin, since they were more likely to accept it after partaking of the Rogers family hospitality. They were interesting guests and he was happy to have their help, even if they were not very knowledgeable of farm work. Still, there were only so many chores he could assign them, no matter how willing they were.

John was also correct that these people had much to learn about the Cherokee world they had stumbled into. They were not stupid; they had understanding of some things that were beyond his understanding, but they were like very young children about the ways of the world, and it would take much teaching to make them think like adults. Benjamin wondered what that said about the future. If these people were some of the brightest, how childlike and naive must the rest of them be?

He did not mind bringing them to New Echota. He had already agreed to attend a meeting with John Carter and the others, and he really did need to go there to pick up supplies. He would be making the run the day after tomorrow, hoping John would have had time by then to quell most of the uproar from his news. He was anxious to speak with some of the others in town and hear their opinions on the Georgia matter.

Before long, Benjamin noticed the women pass by, returning to the farmhouse. They had put aside the planting so they could complete the preparation of the evening meal. The men finished spreading and plowing their field, and Benjamin began directing the group to wrap up the day's field work. Isaac unhitched the plow horses, while the other men loaded the plow into the manure wagon to bring it back to the barn. Once they had gotten the tools and implements stored to Benjamin's satisfaction, they left the removal of the harnesses to Isaac and headed to the farmhouse. The two farm dogs followed the men, sniffing at their heels, apparently attracted to the odor of the manure.

"Get away, dog!" Sal said as he shooed the animal away who was rubbing against his pant leg. "What's up with dogs always trying to roll in something nasty," he asked no one in particular.

"Well, the theory is…" Tom started.

"It figures, dude," Sal interrupted. "Only you would actually have a theory about why dogs roll in crap."

"You're the one who asked," Tom replied. "As I was saying, they do it to mask their scent. Dogs are hunters, and they instinctively try to cover up their own smell so they will have better luck stalking their game. Makes perfect sense, actually."

"Not to me, man. You'd think being stalked by a four-legged turd would scare away more animals than the dog smell." said Sal to everyone's laughter.

When they reached the farmhouse, they saw that Catherine had laid out several buckets of rainwater, scrub brushes, and lye soap on the back porch. Obviously they were expected to clean up thoroughly before entering the house. Catherine and Alice came out of the back door, each with an armload of clean clothes, and set them on the porch table.

"Here are some fresh clothes for you all," Catherine said. "Sal, you are close to Benjamin's size, so I brought you some of his extras. Tom and Adam are about as big as Isaac, so here are a few things I made for him. They are not as nice as your own fine clothes, but at least they are clean."

They thanked her and took the clothes, buckets, brushes, and soap to the side porch where they stripped off their smelly clothing, scrubbed down meticulously, and rinsed off the filth. The borrowed clothing made them look more like farmers than test engineers. Benjamin's clothes were just a bit short for Sal, and Isaac's a bit too large on Tom and Adam, and every piece of clothing had been mended more than once, but as Catherine said, at least they were clean.

Freshly scrubbed and clothed, the men entered the kitchen and took their places at the table. Alice and Sally filled cups with the *gahnohayna* drink for each person. She relayed what Catherine had told her; that it was a traditional drink usually offered to visitors. Tentatively tasting it, they found it to be thick and bland, just a little sour, but refreshing.

"Not bad," said Adam. "Certainly different, and I can see how the taste could grow on you. Thank you for sharing it with us."

"If you are going to work, dress, and eat like a Cherokee farmer," Benjamin said, "you should also learn to speak like one. *Wado* is how you say thank-you in Cherokee."

"*Wado* very much, then," Adam said. He raised his cup in a toast, "here's to the Rogers family and their beautiful farm. *Wado* for making us feel welcome!"

"*Wado*," repeated Alice, Tom, and Sal, joining in the toast.

"And *wado* to you all," said Benjamin returning the toast, "for all your hard work today."

There was not much more for conversation during the meal, other than copious comments about how delicious everything was. The hard day's work, fresh air, and sunshine had given them voracious appetites, and the platters of pork and bowls of boiled vegetables made their way around the table at least twice.

After the meal, the women cleaned up in the kitchen and the men went to the stables to see to the grooming and a few final chores. Tom and Benjamin smoked their pipes as they walked. It was still early, and Benjamin's work day usually went on past dark. He could see his guests were fit, but they were not used to long days of hard work. He decided to let them relax a little early on their first full day as farm hands. Besides, if part of the intention was to educate these newcomers, the evening storytelling would be very beneficial to them. He was surprised at Alice's adeptness at storytelling last evening, and was looking forward to tonight's session. It was his favorite part of the day.

Chapter nineteen

*I*t was still light when they assembled for storytelling on the front porch. They claimed a comfortable seat and watched the setting sun cast colorful shadows from behind the house. Silvey served everyone another cupful of *gahnohayna* before going off to have her evening meal with Isaac. Benjamin brought out two kerosene lanterns and hung them on the posts of the porch. He found himself a comfortable seat, offered Tom another pipe full of tobacco and filled his own. Using a burning stick from the kitchen hearth, he lit Tom's pipe and got his own corncob pipe going with a great cloud of blue smoke, then used the brand to light the lanterns. It was his turn to tell the story for the Rogers family, and his puffing helped set the mood and get his thoughts together before beginning. After a few minutes of silent smoking, Benjamin said that tonight he would tell them two stories. "The first is a short but very important story about how the Cherokee people came to have *tso-lu*—tobacco." Everyone settled into their seats and listened intently.

"Long, long ago," Benjamin began, "when the people and the animals all lived together, there was only one single tobacco plant. That one plant provided all the tobacco for the Tsalagi. Everyone got the tobacco they needed from that plant, and they depended on having it. As you know, tobacco is needed for spiritual offerings and for curing many ailments. There was even one very old woman who was so old that the tobacco was the only thing that kept her alive.

"Everything was fine until one day, the *Dagul-Ku*, the white-fronted geese, stole the plant and took it away with them when they flew south for the winter. Well, this was not good, because all of the people were suffering without the tobacco, and the old woman became very thin and weak and everyone thought she would surely die.

"The other animals knew how important the tobacco was to the people, and they wanted to help. Many of the animals tried to go and get the plant back from the *Dagul-Ku*, but none could because the geese would catch them and kill them before they got to the plant. Even the Mole tried to get it by digging a tunnel underground, but the *Dagul-Ku* saw what he was doing and killed him when he came above the ground.

"Then the tiny hummingbird said that he wanted to try to get it back. The others told him to stop being silly, that he was much too small to try, and he should just go home. The hummingbird begged them to let him at least try, so they told him he would have to show them how he intended to get the plant. They took him to a field and planted a plant there, and said he should demonstrate to them what he would do. Before they could blink, the tiny hummingbird zipped off to the plant, and then in a flash he was back again. The others decided that because he was so fast, they would let him try.

"So the little hummingbird flew to where the *Dagul-Ku* had the tobacco plant. He saw that all the geese were watching the plant. But the hummingbird was so fast, he darted to the plant and snatched the leaves and the seeds off the top before the *Dagul-Ku* could see what he was up to.

"The hummingbird flew straight home with the plant top. The old woman was very weak by then, but they blew smoke in her nose and made her well again, so she didn't die. Then they planted the seeds and the people have had tobacco ever since, thanks to the tiny little hummingbird!"

"Hooray for the hummingbird!" shouted Sally and Billy, and everyone clapped for the story.

"That was your Tsalagi name when you were a boy, wasn't it?" asked Billy.

"Yes, it was. They called me Hummingbird because even though I was small as a boy, I was a very fast runner, and could beat many of the other boys in races. So even if you are a small person, you can still have abilities that make you valuable to the community," he said, giving Sal a quick wink.

"I'm small, too," said Sally, "but Billy is faster than me and always beats me in a race."

"Yes, Billy is very fast," Benjamin concurred, "but you are very beautiful, like *ka-ma-ma*, the Butterfly. Perhaps that is what we should call you—Butterfly."

"Butterfly," Sally repeated softly. "Butterflies are very pretty," she said, clearly embarrassed by her father's compliment.

"Do all Cherokees have a Tsalagi name?" asked Alice.

"Many are given names as a child," said Catherine, "and later may take or earn one or more names in later life. It is the grandmother's right to give a child his first name. That was the traditional way, but now many Cherokee also have a 'white name' like yours and ours. Some families now only use their English names. This alteration is one of the many changes to our culture to try and make us more acceptable to the whites."

"Which brings me to my next story," said Benjamin. "It is also short, and has to do with names."

The sun had fully set, and above the dim glow of the lanterns the stars shone brightly in the dark sky. He pointed to a broad swath of stars overhead. "Do you remember what we call that path of stars, Billy?"

"The Milky Way," he answered.

"That is correct. The Cherokee call it *Gili-utsun-yi*, and now I will tell you how it got its name." He stirred and tamped his pipe, relit it from the lantern, pausing for effect. Then he began the story:

"There was a family who owned a mill where they went to grind corn into meal every day. They would haul the corn from their farm to the mill and fill it every morning, and the family members would take turns pounding the corn. It was much work, but they were grateful for the corn and the mill, and made a good living from it. After a while though, they began to notice that in the morning when they arrived with the corn, some of the meal was missing. It was being stolen during the night. This happened on several occasions, and they noticed that there were very large dog footprints in the meal. They decided that they would catch the dog in the act, so the next night they hid at the mill, and saw a giant dog with wings swoop down from the sky and begin eating the meal. The family jumped out from their hiding place and yelled and kicked at the dog. The frightened dog flew away howling, the cornmeal dropping from his mouth leaving a white streak in the night sky. Each grain of the meal became a star, which we see as the Milky Way. And that is why to this day the Cherokee call the Milky Way *Gili-utsun-yi*, which means 'Where the dog ran.'"

Benjamin watched as everyone on the porch gazed at the constellation, even more brilliant as the sky was now fully dark. It didn't take too much imagination to see the dog running across the sky leaving his trail of cornmeal stars behind.

"Now maybe our guests would care to share another of their wonderful stories," Benjamin said. All eyes turn to Alice.

"My goodness, I think tonight we should give Adam a turn," Alice replied.

"Nothing like putting me on the spot, Alice," Adam said, grinning. "It just so happens I do have a story for you all tonight. I think I can remember all the words. This story is a poem, called *The Lake of the Dismal Swamp*, by Thomas Moore, but it's kind of scary, so maybe it's not really a good story to tell the children..."

"Please tell it!" said Sally. "I love scary stories."

"I am not a child," Billy stated, "so I won't be scared by a story."

A subtle nod of approval from Benjamin and Catherine convinced Adam. "Well, okay. If you're sure it won't keep you awake."

Not to be outdone by Alice's performance last night, Adam went to each of the lanterns and dimmed them as low as they would go. He returned to his seat, building suspense as he solemnly looked into each person's eyes, one at a time. He kept his grave expression as he prepared to tell his story. The only sounds that could be heard were the night sounds of the Georgia countryside, insects chirping, frogs croaking, and an occasional creek, chirp, or groan from some unidentified night creature. He let a long minute pass before beginning, speaking slowly in a low, pensive voice:

"They made her a grave, too cold and damp
For a soul so warm and true;
And she's gone to the Lake of the Dismal Swamp,
Where, all night long, by a fire-fly lamp,
She paddles her white canoe.

"And her fire-fly lamp I soon shall see,
And her paddle I soon shall hear;
Long and loving our life shall be,
And I'll hide the maid in a cypress tree,
When the footstep of death is near."

Away to the Dismal Swamp he speeds—
His path was rugged and sore,
Through tangled juniper, beds of reeds,
Through many a fen where the serpent feeds,
And man never trod before.

And when on the earth he sunk to sleep,
If slumber his eyelids knew,
He lay where the deadly vine doth weep

Its venomous tear and nightly steep
The flesh with blistering dew!

And near him the she-wolf stirr'd the brake,
And the copper-snake breath'd in his ear,
Till he starting cried, from his dream awake,
"Oh! when shall I see the dusky Lake,
And the white canoe of my dear?"

He saw the Lake, and a meteor bright
Quick over its surface play'd—
"Welcome," he said, "my dear one's light!"
And the dim shore echoed for many a night
The name of the death-cold maid.

Till he hollow'd a boat of the birchen bark,
Which carried him off from shore;
Far, far he follow'd the meteor spark,
The wind was high and the clouds were dark,
And the boat return'd no more.

But oft, from the Indian hunter's camp,
This lover and maid so true
Are seen at the hour of midnight damp
To cross the Lake by a fire-fly lamp,
And paddle their white canoe!

Adam closed his eyes and lowered his head, indicating the story was finished. He waited, but heard nothing. He wasn't getting the reaction he expected, but he kept his eyes closed until finally, he heard a cough, followed by a sniffle. When he opened his eyes, he saw Catherine, her arm wrapped around Sally, and both were shedding tears. Benjamin and Billy both nervously tried not to make eye contact with him.

"Way to spoil the party mood, dude," he heard Sal say.

"Oh, my," said Adam, "I didn't mean to upset anyone."

"No, Adam, your story was quite, uh, unnerving, that's all," Benjamin said, trying to keep his voice level. "But I do think it is time for us to turn in. Dawn comes early, and we will have another busy day."

"May I sleep between mother and you tonight?" Sally asked Alice through her sniffles.

"Of course, Sally. I'll tell you a short, happy story about Basil the Beaver before you sleep, so you'll have happy dreams," then to Adam,

"Way to go, killjoy. For heaven's sake, could you think of a gloomier story to depress everyone?"

Chapter twenty

True to Benjamin's word, dawn came early the next morning. All four travelers woke with sore muscles from exertions they were not used to. They were young and fit, so their soreness subsided quickly after a bit of stretching.

Benjamin organized his workers for the day, telling them they would be working in the peach orchard thinning the fruit. He explained that his peaches produced early fruit, and they were already in need of thinning. He demonstrated how to pinch off the unwanted blooms so that those remaining were evenly spaced and would produce large, healthy fruits. The goal was to encourage the peaches to grow large and be ready for harvest as early as possible. The larger and earlier the crop, the better the price he would receive at the market.

Benjamin also showed them how to prune the old, gray, center branches of the trees, so that sunlight could better penetrate the trees. Most of the pruning had been done while the trees were dormant, but there was always some touch up needed. The next serious pruning would not be required until late summer, after the harvest.

They worked in the orchard the entire morning. Alice and Sally joined them after their morning house chores were complete. The fruit thinning was less exerting than the plowing and spreading they did yesterday, but it was still hard, tiresome work. The orchards were planted on the hilly sections of the farm, which meant lots of walking up and down the hills and plenty of stretching overhead to reach the higher branches. No one complained; it was a perfect day to be working outdoors. The weather was beautiful again today, and by the time Catherine and Silvey brought the mid-day meal, the temperature was well into the eighties.

After they ate, Benjamin delighted everyone by suggesting that they show their appreciation for the gift of such a beautiful day. He said they should put aside their work for an hour or two and go fishing.

The Rogers favorite fishing spot was a few miles from the farm, and Benjamin suggested taking the wagon so they could spend more time fishing and less time walking. He told Isaac to hitch up the wagon and load it with all the fishing gear he could find.

When Isaac returned, they piled into the old, open-top wooden wagon, taking seats on the narrow side benches. The wagon was clearly constructed for farm work, with little consideration for the comfort of passengers. It rocked and jarred with each bump in the rutted road, shaking violently as they clung to the sides to prevent being ejected from their seats. Each bump brought a fresh round of laughter. They were all grateful for the break and delighted in the bouncy ride to the river in the warm sun.

The jarring trip came to a sudden halt as Isaac reined the horses to a halt. They piled out of the wagon, grabbed the fishing gear and followed Benjamin down a shady, narrow path that ran along the riverbank. He halted at a spot where several large, flat slabs of granite lined the water's edge.

"We have had good luck fishing in this spot," said Benjamin. "Find yourself a comfortable rock and have a seat."

The team found fishing with cane poles more difficult than the modern casting rods and reels they were used to. After some practice, they mastered flipping the long poles and sat comfortably on one of the warm boulders watching the bobbers.

Benjamin caught the first fish, a medium size black bass that put up a pretty good fight, which he landed expertly. Adam noticed that Benjamin spoke a few words to the fish as he put it onto the stringer, and asked what he was saying. Benjamin explained that he apologized to the fish and thanked it for giving its life so they could have a fine fish dinner. Adam wondered if the fish accepted his apology.

Benjamin had been correct; it was indeed a good spot. It wasn't long before everyone caught at least one fish. In less than two hours, Benjamin said they had caught sufficient fish for the evening meal. They loaded everything back into the wagon for another bumpy ride back to the farmhouse.

While the women prepared the fish, the men spent what was left of the afternoon hours back in the orchard. Benjamin positioned the workers close together so that they could easily converse; wanting to spend more time talking with the team to learn what actions they decided to take. Benjamin and Catherine were very concerned that their visitors were not prepared for the hazards of the world they now found themselves in. Tomorrow he would take them to New Echota, and he was not sure they were ready to face the dangers they would encounter there. Yes, they were good people, but they acted as if they had been sheltered from the harsh realities of the world all of their lives. He felt they would need more patience and strength of character than they arrived with. Benjamin hoped he could urge them to be cautious and discreet. He tactfully eased into his planned conversation.

"Tell me, Adam," Benjamin said, "in the world you are from, has the United States taken a position of prominence in the world?"

"Most definitely," Adam answered. "The USA is a world leader, and is considered to be the strongest, most influential, and wealthiest of all countries. And the USA does everything it can to bring democracy to the people of other countries and lead them away from other oppressive forms of government."

"How do the other countries react to that?" Benjamin asked. "The USA, even in your time, is a young nation. Do not the other countries, who have their own well-established cultures and traditions, resent the US for asserting its philosophies upon them?"

"Well, yes, sometimes that happens," Adam said. "But diplomacy is used more than aggressiveness. Harsh lessons have been learned by the US that it is better to effect change from within. The USA has gained much respect both through its humanitarian efforts, and its use of strength as a last resort. Our country has not always handled things appropriately; there are many shameful incidents in our past, as there have been in every other country. We've done far more good in the world than bad however; we believe more so than any other country."

"Then is it the goal of the USA to make all other countries mirror images of themselves?" Benjamin asked. "Even if the USA believes itself to have the best form of government, is there no room for diversity? Is not the preservation of a country's culture just as important as having an ideal government?"

"Yes, of course," said Adam. "The US doesn't want to destroy anyone's culture. We just want to insure that all people have basic human rights. We want to eliminate the societies where one faction oppresses another. All people should be treated equally."

Benjamin let that comment pass, not wanting to elaborate on how the Cherokee Nation had been treated. "Is not the oppression of some factions a large part of many cultures? For example, slavery in this country..."

"In my time, slavery was eliminated," said Adam. "Not easily; doing so caused a great rift within the nation, and much bloodshed."

"I see," said Benjamin. "I sensed the anxiety of you and the others at the mention of our slaves. There are only a small percentage of slave owners due to the expense, but the large farms and plantations could not exist without slavery, at least the way they operate today. The elimination of slavery must have been devastating to those operations."

"Fortunately, most people believe that basic human rights for all people are more important than plantations," said Adam.

"Did you know that many American Indian people were also sold into slavery?" Benjamin asked.

"I guess I knew that but had forgotten," said Adam. "How can you justify owning slaves then, knowing your own people have been subjected to it?"

Benjamin shrugged his shoulders. "The tribes themselves captured and traded slaves long before the arrival of the whites. Some were treated harshly while others were accepted into the capturing tribe. We have black slaves because the whites tell us that is what must be done to run a farm successfully. As you have seen, many other ways of the whites have been adopted by progressive Cherokee families, such as mine, because we have decided that is the best way for us to deal with the current situation. But there are also many Cherokee who are adamantly opposed to abandoning any of our traditions. They believe we must live by the rules of our ancient customs. It can be difficult for a person to change his ways, simply because someone says his ways are better. As you say, a nation can sometimes get better results using tolerance and example rather than coercion. It would be good to remember that is true when dealing with individuals also."

"I think I'm getting your message, Benjamin. You're warning me to expect that folks in this time aren't likely to accept guidance from us just because we tell them our way is best for them."

"I was only talking to you about the policies of the United States. But you are a wise man to apply that logic to your own situation," Benjamin said with a grin, pleased that his point had gotten across.

Chapter twenty-one

After the fish feast and evening chores, the group once again retired to the front porch. Tonight Benjamin addressed them in a serious voice. Since this would be their guests last evening with them, he wished to express his gratitude for their hard work and good company. He also wanted to speak to them about tomorrow's trip to New Echota.

"But first, I would like to ask Billy if he remembers the story of the Bride from the South," Benjamin said.

"Yes," said Billy, "sure I do. It was when the North went traveling and visited the South, where he met the daughter of the South and wanted to marry her. Her parents objected, and told North that ever since he had come to visit the people had been complaining that it was very cold and they were freezing. North loved the daughter, and pleaded with them to allow them to marry, and her parents finally said they would agree as long as he would take her back with him to his own country to live, which he did. But after they were there for a while, the weather became warmer and warmer, and the ice houses that the people lived in started to melt. The people told North that it was because his new wife was from the South. Her nature was so warm it would soon melt their entire village. So North had to give up his new wife and send her back to live with her parents in the South."

"Good. What do you think is the importance of that story?"

"Well, I think it means that it is not always possible to have what you want, no matter how much you want it."

"That is right. Sometimes we must accept things as they are, because it is their nature. A fish may want to be a deer, because he is tired of swimming and wants to run through the forest, but he can never be a deer because his nature is to be a fish."

"But why couldn't they go live somewhere between the North and the South?" asked Sally.

"Ah, leave it to my little Butterfly to want to find a way to keep the lovers together," Benjamin said, smiling and stroking her long black hair. "Do you think that either of them would be fully happy if neither could live close to their friends and family?"

"No, I guess not," said Sally sadly.

"Sometimes, compromise can be an excellent way to work things out, but not if both sides have to give up so much, or go against their nature so much that neither can be satisfied. It would be good if our guests keep this story in mind when they visit the town tomorrow. I know that the circumstances that put you here are highly unusual, and from the things you have told me, you believe that you are aware of things to come, things that are not pleasant. It is admirable that you have chosen to provide assistance and guidance to our people, to ease the turmoil that you believe they must face. That is a good decision, and I would like to believe that if the roles were reversed, I would have the courage to put others above myself as you are planning to do.

"It is unfortunate that you are likely to find the town much less peaceful than things appear to be here on our farm. The town has changed much in the last few years. It was a promising capital city, but that was short-lived. Many of the homes and businesses there have been abandoned, and most of what is left has already been appropriated by the whites. A stockade fort has been built there. There is much tension among the people, among and between the Cherokee and the Georgia whites, and I have to urge much caution to you. Your demeanor indicates that in the world you are from you may not have had much experience with the type of hostility that exists in our world.

"It is not in the nature of a Cherokee to casually offer advice, and I only do so out of concern for your safety, as in this short time you have all endeared yourselves to my family very much. It is a dangerous time, but you may take some precautions that will improve the likelihood of a hostile encounter. I suggest you keep the clothes we have lent you, as they are less conspicuous than your own, even if they are somewhat ill fitting. Alice, my wife will provide you with a dress, as a young lady wearing trousers is not often seen.

"You must be cautious of the conversations you engage in. It is likely you will hear many things said that you will disagree with, even be abrasive to you. I urge you to hold your tongue in these situations. It may be very dangerous for you to voice an opinion, or even to make a casual remark about something you find disagreeable.

"But my advice is not only in regards to your safety; I hope you will not find that in offering assistance you experience callousness and rejection from the people you want to help. You will do well to remember the story of the bride from the South. Some things you cannot change, no matter how badly you want to change them, if it goes against their nature."

"Thank you, Benjamin," said Adam, "we appreciate your advice and will take it to heart. I'm sure I can speak for Alice, Tom, and Sal when I say that we have become very fond of your family as well, and we are most grateful for the hospitality you have shown us. The little work we have done on your farm can hardly begin to show our gratitude.

"We also appreciate your concern for our wellbeing. While we may appear to be overly trusting and naive, we are also cautious. I admit that none of us has had the experience of such an inflammable situation as this. We hold no grandiose idea that we are persuasive enough to change the way people choose to behave, or prevent the things we believe are going to happen. It is true that we want to help in a larger way, knowing what we know of things to come. It is not completely selfless, however, as we believe that doing so may be the key to finding our way home. We feel that the device led us here for a reason, and once we have completed certain tasks it may lead us back home again. Maybe our being here can make some difference."

"That does sound logical, Adam, but have you considered another possibility?" Benjamin asked.

"We've considered several," said Adam, "but what possibility did you have in mind?"

"It may be that the device, your magic window, has brought you here as observers, giving you a glimpse of some important lesson from your country's past that should not be forgotten. Perhaps the most difficult tasks you must perform will be when you return to your own time."

Chapter twenty-two

The sun was barely over the treetops before they were on their way to New Echota. Isaac had the wagon hitched and ready to go by the time they finished breakfast. Benjamin sternly refused Billy and Sally's request to come along. He could not be certain how their guests were going to react on this trip, or what sort of reaction the townsfolk may have to them. Tensions were already high, and he did not want the added concern for his children's safety. He insisted that the rest of the family would be staying at home this time.

The team said their goodbyes to Catherine, Billy, and Sally, and thanked Isaac and Silvey for their hard work, although accepting their gratitude clearly made both of the slaves uncomfortable. Sally and Alice tearfully hugged, and Sally asked her if she would please come back soon and tell her some more stories like *Basil, the Builder Beaver*.

"Of course I'll try, Sally dear. If I can, I will," Alice said.

"Oh, I hope so." Sally looked solemnly at Alice with moist eyes. The two had become especially fond of each other during their short visit. Alice gave the little girl a final hug before jumping into the wagon.

"*Dodadagohvi*," said Catherine as they pulled away in the wagon. It was a word that loosely translated meant "until we meet again," as there is no actual word for "goodbye" in Tsalagi.

"Goodbye," they yelled back, "and *wado!*" They continued to wave until the wagon rounded a bend and the farmhouse was out of sight.

Benjamin hummed a tuneless song as he drove the wagon, only pausing to occasionally cluck at the horses and give them an encouraging smack with the reins. So far, the trip had been uneventful. The rutted road became a little less bumpy, although it was still far from a smooth ride. They passed by several farms and houses as the area became more populated. Tom asked Benjamin if the smoother road and additional houses indicated that they were getting close to town.

"Yes, there are more farms closer to town," said Benjamin, "and the roads are more heavily traveled. There are even more homes and improvements after we cross the river. Unfortunately, there is no longer any growth in the town, and indeed many of the homes and businesses have been abandoned. The Cherokee who believe our removal is imminent have been fleeing steadily."

"Man, I hope there are a few businesses left. I could really use a pizza," said Sal, patting his stomach. "All this wholesome food and hard work ain't good for my Jersey metabolism, you know."

"Perhaps if you could describe what you are looking for," said Benjamin helpfully, "I could help you find a whole one instead of just a 'piece' of one."

"No, not a piece-a …. Oh, forget about it. I wouldn't want to get sauce on my new country duds anyway." Sal snapped the strap on his suspenders.

"Oh, come on, Sal." said Alice. "The work was good for you, and you know you enjoyed the food at the farm."

"We know you enjoyed it, *gv-li* girl," Sal replied.

"Anyway," Adam interjected to prevent another row. "You mentioned a river, Benjamin. How will we cross it? Is it shallow enough to ride across?"

"No, the river is quite deep and rapid here. There is a ferry just below the confluence of the Coosawattee and the Conasauga rivers. There could be a problem, however, because the operation of the ferry has been inconsistent for the last two years. That is when the McCoy family had to give up ownership of it. The whites who now own it usually have slaves assigned to keep it operating, but not always. The ferry is the only way for us to cross the Oostanaula River without taking a much longer route."

"The Oosta-who River?" said Sal. "Dude, I thought you said it was the Coozy-whatsit and the Cona-sumthin-or-other Rivers?"

"The Coosawattee and the Conasauga rivers come together here to form the Oostanaula River," Benjamin explained patiently.

As if on cue, they rounded the bend and the river came into view. They could see a large, flat-bottom boat, apparently the ferry, docked at the shore. Two black men sat on barrels next to the boat. They could see a heavy rope stretching across the river, which was tied to massive posts on both sides. A third black man sat on the opposite shore.

"It looks as though the ferry is in operation," said Benjamin.

Without a word one of the ferrymen helped to guide the wagon onto the ferry while Benjamin spoke quietly with the other man. He negotiated the fee and handed him a few copper coins. He confirmed that the ferry would still be in operation when he returned. Using heavy, well-worn ropes, they tied both ends of the wagon to anchor points, securing it to the ferry. Benjamin indicated to the others to remain seated in the wagon while he stood at the front calming the horses.

The ferryman used a long pole to shove the boat away from the shore. He then rushed to a windlass mounted on the front of the ferry. The windlass was simply a large wooden spool through which a rope was fed, and a crank to turn the device. The rope was secured to anchors at both ends of the ferry and was connected to a large pulley, which in turn was attached to the main cable running across the river. By cranking the windlass, the ferryman was able to angle the front of the boat upstream, causing the river current to push it across at an angle.

The sensation of the moving current pushing the ferry sideways across the river made sitting in the wagon unnerving. Each time a wave rocked the ferry or one of the horses flinched, the wagon shifted, jogging its passengers.

At one particularly unsettling jolt, Sal yelled to the slave who was controlling the windlass, "Hey, easy there, pal. Is this thing OSHA approved?"

The black ferryman replied with a detached, "Yes, suh," then shook his head and muttered something inaudible under his breath.

"Hold on tightly," Benjamin said.

As they approached shore, the ferryman cranked the windlass to point the front of the boat toward the landing, letting momentum carry it the rest of the way. The wagon shuddered as the ferry hit the river bottom at the landing, and the horses shook the rig as they anxiously strained to get off the ferry. The third black man slowly got up from his barrel seat and helped Benjamin guide the horses and wagon off the ferry and back onto dry land.

"That wasn't so bad," said Adam, "but I'm glad it's over with." Alice nodded in agreement.

"Yeah," said Sal. "I bet that ride would be a big hit at Six Flags."

"It can be a little disconcerting going across for the first time," said Benjamin.

From the riverbank they could see several buildings along the perimeter of the town. The daunting structure of a fort stood on top of a nearby hill, overlooking the town like a feudal castle looming over its fiefdom. It was not an excessively large structure, although its imposing construction of sturdy log walls and defensive guard towers placed at each corner was undeniably intimidating. A United States flag flew from one of the towers.

"Tom," said Adam, nodding toward the fort, "can you see that flag?"

"Yes, I can see it just good enough to count the twenty-six stars."

"That is Fort New Echota," said Benjamin. "The U.S. government put it here under the command of General Wool to maintain order after the so-called treaty of New Echota was ratified, though some feel its presence increased tensions. A while back General Wool was replaced by Colonel Lindsay. They renamed it Fort Wool back in March, in honor of its first commander. Since then Colonel Lindsay has built a new blockhouse and has been recruiting many new troops for his Georgia Guard. He has been very persistent in his demands that the Cherokee voluntarily report for removal. Some have done so. Major Ridge and many of his treaty party were in one of the first groups to leave, but the overwhelming majority refused to report.

"We should avoid the fort as much as possible, as the soldiers there are likely to harass us. There is a trading post here on the main road, operated by a white, where I can get the supplies I need. We will go there first."

New Echota was barely more than a ghost town. Most of the smaller buildings were obviously abandoned and showing signs of disrepair. There were several large, impressive looking homes which appeared to be occupied. Leaving the ferry landing, they walked past a set of stables and a horse corral. Benjamin pointed out a large, two-story, log farmhouse just beyond the landing. The handsome house and substantial stable buildings brazenly depicted the prosperity of the property.

"This was the farm of the family who operated the ferry, before they were removed to the west. These most valuable properties were some of the first to be claimed by whites when Georgia conducted the land lottery."

Further along, they passed a two-story colonial style house, with large chimneys at each end, painted white wooden siding, and a welcoming porch stretching across the front. "That used to be Elijah Hicks' home. He was one of our government leaders and son of Charles Hicks, a principal chief, but he also left for the west last year when his home was confiscated."

"Many of these lovely homes are magnificent," said Alice. "Not at all what I imagined."

"There has been a major effort to paint the Cherokee people as savage and uncivilized, and incapable of living as decent people," said Benjamin. "This was done to ease the consciences of those who wished to seize our land in the name of expansionism." His tone was bitter, despite his effort to keep his voice neutral. He reminded himself that his guests were from a different world, and that they did not seem to share those despicable attitudes. He smiled at Alice and said, "You did not think the town would be full of tipis, did you?"

"No, I paid enough attention to my cultural studies to know better than that," she said, nudging Sal. "But I did imagine that the homes would be much more rustic and impoverished."

"Many are. Just like any other society we have all classes of people, rich and poor, some who choose to live traditionally, and others more extravagantly. You are seeing some of the finest homes here and there are even grander properties. Chief Vann's former home, Diamond Hill, is just north of here. He had one of the most magnificent plantations in the nation—not just the Cherokee nation—the entire country. The home is most elegant, and your president James Monroe once spent the night there. It is said that Joe Vann is one of the richest men in the United States, and is known as Rich Joe."

"You said his former home. He doesn't live there anymore?" asked Alice.

"Rich Joe owned businesses and operated ferries in Tennessee, and he hired a white man to look after Diamond Hill when he needed to be away on business. The Georgia Guard confiscated the home, claiming that Joe had violated the law by hiring a white man without a permit. Rich Joe Vann and his family have since moved to Indian Territory."

Benjamin pointed to another large two-story house, out in the direction of the fort. "That house belonged to Reverend Samuel A. Worcester. He was a Christian missionary who taught the bible and held services in that house. He also served as postmaster. We called him 'The Messenger'. He was not Cherokee, but his home was also confiscated in the lottery."

"How awful! How could they take his home if he wasn't even Cherokee?" asked Alice.

"Georgia has a law that for a white to live in the Cherokee Nation they must obtain a special license and swear an oath of allegiance to Georgia. Worcester refused to do both, saying that he was entitled to live where he chose, and as a citizen of the United States he was not required to take any other oath of allegiance."

"He was right! What happened? Did he try to fight this in court?"

"He was arrested and sentenced to four years hard labor," Benjamin answered. "The case went to the supreme court of the United States, and the Georgia law was declared unconstitutional, but Governor Lumpkin ignored the ruling and kept him imprisoned anyway. Reverend Worcester was finally released after serving sixteen months. He also moved west to continue teaching the bible to the Cherokee."

Alice shook her head, frowned and looked at the ground. "How could people act this way," she asked, more to herself than anyone else.

"Greed is a strong motivator," Benjamin stated. "The perverted philosophy of territorial expansionism has convinced people that god has given them a divine duty to acquire land for themselves."

"Not only land," said Tom. "Many of our country's most shameful acts were committed in the name of Manifest Destiny."

Benjamin shrugged. He had not heard the term before.

They continued walking into the abandoned town center, and Benjamin pointed out a ball field where they used to play a game he called *anetsa*. There were goal posts still standing on the overgrown field, making the area look much like a football field. Benjamin said that the game was played with much vigor and celebration, and it was common to bet on the outcome of the game. The fans would arrive with an abundance of food and drink, and loudly cheer on their favorite team. Many were very passionate about the game, and sometimes violence would break out.

"Awesome. Sounds like an Eagles game," said Sal.

The others chuckled, but Benjamin just smiled courteously. By now he understood that Sal's comments were usually intended to amuse, and should seldom be taken literally. He could not imagine a game that could be played using eagles, and he was certain that asking Sal about it would only result in more ambiguity.

As they walked along the town square, Benjamin pointed out several other buildings, explaining that they were used as a court house, post office, community center, and other government buildings. Nearly all were empty, or had been appropriated for some other use. Benjamin noted another house they were approaching, very similar to the Worcester house.

"This was Elias Boudinot's home. He was the founder and editor of our newspaper, the Cherokee Phoenix. His original name was *Gallegina*, 'Buck' Waite, but he took the name of the man who paid for his education, Dr. Elias Boudinot, one of your first presidents."

"Elias Boudinot was a president of the United States?" asked Adam. "That's one I must have missed!"

"Actually, he is correct, Adam," said Tom. "Elias Boudinot served as a President of the Continental Congress, appointed by George Washington. He technically wasn't called POTUS or elected by the people, but he did hold the presidential title."

"The Cherokee Elias Boudinot created a bilingual newspaper printed in English and Cherokee at the printing office that used to be there," Benjamin continued, pointing at an empty lot. "John Ross refused to allow Elias to continue publishing the newspaper when Elias began printing articles advocating Cherokee compliance with removal. Boudinot had formerly been against removal, but he and Ridge eventually began to believe that relocation would be inevitable. Elias Boudinot was also one of those who signed the treaty of New Echota, agreeing to give up our lands."

"What happened to the printing office?" asked Adam.

"The Georgia Guard confiscated the press, and destroyed the building. They said it was being used to incite turbulence among the Cherokee."

"Up ahead is the trading post where I can get the supplies I need. There is a white man, William Adair, who runs it. He has been here for years with permission from the Cherokee government, and now has a license from Georgia. His motives for being here are strictly for profit-making, which has never been a problem. He is no particular friend to the Cherokee, but I believe he is an honest merchant. Since there are no Cherokee merchants left, I have little choice."

Benjamin stopped the wagon in front of the trading post, a building that looked as if it served as a general store, hotel, restaurant, and dwelling for the owner. He asked Tom to accompany him into the store, and the others to remain with the wagon. There was no one in sight, but he cautioned them again to avoid engaging with any strangers if someone happened to come along.

Upon entering the store, a burly, heavily whiskered gentleman smoking a fat cigar stood behind a counter. He peered over the rims of his wire glasses and nodded to Benjamin.

"Benjamin," the man said in a deep, resonant voice.

"William," Benjamin returned the greeting.

"Still in Georgia, I see. When are you planning to leave?"

"I have no plans to leave, William. I am here to purchase supplies to last the next several weeks."

"It's your money. I don't get it, Benjamin. Most of the Indians like you, who could afford it, have all left for the west by now. What are you waiting for?"

"Justice," said Benjamin bluntly. "I still hold hope that the theft of my land can be prevented."

"Theft? You know the chiefs signed a treaty right here in New Echota to trade for land in the west. They took money for it, too. It was all agreed."

"I never agreed. Neither did most of the others. And the 'chiefs' who signed had no authority to make that agreement."

The storekeeper sighed. "We've been through all this before. Anyhow, Major Scott arrived in New Echota a couple days ago, with a whole lot of federal troops. They're getting the forts ready in case they have to do a roundup. He wrote a letter to all the Cherokees, giving them one last chance to move on their own. Here's a copy of the letter. Sounds like good advice to me," he said, handing the paper to Benjamin.

Benjamin took the letter, folding it and shoving it in his pocket. "I've seen many of the white man's papers. What they say on them can change with the wind."

He knew that William meant well. In his gruff way, he was concerned for the well-being of Benjamin and his family, and could not understand their reluctance to admit defeat. He had tried to encourage Benjamin to take the small compensation the government would provide for his farm and leave, before he was forced to go and receive nothing. William only considered the financial aspect; he could not comprehend Benjamin's determination to stand up for his principles once there was no hope of a successful appeal. He told Benjamin the sensible thing to do was to know when he was licked, and try to make the best of it. It was an impasse they had reached many times before. There was no use in rehashing it.

"I'd like to get my supplies now," Benjamin said, changing the subject.

William grunted, knowing it was useless to continue the argument. "I see you brought along some help." He pointed his bushy chin at Tom and the others outside the door.

"They are visiting friends, and yes, they have been most helpful."

"They'd be most helpful if they were helping you pack," William mumbled through his whiskers.

Benjamin pretended not to hear the remark, and began listing the items he needed. There weren't many things that William didn't have. He pointed to each item as Benjamin went through his list, letting Benjamin and Tom do all the required lifting. A few of the items came in large sacks that were kept in the back part of the store. A shout from William roused a sleepy-eyed young man who wheeled out the required items on a dolly and dumped them next to the door. Benjamin paid for the items while Tom finished carrying them out to the wagon where the others loaded them.

The transaction completed, the farewell was just as curt as the greeting. As they were heading out the door, William said, "Oh, by the way. You haven't seen that friend of yours, John Carter, around lately have you?"

"John was…," Tom started to reply.

"No," Benjamin said quickly. "I have not seen him for a while."

"Well, if you do," William said with a wary glance at Tom, "be sure to tell him that the colonel is looking for him. Seemed pretty hot about it, too."

Benjamin shrugged indifferently, and he and Tom left the store.

"Real friendly chap, isn't he?" said Tom.

"He is not the most cordial person," said Benjamin, beginning to get used to the idea of sarcasm. "At least not to the Cherokee these days. I guess he can't be blamed too much, though. Any show of hospitality toward us will only get him scorn from the other whites who have settled here. He did give us a warning for John Carter in his own furtive way. In his heart he is not excessively belligerent."

Tom thought that the "help you pack" comment was pretty belligerent, but he just nodded at Benjamin in agreement. He imagined that running a trading post in 1838 probably took a lot of grit, and a friendly, helpful salesperson type probably wouldn't stand a chance in this environment. The man did seem to have enough respect for Benjamin not to press his argument too far. And there was something familiar about the guy that Tom couldn't quite place. Adair, he thought; wasn't that a name he had heard just recently?

Benjamin interrupted his thoughts. "I am sorry for interrupting you before, but I think John Carter would prefer that few people know he is in town."

Climbing back in the loaded wagon, Benjamin clucked to the horses and started the wagon rolling with a jerk. He turned onto a deserted side street, and after glancing around to be sure there were no others nearby to overhear his conversation, said, "We are meeting John Carter a short way from the town, at a small farm that has not yet been occupied by the whites. It is important that I explain to you all the potential danger of our meeting.

"As John Carter has already told you, it is illegal for the Cherokee to conduct any sort of meetings. That law can be interpreted loosely, giving the Georgia Guard the power to make arrests at their discretion. The place we are meeting was formerly owned by a friend, so we are very familiar with the farm and its surroundings. As I have said, it is still unoccupied and should be a safe place to meet for discussions for the present time.

"When you first met John Carter, he explained that he was returning from Red Clay in Tennessee, which is where our government relocated when it was forbidden to keep the council here in New Echota. Since there are still many of our people here, John is acting as emissary to bring news to them from the council. According to Georgia law, this is an illegal activity.

"Tom, that is why I stopped you from speaking about John Carter at the trading post. I did not want to put the proprietor in the position of withholding information from the military. I am sure that word of John's mission has already gotten to the whites, and I have no doubt that the colonel would not hesitate to arrest John with only his suspicions as evidence, if he could find him. Therefore, John must remain in hiding. Attending this meeting with him puts all of you in violation of Georgia law as well."

"It seems to me," said Adam, "that just about anything can put a person in violation of Georgia law, especially being Cherokee or even associating with them."

"You are quite correct," Benjamin replied. "It is the intention of Governor Lumpkin to make life as difficult as possible for any of the Cherokee Nation to remain in Georgia. He has made it clear that they intend to remove us from our land, regardless of how he must go about it. Even if that means disregarding federal laws. He had the full support of the former president Jackson, and has gained enough momentum in his efforts that the current president can do nothing to stop him."

"What about the letter from General Scott that the storekeeper gave you?" Tom asked. "Do the contents of the letter change anything?"

Benjamin pulled the letter from his pocket, unfolded it, and began to read it aloud:

> *"Cherokees! The President of the United States has sent me with a powerful army, to cause you, in obedience to the treaty of 1835, to join that part of your people who have already established in prosperity on the other side of the Mississippi. Unhappily, the two years which were allowed for the purpose, you have suffered to pass away without following, and without making any preparation to follow; and now, or by the time that this solemn address shall reach your distant settlements, the emigration must be commenced in haste, but I hope without disorder. I have no power, by granting a farther delay, to correct the error that you have committed. The full moon of May is already on the wane; and before another shall have passed away, every Cherokee man, woman and child in those states must be in motion to join their brethren in the far West.*

My friends! This is no sudden determination on the part of the Presi-dent, whom you and I must now obey. By the treaty, the emigration was to have been completed on or before the 23rd of this month; and the President has constantly kept you warned, during the two years allowed, through all his officers and agents in this country, that the treaty would be enforced.

I am come to carry out that determination. My troops already occupy many positions in the country that you are to abandon, and thousands and thousands are approaching from every quarter, to render resistance and escape alike hopeless. All those troops, regular and militia, are your friends. Receive them and confide in them as such. Obey them when they tell you that you can remain no longer in this country. Soldiers are as kind-hearted as brave, and the desire of every one of us is to execute our painful duty in mercy. We are com-manded by the President to act towards you in that spirit, and much is also the wish of the whole people of America.

Chiefs, head-men and warriors! Will you then, by resistance, compel us to resort to arms? God forbid! Or will you, by flight, seek to hid yourselves in mountains and forests, and thus oblige us to hunt you down? Remember that, in pursuit, it may be impossible to avoid conflicts. The blood of the white man or the blood of the red man may be spilt, and, if spilt, however accidentally, it may be impossible for the discreet and humane among you, or among us, to prevent a general war and carnage. Think of this, my Cherokee brethren! I am an old warrior, and have been present at many a scene of slaughter, but spare me, I beseech you, the horror of witnessing the destruction of the Cherokees.

Do not, I invite you, even wait for the close approach of the troops; but make such preparations for emigration as you can and hasten to this place, to Ross's Landing or to Gunter's Landing, where you all will be received in kindness by officers selected for the purpose. You will find food for all and clothing for the destitute at either of those places, and thence at your ease and in comfort be transported to your new homes, according to the terms of the treaty.

This is the address of a warrior to warriors. May his entreaties by kindly received and may the God of both prosper the Americans and

Cherokees and preserve them long in peace and friendship with each other!"

Benjamin finished reading and stood silently for a moment before saying, "I believe this to be more of an ultimatum than an appeal. It changes very little. It may encourage a few to report to the forts, but I know many of us, myself included, will remain on our land and continue to hope for justice. More importantly, the arrival of General Scott and his troops will certainly embolden the Georgia militia, and cause them to act with even more aggression.

"I tell you of this danger now because this is your final opportunity to avoid becoming involved in illegal activities. You have said you wanted to offer your help, but you must once again consider the danger you are placing yourselves in. Up to now, you have done nothing illegal, except for being in the Cherokee Nation without a permit, which is usually not enforced except when politically convenient. However, if you attend this meeting you are knowingly violating Georgia law, the penalty for which can be quite extreme. I have given you examples of the actions taken against many of our prominent citizens. Some of them had the resources to fight in the courts; you do not. I do not need to tell you that those who could not afford to defend themselves can expect to suffer the full consequences of the Georgia legal system. Being white will probably not help, and none of you have any way to prove your identities, at least none that the Georgians of this time would recognize. It is imperative that you understand what you face, and do not take your involvement lightly."

"I appreciate your frankness," said Adam. "Even though we discussed the severity of the situation before, you have just made it most clear to me that each of us must carefully consider what we are about to do and express any uncertainties now, before we go any further.

"Speaking for myself, I'm prepared to go forward with our plan, regardless of the threat to my own safety. I don't say this lightly. I know the outcome of these events, at least in my timeline, and my conscience will not allow me to stand by idly while this injustice is occurring. However, I can't make this decision for everyone. We all have to agree, once again, that this is the best course of action before we proceed.

"Alice, as a woman, the danger to you may be the most significant. I apologize if I am offending you with a sexist attitude, but in this situation I believe it is a true statement. You know enough history of these times to be aware of some of the shameful actions that occurred, including those intended to cause humiliation to women. How do you feel about going on?"

"I'm not offended," Alice said, "and you just stated one of the most valid reasons that I need to go on. These offenses are not only going to occur to women, but to many people simply because of their race. I'm not sure how much we can change things, if at all, but I'm here, you know, and I have to try."

"I can concur with that," said Tom. "I had the most difficult time accepting that we actually traveled to the past, but I have had to face the facts. I said before, the only other choice is that I'm dreaming all this. In that case, it doesn't matter what I do, I'll just wake up before anything grave happens to me. Don't worry; I'm not counting on that. I'm taking this seriously. I'm certainly no hero, and I don't know for sure how I will react in a life-threatening situation. I'd like to believe that I will respond honorably, having been raised to put others before myself and to always make a stand against injustice when I see it. Well, I see it here, and I am going to make a stand."

All eyes turned toward Sal, who had been listening quietly to the others.

"Sal," said Adam, "it has to be unanimous."

Sal stood looking wide-eyed at each of them, then scowled. "Dude, are you serious?" he said. "When have any of you ever known me to back down from a fight?

"I know you all think I can be self-serving at times, but hey, sometimes you gotta be. But I can recognize injustice and greed when I see it too. You're right Tom, there's plenty of it here to see and it pisses me off. You might think it's out of character for me to give a damn about these folks, but if you do, you really don't know me very well. I couldn't stand by and let this go down without trying to do something to help any more than any of you dudes could. Benjamin here is a good friend, seeing how he taught me all that stuff about growin' peaches and shovelin' horseshit, and I don't abandon my friends. Besides, I've still got to return the favor by teaching him how to appreciate a good pizza or a cheese steak. Maybe for him it'll have to be a raccoon cheeseburger or something.

"I was even starting to get to like that crazy ol' John Squanto, and was kinda looking forward to seeing him again. At least I could rag on him without the nasty comebacks I get from Alice. But to the point, I ain't sure what I'm in for, but I'm in," Sal finished with a wink.

Adam turned to Benjamin and said, "I believe you have our decision, Benjamin Rogers. Please proceed to the meeting."

Chapter twenty-three

B enjamin led the group to a farm about a mile outside of New Echota. The farm was nestled within three foothills, conveniently secluded, making it ideal for their purposes. They followed a winding dirt lane, not to the farmhouse but to a barn; a ramshackle structure that had been built into a cove-like area of one of the surrounding hills. John Carter was standing at the barn door to greet their arrival.

"*'Siyo*," John said, giving them the same sort of half-wave that Benjamin greeted him with when he arrived at the farm.

"*'Siyo*," they answered, returning the wave.

"It is good to see you again, my friends. Thank you for bringing them, Benjamin. I see you were not able to discourage them from coming. I know Benjamin has done his best to explain the severity of the situation you are putting yourselves in and has made you aware of the potential consequences. Even so, I am grateful that you have decided to be here. I am certain you have not made the decision lightly."

"They seemed most determined," said Benjamin, "to become involved in our troubles." As he spoke he removed two large woven baskets from the wagon. "Catherine insisted I bring along this *alisdayvdi* for you. She thought you would be too busy to think of providing food." He handed one of the baskets to Alice to carry, and walked toward the barn door. "Have you been able to share your news with the others?"

"I have, and they received it as expected." John turned his attention to the food baskets. He smiled as he looked under the cover of the basket Alice was carrying. "Catherine is most intuitive as usual. I have not had much time for eating, so the food is most welcome."

A young man emerged from the barn behind John. He looked to be in his mid-twenties, with the long, straight hair, dark eyes, and similar Cherokee facial features to John and Benjamin. He was thinner than the other two men, almost skinny. He was a head taller than John, nearly as tall as Adam. His long hair was not rolled into a bun as John's was, but braided into a ponytail and held in place with a silver clasp. Like John and Benjamin, his clothes were homespun, but well-fitted on his slender frame.

"*Osiyo*, Jimmy Deerinwater," said Benjamin. "I did not know you were here. It is good to see you."

"'*Siyo*," the young man answered. "It's good to see you again, too, Benjamin Rogers."

"Jimmy has been keeping me company while waiting for you to arrive," said John. He turned and spoke to the others. "This is Jimmy Deerinwater, everyone. He and his wife Rebecca have a farm not too far from here. Jimmy, these are the people I told you about."

Jimmy shook hands and greeted each member of the team, smiling and looking each of them in the eye, holding the gaze longer than any of the other Cherokees had. "I'd be most interested in hearing more about the time you came from, and the device that brought you here. It must have been a very traumatic experience for you all, not realizing what had happened," Jimmy said. His manner of speaking was noticeably different than the older Cherokees, more rapid and modern sounding.

"Traumatic to say the least," said Adam. "We were only supposed to be testing a navigational device, not a time machine. We were all quite upset, even disbelieving when we first met John Carter." He glanced at Tom. "I think John and Benjamin's easy acceptance of time travel helped calm us down a little, but we are still very concerned about how we will be able to return."

"It's best you met them before me, then," said Jimmy. "I would most likely have thought you to be escaped lunatics! I would not have believed it if I hadn't heard it from John first. The traditional Tsalagi mythologies talk about many incredible things, but they are only myths after all. I am enough of a skeptic to be amazed at your time travel adventure."

"Jimmy's farm is most modern," said Benjamin. "He has a machine to take the seeds from his cotton, a wind-powered water pump, and countless other devices he believes we will all have one day. So far he has not convinced me to adopt any of them, though." He gave Jimmy a disapproving look.

"You would appreciate the increase in productivity that modern machinery can bring to your farm, Benjamin," Jimmy said defensively, "if you would just give them a chance."

"I believe I'll stick to my old ways for now. It seems to me that you spend more time repairing your machines than you gain in productivity." That statement brought a look of embarrassment to Jimmy and a chuckle from John Carter.

"You both may be interested to know," said Adam, "that even in my future the debate about modernization goes on. Most new machines and techniques are met with reluctance, then acceptance when the increase in productivity is proven. But increased productivity isn't always acknowledged as an improvement. There are many who like to see things done the 'old-fashioned' way."

Jimmy nodded his agreement, which got him a scowl from Benjamin.

"As fascinating as a discussion of farm machinery may be," said John Carter, "we should probably move our group into the barn. The Georgians would like nothing better than to catch us in an illegal gathering. We have much more pressing issues to discuss, and I for one am anxious to enjoy the wonderful food Catherine has provided," he said, rubbing his hands together. "One other, Gvnigeyona, will be joining us soon, so we can eat while we are awaiting his arrival."

"Then you will have to eat very fast," said a man standing not more than a dozen feet from the group, "because he is already here."

The old man's sudden appearance startled everyone; he seemed to have appeared out of nowhere. They quickly turned to face him. His features were as astonishing as his abrupt arrival. The dark brown skin of his deeply wrinkled, leathery face gave him the appearance of being well advanced in years, though his dark, flashing eyes, like shards of polished obsidian, revealed the vigor and liveliness of a much younger man. He was medium height and barrel-chested, with the thick arms, stocky legs, and powerful hands of someone who had been, and still was, a very physically powerful man. He wore buckskin leggings and tunic instead of the cotton clothing, and on his feet were moccasins instead of leather boots. Strands of his long, silver-white hair flowed down his back, hanging below a turban of red and white cloth meticulously swathing the top of his head. Over his shoulder was a longbow and quiver with several arrows.

To the team, his attire was an unexpected combination. His clothing was a blend of traditional Native American garb and a middle-eastern touch added by the turban on his head.

"'*Siyo*, Gvnigeyona!" said John. "I see you are as stealthy as ever."

"*Osiyo*, John Carter," the old man replied. "Were I not stealthy, I would most likely be in the *yonega's* stockade by now. Besides, you were all making enough noise to easily cover the sound of a noisy approaching bear. I have explored the surrounding area and there are no others nearby, but I do not recommend remaining out here in the open." His look was serious and stern.

"You are right, Yonah," John agreed. "We will go into the barn now. We were just planning to do so."

He introduced Gvnigeyona to each of the team as they filed into the barn. Gvnigeyona nodded to each, very briefly making eye contact as Cherokee politeness requires. He kept a serious look upon his face, although a slight flutter of the wrinkles around his eyes indicated some amusement when he heard Sal's name. John Carter explained that *Gvnigeyona* meant "black bear" in Cherokee, and he slowly repeated it phonetically as *Ga-na-gay-yoh-nah* to help them with the pronunciation.

"You may call me Yonah if you wish," Gvnigeyona said. "Easier to remember and white people can say it better. Most of the black has abandoned this old bear anyway." His eyes gleamed as he held up a handful of his silver hair to illustrate his point.

They pulled Benjamin's wagon and horses into the barn, which was empty except for John's horse and one other belonging to Jimmy Deerinwater. Dragging together several bales of straw to use as seats and a table, they laid out the food from the baskets. As they ate, they conversed socially about trivial matters—farming and hunting mostly, and more than a little friendly gossip about family and neighbors. Benjamin told them how their new friends had helped with chores around the farm, and lauded them for their storytelling abilities, which impressed the others most of all. There was a casual mention of the team being from a future time, which they had apparently all been made aware of beforehand. The team had learned that the Cherokee culture saw nothing unusual about time travel, but it still astonished them that it was accepted so easily.

Once an appropriate period of polite conversation—and their appetites—had been attended to, a pause in the chatter indicated it was time to begin a serious discussion.

John Carter began his solemn discourse, keeping his expression neutral and not looking at anyone in particular. He spoke in a clear, resonant voice that commanded attention. He told them that he had delivered his messages from Red Clay to the nearby families, and they will spread the information to the rest. He said that many are disheartened by the news, as could be expected. Many remain committed to John Ross's direction to stand firm against removal and will not voluntarily cooperate. A few had decided to report to the forts as they had been ordered, out of fear of retaliation. Nearly all agreed that they should not take up arms against the soldiers. Their resistance will be passive.

He told them that the military were building additional forts in preparation for carrying out their orders to forcefully remove the Cherokee, and that Major General Winfield Scott had been ordered to supervise the construction. "While I am still hopeful that John Ross can negotiate further to avoid removal, I am not expecting that he will be able to do much more than get better terms for our land. I have seen no indication, other than from the few whites who have argued for justice, that there will be any hesitation to remove us by force." John Carter paused as he let them mull his grim statement.

After a moment he continued. "There has been bickering and accusations from both the Treaty Party and Ross's supporters. Major Ridge has been advocating that we must accept the inevitable, and relocate before we are moved by force. Ross believes we must stand on principle and peacefully resist. Both sides know that we are helpless against a forced removal. We have been forced into treaties before by a militia that is so powerful that we stand no chance against them.

"The United States government remains committed to enforcing removal. Most of you know that General Scott arrived in New Echota with many troops to complete the construction of the forts. He delivered an address to the Cherokee, in the form of a letter, urging all full-blood Cherokees to voluntarily report to these forts before May 23rd or face forced removal by his troops. I see you have a copy," he said, seeing Benjamin pull the crumpled paper from his pocket and pass it to the others.

"That deadline is close at hand. I have attempted to convey information between the various parties about what is occurring here, in Red Clay, and in Washington City, so that all factions know the minds of the others. Each individual is, of course, entitled to determine what he believes to be his best course of action. You are among my closest friends, and I would welcome any thoughts you may wish to share." He stopped speaking, and glanced at the others indicating the floor was open if they wished to make a statement.

Benjamin coughed politely indicating his intention to speak. He retrieved his pipe and tobacco pouch and prepared to smoke, providing a dramatic pause before he began talking. "As are all of you, I am torn apart by our desperate situation," he began through a blue cloud of tobacco smoke. "I have watched the mounting greed of the settlers, and have felt the malevolence toward us; stealing livestock and supplies, confiscating land, even acts of violence, intending to make our lives miserable to induce us to abandon our homeland. I have felt the hopelessness of remaining on my own land, working my own farm, knowing in my heart that I will soon be dispossessed of all I have worked for. I know that I am powerless to fight against the overpowering aggression. Any resistance I offer will be futile, but I am also overwhelmed by the injustice and yearn to stand against the threat to what is honestly my right, no matter how insignificant my protest would be. John, my friend of many years, are you now advocating that we go the way of the treaty party and comply with removal?"

Jimmy Deerinwater and Yonah both shook their heads and mumbled disapproval.

"I am not," said John. "I simply speak the facts, so that you may consider everything and determine your own course of action. I believe that here in this barn we have men and women possessing great faculty of mind. It is far too late to develop a plan to prevent what is happening. Between us, however, I believe it may be possible to reach an agreement about what we should do to help ourselves and our neighbors. I freely admit that I am as overwhelmed as you, Benjamin."

The air in the barn was filling with tobacco smoke, as Tom and Jimmy had also joined with Benjamin in lighting up their pipes. Yonah produced a hand-carved pipe of his own and filled it with strong smelling tobacco from a small pouch. He did not speak, but made a show of filling and lighting his pipe, then exhaling the smoke toward Sal. It seemed that Yonah had selected Sal as an outlet for his resentment of the *yonegas'* misdeeds.

"Phew, dude, what're you smokin' in that pipe? Old socks?" said Sal, waving the cloud of smoke from his face. "Are you sending smoke signals, or what? I thought you guys used a blanket and a campfire for that."

"Quit your chattering, squirrel-man," said Yonah. "We have serious business to discuss which will benefit from this good smoke."

"The surgeon general might disagree with you," mumbled Sal, "and whadaya mean by..."

"If we can get back to business," Jimmy interrupted. "You all know my feelings. I've spent much money and plenty of effort to build one of the most modern farms in the Nation. It's far from the largest, but Rebecca and I have put everything into it, and I'm not at all happy at the thought of walking away and turning it over to some Georgian *yonega*. I know I've been ignoring the warnings and putting up with the abuse for years, but I've had faith in the leadership of John Ross and believed that the lawmakers in Washington City would eventually be reasonable and just. Now I can't fight and I can't just walk away from everything; same situation as you are in Benjamin. The only option I have is to wait and hope that Chief Ross will come through for us."

"I have some thoughts to contribute—if I may be permitted to speak?" asked Adam.

"You may. It is customary that everyone may contribute to the discussion," said John Carter. "We would be appreciative to hear your thoughts."

"And as long as they are relevant," said Yonah. He gave Adam an austere look, and then turned his menacing glance toward Sal, who returned the stare.

"Of course, I believe they are pertinent. John and Benjamin have explained to us that the Cherokee people believe our version of the future, the one we came from, could be different than the one you will experience. But there are certain things that will remain basically the same, and I think it is important to keep this in mind."

"John has told us about your version," Yonah said, "and it is not very encouraging. Are the things you want us to keep in mind that we should despair because there is no hope?"

"Certainly not," Adam replied evenly. "What I think you should keep in mind is that human nature remains the same, whether you believe my version of the future or not. The greed for your land by those who want to take it from you does not depend on the specific path that the future takes. It will be there regardless, and will have to be dealt with. There is also the human nature of your own leaders to consider. In my version of the future, the case could be made for either party, Chief Ross or Ridge, as they both probably had the best of intentions for their people. On the other hand, neither one is immune to temptation, as they are human. Both have something to gain—power, money, whatever, so their guidance may be influenced by those things. The leaders of both factions are successful and powerful, and did not become this way through compromise."

"What you say is logical," said John Carter. Jimmy and Benjamin nodded in agreement. "But how does knowing those things help our situation? Are we to distrust all of our leaders because they may put their own interests before ours?"

"No, I'm actually saying just the opposite. I think that each person must pick the path of the leader they believe in. All leaders are influenced by their own self-interest to some extent, even those who have dedicated their lives to those they lead. You know these men personally. I only know them historically. The knowledge you have of their personal motivations can help you determine what the outcome of their leadership may be, understand what they will settle for, and what their true goals may be.

You must also remember that those being led also have their own self-interest in mind, and will be prone to make their decisions based on those interests." Adam crossed his arms over his chest and continued.

"I don't see how any version of the future will be less than disastrous for the Cherokee people. If you stay, you risk the violence of the soldiers. Even if Chief Ross is successful in delaying their action, you will still face their anger and greed. If you leave, you give up a homeland you love, and face an unknown future in an unknown territory."

When Adam paused, Yonah said, "You are speaking of doom and despair as I predicted. And you also left out an option, the option to fight. We could act like the valiant warriors our ancestors were." Yonah had had enough dealings with the whites to know better than to trust them easily. He was not about to take advice from these *yonegas* from the future incontrovertibly, not without knowing more of what was in their minds and hearts. He suspected the only counsel these soft-looking hatchlings would offer would be squawks of cowardice.

Adam held his ground. "I believe at this point that option has even more dire consequences. There is the obvious problem of being massively outnumbered. The young, unattached men may be able to successfully wage a guerrilla-style rebellion against the military for a while if they were willing to give up their present lifestyle and live in hiding. But if I recall my history correctly, this part of the country has had so much of the game depleted that living off the land for any length of time is hardly practical, especially if they must remain in hiding. They could stage raids for resupply, but what of those with families and small children to care for? Even Chief Ross is not advocating violence."

"As you said, he has his own agenda to consider," Yonah said sternly. "Some things are worth fighting for, even though all odds are against you. Do the people of your time have no honor? Honor is something that used to be important to the Tsalagi." In truth, Yonah knew the question of armed confrontation had been resolved long ago. It was not an easy admission for those of warrior blood, as he was, but he had ultimately come to grips with the realization that the only sane option left to them was passive resistance.

"It is still important," Adam countered. "Yes, we value honor—and freedom above all. Many of our brave soldiers have fought and died defending our country against those who would deny us our freedom. Surely you recall the Revolutionary War."

Yonah puffed out his chest. "Do you not believe our warriors are entitled to the same privilege of defending their nation against aggressors? Our ancestors also fought in that war!"

Adam knew he had read Yonah correctly—the man was testing him. He had often been in meetings where someone played devil's advocate, challenging his every statement. He knew how to handle his type, even if the subject matter was different. Yonah had reacted to Adam's last remark just as he expected he would. "I believe that they not only are entitled, but they have a duty to defend your nation."

Yonah's voice became confrontational. "A moment ago you claimed to be against armed resistance," he scoffed. "Now you are in favor of it?"

Adam continued undaunted, without hesitation. "I am not in favor of reckless violence. What good is sending warriors against an enemy that they have no hope to overcome? It would be foolish, if not immoral. I have studied battles in which the Cherokee fought alone and outnumbered, and other battles together with whites, in which they played significant roles, just as you said. Those battles would have been lost without the cunning and fierceness of the Cherokee. I have never heard of any battle they won by rash suicide."

Yonah would not be won over with false bravado, but Adam's remarks contained enough insight to merit further listening. He folded his arms across his chest and grunted at Adam. "We have already expressed the hopelessness of our situation. What good does it do to tell us these things?"

"I'm not just pointing out negatives, Yonah. You know better than I that not all battles are won on the battlefield. I believe that if the Cherokee Nation is committed to passive resistance by refusing to relocate until they are forced, there will still be great danger to them. Certainly the best thing that could happen would be a last minute reprieve, sparing the Cherokee from a forced relocation. If that reprieve doesn't happen soon, things will get very ugly fast. In that event, the goal will be to prevent as much tragedy to the Cherokee as possible. First get the people safe, then regroup and strategize your most effective options without the pressure of this tense situation. I know you have all already thought this through."

Yonah continued to stare at Adam, arms folded. His stern face did not betray the smallest hint of a reaction while he considered that perhaps this man was more perceptive than he looked. The harshness in his voice mellowed slightly. "Go on," he said.

"I would like to propose some positive action my friends and I can take. As has been said, the Cherokee people are in the position of having only unacceptable options. It will be up to each person or family to make the decision how they will best cope with the transgressions. It is a highly stressful situation, and not conducive to making good decisions, especially for those who, unlike yourself, have not been tempered by battle.

"The four of us, even though we are in our own stressful situation, are not facing the catastrophic circumstances of your people. Unfortunately we have no political influence to use to dissuade the government from going forward with their plans. My suggestion is that you allow us to provide encouragement and support in whatever small way we can. That may mean doing nothing more than helping out on someone's farm, like we did for Benjamin, or helping with any other tasks that need to be done. I know that doesn't seem like much, but we would like to be able to offer some help to those who are facing such calamitous prospects. It could be just enough relief to prevent rash, stress-induced decision making. I am afraid there is nothing we can do to prevent this disaster, but *some* things can be done to ease the suffering that I believe will occur."

Yonah turned toward Benjamin. "You have spent the most time with them, Benjamin, and have said they were helpful to you. Is that truth, or simply politeness?"

Benjamin rubbed his chin, carefully choosing his words before speaking. "In truth, they do not possess much knowledge of the running of a farm. But what they lack in knowledge they make up for with an abundance of cleverness and determination. They were able to quickly grasp what was needed of them, and they did not hesitate to exert themselves. On a farm, anyone who can do that is useful. An extra hand is always welcome."

Yonah nodded curtly and said, "Then I am indifferent. If they wish to play at being farmhands, I suppose it will do no harm."

"I can see how your suggestion could be beneficial, Adam," said John Carter. "I see no reason to not take advantage of your offer to help. There is also another reason, more than just having your help as simple farmhands. It is undeniable that a great power has brought you here to us at this particular time, for some reason that is still not clear. We should keep you close at hand until it is."

Yonah, Benjamin, and Jimmy exchanged thoughtful glances and murmured their agreement. John Carter had made a strong argument. This was not superstition; it is a part of Cherokee spirituality that teaches everything has a purpose and a destiny to fulfill. Something even Yonah would not deny.

"I wonder, though," John continued, "if you have considered that for you and your friends to be most effective, it would mean being separated. Each of you would need to spend time with a different family or individual. Is that something you all would be willing to do?"

"Tom? Alice? Sal?" Adam said. "What do you say?"

"We all agreed," said Alice, "that we would do whatever we could to help. I have no problem trying to help a family however I can." The others nodded agreement. "But we also have our own interests to serve. Our ultimate goal is to get home, which we think we can do by finishing whatever quest the LANav has given us, and we need to follow the beacons to determine what those are. Adam, have there been any changes to the display?"

"Good thinking," Adam said, pulling the LANav from his pocket. "Hmm," he scratched his head as he studied the display, "I don't see how it could be any clearer." Adam held up the device for the others to see. There were four separate beacon indicators now flashing on the LANav's display.

"I ain't so sure I trust that crazy thing anymore, dude," said Sal, "but I guess if it's more effective for us to split up, then it's okay by me. Whatever the heck we can do to speed up getting out of here and back home, I'm all for. Uh, not that I don't enjoy your company," he said, casting a sarcastic look at Yonah. "I'd just like to get back before the manure spreading season is over, ya know?"

"I guess we should give it a try." said Tom, "I'm also anxious to return home, but since we're here I think we should study and observe as much as possible about this period. My scientific curiosity needs to be satisfied, and we must try to look at our situation as an unprecedented research opportunity. Each of us going to a different household will expedite our investigations."

"You're beginning to sound like your old self, Tom," said Adam, "and you're right, if we can put aside the distress of finding ourselves nearly 200 years in the past, it is an unprecedented opportunity. John, it sounds like we are in agreement, but I'm a little concerned about not having a way to communicate between us."

"I am sure in your time," said John, "there are excellent methods of communication. I have been told about an invention called an electrical telegraph, but we currently have nothing like that. I'm afraid you will not have a way to send messages, that is, without sending a messenger. I will do what I can to convey messages for your group, but under the circumstances it may not always be possible."

Adam shrugged. "I suppose that will have to do. Do you have any thoughts about where you would like each of us to go?"

"Yes, I have been considering a few possibilities. If they are willing, I believe Jimmy and Rebecca Deerinwater would find your assistance most helpful."

"Of course," said Jimmy, "we would be happy to have you with us for a while. Rebecca has been understandably troubled about the threat of removal, and the distraction may be helpful for her. I can always use an extra hand on the farm, and I'd be pleased to show you some of the modernization I have implemented. Perhaps you can give me some further ideas from the future."

"Alice," said John, "Benjamin tells me that you were quite useful to him and Catherine, and have formed a special friendship with his daughter Sally. Perhaps you would return with him to his farm."

"Sure, I'd love to spend some more time with Benjamin's family. They're wonderful people, and the food is great!" she said to laughter and nods of agreement.

"My suggestion for you, Tom," John continued, "is to go to the home of Guwaya and Woyi Ward. They live somewhat traditionally, so you may satisfy some of your research curiosity by learning something of their lifestyle. They have two small children, and Guwaya's mother also lives with them. I am going in that direction from here, so you can travel with me to their home.

That leaves Sal, whom I believe would be most beneficially paired with Yonah."

"Yo!" cried Yonah, eyes wide in astonishment. "I have no need of a farmhand. I have serious business to attend! Why would you think I need the help of this squirrel-man? I am Gvnigeyona, a proven warrior who has fought at Horseshoe Bend with Chief Junaluska to win the battle for Old Hickory. What need does a bear have for a rodent?"

"Look here, Tonto," said Sal, puffing himself up and eyeballing Yonah. "I'm willing to go wherever I'm needed to help out, and I don't need you breakin' my balls..."

"Of course, Yonah," John Carter interrupted. "I am well aware of your record of outstanding accomplishments, although, respectfully, that was many years ago. If you would trust me, I believe you will find that Sal has a strong spirit when called upon, and will prove to be a value—even to you. I also believe he will gain immensely from an association with you."

"He will gain if he can prove himself worthy. My road is long and littered with perils." Yonah answered, ignoring Sal, who was still staring at him. "I will trust you with this, John Carter, only because I have never been disappointed by your judgment before. I only hope that this time you have not lost your senses."

Yonah turned to Sal, returning his stare at last. "I mean you no insult, squirrel-man, but my life is not an easy one. You may be of some use to me, though you should know that I have no time to coddle an *usdi*. I need no infants with me. But I will show you how to survive in my world if you are certain you can endure it."

"My life hasn't been a picnic, either, Tonto," Sal said. "I may not have your knowledge of the wilderness and warfare, but I can hold my own on the streets. Given half a chance, I'll endure. Maybe even show you a thing or two, old man."

"We shall see, squirrel-man." Yonah smirked, his voice was without conviction. He turned to Adam, puffed his cheeks, and said, "I will accept your friend as helper and teach him as I would a young warrior. I will do my best to return him to you safely."

"That would be a good thing," said Adam. "He's somewhat high maintenance and ornery, but we would like him back in one piece. Don't let his sharp tongue fool you; his wit is just as sharp. His resourcefulness can be surprising."

"Oh, my yes," said Alice. "He might be crass, tactless, and impertinent, but he's our squirrely friend and we don't want him broken."

"Gee, you're so thoughtful. I didn't know you cared. Hey, what the heck is with the squirrel-man stuff anyway?" Sal asked with irritation.

"It's your name," Alice snickered.

"My name? Whadaya mean?" said Sal.

"Sal Lolliman," said Alice. "Back at the farm Sally told me that in the Cherokee language *saloli* is the word for squirrel, so that makes you the squirrel-man."

"Perfect," said Sal, rolling his eyes. "I guess that's what I get for hanging out with a bunch of nuts."

Chapter twenty-four

The mood in the barn grew doleful as the group's discussion turned to the disheartened mood of the community. They agreed that it was most important to prevent people from falling into despair, lending merit to the decision to let Adam and his team become helpers for a few families.

They decided that it would be best to keep knowledge of the unusual circumstances about Adam's group limited to only those who already knew. John Carter felt that the others would most likely accept it as easily as he had, but folks already had enough on their minds as it was. For now, they would simply tell the others they were visiting from up north, from Philadelphia or Delaware. Most of the Cherokees in Georgia had never been to those places, so they would attribute their peculiarities to being whites from a northern city.

The four Cherokees continued their discussion of several community issues. John Carter conveyed several bits of society news from his trip to Red Clay, and then conferred with Yonah on the matters he would relay. Yonah would be traveling toward the western boarder of the Cherokee Nation, and would carry news to those who lived there.

After the tribal business John turned his attention to Adam's team, filling them in with some more details about the people they would be with. He drew a map on the dirt floor of the barn to illustrate the general location of each family so that they could get a sense of where the others would be.

The meeting concluded, they loaded the empty food baskets back into the wagon, and made preparations to go their separate ways. While they were outside, Yonah caught John's eye and pointed his chin to a place away from the others where they could speak privately.

"What are you thinking, John Carter? I do not understand why you believe any Real People need the help of these *yonegas*. They can barely look after themselves. I suspect you have ulterior motives." The wrinkled folds of skin tightened around Yonah's eyes as he squinted warily at John.

John Carter placed his hands on his hips and feigned a scowl. "Always the suspicious one, eh, Yonah? You are right, they are not familiar with our ways, and are disoriented because they are not even from our time. However, you of all people should comprehend my ulterior motive. I wish to determine the reason the Creator sent them on such a strange journey. He sent them to us, and they don't know why. It is up to us, those who understand the ways of the Great Father, to figure it out."

"It is not always possible to understand His intentions. What do you believe you have figured out?" asked Yonah.

"Very little, so far," he admitted. "Perhaps His purpose is served when they return to their own time. Our part may be to have them experience our plight. They should be shown how we are in this time, and see that we suffer this injustice in spite of all our attempts to live among the whites and all the appeals to the white government. It may be that His purpose is to have them take those experiences back to their own time, so people do not forget; so that the things that happen in this time will not happen again."

"Mmm, perhaps," said Yonah, rubbing his chin. "Perhaps you are right. I suppose that is better than the alternative."

"Which is?"

"That they were sent to show us we have no place in their future."

Chapter twenty-five

Yonah and Sal were the first to leave. They had the furthest to travel, starting out on foot through rugged mountain trails. Sal said his goodbyes to the others, cracking jokes as usual, attempting to reveal no indication of anxiety about spending time with Yonah, although the nervousness in his voice belied his effort. They bid him and Yonah farewell, and made Sal promise to be extremely cautious. Naturally, he shrugged their warnings off as inconsequential. The rest of the group watched as the pair ascended the hill behind the barn, Sal turning for a final quick wave before disappearing from view over the hilltop.

"My goodness, I'd give anything to have a video of Sal's next couple of days," said Alice, eliciting laughter from Tom and Adam.

"Yeah," said Adam, "I'm not sure about your reason for partnering those two, John. They seem to irritate each other considerably. Unless you thought it would be amusing."

"I admit that their partnering may be somewhat entertaining," John Carter answered, "but I believe they will come to find they are much more complimentary than they realize. Like you, I also see great potential in Sal, and what he will learn from Yonah in a few days will add greatly to his character. I also believe that Yonah will benefit from Sal's wit, so he may learn to see humor in serious situations. Sometimes things that don't mix well can together create something good, the way oil and vinegar are combined to make an excellent salad dressing."

Adam wasn't totally convinced. "I just hope that Sal doesn't come back as coleslaw."

John and Tom were the next to leave. Tom borrowed Jimmy's horse so he could ride with John to the Ward place, while Jimmy and Adam would hitch a ride home in Benjamin's wagon. The Ward farm was several miles from town, and even on horseback it would take them several hours to reach it. Tom was an experienced rider, but out of practice. He checked the saddle, gracefully mounted the horse, and trotted around the barn once to refresh his horsemanship skills. "Just like riding a bike," he said.

John Carter mounted his horse and said, "We should be going, now. It is not good for us to gather for so long in one place."

"*Howa*, very well," said Benjamin. "Ride with caution, my friends. John, I suppose you know that the colonel is looking for you."

"*Uh*," John affirmed. "Yes, I have heard. I don't think I'll give him the pleasure of my company today, though. *Dodadagohvi*, my friends, we will meet again soon."

John and Tom set off trotting down the lane. The others loaded into the wagon, following them, but turning the opposite direction at the end of the lane, toward New Echota. They had to take a slight detour to reach Jimmy's place before returning to town. Adam and Jimmy would ride in the wagon as far as the cutoff to the Deerinwater farm, and then walk the rest of the way. The farm was less than a mile from the cutoff, and walking would give Jimmy a chance to show off some of his modernized farm.

When they stopped at the Deerinwater cutoff, a group of about a dozen men on horseback rounded the bend in front of them at a gallop and surrounded the wagon. Through the great cloud of dust kicked up by the horses, they could see that they were not wearing uniforms, but were dressed in civilian clothes and appeared to be farmers or townspeople. Some had shoulder-length hair, and many were bearded. They were all armed with pistols and rifles. Several had their weapons drawn, and they pranced their horses around the wagon to prevent it from moving.

"Well, just lookee what we got here," said one of the men, evidently one of the leaders. "Looks like a bunch of injuns out for a picnic. Or maybe they been havin' them a political meetin'. We just might hafta run 'em in for that!"

"Yeah, Jeb," said one of the other men, "or maybe it'd be best jus' to shoot 'em right here!"

"Not all of 'em, though," said Jeb. "I got a better use for that there little blonde half-breed," he said, flashing a toothy, leering grin at Alice. "I betcha wouldn't mind sharin' some of that injun coochie your sittin' on with all o' us, would ye'?"

Adam stiffened and started to act in response, but Benjamin placed a restraining hand on his arm as a warning not to speak. The man Jeb smiled and waved his pistol as if he would like nothing better than for Adam to give him a reason to use it. Alice gave the man a cold, disgusted look, then summoned all of her willpower to lower her eyes and refrain from making a sharp reply. She knew how to handle ignorant comments from rude men, but these men were armed, and she was not ashamed to let her fear guide her actions in this case.

"We are simply giving our friends a ride home, before we return to our own home. We are not breaking any laws or causing anyone harm," said Benjamin.

Jeb responded with a snort. His face told Benjamin that it didn't make much of a difference whether they were breaking any laws or not. These men would find a way to detain them, or worse, if they wanted to.

"I know'd them two," said one of the other men through a wad of tobacco in his cheek, indicating Jimmy and Benjamin. He spit out a long string of brown juice, most of which dribbled into the slimy stain already in his beard. "That there is Rogers from 'cross the river, and that 'ns Deerinwater who lives down there a piece. At least that's where he *used* t' live. I don't know'd who them others are. I ain't never seen 'em before."

"That right?" said Jeb. "I know'd the man what really owns that Deerinwater place—won it long ago in the lottery. He's been a-waitin' for them redskins t'clear out. Been me, I'd a done run 'em out by now. I seen that other place 'cross the river, too. That's some good land. Maybe I ought a just shoot this injun an' go claim it for myself."

"There is still time to leave before the deadline," Benjamin stated.

"It's way past your deadline, injun. We been waiting years for ya'll to git your damn red asses out-a here. All of you what don't git will be a-gettin' new homes, though. General Scott's a-buildin' 'em for ye' now. Look like pig pens. Ought a make ye' filthy savages feel right t' home.

"Ya'll is lucky today, though, seeing that we got us some other business to tend to. We ain't got time t' mess with ye right now; but ye best be a-headin' fer the injun territory afore we see ya'll agin'. Lest ye want our help leavin'; feet first, that is. Ye kin leave lil' blondie here fer me, though. Ah bet a bottle o' *wisgi* helps her git real friendly," he said, winking at Alice and grabbing at his groin. Alice silently seethed, but did not look at the man.

"Come on, boys. We got more important things t' do with our time than t' be a-foolin' with these redskins. Blondie, ya'll keep it warm fer me an' ah'll shows ya a real good time next time ah sees ya." He wheeled his horse around and galloped off. The rest of the men followed, hooting and shouting as they kicked up a cloud of dust and disappeared down the road.

"I had hoped to avoid any confrontation with the Georgians," Benjamin said. "I should have taken a more indirect route to Jimmy's place. I am sorry you had to endure such behavior."

"Don't blame yourself," said Adam. "You warned us that we might have to face this sort of thing, and we came anyway. I am ashamed to admit feeling frightened and helpless facing that much anger and loaded weapons."

"That was nothing," said Jimmy Deerinwater. "Usually we have to face much more than just their verbal abuse. Several of my friends have been dragged from their homes by *yonegas* who claim they are now the owners of the property. Others have felt free to steal anything they want from us, as we are no longer permitted to use the Georgian courts. Men like those have been doing their best to intimidate us into leaving for the last several years. It was fortunate for us they seem to be in a hurry."

"They are disgusting animals," said Alice, still seething at having to hold her tongue. "Good heavens! If the women have had to put up with that type of abuse," she said, "I can't blame them for being tempted to just leave. Don't feel bad for being frightened, Adam, I certainly was. You know I normally wouldn't put up with that sort of nonsense from anyone, but I got the message loud and clear that they wouldn't hesitate to use violence."

"Yes," said Benjamin. "With that sort, it is usually best just to not respond to them, and try to ignore their verbal taunts. You were wise not to respond to them, Alice. Of course it would be a different matter if they began to act out their aggressions; unfortunately, since we have no weapons, our resistance would likely be short-lived."

"If you face that kind of aggression every day," said Adam, "I'm surprised you don't all carry guns."

"The Georgia military ordered us to turn in all our arms some time ago," said Benjamin. "They were collected by General Wool at Fort New Echota. Of course not everyone turned in their weapons, although the penalty for being caught in possession of a firearm is dire. I suggest we save our further discussion for another time and place. Danger is no longer imminent and I do not believe we will be troubled further by them today, but we must be getting underway to reach the ferry and make the crossing before sundown."

"Guess that's our cue to get going, Adam," Jimmy said jumping from the wagon. "It was a pleasure to make your acquaintance, Alice. I hope we can meet again and you have the opportunity to meet my wife Rebecca sometime. *Donadagohvi*, Benjamin, and safe journey."

Jimmy and Adam gave a final wave and headed down the dirt lane to the Deerinwater place. Alice and Benjamin watched Jimmy pointing enthusiastically, already beginning Adam's tour of the property surrounding his farm.

Benjamin had correctly foreseen their unmolested and relatively uneventful trip back home. When they reached the ferry, they were grumbled at by the slaves who were preparing to discontinue operations for the day, but Benjamin soothed them with an extra coin and some of the leftover food from Catherine's baskets. He spoke to Alice of his appreciation for the time she was willing to spend with his family, and told her it would be especially rewarding to Sally, who had quickly grown very fond of her.

"I'm fond of her too," Alice told him. "She's quite a darling and bright for her age. I enjoy sharing the stories with her. I just hope when all this is settled she will get a chance to make use of her intelligence and charming personality. She deserves a chance for a happy and productive life, as do you all."

"I wish that as well. I believe that your companionship will be most beneficial during the difficult times she must face. I also hope that you do not underestimate the danger to yourself. Simply because my farm is across the river from town does not mean that it is any less threatened. We have had incidents there as well, so you must be on your guard at all times. Do not let the serenity of the farm lure you into a false security. Yes, the open acreage around the house and our *gilis*, our dogs, give us warning when a threat is approaching, but it does not eliminate the dangers. And as I have said, we have been deprived of most of our weapons and have insufficient means to defend ourselves."

"Don't worry," Alice said. "Gracious, after the scare I got today I'll be on my guard. You know, I've read about these events happening in my version of history, and I knew it was a terrible and shameful episode for our country, but I never considered how much courage it took for the Cherokee people to stay and face this terrorization. Many people say they would defend their home against someone trying to take it from them, but risking your life to preserve your homeland against such overwhelming force takes remarkable bravery."

"Let us hope," said Benjamin, "that it is not all in vain."

Alice didn't have the heart to tell him that in her history, it was.

Chapter twenty-six

You ride well, Tom," said John Carter.

They had been traveling at a quick gait since leaving the barn. After the first mile or so, Tom had no trouble controlling his horse. He was actually enjoying his ride on the well-trained steed, despite the seriousness of their mission. He was also enjoying his dialogue with John. They rode side-by-side so they could converse.

"I used to ride quite a lot," Tom replied. "My parents have a place in central Virginia, where I grew up, and they've always kept horses. I haven't had time to see them much lately, so I've gotten out of practice."

"You live far away from your parents?"

"Kind of far; it takes about four hours to get to their place from mine. Of course that's by car, er, motorized transportation. If I had to go by horseback it would take much longer."

"It would be most unusual for a Cherokee to live that far from his family. I can see how that might not always be the case in the future, as we become more integrated with the white culture."

"It's still not something that most families like doing, even white families." Tom said. "But in our society it is sometimes necessary to move away to a larger city in order to find work, as in my case. I think most people would prefer to live close to their family."

"It would not be very pleasant for me," said John. "It is bad enough to be away for so long when traveling. I do not think I could bear to live apart from my family all of the time."

Abruptly, John held up his hand, signaling Tom to stop. He reined his horse to the side of the road. John looked back down the road in the direction they had come. Tom followed his gaze, and could see a dust cloud being raised by something coming along behind them. Listening closely, he could hear the hoof beats of at least several horses in the distance.

"I think it would be prudent for us to avoid whoever that is." John's voice was tinged with uncharacteristic nervousness; he seldom showed any sign of unease. "If you feel you can handle a short gallop, there is a place up ahead where we can get off the road and remain out of sight until they pass."

"Lead on," said Tom.

They kicked their horses into a gallop, and Tom did his best to keep up with John's pace. He was exhilarated by the speedy ride, yet he was apprehensive about John's sudden urgency to steer clear of whoever was behind them. His exhilaration was short lived; after only about a mile John reined his horse to a quick stop and dismounted. He pointed through the roadside brush to a small creek about ten yards from the road.

"We can leave the road at this point and use the creek to cover our tracks," John said. "We will have to walk from here, and lead our horses through the creek a short way. If you would go first, I will follow and cover our tracks leaving the road."

Tom dismounted and led his horse to the creek as John directed. John used a leafy branch to brush out their tracks leading from the roadside, and took precautions to assure the vegetation they walked through was disturbed as little as possible. He joined Tom at the creek and said, "If a good tracker is following our tracks, I doubt this would fool him. It is likely they are simply traveling along the same road, and not following us. I do not want to make their acquaintance in any case. My hope is that there are enough other tracks on the road that perhaps it will not draw attention to ours suddenly coming to a stop."

They walked along the creek bed until there was enough cover to keep them well hidden yet still have good visibility of the road. "Let us wait for a moment here," said John, "and watch as they pass."

Within minutes, a dozen horsemen thundered by; the same group of men who had stopped Benjamin's wagon. They did not pause at the point where John and Tom had left the road, to Tom's great relief. Both men now breathed more easily, but Tom sensed that John was still tense.

"It looks like your trick worked, John."

"Yes, we were fortunate. I recognized the man at the front of that group. He is Jebediah Barnett, a quite nasty character from New Echota who is at the center of much terrorism. He is often used by the colonel to perform disagreeable duties that could not be assigned to the federal troops. I expect he may be on a mission for him now, perhaps to locate me, since the colonel has been looking for me. We seemed to have evaded him for now. I hope that none of the others encounter him today."

"Is this man dangerous? Would he assault them?" asked Tom.

"He can be most dangerous, but do not be too concerned. Both Jimmy Deerinwater and Benjamin have enough wits about them to keep calm and endure his verbal abuse. They will avoid provoking him to violence. If Jebediah is on a mission to find me, he would not waste much time with the others. I am more concerned about his encountering Yonah and Sal, since they can both be somewhat inflammatory individuals. Fortunately they are traveling overland, and the chances are slim that they have crossed paths today."

"Hopefully," said Tom. "Do you have any idea why the colonel is looking for you?"

"I am sure he suspects me of carrying messages from Red Clay to the people here, and of holding illegal meetings among the Cherokee. I believe that the closer we get to the deadline for removal, the more anxious Colonel Lindsay will be to have me incarcerated. He is surely under orders to purge all those who are engaged in organizational activities."

"Purge? Is that a euphemism for murder?"

"I think that would only be a last resort. But I am certain he would like for me to be locked away safely in his stockade."

"I guess it's a good thing we got off the road then, before they caught up to us. Should we risk traveling on it further?"

"They will eventually return to New Echota, and most likely use this road to get there. It would be best if we avoided the road the rest of the way. We can follow this creek for a couple of miles and reach a much less traveled path. It will take us a little out of our way to reach Guwaya's place, and our pace will be somewhat slower."

"Slower is better than not getting there at all."

"Agreed. See how your wisdom is growing just from being with the Cherokee for a short time?" he said to Tom with a half-smile.

Chapter twenty-seven

It was nearly dark by the time they reached Guwaya Ward's cabin. Tom had studied the topographical maps for this part of Georgia in preparation for their trip, but the lack of modern roads and landmarks made it difficult to determine his location accurately. From what he could remember of the landscape, and the northwest direction they had been traveling, he guessed that they were somewhere north of Dalton, Georgia. Possibly they had gone as far as Caloosa County. Or at least where those places would be someday. John told him that if they had stayed on the road, they would have followed a more northerly route, and dropped back southward to reach the Ward place. The alternate route they took was a circuitous path that followed hunting trails coming up from the south.

He remembered that Tunnel Hill was located somewhere in this vicinity, thinking at the time that it might be worth a short historical side trip. Tunnel Hill was the place where the first southern railroad tunnel was built, through Chetoogeta Mountain. It played a major role in the Civil War, obviously as an important railroad supply route for the Confederacy. The tunnel was also part of *The Great Railroad Chase*, a Civil War event where Union civilians hijacked a locomotive intending to disrupt the Confederate supply lines. He laughed to himself when he realized that if he wanted to visit the site of this historical event now, he'd have to wait about thirty years for it to happen.

He began to enjoy the journey again as he got over the anxiety of the close brush with John's pursuers, relaxing as he rode the trail through Georgia's northwest hill country. After leaving the road, they rode silently, following the narrow trail through the dense forest as they made their way through valleys and across the hilltops. When they crested the hills he could see a mountain range not more than a few miles to the west. Most likely, he thought, the border of what would become the southern part of the Chattahoochee National Forest. The countryside was astoundingly beautiful. Horseback riding through this remote part of Georgia, unencumbered by all of the modern paved roads and established towns—was an equestrian dream come true. It was as if nearly the entire state was a protected wilderness area. He understood that progress demanded the growth of towns, cities, and highways, and he was happy to have the advantages of modern life, but there were times when he longed for such an opportunity; a chance to experience the pristine beauty of the pre-industrial South.

Tom began to notice more signs of wildlife activity as evening approached, especially in the low-lying areas between the foothills. They had startled several small herds of deer out for their evening forage, and came across a large female black bear and her cub. Both experienced woodsmen, they kept their distance from the bear, even though she showed more interest in sharing a meal of termites from an old log with her cub than she did in the two humans. The black bear made Tom wonder how Sal was getting along with Yonah. In a way, he was a little envious. He was sure Sal and Yonah would have nothing short of an incredible adventure—if they didn't strangle each other first.

As he topped one of the larger hills, he was treated to a spectacular pre-sunset view over the mountain range to the west. The glowing orange globe of the sun, not quite touching the top of the highest peak, lit the soft silhouettes of the tree line horizon across the mountaintops in brilliant gold. Ironic, Tom thought, the brilliant gold of the western sky forewarned of an infamous tragedy about to occur, one of unpardonable human suffering that would be inflicted on the Cherokee people, brought on in part by the brilliant gold beneath the Georgian ground.

John broke the silent contemplation of their ride. "Guwaya's cabin is just ahead."

As they left the cover of the woods and entered the clearing at the front of the cabin, John paused courteously waiting for recognition from the occupants. A man chopping wood in the front yard shielded his eyes from the glare of the setting sun to get a better look at the two visitors approaching on horseback. His face bore a stern countenance which quickly changed to a wide grin when he recognized John Carter.

"*'Siyo*," the man called to John. "*Tsilugi, to-hi-tsu*? Welcome, are you well?"

"*'Siyo*, Guwaya," John said as he dismounted and walked up to the man. "*Tdo 'hi quu*, Yes, I am well. *Ni-na*? And you?"

"*Osda*, good," Guwaya replied. "I am happy to see you! I expected you may be coming for a visit, and we were concerned about your safe arrival." Tom wondered how the man could possibly have been expecting them, out in this isolated wilderness. These Cherokee seemed to have mysterious ways of communicating.

"*Tla utso-a-se-di*, no trouble," said John. "I would like for you to meet my friend, Tom Woody. *Tsi`tsa-ne-lv*, I rode with him today, and journeyed with him before on the trail back from Red Clay. He has been staying with Benjamin Rogers, helping out at planting time."

"*Osiyo*, Tom Woody," said Guwaya, shaking his hand.

"*Osiyo*, Guwaya," Tom replied.

"*Hi-tsalagi-s?*" Guwaya asked.

"Uh…," said Tom, looking perplexed.

"Guwaya asked if you are Cherokee," John interpreted with an amused smile.

"Oh, no, I'm not. Well, actually I guess I don't really know," he stuttered. "My family has American Indian ancestry, but I'm afraid I don't know much about my genealogy. I only know a few words of Cherokee that John and Benjamin taught us, like hello and thank you."

"Tom is not Tsalagi," John expounded on Tom's answer. "He is from up north. He is aware of the conflict over our people's rights, is sympathetic to our cause, and offers to be helpful in whatever capacity he can."

"I see," said Guwaya with a shrug. "You are most welcome, Tom from up north. And I will try to remember not to speak Tsalagi to you unless it is to say hello or thank you." His eyes sparkled as he grinned at John.

Guwaya was about six feet tall, about the same height as Tom and John Carter. His build was leaner than John's, though his well-muscled arms were evident beneath his thin sleeveless shirt. He had the darkest complexion of the three men. His black hair hung loosely past his shoulders, and he wore a red and black headscarf, similar to Yonah's but tied in back rather than in front. Tom thought the man look less middle-eastern than Yonah, and a bit like a biker. He could easily imagine him astride a Harley, clad in motorcycle boots and sporting a "Born to Ride" tattoo on his bicep.

"Please come inside and rest from your long ride," Guwaya said. "*Ja-yo-si-ha-s*? Excuse me, Tom. Are you men hungry? Woyi must be nearly ready with the evening meal."

"*A-gi-`yo-si*, yes, I am hungry," said John. "But perhaps we must make Tom learn some more Cherokee words before we give him any food," he said as they entered the cabin, laughing and placing his hand firmly on Tom's shoulder.

The cabin was much smaller than Benjamin's farmhouse. The furnishings were rustic, and the place was immaculately clean. The air in the cabin was filled with delicious smells, none immediately identifiable to Tom, but appetizing nonetheless. They passed through the front room into the kitchen, the largest room in the cabin.

In the kitchen were four other people. Sitting in a rocking chair was an elderly woman with a dark brown face so creased and wrinkled her skin looked like distressed leather. She wore a white dress decorated with a colorful pattern of morning glory vines. The old woman rocked slowly, murmuring into the ear of a very young child who had climbed into her lap when the strangers entered the room. She did not acknowledge their presence, but the little boy kept a wary eye on them, quickly turning his face into the folds of the old lady's dress if anyone dared to look back.

A younger woman stood over the enormous hearth tending an eclectic collection of cooking pots and kettles, each simmering, frying, or roasting some kind of victuals, providing the source of the mouthwatering aromas. Her jet black hair was pulled tightly into a single ponytail, revealing her round, youthful face and strong jaw line. She wore a plaid, threadbare dress, and around her neck was a single ornament, a wide, choker necklace made from four alternating rows of polished black and white beads. The fourth person, a tiny infant, was strapped to the back of the young woman, its head bobbing as she went about tending the cooking pots.

"I thought I heard voices," said the young woman. "*'Siyo*, John Carter, *tohitsu?*"

"*'Siyo, tohigwu*," John answered. "*Nihina*, Woyi?"

"*Osdi*," Woyi answered, "very worried about what will become of us, but mostly good. I heard laughter as you came in. Do you have good news to share?"

"Unfortunately I do not," John said. "We were just joking around. '*Siyo*, Ahni."

"*Osiyo*," answered the old woman. Her voice creaked like the rocking chair she sat in. She nodded at John, but did not look at him.

"I would like you to meet Tom Woody, my traveling companion. Tom, this is Woyi, Guwaya's wife, and Ahni, who is Guwaya's mother. The little one on Ahni's lap is Sagi, their son."

"*Osiyo*, Tom Woody," said Woyi and Ahni.

"*Osiyo*, ladies," Tom answered. His steel-gray eyes focused on each face, giving them a long, friendly look, believing he was being a courteous southern gentleman. "And *osiyo* to you, too, little Sagi," he said, bending down to the child and giving his hand a gentle shake.

"'*Siyo*," replied Sagi in a tiny voice, giggling and swiftly turning his face back into his grandmother's dress.

"Tom doesn't speak Tsalagi," said Guwaya, "before anyone else makes the same mistake I did."

"I told Guwaya that so far I only know how to say hello and thank-you," Tom added.

"Then you should get along fine with Sagi," Woyi said. "He does not say much more than that, except to say is *A-gi-'yo-si*, which means 'I'm hungry!"

"That is not surprising," said John. "Woyi is an exquisite cook and her meals are most satisfying. If Guwaya wasn't such a hard worker, he would be as big as a *yansa*!"

"*Ha!*" said Guwaya, feigning insult. "If I used my mouth to eat as much as you use yours to talk, I would indeed be as big as a buffalo!"

They all laughed and made themselves comfortable in the kitchen, talking about the planting chores and the good weather they'd been having so far this season. They explained to Tom that Ahni spoke mostly Chero-kee, and repeated everything in both languages so neither she nor Tom would be left out of the conversation. Ahni actually understood many English words, but she found them difficult to pronounce.

After some polite talk, the discussion turned to the more serious topic of the impending deadline, and did anyone still have any hope that it could be avoided. John reiterated the conclusions of his earlier meeting; that each family would have to make their own decision and take action accordingly. He explained that Tom was willing to stay with them for a while, if they would have him, to offer any assistance he could, whether that be moving west or staying put. The Ward family said they would be most happy to have Tom as a guest, and were appreciative of his support.

Sagi began to get more comfortable around Tom and John, and climbed down from his grandmother's lap to scurry about the kitchen. He cautiously stole glances at Tom, curiously checking him over whenever he thought Tom wasn't paying attention.

Tom was almost equally curious about the baby, bobbing along on Woyi's back, thinking that it was quite well-behaved for having its move-ments so restricted by being strapped to its mother's back.

"What is your baby's name?" Tom asked Woyi.

"We just call him *Usdi*," said Woyi. "Except for his secret clan name, he hasn't earned another name yet."

"*Usdi* is just a word for little one," John explained. "A child gets a name when he is born, given to him by an elder woman of the clan, but that name is known only to the clan. He will get a real name once he gets a little older and starts being a person. Sometimes a boy doesn't get a name until he reaches puberty. He is just called 'boy' or 'chooja' until he earns himself a better name. But I don't think Woyi and Guwaya will make him wait that long, since they have already named Sagi and he is only two. His name means Onion."

"He earned that name," said Guwaya. "He is always crawling around outside pulling up wild onions and eating them."

"He won't have to eat onions tonight," said Woyi. "This meal is ready for anyone who wants to eat it."

"Great!" said Tom. "*A-gi-`yo-si*! I could eat a *yansa*!"

"A-ha!" said Guwaya. "Tom has earned his food today. He has learned two more Tsalagi words! Very good!"

"*Wado*," Tom said, to everyone's laughter. He took a place at the table, looking over the mouth-watering food and anticipating a delicious meal.

During the meal, Ahni, using Guwaya as interpreter, asked Tom a few polite questions, such as if he had traveled far and if he was enjoying the meal. Tom replied to her, courteously answering directly to Ahni, speaking slowly so Guwaya had time to translate. Ahni kept her eyes lowered to the table, and suddenly spoke a few sharp sentences of Cherokee to Guwaya. He did not immediately translate, giving Tom an uncomfortable look.

"What is it?" asked Tom. "Did I do something wrong?"

John, who had been listening to the exchange, began laughing so hard he nearly choked on his food. "It is not customary to look someone directly in the eyes when speaking to them, and can be considered impolite or threatening. I know that for whites the opposite is true, so I will explain that you were trying to be polite."

"Please do," said Tom, ashamed that he had not considered the cultural differences. "I did not intend any discourtesy and I'll try to keep that in mind when speaking to her and other Cherokee. Thank you for telling me, but why is it so funny to you that I offended her?"

"It wasn't that," John said after relaying Tom's apology to Ahni. "It was what she said. Your name, Tom Woody, sounds like our word for hawk, *tawodi*. She asked Guwaya if you were named after a hawk because you stared at people so intently, as if you were getting ready to swoop down and capture an unsuspecting mouse," he told Tom, still laughing.

"In Ahni's case," said Guwaya, "the hawk would be swooping down for a strawberry, since that is what her name means in English.

They were all laughing now, especially Ahni when she heard Guwaya's translation. Even Tom laughed at the apt metaphor, relieved that Ahni had not been offended by his blunder.

There was a noticeable contrast between the spaciousness of Benjamin Rogers' farmhouse and the Ward's tiny cabin, although there were many similarities between the two families besides the apparent tribal connection. The emphasis on good and plentiful food, the open, friendly manner toward guests, and the cleanliness and order of the house were qualities that were present in both homes. Tom did not know the details of the Cherokee social structure, but Guwaya Ward and his family were undeniably on a different economic level. The furnishings of the cabin were sparse, and nearly everything was handmade. There was much less ornamentation around the house. Nearly everything was functional; the decorative items were limited to recently picked flowers and some small needlepoint wall hangings. Their clothing was heavily worn, showing the signs of multiple attempts at mending.

While some people may have felt uncomfortable around such meager surroundings, Tom had no problem in this regard. As a Southern man from a farming community, many of his friends and neighbors had different levels of prosperity. The Charlottesville, Virginia area was unique in that it had college students from all over the world, drawn by the university, as well as a farming community, many affluent business folk, and even several music and movie stars who called the town home. In the surrounding countryside many working farms could still be found, adding to the appeal, and the prosperity, of Charlottesville. Tom's family, being farm owners for many generations, never really considered themselves to be affluent. They had benefitted from the rising and falling property values created by the nearby town, but not everyone in their community had the cleverness to take advantage of it. Tom's family believed that good friends were something to cherish, regardless of the size of their bank account. His friends ranged from folks who could barely make ends meet to those who lived in pampered luxury, and he was comfortable among all of them.

Tom turned his attention back to the conversation, which had taken a more somber tone. He listened as Guwaya questioned John Carter.

"Is there still a chance that Ross will be able to successfully prevent a forced removal?"

"Of course that is what we are all hoping," John answered, "but it is looking more doubtful by the day. This letter to the Cherokee from General Scott was being passed around in New Echota, and it has the tone of a final warning." He handed a copy of the letter to Guwaya who read it aloud, in Cherokee, to his family.

They sat silently for several minutes before Guwaya spoke again. He seemed to be hesitant about saying something to John. At last, he decided to speak. "I have discussed with my family what we would do if the whites insist on enforcing this removal. This land is all we have. You well know that it was given to us, our ancestors, by the Creator, and no one should be able to take it from us. We should not be expected to trade it for other land in some place we have never seen."

John Carter looked at his friend with concern. "I agree with you, Guwaya, as do many others. But if the whites are adamant to force us to leave, we have little option but to comply. It would be suicide to forcefully resist, if that is what you are thinking."

"It would be an honorable thing to give my life defending my land," Guwaya responded with pride. "But no, I will not sacrifice the lives of my family. I will do the next best thing."

John raised his eyebrows. "Which is?"

"We will go into hiding."

Chapter twenty-eight

The Deerinwater farm was situated in a small valley, between the hills that bordered a bend in the Oostanaula River. Jimmy Deerinwater pointed out the boundaries of the land he was entitled to farm as he and Adam walked along the lane. His farm was smaller than Benjamin's, although it was still large enough to provide a living for them. Running the farm with just the two of them was a challenge, and it was going to be more challenging for Jimmy shortly. Now that Rebecca was expecting, he told Adam, she would not be helping him with the farm chores as much. Jimmy said he didn't mind the extra work for a while in order to get his family started. He was looking forward to beginning a family, and the excitement of their first child showed in his eyes when he spoke.

As they walked along, Jimmy pointed out that he had chosen different crops than Benjamin Rogers. He had some peaches, but the majority of his orchards were planted with apple trees. Like the other farms, he had a small field of tobacco, and another of cotton. Jimmy explained that cotton would be his cash crop of choice, but the cotton they grew was mostly for their own use. Cotton was a very labor intensive crop, and they could not afford the additional labor costs.

"I prefer to make my investments into technology, rather than slaves," Jimmy said. "Not that I could afford a slave. Most folks can't. I did invest in a cotton gin, as Benjamin mentioned. I don't really grow enough to justify the machine, but I think there might be an opportunity to offer the service to the other farmers. I'd like to be able to reduce my dependency on how well the crop does, which can be unpredictable, and have a more secure income from offering an agricultural service. I would still be somewhat dependent on the bounty of the crops, but not so much that a single bad year could wipe me out."

Jimmy showed Adam his second largest crop—peanuts. He explained that both peanuts and tobacco were labor intensive. He felt that the developing technology would soon offer ways to reduce that labor, giving him other agricultural service possibilities. He had heard that someone had invented a corn planting machine, and told Adam he didn't think it would be long before someone came up with machines for planting other crops as well.

"A real breakthrough would be a machine to harvest peanuts," he said. "There's a lot of manual labor in the digging and shelling of peanuts.

"I don't think that the average farmer is going to be able to afford all the new machines. He is going to have to find a solution, because those who can afford them will easily out-produce those who can't. That's why I think there will be a good living for someone who provides the service of these new inventions to the farmers who don't have them. Perhaps a cooperative of a sort."

Adam admired Jimmy's entrepreneurial spirit, and was even a little bit envious that Jimmy was going to be living through one of the most revolutionary periods of industrialization. Over the next few decades, the country would experience a major change from agriculture to industrial, and Jimmy was preparing himself to be at the forefront. Adam's envy quickly turned to dismay, however, when he considered the more pressing events Jimmy was going to have to live through. Was this really going to happen? Would Georgia drive this energetic and visionary young man and his family from his home and squash his dreams? Even worse, would society lose the contributions he was surely going to make?

"Jimmy," said Adam, "have you thought about what you will do if they go through with the Indian Removal? If all your people are moved west, your ideas will still be valid and maybe even more lucrative in an area with more need and less competition."

"No, no," said Jimmy. "There will be more need and less competition, as you say, but everything I've invested in is here. How would I learn about effective agricultural technology without my farm? Not to mention that I am well known here. Even some of the white settlers here come to me to share ideas and discuss the new inventions."

"But if you have no choice…" said Adam.

"I can't allow myself to believe that will happen," Jimmy said. "Certainly justice will prevail before the government allows our lands to be taken from us. I know countless treaties have been broken, and often we are not given an equal status with the whites, but both the white nation and the Cherokee nation have progressed over the years. Besides, isn't that what this country is supposed to be about; freedom and opportunity for all?"

Adam didn't reply. Jimmy was correct about the freedoms our country promised, but he was forgetting that during this period much of the country had strong ambitions of expansionism. The indigenous people in this country had been set up as sovereign nations, and many leaders believed they were not accorded the same rights as American citizens. The Indians were seen as impediments to their divine right to expand the country, and the people were convinced it was their Christian duty to eliminate any obstacles. Adam knew there was no appropriate response to justify the misguided, heinous actions his country was about to commit.

They reached the farmhouse after making a quick stop at the windmill so Jimmy could show Adam how easy it made getting water. The house was a simple, one-story frame house with board siding painted white, and a pitched roof covered with wooden shingles. A neat, spacious front porch was adorned with the obligatory pair of rocking chairs, and a Cherokee *kanona* for pounding cornmeal. There was also a weaving frame loom with skeins of yarn and some partially finished fabric in place.

Jimmy called out to Rebecca, but there was no answer and the house was quiet. "Let's check around back," Jimmy said. As they rounded the corner of the house, they nearly ran into Rebecca. She was returning from the vegetable garden carrying a large basket full of carrots, beans, onions, greens, and strawberries. She hoisted the basket onto her shoulder, gave Jimmy a kiss, and said, "Oh, there you are! I thought I heard you calling." She flashed a gleaming smile at Adam and said, "*Osiyo.*"

She was strikingly beautiful. Tall and willowy with long jet-black hair reaching nearly to her waist, her athletic, pulchritudinous figure graced the homemade cotton dress as well as any photographer's model sporting the latest feminine fashions. She radiated the healthful look of someone who spent a great deal of time outdoors. She showed no signs of being pregnant, or if she did, she hid it well.

"*Osiyo,*" Adam stuttered. "I'm pleased to meet you."

Back home, Adam thought, Rebecca would have had a difficult time not winding up as someone's trophy wife, especially if her personality was as dazzling as her looks. He was beginning to feel envious of Jimmy again.

"This is Adam Hill," said Jimmy. "He's one of the people from the future I told you about. Only don't tell anybody. John and Benjamin don't think it's a good idea."

"I won't tell anyone," Rebecca said. "Do they think people will not understand? I think most would accept it just fine."

"Yes, me too. I guess it's like one of those secrets everyone already knows. I think they mostly want to avoid too much talk, which might draw attention from the whites," Jimmy said. "We're supposed to just say they're from up north.

"Adam is going to stay with us for a few days. He has offered to give us a hand with chores for a while, and I hope he will take a look at some of my machinery."

"Very well," she replied. "If he is going to help with chores, though, maybe he'll start by taking this heavy basket of vegetables."

"Of course," said Adam, clumsily taking the basket. As soon as Rebecca was free of the basket, she and Jimmy embraced, circling their arms around each other's waist.

"You shouldn't be carrying that anyway," said Jimmy, giving her a hug.

"Now Jimmy," she said with mock sternness, "do not start that again. You know the baby is a long way off, and I'm perfectly able to do my chores. Would you have me sit around and do nothing but grow fat for the next six months? Honestly," she said to Adam, "sometimes he's like an old mother."

"I'm sure he's just concerned for your welfare and the health of the baby," Adam said, shifting the weight of the basket and beginning to regain his composure. "Jimmy spoke very proudly of you and his future child on our walk here."

"Oh, I know. He is just being my big, strong protector," she said, tightening her grip on Jimmy's waist and winking at him. "You must be getting tired of holding that basket by now. Please bring it into the kitchen, then you men can rest and talk on the porch. I will bring some *gahnohayna* for you to drink and begin preparing our evening meal."

They entered through the back door of the house, directly into the kitchen, where Adam dropped off the basket of vegetables and then followed Jimmy to the front porch. For a nineteenth century farmhouse, it was remarkably contemporary. The kitchen had a huge woodstove for cooking, a very modern item for 1838. Most people during this time, other than the very rich, still cooked on a hearth. The furnishings were still wooden, hand-made pieces, and they closely resembled the antique furniture Adam associated with New England style. More finely carved decorations, chairs with delicate spindles, and cupboards rather than the plain, austere board shelves in Benjamin Rogers' kitchen. One cupboard even had mullions dividing an opening in the cabinet door, although no glass had been installed.

They took their seats on the porch, and Jimmy retrieved his pipe and filled it with tobacco from a small pouch. He held out the pouch to Adam and offered it to him.

"No, thanks," Adam said. "You know, in my future, they have determined that smoking is bad for you and can shorten your life. There are many people who don't smoke, and many places where it's prohibited."

Jimmy raised his eyebrows. "That is too bad. The Cherokee make many important decisions while sharing a pipe, and many treaties were sealed with smoke. It seems the treaties were worse for our health than the smoking. Might be better to outlaw them rather than tobacco."

Jimmy pulled a small box from his pocket, and held it up for Adam to see. "These are probably a common item for you in the future, but now they are rare." He opened the box, and took out a stick with a glob of chemicals on the end, and struck it on the side of the box. The match sputtered into flame with a cloud of smoke that smelled like old, burning tires. Jimmy lit his pipe with the flickering match, adding to the smoke billowing around his head. "They are called Lucifers," he said, "probably because they smell of brimstone. I think they will become more popular if they can make them smell less obnoxious."

"That's for sure," said Adam, waving away the foul-smelling cloud. "You might not want to breathe too much of the smoke from those things," he said, remembering that the original matches were made from some pretty hazardous chemicals. "I think the tobacco is a lot safer than those fumes."

"The future must be a very dangerous place," said Jimmy, "with so much concern about such a simple thing as smoking."

Adam considered telling him about the advances that had been made in public health. Considering the exceptional health of everyone he had met here, compared to the sedentary lifestyle of many in his own time, he decided it was best to change the subject. "You are a very fortunate man, Jimmy. You have a fine, elegant home, a very beautiful wife, and a keen sense for business."

"I can agree with the beautiful wife part," said Rebecca, overhearing as she delivered the mugs of *gahnohayna* and embarrassing Adam once again.

"Thank you," said Jimmy. "But try not to spoil Rebecca with such talk." He gave Rebecca a wink. "Yes, I sometimes can't believe my good fortune. I worry that one day Rebecca will realize she is much too beautiful for me and go marry a rich chief like Joe Vann."

"Now why would I want a smelly old leathery chief when I have a strong, handsome man like you?" she said. "And today I am lucky to have a handsome visitor as well, so what more could a woman want," she winked at Adam. "Now I must go prepare a fine meal for two handsome men," she said. The two men admired her lithe form sashay back to the kitchen.

They sipped their drinks, Jimmy puffing his pipe, and sat in silence for a short time. Looking out over the farm, Adam could see several out-buildings, and a flock of sheep grazing in one of the fields. "Do all those sheep belong to you?" he asked.

Jimmy exhaled a ring of tobacco smoke and nodded. "Yes, they are one of our best sources of income. I raise sheep for both meat and wool. The breed I have is good for both. You can see some of the fabric Rebecca is weaving there in the loom," he said, pointing his pipe at the weaving frame. "The wool cloth she makes is very much in demand, and provides us good income."

"I guess the wool crop is a lot less labor intensive than cotton," said Adam.

Jimmy looked at Adam incredulously, nearly dropping his pipe. "I see you have no experience with sheep," he said. "Wool production is highly labor intensive, and is another opportunity for modernization. A person good at shearing could make a living doing that alone!"

"I can see where the spinning and weaving could be pretty time consuming, but don't you just cut the wool off of the sheep, and then spin it into yarn?"

"There are many steps the wool must go through before it is ready for spinning," Jimmy said. "Cleaning the fleece isn't as easy as it looks, and then it must be picked, carded or combed, then roved, and possibly dyed…" He studied Adam for a moment, and flashed an impish smile. "But you are in luck. We still have sheep to be sheared, so you will be able to experience the full process for yourself. We have just enough time to get started before Rebecca is finished preparing the evening meal."

Jimmy shouted through the door to let Rebecca know where they would be, and then motioned for Adam to follow him toward the barn. They walked to a pen area adjacent to the barn where two sheep stood, warily watching the men approach.

"I use this area as a catching pen," said Jimmy. "These are the next to be sheared, so the first thing we need to do is catch one. Good luck," he said, holding open the gate for Adam.

"Uh, okay," said Adam. "I just pick one and catch it? Any particular way?"

"Anyway you can," said Jimmy. "Try not to pull their wool too much. They don't like that."

"Are they going to try to bite me?" Adam asked tentatively.

"No," said Jimmy, "that's not likely. But watch out for their hooves. If you make them really mad they might try to kick you."

"Great," mumbled Adam.

Adam entered the pen and looked at the sheep. The sheep looked back at him. One sheep was slightly smaller than the other, so he selected that one as his target. He figured it had smaller hooves, so getting kicked might hurt less. He approached his intended victim slowly, until he got to within about ten feet, and then darted toward it. The sheep easily dodged him, running together with the larger sheep along the wall of the pen. Adam swerved, made another dive toward the sheep, and came no closer than he did the first time.

"They're fast little critters," he said to Jimmy. "I can see I'm going to have to be quick."

Jimmy hooked his thumbs into his pockets and flashed Adam a roguish smile. "You'll never be quicker than they are; you have to be smarter."

"In that case I might be in trouble." Adam took a breath, and tried to nonchalantly saunter up to the animal. He stole a sideways glance at the sheep and was sure he could see amusement in the creature's rectangular pupils. He walked sideways, trying to approach from behind, but the two animals just continued to circle around the walls of the pen, never allowing Adam to get close enough to grab them.

Next he tried walking away from the pair. The sheep watched him suspiciously, holding their position. Adam stopped, keeping his back to the animals, and flexed his knees slightly. He abruptly pivoted toward the sheep and sprang toward them in a flying leap. The sheep simply stepped aside, leaving Adam to land chest first in the mud and manure of the pen. The sheep looked at him and made an undulant bleating noise, sounding a lot like laughter to Adam. Jimmy stood stoically outside the pen watching, a slight smirk the only indication of his amusement.

Adam huffed as he pulled himself to his feet. "Ok, I get it; catching a sheep isn't as easy as it sounds. How about a quick lesson?"

"You're giving up already? I was just beginning to enjoy the show," Jimmy laughed as he stepped into the pen. "You have to remember that sheep are herding animals. Whenever they are threatened, they will run to the others for protection. Or if there is no herd, they will run toward a wall."

"I noticed that." Adam tried to brush off some of the muck, succeeding only in smearing it down the front of his shirt. "I couldn't figure a way to make it work for me though."

Jimmy calmly walked toward the sheep, keeping his knees slightly bent, extending his arms perpendicular to the ground. "You got them a little stirred up, but I should be able to catch one with little difficulty." He continued walking evenly toward the animals. As he approached, they began darting back and forth along the pen wall. When they ran to the left, Jimmy moved his left arm toward the wall, causing them to turn and move back to his right. He used his right arm to grab one of the sheep around the neck, and quickly brought his left hand under the animal's front legs, capturing it with skilled ease.

"Aha!" cried Adam. "I get it now; the old wraparound maneuver! Can I try again?"

"Be my guest," Jimmy answered, letting go of the sheep. He sniffed Adam and wrinkled his nose. "Maybe you'll have better luck now that you smell more like one of them."

Jimmy stood back out of the way as Adam got himself into position. He extended his arms while slowly and steadily approaching the pair of sheep, just as Jimmy had done. They slipped past him the first couple times, but on the third try, he angled just right and managed to crook his right arm around his target's neck. The animal bleated and stomped as he tried to get control of it.

"Grab it under the front legs with your other arm, and lift. Just remember to watch out for the hooves," Jimmy shouted over the bleating sheep.

Adam did as he was told, holding tightly and lifting the animal's front legs from the ground. As he did, the sheep calmed and gave in to capture.

"Ho!" cried Jimmy. "Very good! You may have a future as a sheep farmer."

Feeling confident, Adam relaxed his grip, and as he did the sheep lurched, wrenching free and knocking Adam back to the ground. He saw the sheep lurch toward him as it jumped over his body in its attempt to escape, and reflexively flattened himself against the ground and covered his face with his arms. He had avoided being struck by the animal's hooves and wasn't injured, but he could hear Jimmy's muffled laughter through the caked mud now lodged in his ears. He sat up, wiped the muck from his eyes, and saw Rebecca standing akimbo next to Jimmy, hands on her hips.

"What are you doing to my sheep?" she asked him.

Jimmy doubled over from laughing so hard, tears flowing from his eyes, pointing at Adam. Rebecca, neither amused nor sympathetic, just stared at him waiting for an answer.

"Uh," he said, feeling foolish sitting in the mud and manure of the pen. "I was catching one."

"That's a strange way to go about it. The sheep are now quite disturbed. If you boys are finished horsing around, the evening meal will be ready very soon. Jimmy, please show your friend where to clean up. He has gotten himself completely filthy, and I will not have that mess brought into my kitchen." She turned without further comment and headed back to the house.

"I don't think I made a very good impression," said Adam.

"I wouldn't worry about it," said Jimmy. "She never stays mad for very long. Besides, I see you've made a new friend." He pointed with his chin toward the sheep, which was now standing next to Adam nibbling on his pant leg.

"Great," he smirked, patting the sheep on its wooly head and brushing off some of the drying mud from his clothing. "Just marvelous."

"Come on," said Jimmy, laughing again. "I'll show you where to wash up."

Chapter twenty-nine

A dam cleaned off the majority of the muck with a washbasin and broom, at least enough to pass Rebecca's inspection before he was permitted to enter her kitchen. Jimmy said he would show Adam how to shear a sheep after they ate, and not to worry about cleaning up too much. "You'll get plenty dirty again this evening," he said.

The aroma from the kitchen was exquisite, and Adam tried to make amends to Rebecca by commenting on the great smelling food.

"You should really enjoy it," she said with a glare. "It's mutton stew."

Adam winced, staring dolefully at the bowl of stew Rebecca placed in front of him. His expression set Jimmy laughing once again. His laughter was infectious; Rebecca could no longer keep up her pretense of being upset and burst into laughter as well. Adam was relieved that no one was really annoyed with him, and he too joined in the laughter.

Everyone had several helpings of stew, eating and joking about Adam's first experience with the sheep. Adam admitted that he had never eaten mutton stew before and he found it to be delicious. He remembered how good Catherine's cooking had been, and wondered if good cooks were common among the Cherokee women.

Jimmy and Rebecca told Adam that they were very pleased to have him staying with them, since things had been so serious lately and they were glad to have such an amusing houseguest. It was a pleasant distraction. Adam said he really enjoyed their company as well, although he wasn't sure he had the energy to be their source of amusement for too long.

"I think you will enjoy working with the wool," said Jimmy. "It's still exhausting work, but the sheep usually relax once the shearing begins, and once the fleece is no longer attached to a sheep it's a lot easier to catch," he said, starting the laughter again.

After dinner all three of them headed back to the barn, where Jimmy demonstrated the process of sheep shearing. He showed Adam the shears, which looked like a heavy-duty pair of scissors, except they were hinged at the bottom with a metal spring. Jimmy expertly used the shears to remove the fleece, leaving a much smaller looking animal and a large pile of wool. The entire process took him less than ten minutes. Jimmy grabbed the second sheep and handed the shears to Adam, showing him how to control the shears by running them close along the animal's skin. At first, Adam was nervous that he would injure the animal, but Jimmy held on tightly and the sheep cooperated by holding still. Once Adam had the feel for handling the shears, Jimmy took them back and showed him how to trim around the animal's legs and hindquarters so the entire fleece could be removed. Adam was embarrassed to remember his naive belief that removing the wool was a simple task. For one man to both hold and shear, and do it quickly, was a skill that would take plenty of practice to master.

Jimmy continued the lesson with the wool washing process, explaining how dirt, organic matter, and especially the lanolin—the grease secreted from the skin of the sheep—had to be removed or it would harden and ruin the wool. Rebecca demonstrated how the fleece needed to be carefully placed into a very hot water and lye soap solution and soaked several times. When the wool was clean and the lanolin removed, it could then be rinsed and set aside on a rack to dry. She explained that sometimes they used abrasion when cleaning in order to felt the wool. The felting process would turn the wool into a fabric, and was only performed when it was not going to be spun into yarn. Once the washed wool was dry, it needed to be carded, or combed, with metal-toothed brushes to separate the fibers and get it ready for spinning.

"I have to admit," said Adam, "I never really gave much thought to all the effort that went into making cloth. Whenever I need some new clothes, I just go to the store and buy them. Much of this labor has been automated in my time, and we now have many man-made fabrics. The wool processing is still fascinating, whether it's being done by man or machine.

"Speaking of automation, Jimmy, you said before that you purchased a cotton gin. Is processing cotton done the same way as wool? What exactly does a cotton gin do?"

"He has been hoping you would ask him about that," said Rebecca. "Most people learn not to make that mistake twice."

"I admit I get excited about new farming innovations. Especially my cotton gin," Jimmy said. "I promise to not talk you into boredom."

Despite his promise, he took a deep breath, preparing to speak for quite a while. "A big part of the cotton crop is picking it, of course, which is difficult, back-breaking work. The growers may use new immigrants to this country to do this work, but they learn quickly try to find something better to do for a living. Those who can afford it use slave labor. All of the large cotton plantations must use slave labor to be successful, since slaves don't get a choice about the type of work they have to do.

"Once the cotton is picked, the seeds have to be removed from the bolls, another very tedious process, and that is where the cotton gin comes in. It works by using comb-like spindles to separate out the seeds from the lint. That is the part you want to keep—the lint. The cotton lint still has to be carded, just like wool, to separate the strands of fiber for spinning."

Jimmy directed Adam's attention to a wooden box, about the size of a large shoebox. It had a crank on one side, and a cluster of pulleys and belts on the other. He flipped open the top, exposing a metal-fingered spool and a comb-like device. "The gin I have is a small model, which I got mostly so I could understand how it works, and to process the cotton for our own use. Even this small machine greatly reduces the amount of time it takes from picking to spinning cotton. Some of the others, as you heard Benjamin, scoff at me for purchasing such an extravagance. They do not understand the great potential I see in it. I had to have one." He patted the machine reverently.

"Jimmy," said Adam, "in my time you would be a geek, for sure."

"A geek?" asked Jimmy hesitantly. "Is that some sort of vegetable?"

"Some kind of nut would be more appropriate," said Rebecca.

"You're pretty close to right," Adam laughed. "A geek is what we call a person who is 'nuts' about new technology. Someone who is very excited by new inventions, and is compelled to own them. We're alike in that regard, Jimmy. I'm often accused of being a geek too."

"You two can be geeks later," Rebecca groaned as she lifted the heavy wool fleece. "Come and help me with stacking these heavy fleeces and I'll let you both have some of the grape dumplings I made as a special treat."

"Grape dumplings, yum!" said Jimmy, sounding like a kid who had just been promised a piece of his favorite candy. "Lead the way, my beautiful wife."

"That always works," said Rebecca to Adam, "I've saved many visitors from the agony of sitting through hours of Jimmy's stories with the promise of a few grape dumplings."

They made quick work of the chores and headed off to the farmhouse, where they feasted on grape dumplings. The dumplings were made from mashed grapes mixed with cornmeal and rolled into bite-size balls. Adam had to agree with Jimmy, they were as sweet as candy and quite delicious.

By the time they finished the dumplings, the sun had set and Jimmy was charged with lighting some lanterns. Rebecca ordered him not to use "those stinking Lucifers" for which Adam was grateful. Lamps lit, they took seats in the small living area of the farmhouse while Jimmy performed the ritual of filling and packing his pipe, lighting it with a brand from the hearth instead of a Lucifer. Rebecca sat with them, tranquilly carding wool, and demonstrated to Adam how the two combs pulled the fibers into fluffy white mats.

As he puffed his pipe, Jimmy told Adam that even though he and Rebecca had adopted many of the ways of the whites, and appreciated the modern inventions that made farm life a little easier, they still tried to keep and respect many of the traditional ways of the Cherokee. He said that many of the people who lived strictly traditionally chastised them for their lifestyle, but they felt it was important to learn and utilize both the white and traditional Cherokee ways. They believed that by doing so, both cultures could someday come to understand and respect each other's customs.

Jimmy said that one tradition they found most gratifying was storytelling. Cherokees were well-known for their fascinating and expressive stories. Often repeated, they never tired of hearing them. "The children really love hearing the stories. It is the way our history has been passed along from one generation to the next for hundreds of years. We're looking forward to telling them all to our own children. Other tribes have a tradition of evening storytelling, but for the Cherokee, any time of day is good for a story. Evening just happens to be the best time for us farmers." He said that this evening it was Rebecca's turn, if he would care to listen.

"Sure I would," said Adam. "I heard a few of the delightful Cherokee stories at Benjamin's farm, and would love to hear another."

"Then I know just the story," Rebecca said, "and I have the perfect accompaniment for it." She set aside her wool carding brushes and went to the kitchen, returning with a large bowl of fresh strawberries from the basket Adam had carried in that afternoon. They passed around the bowl and each took several of the ripe, bright red berries.

The strawberries were irresistibly juicy and lusciously sweet, even after the grape dumplings they had just enjoyed. Adam was learning that the Cherokee enjoyed eating just as much as storytelling.

"I'd like to tell you the story of how the first strawberries came to be," she said.

"Yes, perfect," said Jimmy. "That's one of my favorites, especially when there are fresh strawberries to go with it!"

"You like any story that comes with food," she said with a snort.

"That I do, my beautiful wife," Jimmy admitted, popping another plump strawberry into his mouth.

Rebecca shook her head with an amused smirk and began her story. "This story starts with the first man and the first woman. Now they were very happy together, and loved each other very much, which was a good thing since there wasn't much of a choice of anyone else to be with. But they were like all couples, and once in a while they quarreled and got angry with each other, probably because the man did something stupid or ate all the food."

"Hey," said Jimmy, fumbling his pipe, "I don't remember that being part of the story."

"Who's telling this story, me or you? Now don't interrupt," she scolded.

"Yes, my darling. Please forgive me. Go right ahead," Jimmy said, dabbing some strawberry that was dribbling down his chin.

"Where was I? Yes, I remember. So this time when they quarreled, the woman just had to get away from first man for a while. She decided to take a long walk until she got her temper under control, and started walking down the road. Maybe she was just going to go for a stroll and think about how silly men could be.

"Anyway, first man got lonely really quick and decided to follow her, but she just kept walking and didn't look back at him. He thought that maybe she was never going to come back so he started pouting with his head hanging down while he walked. He was really sad because he had been acting like a spoiled little child, but first woman just didn't want to deal with him right now. She just wanted to be by herself for a while.

"Well, *Unehlanahi*, the Sun-god who created first man and first woman, saw first man sadly shuffling along and asked him what was the matter. First man told him about the quarrel. He said he was afraid and lonely because first woman walked away and left him. And he was getting really hungry and might starve to death if she didn't come back soon. *Unehlanahi* told him that if he didn't act like such a baby she might not have left, but he felt sorry for the pitiful first man. *Unehlanahi* was a man too, after all. *Unehlanahi* asked the man if he would like to help him get first woman to come back. First man said yes, he would really like that and he'd be really grateful to him and maybe they could have a smoke and swap hunting stories sometime. *Unehlanahi* said that he'd see what he could do to fix things up with her.

"*Unehlanahi* knew that first woman really liked sweet fruits, so he made a blueberry bush full of fat, ripe blueberries appear in the road ahead of her. First woman just kept walking, though, as if she didn't even see them, so *Unehlanahi* tried to tempt her with a clump of sweet huckleberries. She didn't pay any attention to those either, so one by one *Unehlanahi* made all sorts of fruits appear, but first woman just ignored them all. She really just wanted to take a nice, peaceful walk. Perhaps later she'd stop to pick some herbs or sit under a hickory tree for a while.

"*Unehlanahi* scratched his head, trying to think of something he could tempt her with. He was starting to think that this woman was pretty stubborn and maybe the best thing for first man would be to just let her go. But then he got an idea for a new kind of fruit and made a whole field full of strawberries appear for first woman. Well, this was just too much for her to resist, since she had never seen a strawberry before and they looked so plump and red she just had to stop and try one. When she tasted one, they were just so delicious that she picked as many as she could carry. She forgot about wanting to be alone and what had made her mad. She turned around to find first man so he could taste the new fruit. It didn't take her long before she met up with first man, and they both walked home, eating strawberries and happy to be together again."

"So now you know, my friend," said Jimmy as he puffed a cloud of tobacco smoke, "how strawberries came to be. And you can also understand why the Cherokee are a matriarchal society. Our women are so strong-willed the creator had to invent a new fruit to get one to change her mind!"

"I guess we should be thankful that they are," said Adam. "I'd hate to think of a world without these delicious strawberries. And thanks for the great story, Rebecca. It was very entertaining, especially with your added interpretations. I think your story would appeal to the feminists in my time."

They finished off the strawberries and talked more about farming and raising sheep, with Jimmy listing off a number of chores he hoped to get done tomorrow. Adam was pleased when he suggested turning in for the evening; he was feeling the aches and bruises from the earlier encounter with the sheep. He hoped a good night's sleep would leave him feeling refreshed for helping with tomorrow's chores. Rebecca provided him with a straw-filled mat for sleeping in a private corner of the house.

Jimmy and Rebecca retired to the sleeping loft Jimmy had recently added for them and the new child.

As he lay on the sleeping mat, Adam thought about how open and trusting of him these people were. It was a stark contrast to the way he would expect to be treated by strangers in his own time. He wondered if the world had really become so much more evil over the years, making people wary of anyone they didn't know. Or was it that the Cherokee people were simply overly trusting and naive? He fell asleep thinking that if the latter was true, the United States government was about to harshly punish them for it.

Adam woke to the sound of Jimmy and Rebecca's laughter echoing through the farmhouse window. Apparently he had overslept, the sun already streaming brightly through the window. He slept soundly after the previous day's exertion; he felt as if he had just closed his eyes. His muscles were still tender from wrestling with the sheep last evening, but he eased their aching with a few stretches. He dressed quickly and went outside, noting that the sun had already risen well above the horizon. He shielded his eyes from the shining sun and mumbled a good morning to Jimmy and Rebecca.

"*Osda sunalei!*" they answered as brightly as the sunlight.

"That means good morning," said Jimmy. "Another phrase for your Cherokee vocabulary."

"Mmphh, *osda sun...*" said Adam, still trying to wake up.

"*Sun-ah-lay*," said Jimmy.

"Did we wake you? Good! We thought you would sleep all day!" Rebecca chided cheerfully. "Jimmy and I have already been to the water, and the morning is passing quickly. I set out some of Jimmy's spare clothing for you," she said, pointing to a neatly folded pile of clothes. "Jimmy can show you the path to the river where you can wash, and I will prepare us something to eat."

"Thanks, er, I mean *wado*," Adam said. He grabbed the clothes and followed Jimmy down the trail.

As they walked, Jimmy told Adam that they were fortunate to be on the river so they could come each morning if they chose. He explained that "going to water" was a Cherokee tradition that they found to be an exhilarating way to start the day, and that they tried to keep the tradition in all but the coldest part of the year. When they reached the riverbank, Jimmy showed Adam several places among the rocks that formed natural pools, and led him to one of their favorite spots, an isolated pool formed by a semi-circle of half a dozen boulders. The water was crystal clear, and Adam could see the sandy river bottom below through at least ten feet of water.

"There are some places where you can wade in slowly," said Jimmy, "but on a warm day like today I like to just jump into one of these deep pools. I'll leave you to your privacy and meet you back at the house. Just follow the trail back," he said as he turned and headed up the path.

"Okay, great," he said to himself as he started to undress. It wasn't the first time he bathed in a river. He'd done so often while backpacking in wilderness areas. "I guess in the 1800's pretty much all of Georgia is a wilderness area," he chuckled to himself.

He stood on top of the boulder, picked a spot in one of the deep pools, and jumped.

He would have screamed the instant he hit the water if he had any breath in his lungs to do it with. The biting cold shock of the frigid river left him breathless. As he submerged, Adam figured the temperature of the gelid water was nearly thirty degrees colder than the air, something he now realized he should have considered before plunging headlong into the icy pool. He briskly stroked his long arms and kicked his feet, clawing his way upwards, gasping for breath as he broke the surface.

"Wow!" he gasped. "Brrr, did Jimmy call this exhilarating? I'll say!"

He caught his breath and eventually adjusted to the temperature as he swam vigorously through the chilly water. Once he became used to the cold, he began to enjoy his swim, diving several times and then floating silently, taking in the serenity of the wooded stretch along the riverbank. He dove back under, discovering that the pool was deeper than it appeared. He grabbed some sand from the bottom and used it to rub the grime from his body, then swam some more. He was fully awake now and the cold water had erased any remaining muscle soreness. He climbed out of the water and lay naked on a sun-heated boulder, letting its warmth dry him before donning the fresh clothes.

Striding energetically back to the house, he could smell coffee brewing and breakfast cooking. At the table set up on the porch, Jimmy sat with a mug of steaming coffee, eating a huge plate of biscuits smothered in gravy.

"Now you look much livelier," he said, motioning to Adam to sit down and pouring him a tin mug of coffee. "Did you enjoy the water?"

"Very much," said Adam, "once I recovered from the shock. That's some cold water!"

Jimmy shrugged. "You should feel it in February." His words were muffled by a mouthful of biscuit.

Adam thought he would prefer not to. He helped himself to a plate of eggs and sausage, along with a couple of biscuits. The coffee was hot and strong, and between the caffeine and his cold dip in the river he was getting anxious to get started on the day's chores.

He thanked Rebecca for the breakfast as he cleaned the last of the eggs from his plate, and rushed to join Jimmy who was already heading to the barn. Adam knew there was a full day of farm work planned. He was enjoying the vigorous lifestyle, the great food, and Jimmy and Rebecca's company. He also was concerned about looming disaster yet to come, and the effect it would have on them. Adam wasn't foolish enough to believe that helping with farm chores was going to make any difference to the outcome, but he would do his best to respect the Cherokee's preference to deal with things as they arose rather than fretting about things that might never occur. In a way, he envied their attitude, wishing he could prevent his knowledge of the devastating removal from weighing heavily on his mind. As he ran to catch up to Jimmy, he wondered how his other friends were doing. He hoped they were being treated as well as he was.

Chapter thirty

Sal wasn't about to give Yonah the satisfaction of knowing how much his leg muscles ached from the brutal hike. There wasn't much he could do to hide his panting though. His lungs burned from the exertion and the thinning air of the high altitude made it even more difficult to catch his breath. They had followed a series of trails for the last few hours, most of them ascending, without stopping for a break. The last mountain path Yonah had taken was a steep climb of about 600 feet in elevation gain in less than a half mile. They now stood on the top of a ridge.

"Still with me, Squirrel-man?" Yonah said, making no attempt to conceal his sneering tone. He was not winded in the least.

Sal struggled to breathe normally. "Right behind you, Tonto. It'll take more than that little climb to lose me."

"Losing you is not my intention," Yonah replied. "I would only have to waste my time looking for you. I just have not heard your chattering for a while. We have much farther to go, so we will stop here for a few moments before going on. I have brought some supplies from the food Benjamin provided so we may also enjoy a small meal." He removed a small bundle from a pouch he was carrying and handed Sal a strip of dried venison and a handful of *gahawista*—kernels of dried, parched corn.

Sal was exceedingly relieved they were taking a break, but he just shrugged and said, "Whatever, dude. You're the chief."

He sat on a convenient boulder and used his teeth to rip off a small piece of the tough meat. It took some chewing to get it soft enough, but he was finally able to swallow it. He popped a couple of the corn kernels into his mouth and began working on crunching them up. They were hard as pebbles, and had about as much taste.

"I thought you Indians hunted for your food," Sal remarked as he crunched on the corn.

"We do. Although there is no longer enough game to live entirely by hunting anymore, now that so much of our land has been ceded to the white settlers." Yonah knew that the game had been depleted from overhunting by both white and Indian hunters. He avoided elaborating on the subject to Sal, though. "The venison you are eating was hunted by Benjamin and his son. It has been dried to make it better to carry on a long journey, and the *gahawista* is excellent for travel."

As he spoke, he reached into his pouch and retrieved another small bundle, which he nonchalantly unwrapped to reveal a fat ham sandwich. He made a show of relishing each bite he took.

"Hey, man!" said Sal, glaring. "How come you get the fresh sandwich and I get the hard gah-whatsit corn nuts and shoe leather?"

"It is gahawista," he corrected. "And I have the sandwich because I am the one who thought to bring it." Yonah answered matter-of-factly, smacking his lips as he ate the sandwich. "When we stop for the night we will eat again. Then you may get to see an Indian hunt, and if the spirits are obliging we will both have fresh meat."

Sal grumbled under his breath, but pretended to enjoy the food as if it were the finest meal he ever had. He regretted his outburst, realizing that he had fallen for Yonah's baiting. He washed down some of the crunchy, dry corn with some water. At least he had thought to grab one of the skins of water from Benjamin.

"Just how far are we going on this little walkabout?" Sal asked.

"The journey will last several days. By tonight we will reach the water and will use the river for travel for much of the rest of the way. The end of our journey will bring us within what you call the state of Alabama. That is, if you can make it."

"Just lead the way, Tonto. That is, if you can find the river," Sal retorted. Alabama! He hadn't expected to travel so far. He kept his expression neutral, not allowing Yonah to see his shock. At least most of the trip would be by boat.

After the short break, they continued walking southward along the ridge. It was another warm, sun-filled day in May, and nothing worked better to mellow Sal out than a long hike on a beautiful day. His irritation at Yonah was soon replaced by the delight of the surroundings. The elevation gave them a spectacular view of the valley below and the next mountain range to the west. Yonah seemed content to travel in silence, which suited Sal just fine. In his own time, he would likely hear traffic noise or other sounds of civilization, even in this remote spot at this high altitude. Today, other than the occasional insect or animal noise, the only sounds were those made by their own footsteps.

Sal determined he was in the vicinity of Lookout Mountain, somewhere between Georgia and Alabama. Yonah moved forward with confidence, so he wasn't too concerned about getting lost, and felt sure he could back-track his route if he had to. That thought gave him some comfort. The alternative was to admit he would be completely lost without Yonah.

They hadn't traveled long before Yonah took a switchback path descending down the western slope, leading them to some relatively flat terrain. It was much warmer in the valley, and the blazing midday sun made Sal thankful he still had the straw hat from Benjamin. Even so, he was sweating profusely by the time they reached the first creek crossing. Swollen from the spring runoff, the creek was waist-deep. Sal was cooled by the chilly water, but the sun dried him quickly. With several creeks and small rivers to cross, he was never too hot or too wet for very long.

The warm sunshine and long stretches of trail also began to have an effect on Yonah, who abandoned his silent march and began to sing. Initially, it sounded like unintelligible chanting to Sal. As they walked, the rhythm of the Tsalagi song matched their stride and Yonah's quavering voice became a hauntingly eerie melody as it echoed through the forest. It seemed to push them along, making the hike feel less strenuous. Anything that took his mind off of his aching legs was okay with Sal.

Before long they were ascending another mountain. This range was higher than the last, but mercifully the switchbacks of the trail made the ascent less grueling. It was still a strenuous climb, and at a point about halfway up the mountain they paused next to a pile of huge boulders, Yonah allowing them a moment to rest and take a drink of water. Grateful for the breather, Sal stepped up onto one of the boulders to take in the view.

"*Si*! Wait!" Yonah cried urgently.

Sal heard the agitated rattling at the same instant. He looked down to see a sunbathing rattlesnake coiled on the boulder not more than four feet from his boot. He froze, mesmerized by the spiraling patterns of the snake's markings as it coiled. Its tail was erect, vibrating urgently and demanding attention.

"Don't…" Yonah began.

"Shhh!" Sal whispered firmly, still frozen, keeping his eye on the snake and trying to judge its size and distance from him. Keeping his body stiff, he cautiously backed away from the snake, as slowly and as far as he could until he reached the edge of the boulder. He then gingerly stepped off of the rock. As he did, the snake swiftly uncoiled and shot off in the opposite direction.

Yonah sighed in relief. "Let's not meet each other again this summer, *Utsanati*," he spoke in the direction of the retreating snake. "Well done," he said sincerely to Sal. "I am surprised you did not panic or try to kill it."

"Hey, dude, I'll admit my heart rate went up a bit, but I was pretty sure that I was outside of his striking range. Most of the time and given a chance, a snake will prefer to retreat rather than strike a human. Kill it? Why the heck would I do that? These are his digs; I'm just passing through."

Yonah looked at Sal with a raised eyebrow and grunted. He pondered the possibility that this worthless *yonega* may have some merit after all. A very remote possibility, he thought, and he was not about to give Sal any indication of further approval beyond his "well done" remark. He would, however, reward the respect Sal had shown for the rattlesnake by sharing a story with him.

"You may not know this, Squirrel-man," Yonah began, "but *Utsanati*, the rattlesnake, holds a position of high regard with the Cherokee. It is said that the killing of a rattlesnake will bring about the death of the killer, at least if it is done without proper preparations. That belief began with the story from long ago, back when the animals could speak to men. I will share this story with you.

"It seems that a man was out hunting and came across a clan of rattlesnakes who were all making a terrible wailing sound. When the hunter asked them what the trouble was, they told him that his wife had just today attacked and killed their chief, believing him to be dangerous to her children. They told him that they were planning to send another snake to take revenge, and he must help them by sending his wife out for water, where she could be bitten. If he did not do this, they would just kill him here and now.

"The hunter told the snakes he was sorry that their chief had been killed, and although he did not want to lose his wife, he knew that what they were asking was just. He agreed to return to his home and send his wife outside so the snake could take his revenge.

"He did what they asked, and in return the snake promised not to bite any men unless they were threatened, and taught him a song that could be sung over a person who had been bitten to help cure him."

"Man, that's like a pretty hefty fee," Sal said, "just for killing a snake. Anyhow I'm pleased as punch you don't have to sing any songs over me. I think the bite would be painful enough, Tonto, without having to listen to more of your caterwauling. But I agree that creatures oughta be treated with respect, especially the ones with poisonous fangs, dude."

Yonah nodded, mentally giving Sal credit for the remark, and showing only a slight suggestion of a smile at the criticism of his singing voice. "If you are bitten you had better hope I remember the words."

They continued their trek up the mountain path, being a little more vigilant about where they stepped, Yonah not wanting to insult *Utsanati* after promising not to see him again, and Sal not wanting to get bitten. They were on the east side of the mountain range and the shadows grew long as the sun descended below the mountaintop. When they crested the peak they were once again in full sunlight, while the valley below was bathed in the early evening's orange glow.

Turning southward once again to follow the ridgeline, the chilly breeze of the higher elevation was at their backs. They had not gone far before Sal saw the orange sunlight glistening off of a small mountaintop lake. He followed Yonah to a tiny campsite on the lakeshore, nestled in an isolated cove. Sal could see the small darkened spot ringed with rocks that served as a fire pit, and a small lean-to, crudely made from boughs and tucked into a stand of three pine trees. Down at the lake edge, pulled up into the trees, was a canoe.

"We will camp here tonight," Yonah declared. "From this lake, we can follow the Little River to my home near Dog Town."

"Awesome!" said Sal, as he plopped down on a stump next to the fire ring. "A downstream paddle the whole way. I've had my fill of walking for a while."

"Make no mistake, Squirrel-man," Yonah warned. "It is an arduous journey with many portages around waterfalls and non-navigable rapids. There are several portages that require a steep climb, and getting to my home, which is on a mountaintop, is also a strenuous ascent."

"Of course," said Sal sarcastically, "where else would you live but on a mountaintop."

Yonah ignored the comment. "Gather some firewood," he said, dropping his bundles. "I will return soon with meat," he said as he headed into the woods with his longbow.

"Right," said Sal, speaking aloud to himself as soon as Yonah was no longer within earshot. "Whatever you say, Tonto, you're in charge. I'll just hang here and gather firewood," he grumbled as he began picking up pieces of deadwood. He piled the collected wood next to the fire ring, and broke up the longer branches so they would be the right size for a campfire. Once he had enough wood, he took some dry twigs and, using his pocketknife, he made a small pile of wood shavings and twigs in the center of the fire ring.

He decided to take a shot at starting the fire. He did not have matches or a lighter, and the fire-steel he bought from a camping store had been left behind in the SUV with the rest of the twenty-first century gear. He'd never had the chance to use it before anyway, since someone always had matches to light the fire. He knew the secret would be to create a spark, one hot enough to ignite the kindling, which he figured he could do by banging a couple of rocks together. It might not be easy, but it would give him great satisfaction to get the fire started before Yonah returned.

There were certainly plenty of different types of rocks around. He experimented banging a few different kinds of rocks together until he found some that seemed to generate a spark if he banged them together hard enough. He took the rocks to the fire ring, and began to strike the rocks together as close to the kindling as he could get them. With much effort he was able to make sparks, but they were just landing harmlessly on the kindling and dying out before catching fire. He needed something that would catch fire more easily. He set aside the rocks and found a rotten log. Peeling away a layer of bark, he scraped out some of the dry, white, fluffy material underneath and added it to his pile of kindling. He picked up the rocks again and resumed striking them together with the same result—a few weak sparks, not nearly hot or enduring enough to ignite the kindling.

"Man, this is tougher than I figured," he thought. "I guess I need to smack these rocks together harder."

He firmed up his grasp on the rocks. Holding one against the ground with his left hand, he drew back his right hand with the other rock over his head and brought it down with all his might against the other.

He screeched in pain as the rock struck his fingers. "Yeow!" he cried, dropping the rocks. "Damn!" He tried to assess the damage through the blood oozing from his three smashed fingernails, and then quickly turned at the sound of laughter coming from behind him.

"Are you so hungry you are going to cut off and eat your own hand?" Yonah said through his laughter. "I told you I would be back soon with meat. Could you not wait?" he said, still laughing as he dropped two freshly killed rabbits next to the fire ring.

"I was lighting the fire, dude." He did his best not to wince at the pain throbbing in his fingers.

"Lighting the fire?" Yonah said, laughing even harder. "I know you are hot-blooded, Squirrel-man, but I didn't know you could light fires with it!"

"You're a real freakin' riot," Sal snapped, washing some of the blood from his fingers with water from his drinking skin. "At least my fingers aren't broken. Thanks for your concern."

"You will feel better after you eat, Squirrel-man. Tend to your wound and I will prepare the meal."

Yonah retrieved a metal tin from his pocket and twisted it open. Inside the tin were several small pieces of black cloth and a piece of red flint. Using his hunting knife to strike the flint, a single stroke sent sparks onto the black cloth, causing it to smolder and glow. Yonah flipped the burning cloth with his knife into the pile of kindling Sal had made. He blew on the kindling, added a few more twigs and some larger sticks, creating a fire in less than a minute as Sal watched in frustration.

"What's that black stuff?" he asked.

"It is char-cloth. Just a few pieces of cotton that have been 'charred.' It readily catches fire from a good spark and smolders long enough to catch the kindling. And a good piece of steel against a flint rock is much better than smashing your hand with a rock, although you may not want to use a knife without some more practice," he said, smiling and pointing with his chin to Sal's bleeding fingers.

Yonah skinned and cleaned the rabbits, threading them onto a spit he rigged above the fire, slowly roasting them while Sal went down to the lake to tend his fingers. Sal held his hand in the cold water until the bleeding stopped and the chill of the water took away the throbbing pain. He examined his fingers once again, noting that no serious damage had been done, other than to his pride at having failed to start the fire and getting laughed at by Yonah. He cupped his hands and filled them with lake water, throwing it onto his face several times as if it could wash away his humiliation. He sat on a rock next to the lake, watching his reflection become clear in the lake water as it stilled. He liked what he saw, of course, and a few moments of self-admiration was enough to reenergize his high-voltage ego. The delicious aroma of the roasting rabbits stirred his appetite, driving any remaining embarrassment from his mind. His confidence returned, knowing that sooner or later Yonah would realize how fortunate he was to have him along.

"Smells good, Tonto," Sal said, walking back to the camp. "When do we eat?"

"Soon, Squirrel-man, very soon," Yonah answered, shaking his head in amusement as he rotated the rabbits over the fire.

Chapter thirty-one

The next morning Yonah erased all traces of the camp. He told Sal that he may want to return to camp in the same spot, and didn't want any surprises waiting for him if he did. Sal didn't think it was likely that anyone would take the trouble to stake out a campsite hoping for the possibility of Yonah's return, but he shrugged and gave him a hand restoring the camp back to its natural look. They secured their few small bundles in the canoe, and launched it. Sal had plenty of canoe experience on his camping and backpacking adventures, and he used a canoe a few times to reach some island geocaches. After handing him a paddle and pointing to a position, Yonah did not offer any further guidance, sensing that Sal had some paddling experience. They made their way across the lake and headed toward the outlet into the river at the southern end.

"This lake empties into the Little River, which we are about to enter," said Yonah. "There are two branches at this end of the river, an eastern and a western fork, which meet further to the south. We will follow the western fork to the confluence, and travel beyond that into a deep canyon area where we will find the path to my home. We will pass through some of the most rugged and most beautiful country in the Cherokee lands. As I have mentioned before, it is not an easy passage and there are many dangers. However, there is much beauty to be enjoyed by a stout river traveler.

"I have made the journey several times, so I ask that you follow my instructions closely when we reach the treacherous parts of the river. I ask this not to demean your skills, but to provide the benefit of my experience with this river for the sake of safety."

"No problemo, Tonto," said Sal. "Hey, I can appreciate the value of your experience with this river. I've canoed plenty of times, but my experience with white water is limited. So you're the boss, dude."

Despite Yonah's ominous warning, the journey began as a silent, pleasant paddle. The river began at a high elevation, meandering down along the ridgeline of Lookout Mountain, following the Tennessee Valley Divide from the western edge of Georgia into northeastern Alabama. It wiggled its way along the mountaintop, passing through several other small lakes and ponds, and slowly decreased in altitude as they paddled southward. The river carved through sandstone cliffs and wrapped around huge granite boulders. There were several small waterfalls along the way, most navigable, although a few required them to head to shore and portage a short distance. It was truly a wild river, one that would have been challenging to Sal in several places, but following Yonah's direction they passed through without incident. There were several long stretches of peaceful river where the two men paddled along easily in silence, taking in the splendor of their surroundings. As much as Sal relished the magnificence of the river, there was a limit to the amount of serenity he could withstand, and so he decided to risk agitating Yonah's temperament by striking up a conversation.

"Hey, Tonto, you mentioned the battle of Horseshoe Bend back at New Echota," Sal began. "If I remember my history, that was part of the War of 1812, wasn't it?"

Yonah spoke without breaking the rhythm of his paddling. "It was the final battle of the Creek War, which you may consider to be part of that other war, but in reality was a civil war among the Creeks. The root of the Creek War was due to a clash between the Creek chiefs and a faction called the Red Sticks, who wanted to turn the Creeks back to their traditional way of life. The Red Sticks were so resolute in their beliefs they began to attack the white settlers, seeking to destroy all symbols of white influence. They even attacked some of their own people who did not want to reject the whites. The Red Sticks claimed to have received signs from the spirits, guiding them in their beliefs. There was a big earthquake that they claimed was one of the signs. They received much encouragement from the British, who thought it would be a good idea to set some of the Indians against the French, Spanish, and the Americans. The British wanted the Indians to have a neutral state they could trade with, and most of all wished to slow down the American expansion.

"The Americans first became involved when they attacked a band of Red Sticks returning from Spanish Florida with supplies. Because the Red Sticks were attacking settlers, the United States felt compelled to send their military to put an end to the uprising."

"Didn't the Cherokees also want to get back to their roots? You know, return to their traditional ways?" asked Sal.

"Some of the Cherokee agreed with the Red Sticks at first, and wanted to go back to the old ways. There was a Cherokee prophet who began to encourage people to destroy all of the trade goods they had from the whites, and he told the people he was going to create a big storm to wipe out all of the non-believers. He told all his followers to abandon their farms and go to the top of a mountain so they would be safe from the storm. A lot of them did, but when the time came and went for the big storm and nothing happened, the people realized he was a false prophet and they all went home."

"So how did the Cherokees get caught up in the war?"

"The Americans sent Andrew Jackson and a few others with the army to put an end to the Creek War. They did well in some of the battles, since they had cannons and more men than the Red Sticks did. After a while the Red Sticks started doing a lot better, and they really kicked Jackson's butt down in Alabama and ran him all the way back to Georgia. So some of the Creeks who were still friendly with the whites, along with the Cherokee, thought they should help out the Americans. They put a bunch of us under the command of Colonel Morgan."

"What about this Horseshoe Bend place? What happened there?"

"Horseshoe Bend is a big loop in the Tallapoosa River, and inside the loop is about a hundred acres of land. There were about a thousand of Chief Menawa's Red Stick Creeks at the Bend. They built themselves a barricade, a wall of logs about eight feet high, from one edge of the river to the other. That closed off access to their camp, with the wall on one side and the river on the other. They took a bunch of canoes and lined them up in the river, just in case they needed a way to retreat to the other side.

"General Jackson, now that he had reinforcements and about six hundred of us Indians to help—about two thousand men in all—cut his way through the forest to Horseshoe Bend, set up his cannons, and commenced blasting the hell out of the Red Sticks and their wall. He sent us Cherokee with General Coffee around to the other side of the river so we could catch any Red Sticks that tried to get out that way. But after about two hours of cannon fire, they had hardly made a dent in the wall. I guess them Creeks can build a pretty good wall. My friend, Chief Junaluska, a chief from Carolina, thought it would be a good idea for some of us Cherokee to swim across the river and grab a few of the canoes. So that was what we did. Chief Junaluska led a bunch of us across the river, and we kept running the canoes back and forth bringing men across the river until there were enough over there to attack the Red Sticks from the rear. After that, there was no way for them to escape, so it was pretty much a massacre. We took about three hundred prisoners, but only three of them were men. All the other warriors had been killed. The rest of the prisoners were women and children who were living there. Two weeks later, the Red Sticks leader, Red Eagle, who was also called William Weatherford, came in and surrendered to General Jackson.

"Jackson let Red Eagle go, but not before making the Creeks sign a treaty that gave up twenty-three million acres of their land. He even took the land from the Creeks who were on his side. Some of that land had been ours, and we got it back as part of the treaty, paid for with our blood. But now that son of a bitch Jackson wants to take that from us, too. He wants to take all the land from the very people who saved his ass at Horseshoe Bend and helped him win enough honors to become president."

"Uncool, man. That dude was unrighteous. Not very grateful for your sacrifices," said Sal.

"We do not need him to be grateful," Yonah snapped. "But principled and honest should not be too much to ask. And it seems the new president is no better!"

Sal grunted his agreement, but said nothing. He remembered enough history to know there was more to it than that. Jackson faced a country bent on expansion, and he probably believed that the only solution was to move the Indians to the west. Settlers had been constantly ignoring the boundaries of Indian land, leading to more friction between them. Sal also knew that Jackson wasn't above using the situation to advance his own political career by telling the settlers what they wanted to hear—that he would enforce removal of all Native Americans east of the Mississippi.

Of course he wasn't about to get into a conversation with Yonah that suggested he should consider Jackson's point of view. Sal enjoyed conflict, but he wasn't stupid. It would be like trying to justify to a war veteran why the politicians didn't keep promises made to them. In fact, it was exactly like that. Even worse—it would be like trying to justify why they wanted to take away his home and give it to someone else.

He also understood that Yonah had firsthand knowledge of the situation, and may have even met Andrew Jackson. Sal only knew what he read in history books, and what he had discussed with the other members of the team to refresh his memory of the period. The history he knew was written by the descendants of the American settlers, and he suspected that it might read quite a bit differently had the Indians written it.

Sal thought about how Yonah was going to feel about the whites when history played out the way he knew it was going to. Even the most callous individual could not justify what was done to the indigenous people in the name of expansionism and so-called manifest destiny. He thought about how he would react if he were in Yonah's place, and wondered if he would be able to accept the unfairness and maintain his dignity. It occurred to him that there would be little choice but to accept it.

They were making good time, helped along by the flow of the river. In several places the portage required a steep climb while carrying the canoe, but nothing that exceeded Sal's abilities. He enjoyed the physical exertion, and loved the magnificent scenery along the pristine river. The river level was high and the water exceptionally clear and cold. Yonah directed their paddling, leaving him free to delight in the shimmering reflections of the landscape in the mirror-like surface of the river as they rolled by. Many of the rivers back east were murky and full of green silt. This river reminded him more of pictures he had seen of the clean, clear rivers in the Canadian wilderness.

Yonah told him that they would soon reach Indian Falls, a waterfall with a hundred foot drop over a concave rock cliff. Here they could expect a demanding portage. Sal was looking forward to seeing the falls; Yonah made them sound spectacular, and he didn't mind making the portage. How difficult could it be? After all, they would be going downhill. Yonah planned to make camp somewhere near the falls, and continue the journey in the morning, which was just fine with Sal. The thought of a swim in a clean, cold pool beneath a waterfall sounded invigorating after an exhausting day of canoeing.

They guided the canoe around a wide bend in the river, and as they cleared the turn, the flow of the river increased slightly. Sal sat upright, looking over Yonah's head to the river beyond, checking for signs of the waterfall.

"There is still some distance to go before we reach the falls," said Yonah, noticing Sal's nervousness. "There is a landing ahead, well clear of the falls, where we can begin our portage."

"Okay then," said Sal. "I'll trust you not to let us go sailing over…"

"Asduda! Hush!" Yonah said sternly. "I hear someone speaking on shore."

Yonah noiselessly back-paddled, slowing the canoe while he searched the shoreline for the source of the voices. He spotted two men sitting on a rock by the shoreline, passing a jug back and forth. He drew Sal's attention to them with a jerk of his chin. They could hear their voices, talking loudly and laughing, although they were still too far away to make out what they were saying. Yonah spotted a pair of flintlock rifles leaning against a tree next to them.

"They are armed," he whispered, "and apparently drunk with whiskey. We will move as far away toward the opposite shore as possible, and try to use the boulders in the river to shield us from their view. We must go quietly. Unfortunately, the river is not wide enough at this point to get out of range of their rifles."

"Do you really think they'll shoot at us?" asked Sal quietly, unable to mask the tension in his voice. "They just look like a couple good ol' boys out hunting who stopped for a drink."

"I do not want to find out," said Yonah. "Many of your 'good ol' boys' consider Indians no better than game to be hunted."

They quietly paddled as Yonah directed, moving as stealthily as possible from rock to rock. There were fewer large rocks as they approached the two men, and they attempted to drift past them silently, using the paddles only as rudders to keep the canoe on a steady course. Unfortunately, they would be completely exposed as they passed directly in front of them.

"They'd have to be blind not to spot us," he thought to himself, not daring to make a sound. "With luck they're blind drunk."

At that moment, one of the men pointed at them and yelled, "Lookee there! Injuns!" He staggered to his feet, grabbing for the rifles leaning against the tree.

"Paddle hard," cried Yonah. "They will only have two shots if both guns are loaded. They will not have time to reload before we are out of their range. And keep your head down!"

"Only two shots!" Sal said as he slouched down and began digging in with his paddle. He knew the flintlocks weren't all that accurate, but they were well within range, even for a couple of drunks.

Sal glanced toward the men and saw one of them taking aim, while the other was slipping across the wet rocks and grabbing for his rifle. He heard the muffled crack of the rifle shot, and gasped as a chunk disappeared from the gunwale of the canoe. He felt a stinging on his hands and neck from the splinters of the shattered wood, relieved that it was wood and not lead. He paddled faster and harder all the same. Yonah ignored the shower of splinters and tried to jog the direction of the canoe to make them more difficult to hit, while at the same time keeping the canoe heading downstream and moving as fast as possible.

"Dang, ah missed 'em," they heard one of the men shout.

"I won't," the other bragged.

Sal watched the second man, who was now in a crouching position, take aim. They were no longer directly across from the men, but still within shooting range. "Just a few more seconds of paddling should put us out of reach," he thought, paddling with all his might.

He heard the crack of the second shot, and felt the breeze of the slug as it zinged past his ear. A warm wetness splashed on his face as Yonah dropped his paddle with a grunt and grabbed his shoulder. As he did, the fast-moving canoe slammed into a rock, tipped sideways to the flow of the river, and instantly filled with water. Sal and Yonah were abruptly displaced as the canoe filled, dumping them into the cold, swiftly flowing river.

"Ye-haw! Told ya I'd git 'em!" Sal heard the man bellow.

"Should we go finish 'em off?" the other man asked.

"Hell, no. What for? They'll be over them falls in a couple minutes. No injun's gonna live through that!" he answered.

Sal fought against the current that mercilessly thrust him against the river rocks. He saw Yonah struggling to swim with one arm, the other hanging useless. They were moving fast, and even with two good arms it was impossible to avoid being bashed into rock after rock. They were not far from the shore, but the current kept trying to sweep them out to the center of the river. Yonah had barely begun his painful struggle against the current, slowly making his way to the shore, when he was unexpectedly pounded by a crashing wave, smashing him head first into a rock. Sal winced as he saw Yonah's body go limp, no longer struggling. Unable to resist the power of the river, the Indian tumbled helplessly, bouncing against one rock after the next.

"Hold on, Tonto!" he yelled, getting no response from Yonah.

He made his way back toward the center of the river, dodging rocks while trying to quickly close the gap between him and his unconscious companion. He grimaced as he saw the river slam the old man into yet another rock. Luckily the force of the water held him against it, giving Sal the chance he needed to swim close enough to reach him. Sal looped his arm around Yonah's neck and gripped a fistful of his drenched shirt. Yonah gave no response, and for a moment Sal worried that the Indian might be beyond saving. The cold river water had slowed the flow of blood from Yonah's gunshot wound, but there was no way to determine his overall condition while battling the current in the middle of the river. He also had no idea whether the shooters would pursue them downriver.

Sal resolved himself to get them both to shore. Committed to the task, he set his jaw in determination and pushed himself away from the rock, dragging Yonah behind. Without the protection of the rock, the full force of the river pounded against them. The dead weight of Yonah's body pushed against him as the current hurled them both toward the next boulder. Sal tightened his grip on Yonah and struggled to put his own body between Yonah and the swiftly approaching rock. His back struck painfully against the rock as a wave slammed Yonah into his chest, knocking the breath from him. The current was becoming stronger now, and the whitewater foamed around him as he tried to regain his breath. He clung to the slick boulder and tightened his grip on Yonah. He began to panic when he realized he was in the rapids, remembering Yonah's description of the hundred foot waterfall ahead.

"I'll be damned if I'm going to let a couple of rednecks send me over these falls!" he screamed with characteristic spunk. "C'mon, Tonto, we're going to shore!"

Sal lodged his feet against an adjacent rock, held tight to Yonah, and kicked himself away from the stone they had slammed against. This time, he summoned all his strength to fight the current and managed to stay parallel with Yonah, keeping his own feet pointed downriver. Sal kept his knees bent to cushion the blow when his feet struck the next rock, hoping to soften the punishing impact. His teeth jarred when his boots slammed into the boulder, and he struggled to keep his grip on Yonah's sopping shirt. Gasping for breath, he gulped air between the waves that crashed over his head, trying not to swallow more water. He secured himself against his new perch and glanced over his shoulder to the rock he had just left. He judged himself to be about twenty feet closer to the shore, but he had traveled another hundred feet further downriver. Measuring the remaining distance to the shore, he estimated it would take him at least two more caroming jumps to reach it.

"I wish Tom were here," he thought. "He could probably calculate if there's enough river left before the falls to make it to shore. Come to think of it, I wish anyone was here besides me!"

"Okay, old dude, here we go again!" he said aloud to the inert Yonah. Once again he kicked himself away from the rock.

He felt the current accelerate him downriver as he desperately sought another rock to stop his careening advance. He clutched Yonah and kept his legs ready to accept the next rock. Sal felt a severe thump against the back of his head as it struck a rock just below the surface. The blow caused his vision to blur, and water rushed into his nose and mouth when he shrieked in pain. Coughing and gagging, trying to clear enough water from his air passage to take a breath, he caught sight of his target rock. He expelled the remaining water from his lungs, spouting water like a whale, and sucked in a huge breath of air. Once again his feet slammed into the rock. This time, due to his blurred vision, he hit it slightly off center and his feet slipped off of the wet boulder, one on either side. The full force of the water propelled him groin first into the rock. He gasped in agony, almost losing his grip on Yonah as the nauseating pain nearly caused him to vomit.

"Sonofabitch!" he panted, trying to get his feet back on the rock and stop the river from bouncing his crotch against it. Unable to do so, he twisted off the rock entirely, still clutching Yonah and hoping for a better purchase against the next one.

"Damn, I'd rather go over the freakin' falls than do that again!" he thought.

The next rock was a larger boulder, and he hit it squarely with his feet. Several more boulders and large rocks were now shielding him from the raging river, dampening the turbulent water flow. He used his legs and his free arm to claw at the rocks, making his way toward the shore. He felt the gravel of the river bottom beneath him, and used the last of his remaining strength to pull himself and Yonah far enough ashore to get the top half of their bodies clear of the river. He lay there bruised, battered, and exhausted, the side of his face pressing into the gravel. He relaxed his grip from around Yonah's neck, feeling the stinging tingle as the blood rushed back into his fingers.

"We did it, Tonto. We made it," he said breathlessly as consciousness slipped away.

Chapter thirty-two

The farm dogs barreled out to meet Benjamin's wagon as he and Alice turned up the lane. They gave a few short barks of greeting, and then fell into step alongside the wagon, prancing dangerously close to the wheels and the horse's hooves. Sally appeared next, enthusiastically running to greet her father and becoming even more excited when she saw that Alice had returned. Benjamin kept a wary eye as he brought the wagon to a stop, cautious that Sally's exuberance did not cloud her good sense to keep clear of the moving horses.

"Alice!" she cried, beaming a wide smile. "You came back!" She hopped into the wagon and gave Alice a hug.

"That I did, honey," Alice said. "My goodness, I just missed you so much I decided to spend some more time with you guys."

"A very good idea!" she said. "Where are your friends?"

"Hey! What about me? Are you not glad to see me?" said Benjamin, feigning hurt feelings.

"Of course I am, daddy!" she said, jumping into his lap and giving him a big hug. "But where are the others?"

"Well," said Alice, "they went to visit some of our new friends. Adam is staying with Jimmy and Rebecca Deerinwater, Tom went with John to visit the Ward family, and Sal went on a trip with Gvnigeyona."

"Yonah! Sal is with Yonah?" she said with a perplexed look, then began to giggle. Even Sally realized the absurdity of that mismatched pair.

"Where are your mother and brother?" asked Benjamin, changing the subject before Sally said something embarrassing. He slapped the reins to start the wagon moving again.

"They were working in the orchard," she answered, "but now they are on their way home. Billy promised we would go bird hunting later."

They met Catherine and Billy at the barn, just returning from the orchard. Sally ardently relayed Alice's information about the disposition of the others, flaunting her knowledge of the details. She put emphasis on the pairing of Sal and Yonah, enjoying the amused reaction from Catherine. Billy just nodded, not wishing to give too much importance to any news his little sister had. After the news from New Echota had been shared, Billy was charged with the care of the horse and wagon and led them to the stables. Sally and Alice gathered the empty food baskets from the wagon and carried them to the farmhouse, leaving Benjamin and Catherine alone in the barn.

"How did everything else go?" Catherine asked. She could tell he wanted to speak alone to her, easily reading his body language.

"About like you would expect," Benjamin said. "There are mixed reactions about the news John Carter has brought. Most are upset, but it is just more upset piled upon all the rest. It is not as if it were unforeseen."

"What purpose does it serve for our new friends to spend time at other households?" asked Catherine. "John does not really believe there is anything they can do to alter the situation, does he?"

"Not really, but he believes that they truly want to help. It may be that the best thing they can do is to bring firsthand knowledge of these events back to their own time. Regardless, they are here and want to be helpful, and there is always plenty of work to be done."

"What about Sal with Yonah? That seems a very unlikely combination."

"To me as well. But John sometimes can see harmony in situations where others can only see discord."

"Hmm; I suspect whatever song they sing together will be more cacophonous than harmonious."

"It will certainly be anomalous," Benjamin laughed.

Catherine chuckled at his word play. "I am pleased to see Alice here with us again. She gets along very well with Sally, and helps to keep her in good spirits. And she is very helpful to me."

"She also showed good sense when we encountered the ruffians in New Echota," said Benjamin.

"You were accosted?"

"They were not physically violent, although they threatened us, and they were especially abusive to Alice. They made very crass and rude remarks to her. You have experienced their ignorance. She was of course intimidated, but did not let them see her fear or provoke her to react foolishly. I believe she handled the situation as well as anyone could expect. Better than most."

"It is unfortunate she had to experience such shameful verbal taunting. At least she was spared physical abuse."

"Mmm," Benjamin nodded his agreement. "Still, I believe the encounter affected her more than she lets on. Some words from you may give her comfort."

"Yes, of course," she agreed. "I will speak with her. If only there were someone to utter words of comfort to sooth our minds as well."

Benjamin and Catherine left the barn and walked in silence to the farmhouse. Each knew what the other was thinking. They had discussed their situation many times; so many times no further words were necessary. How could they be expected to leave their home, the land that had been theirs and their ancestors longer than anyone could remember? Had they not done everything asked of them? Their people had changed their form of government, their religion, even their basic society from matriarchal to the patriarchal system of the whites. They had done this knowing they had no choice; they must become like the whites if they wanted to be allowed to exist.

The times of violent resistance were long past. The efforts of the charismatic war chief Tsiyu Gunsini, known as Dragging Canoe, who relentlessly led the Chickamauga against those who would invade the Cherokee homelands, had accomplished little but a delay of the inevitable. Dragging Canoe, now dead for nearly fifty years, had predicted that the insatiable greed of the whites would eventually drive them to claim all Cherokee land. The homeland was essential to the Cherokee; it was part of their soul, and nearly all of it had been taken away. They had capitulated many times, and still it was not enough. The whites would not be happy until they had it all. Benjamin and Catherine had no need to speak of this to each other again; it no longer served any purpose. All they could do was wait and hope for an unlikely miracle.

Immediately upon reaching the house, Catherine and Alice began preparations for the evening meal. Benjamin headed back out to the fields, wanting to tend to a few chores that could be addressed with the supplies he brought from town. Catherine made use of her time alone with Alice to offer a few comforting words as Benjamin had suggested. From Alice's reaction, Catherine determined that it was not comforting words that she needed, it was retribution. Alice made it clear that she was angrier about having to hold her tongue than she was about the childish behavior of the men. That impressed Catherine; Alice was even stronger than Benjamin believed her to be.

When Billy arrived at the house, he retrieved a four foot long wooden stick that was hanging above the door, and grabbed a pouch from a hook on the wall beneath it.

"Are we going bird hunting now, Billy?" Sally asked.

"We can go as soon as you are ready," he answered.

"I'm ready," she replied excitedly. "Alice, won't you come with us?"

"Yes, please come along," said Billy. "We will show you how to hunt for birds."

"I'd love to, honey," said Alice, "but I think I should stay and help with the meal."

"You should go," said Catherine. "I will take care of the meal, and Silvey will be along soon to help. It will help put your unfortunate experience out of your mind, and will do you good to have some fun. Go with them."

"Okay, I think I would like to go," Alice said. "Won't you need a gun? What's that long pole for?"

"Come on; we'll show you," said Billy. "We have everything we need."

Alice and the two youngsters trotted off toward the woods beyond the edge of the cotton fields. As they walked, Billy explained his bird hunting technique.

"This tube is a piece of river cane. There's plenty of it growing around here along the creeks and rivers. The Cherokee have used it to make blowguns as long as anyone can remember. A *tugawesti* is a great way to hunt small animals, especially birds, and almost every young Cherokee has one. It takes a while to get the hang of shooting a dart, but it works really well. It's very quiet too; so if you miss, you often can take a second shot."

He handed the blowgun to Alice for her to examine. It was straight and hollow all the way through, and the outside had been decorated with painted bands and symbols. There was soft jute wrapped around one end to make a mouthpiece.

"When you first cut it you have to ream out a couple of places to make it hollow all the way through," he told her. "Then you can decorate it anyway you like.

"In this bag I have my darts," he said, removing one of the eight-inch long sticks from his bag. To Alice, the darts looked a lot like the pointy wooden skewers she used to make kabobs on the grill, only each one had a bit of fluff tied onto the end.

"We make the darts from the wood of locust trees because it is very hard and I can make an extra sharp point on it. I tie a piece of cotton on the end for fletching because we have plenty of cotton, but you can use thistle down, too. That's what they used in the old days."

"So you just put one of those darts in the tube and blow it at a bird?" Alice asked.

"That's about it," Billy said. "Like I said, it takes a little practice, but it's pretty easy. Sally is getting pretty good at it, so I'm going to help her make her own blowgun and darts. We'll show you how it works before we go after the birds."

"Don't you have to dip the darts in poison or something?" Alice asked.

"No, not usually. Some people boil tobacco leaves to coat the darts, but I just use plain darts."

He pointed to a birch tree about twenty-five feet away at the edge of the woods, and said, "I'll put a target on that tree and we can practice."

He walked to the tree, found a two foot-square piece of the smooth, white bark that the tree had shed, stood it against the base of the tree, and then returned to where the two girls were standing. He put one of the darts into the blowgun until the fluffy white stopper was just past the mouthpiece. He inflated his cheeks with a deep breath, placed the blowgun against his lips, and blew a quick, sharp puff of air into the end of the tube. The dart stuck firmly, going about halfway through the center of the piece of bark.

"Let me try," said Sally.

She took the blowgun, put in a dart, aimed, and puffed into the end. The dart struck the bark just a few inches from Billy's shot.

"Your turn," Sally said, handing the blowgun to Alice.

"Oh, dear. I'll try," Alice said tentatively. She took the blowgun and a dart from Billy, placing it into the tube as she was shown. Aiming carefully at the bark, she blew into the tube, only to watch the dart drop from the end not more than two feet away.

"Oh, my," she said, laughing. "I guess I'm not going to be much of a hunter!"

"When you blow through the tube," Billy instructed, "be sure to take a deep breath and use lots of air. When you blow, puff sharply to give the dart a good push." He demonstrated making a sharp puffing action with his mouth, without the blowgun. He retrieved the dart and replaced it into the blowgun for her, and said, "Try again."

Glenn R. Petrucci

This time Alice inhaled a deep lungful of air and took aim. She sent the dart through the tube with a tremendous puff. The dart struck the bark and continued on, sailing completely through it.

"Good!" said Billy and Sally in unison.

"That was quite a shot," said Billy. "You must have powerful lungs."

"Probably from arguing with Sal so much," she laughed.

They each took a few more shots. Once they were all hitting the target consistently, Billy said they were ready to go hunting. "Enough practice. Now let's get some birds for our dinner." They gathered up the darts and headed into the woods. "I know a spot where we will have good cover and usually has many birds," said Billy.

He led them to a clump of bushes, crawled inside, and used his hunting knife to hack out an area for them to sit. He situated Alice and Sally where they would be well camouflaged, then crouched into a position where he would have a good view of a small clearing in front of the bushes. The low-growing shrubs had been overtaken by wild grape vines, and the huge grape leaves formed a natural hunter's blind, concealing them from view of any game that might enter the clearing. The corkscrew grapevines hung around them like bouncy green springs, and Alice could smell the moist sweetness of damp earth beneath the dripping vines. Even though it had not rained, the immense leaves collected moisture from the air, keeping their supporting bushes well watered.

"You have to be very still and quiet," he instructed them.

The three hunters waited silently behind the foliage. Within minutes they heard the distinctive bobwhite call of the quail. Sally grinned and nodded at Alice. She pointed in the direction of the sound and whispered "*guque*," which earned her a stern frown from Billy, placing his finger to his lips. Billy returned his attention to the clearing, not seeing Sally scrunch up her face and stick out her tongue in response to the reprimand. Alice gave Sally a wink, turning her frown into a cheerful grin.

They heard the sound of rustling leaves as the quail foraged just beyond the edge of the clearing. The hunters sat stock still, waiting patiently for the birds to enter the clearing. Billy slowly raised the blowgun, pointing its lethal end through the bushes in the direction of the rustling.

Oblivious of the hunters, the covey of quail entered the clearing, pecking at the ground as they foraged. Billy waited, letting the birds become at ease with their exposed position. Alice noticed his lips silently moving as he selected his target, as if he was saying a prayer. He filled his cheeks with air and placed the end of the blowgun into his mouth. He aimed carefully, puffed sharply into the tube, and sent a dart flying toward his target. The dart struck the bird in the center of its chest. Immediately the silence was broken as the quail's legs collapsed and the bird flapped wildly about, slapping at the ground and raising a cloud of dust. The deafening flutter of wings added to the din as the other birds took flight in a panic.

"You got it!" Sally cried, as the three crashed out of their cover and ran to the clearing.

Billy knelt by the quail, and Alice saw that he once again mumbled a few words before picking up the still twitching bird and gave its head a sharp twist, ending its movements with finality. He dropped the bird, dart and all, into the bag he was carrying.

"That's one," he said. "We'll do better if we move to a different place for the next one. I know of lots of good hunting spots for birds."

"Billy," said Alice, "I couldn't help but notice… It looked like you said something to the quail before you picked it up. And before you shot."

"Yes, of course," he answered. "As my father taught me, I say a hunter's prayer to guide my dart before shooting, and then of course I must apologize to the quail for killing it."

"You apologize to the quail?"

"Yes, certainly. And I thank him for giving up his life. It is necessary for us to have food, so I explain that to him so he will understand."

Alice didn't think the quail was very likely to understand being shot, and would most likely prefer to be left alive. She could tell from Billy's fervent look that the killing of game was not something he took lightly, and that he considered the prayer to be an important part of his hunting ritual. Her previous hunting experiences had been all about the sport, the challenge of tracking and shooting. Billy's outlook was more spiritual, and reflective of a culture more closely tied to the earth, one that still remembered to be thankful for the bounty nature provided. It was a realistic attitude toward the harsh actions necessary for all living things to survive.

"Let's go," said Sally impatiently. "I want to get my bird next."

"Remember what I told you about hunting," said Billy, "and how it is important to be patient. But we do need to get to our next spot and get under cover."

The trio spent the next few hours hunting. Sally and Billy both bagged a pair of quail, and they insisted that Alice give it a try. After several attempts, she was finally able to accurately place a deadly shot, to score a kill of her own. She was not averse to killing a bird; she had been hunting for both large and small game before.

The uniqueness of the blowgun gave her some difficulty; it took some effort to hit a live, moving target instead of a stationary piece of bark. Once she discovered that aiming took more "feel" than sight she could place the dart accurately. The youngsters applauded her achievement, praising her skill and learning as quickly as she did.

They each bagged an additional quail and now that they had plenty of birds for everyone's dinner Billy declared that it was time to head for home. Alice was so intensely involved in the hunting she nearly forgot she hadn't eaten since New Echota. She was looking forward to a meal of wild bobwhite quail and whatever else Catherine was making to go along with them. Catherine had been right to suggest she go hunting; she enjoyed the afternoon with Billy and Sally. Her fury at the encounter with the offensive riffraff in New Echota was beginning to fade.

Once they were back to the farmhouse, Billy handed the bagful of quail to Silvey who made quick work of cleaning them. Alice was still uncomfortable with the idea that this family could accept slavery so readily, but she thought that having a servant, a paid one, would be something she could get used to quite easily. She enjoyed hunting, and loved to prepare meals with wild game, but cleaning dead animals was not a chore she looked forward to. It amused her to imagine herself as the Lady of the Manor—she'd love to be able to go hunting, hand the game to a servant, and have it served to her at a great long table on silver trays. "I've been watching too many BBC classics," she chuckled to herself.

The quail became the main dish of the evening meal, having been roasted on a great spit in the hearth and stuffed with a mixture of cornbread and herbs. As usual, there were also plenty of side dishes of vegetables and other cold meats that Catherine and Silvey had prepared. Benjamin lavished the hunters with praise for their successful outing, promising Billy that he would take him soon for deer or possibly a spring turkey.

As per tradition, they finished up their evening chores and settled down for storytelling. Benjamin said that he would honor the hunters with a special hunting story.

"This story," Benjamin began, "starts with the bears. Long ago, when men were first starting to invent things like blowguns and bows and arrows, the bears all got together to complain. They didn't like the fact that the men were inventing these things. 'They make it too easy for them to kill us,' they complained to their chief, the great white bear. After some discussion, the bears decided they would learn to use weapons themselves, and one of them made a bow and arrow that they could use to defend themselves against the men.

"When they tried to use the bow and arrow, they found that their long claws got in the way. No matter how hard they tried, they couldn't make the arrow go straight. One of the bears trimmed off his claws and tried again, and this time the arrow flew straight and true. 'We just have to all cut off our claws,' they decided. But the chief bear told them that they couldn't do that, because they depended on their claws to fight and kill the other animals, and they would starve if they didn't have claws anymore. They never did come up with a solution, so they just gave up and went home. If they had not given up, we would be at war with the bears. But since they did, a hunter can kill a bear without even needing to ask his forgiveness.

"Next, it was the deer who met, having the same grievance. 'Too many of us are being killed by the men without any thought given to our sacrifice,' they complained. The chief of the deer was called the Little Deer. He told them that what he would do is every time a deer was killed, he would run to the spot and ask the deer's spirit if the hunter had asked the deer's pardon. If he had, all would be well. If not, the spirit of Little Deer would follow the hunter, and when he caught up with him he would strike him down with a crippling disease, like rheumatism. That's why it is important for a hunter to apologize to a deer whenever he kills one. If he forgets, or wants to make extra sure the Little Deer spirit doesn't follow, he must stop and build several small fires in his path along the way home.

"The other animals liked this idea, so they all started coming up with their own diseases to inflict man with. Each animal named one, and soon there were so many new diseases that men might not have been able to survive if it was not for the plants, who were good friends with man. They decided that each one of them could be used as a cure for each disease the animals came up with. There are a lot of cures, and men don't know them all, so sometimes the doctors have to communicate with the spirit of the plants to determine which plant cures which disease."

Everyone, except Alice, had heard this story many times. No matter, they all enjoyed hearing it as often as someone was willing to do the telling. Alice especially enjoyed the part about the plants, and it led to a discussion about the various types of plants in the area and how they were used. She recalled how plants played a part at the very beginning of this adventure, remembering the poultice John Carter had made for his horse, and that his reason for being in the tiny valley was to gather those plants. Most of Alice's interest in botany was in their use as a food source, but she was also intrigued by their many medicinal properties. She had once volunteered her time to a botanical exploration group whose focus was on discovering new plant species in the world's rain forests. She had done some reading about the many plants, some still yet unknown, that had a possibility of use for cures of disease. She hadn't given much thought to the medicinal plants in the forests of her own country. She asked her hosts if there were many types of medicinal plants in the woods nearby.

"Yes, there are many," said Benjamin. "One of the most in demand is Ginseng, which grows up high on steep mountainsides. We call it the 'little man' because the root looks like a little old man. In the old days, it was only permitted to take every seventh plant, which meant you had to find at least seven to take one. Since the plant is scarce, that would assure there was always some available for the next person. But ginseng has become a much sought after herb, and now people take all they can find."

"Snakeroot is another that is collected," said Catherine. "We use it to treat snakebites and fevers, among other things. Also, orangeroot, or what you may call goldenseal, is a very important herb that can be found nearby. John probably used some Orangeroot in his horse's poultice, as it can help reduce swelling. Goldenseal can also be used to treat cancer."

"I think I've heard of people using goldenseal as a cancer cure, but medical research has determined that it doesn't really work," said Alice.

"That will be a disappointment to the people who have been cured by it," Catherine said with a sly smile.

"Some of the other medicinal plants are black cohosh, cone-flower, may-apple, boneset, pinkroot, and witch-hazel," Catherine continued. "We use partridge moccasin to treat worms, and milkweed juice to treat sores on our children's heads. Catgut will strengthen your hair and skin. The ballplayers use that to toughen up their skin before playing."

"If you are very interested," said Benjamin, "a good person to speak with is Rebecca Deerinwater, Jimmy's wife. Adam is visiting with them. Rebecca is *Ani-Sahoni*, Blue Holly clan, and has a lot of experience with making medicine from herbs and grows many of her own for that purpose. Her clan is well-known for their expertise at that."

"I think that would be very interesting, Benjamin. I'd love to meet her, and hope I get the opportunity," Alice said.

Sally and Billy had sat listening quietly to the discussion of medicinal plants, but Sally clearly had something else on her mind. "Will you tell us the story of *Basil, The Builder Beaver* again, Alice?" she pleaded. "I love that story."

"Yes, of course I will, if that's what everyone wants," she said, looking around the room at the others.

"Please," said Billy. "I liked it also."

"We would all enjoy hearing it again," said Benjamin.

Alice proceeded to tell the story again, using all the characterizations and sound effects that she used before, except this time the rest of the family joined in, each picking an animal from the story to imitate. By the time she finished, everyone was exhausted from the storytelling and laughter.

Benjamin yawned and stretched, and Catherine declared that bedtime had arrived. Sleep came easily for them all.

Chapter thirty-three

*A*lice was awakened from a sound sleep by the aroma of cooking food. Jumping from bed, she quickly readied herself and headed to the kitchen, where Catherine, Silvey, and Sally were busily executing the morning kitchen chores. "*Osda sunalei,*" they said, greeting her with bright smiles.

"Oh, good morning. I didn't mean to sleep late," she said. "You should have wakened me."

"I thought you could use some extra rest after your long day yesterday," said Catherine, "but don't worry, there's always plenty to do! Benjamin and Billy have already eaten and gone to tend to the horses. We'll join them in the fields later."

Silvey set a place for her at the table with a huge plate of eggs and sausage, steaming coffee, bread, and a number of bowls with a variety of side dishes. Alice's healthy appetite usually didn't kick in until later in the day, and she normally did not eat more than a quick snack in the morning. This morning, however, she was ravenous, her appetite stimulated by all the fresh air and exercise she had been getting. She attacked the meal like a starved wolf with a fresh kill. She downed the strong, hot coffee with the same vigor, and the caffeine cleared away her remaining drowsiness.

While Alice finished her meal, Catherine began listing the chores for the day, mostly for Alice's benefit, since much of it was routine for the others. There were the normal kitchen and household chores, along with livestock to feed, milking to do, buckets of water to fetch, firewood to stack, the kraut-barrel to see to—a seemingly endless list of routine chores—all before they got out to the fields. Catherine's plan was to complete these chores, prepare a mid-day meal to bring to the men, and then spend the afternoon helping them to clear a neglected field of brush. It would be a typically full day on the Rogers' farm and Alice needed no prompting to get started. She may have been less enthusiastic if this was her normal routine, but for now she was enjoying the change of pace. The sedentary routine of her regular job required her to fit in exercise during her leisure time. The physical labor required for this lifestyle was hard, but it was a wholesome feeling. Life on the Rogers' farm was basic. The work was tough and the pleasures were simple. There were problems to be dealt with, but most were the kind of problems people could solve using their own labor and ingenuity. The way things should be, she thought. The way they were before the daily mundane chores had been replaced by the complexities of modern life. Sure, she appreciated the advantages of modern conveniences; she wasn't so childish as to suggest technology should be abandoned. Rather she felt it was beneficial for her to temporarily do without, making her appreciate them all the more.

Here she also felt more connected to the people, the animals, even the land around her. In just this short time, she was beginning to get a true understanding of what leaving behind the land that people had worked for their entire lives, and the entire lives of their ancestors, would mean to them.

The morning passed quickly. They hauled the mid-day meal out to the fields and served it in the usual spot under the oak tree. While they ate, Benjamin explained to Alice that the field he wanted to clear was a spot that had been neglected, and ridding it of the overgrowth would be laborious. He planned to make good use of the field for the late summer vegetables he wanted to plant. He told her that he expected the clearing to take several days, although because the days were getting longer as summer approached, with the extra daylight they may be able to complete the job in less time.

The field was about six acres and had been lying fallow for about three years. There were not any large trees to remove, although the brush had thrived. The majority of it could simply be cut and hauled to a burn pile. The larger roots had to be dug or chopped out of the ground with a mattock to prepare the field for plowing. While the men chopped at the roots, the women carried and dragged the cut brush to a huge pile, where it would be allowed to season and set on fire.

They worked hard and managed to complete the job in a single afternoon. Now Benjamin would have his extra field, ready to be plowed and planted. The workers stood looking at the field, taking a few moments to admire the results of their hard work. A passerby might wonder at seeing seven people silently gazing at an empty field, but to the exhausted workers it was a glorious site. The workers themselves, haggard and fatigued, were far from glorious. Every bit of exposed skin was covered with a mixture of dust and sweat; faces streaked and smeared where it had been wiped away from their eyes, nose, and mouth. Their clothing, also covered in dirt, suffered from every sort of abuse—tears, rips, snags, and frays.

They dragged themselves back to the farmhouse after a quick stop at the barn to put away their tools. Elated with the progress on the field, Benjamin suggested that tomorrow they might suspend their chores for an hour or two and take another fishing trip. His suggestion energized them all, animating their previously quiet and sluggish procession into a lively discussion of fishing holes and techniques.

They used several buckets of water from the rain barrel to remove as much of the dirt from their hands, arms, and faces as they could. The strenuous work had given them all a healthy appetite, so a thorough washing was going to have to wait until after they ate. There had been no time for extravagant food preparations, which meant that their evening meal would be pottage, a meal that all farming families ate every now and then, even the more prosperous ones. Pottage was made from the choice leftovers of the last several meals, which were put into a massive iron pot, seasoned well and kept simmering over the fire, resulting in a hodgepodge stew that was always ready. In the case of the Rogers family, it was also always very tasty.

The discussion of tomorrow's fishing outing continued while they served up bowls of the savory stew and great slabs of leftover cornbread. With everyone talking, Benjamin didn't notice the dogs barking until they became loud and persistent enough to catch his attention.

"Billy," Benjamin said, "go and see what those dogs are on about, please. It is probably just another 'coon that has wandered up to the house, but we should make sure it is not a fox up to some mischief."

Billy reluctantly put down his spoon and headed toward the front door. No sooner than he left the table, Benjamin heard the sound of hoof beats thundering up the lane to the farmhouse.

"Sounds like we have company," he said, trying to sound nonchalant, but unable to keep an edge of alarm from his voice. He flew to the front door with all the speed of the hummingbird, his boyhood namesake.

"Get out! What do you want!" they heard Billy's cries coming from the front of the house, followed by Benjamin's authoritative voice, "How dare you enter my home!" then lower, "Get behind me Billy!"

Startled, the others sprang from the table and rushed toward Benjamin, who held up a firm hand indicating for them to remain behind him. He was facing three uniformed men who had entered the farmhouse.

Benjamin stood waiting for a response to his question, his small but sturdy body like a rampart between the men and his family. The three men wore gun belts, their pistols holstered, although two of the men kept their hand on the stock of their gun. Through the door they could see a half dozen other men, still mounted, who were armed with both rifles and pistols. The men outside were not wearing uniforms, and Benjamin thought he recognized a couple of them as townsfolk from New Echota. They were not the same men they had encountered with Jebediah Barnett, nor was Jebediah among them.

"Are you Benjamin Rogers?" asked one of the soldiers who had entered the house.

"I am, and you are trespassing on my property," Benjamin said sternly.

"I'm afraid it is not your property any longer," the soldier said. "You and your family must come with us."

"Come with you where? Why should we?"

"You are being ordered to come to the fort at New Echota. My name is Captain James Martin, of the Georgia Guard. We have no wish to cause you any harm, but my orders are to bring you and your family to Fort Wool for relocation. Peaceably, I hope, for the sake of your safety and that of your family."

"We were told we had until May 23rd. Today is only the 18th," said Benjamin.

"The Georgia Guard has been ordered to begin the roundup of all Indian people today. The federal troops are making the final preparations of the relocation forts, and will begin assisting with the roundup soon.

"We have much to do today," the captain continued. "I would like to be patient, but I have not been allotted time for discussion. Will you and your family cooperate, or must I order my men to move you by force?"

The look in Captain Martin's pale blue eyes and the stern tone of his voice implied that he preferred not to use force against this family, but he would be willing to do so if pressed. The men standing outside the door were already fidgeting, and Benjamin did not doubt that they would be willing to do the captain's bidding; some of them would possibly even enjoy using violence against defenseless civilians.

He turned and looked at his family. Billy stood boldly, but fear showed through his defiance. Sally was crying, holding tightly to her mother's skirt. Alice looked disbelieving and full of anger, ready to verbally engage the captain, though wisely remaining silent. He glanced at Catherine and noted that this was one of the few times he had seen her without a smile, struggling to keep her fear and anger hidden. She exchanged a look with Benjamin, slowly nodding her head, lowering her eyes to the floor.

"We will cooperate," Benjamin said. The words left a foul taste in his mouth.

"That would be for the best. I will give you ten minutes to gather personal items. You have a wagon, and you may load your things into it. Everyone, including your slaves, will be escorted to the fort."

"Ten minutes!" Benjamin cried. "How are we to get all our belongings into a single wagon in ten minutes?"

"Consider yourself fortunate that I am allowing you that," said the captain. "Do not waste the time you have." He turned and walked out the door, followed by his two companions.

The family stood looking at Benjamin in shock, feeling as if their world was coming to an end. The feeling was not far from the truth. It would take every bit of his willpower, but Benjamin knew he had to set aside his anger and humiliation, at least for the next ten minutes. He suppressed his initial inclination to oppose the men, to show them he was no coward and greet their aggression with fierce resistance. It would only be foolishness. He knew he was no coward, and so did his family. He did not need to prove anything to these men. His immediate priority was to get his family safely to the fort. He knew they were as angry as he was, and it was clear they had no choice but to capitulate to the wishes of the Georgia Guard. He gathered his thoughts and began directing the preparations, firmly and without emotion.

"Catherine," he began, "gather what you can of our clothing and blankets, those things may be the most important. Also whatever household items you think are essential. You must leave behind sentimental items, we have limited room with a single wagon, and it cannot be overloaded if we are truly expected to make a long journey. Keep Sally with you.

"Billy, you will come with me to prepare the wagon and help gather a few of our most important tools. We will inform Isaac and Silvey of the situation and I will send Silvey back to help Catherine.

"Alice," he lowered his voice to not be overheard by the men outside, "they may assume you are part of the family, which at the moment may be for the best. I do not believe that trying to explain anything else to them is advisable at this time."

With her blonde hair and blue eyes, Alice hardly looked like a Cherokee, although many of the mixed-blood Indians had European features. She was still wearing the tattered and dirty clothing from working in the field, giving her the appearance of a farm laborer. Most likely, the Captain just didn't want to take the time away from his roundup schedule to deal with individuals.

"Yes, you're probably right," Alice answered. "I'll help Catherine pack, and go along with you all to New Echota."

"Very good," Benjamin said. "I will bring the wagon as soon as it is ready."

Captain Martin sent a couple of his men along with Benjamin to the barn. They did not offer any help, but neither did they interfere. Benjamin could not imagine the purpose of sending the men to the barn. Did this captain think that he would run off and leave his family behind? He put the thought from his mind, and set about his tasks.

They brought the partially loaded wagon to the house, where the women had begun stacking a pile of items to be loaded. Benjamin was not sure how much of his ten minutes he had used. The captain watched, expressionless, as they loaded the wagon. He was clearly impatient but was so far uncomplaining of the progress.

Several of the men nudged each other and pointed to the tree line across Benjamin's fields. The captain could see that another group was gathering there—scavengers, ready to swoop in like buzzards to help themselves to whatever Benjamin left behind. This assignment was not one that Captain Martin enjoyed. He had many Cherokee friends at home back in Tennessee, but he was a soldier and had no choice, it was his duty and he would do it as best he could. He called his men to order and turned his attention back to the Rogers.

"That will do," he said to Benjamin. "We're moving out."

They had not finished loading the wagon, and Catherine started to protest, but Benjamin held up a hand and shook his head. He was sure their ten minutes had long passed.

"We are as ready as we can be," he said to the captain.

In addition to the two horses pulling the wagon, Benjamin had brought up two additional horses. He and Billy rode on one, while Isaac mounted the second. The women squeezed into the wagon, with Catherine at the reins. They headed down the lane, the captain placing several of the men in front and several behind the wagon. When they reached the end of the lane, Benjamin paused.

"Captain?" he said, nodding his head toward his family.

Captain Martin looked at Benjamin and the grief-stricken faces of the rest of the family. He was a soldier, but not completely without sympathy. He signaled his men to halt, and said to Benjamin, "I can only give you a moment."

"That will be long enough," said Benjamin.

The Rogers family turned for a final farewell to the farm that had been their home for so many years. So much more than a few acres of land and a handful of buildings, the place was part of the family, full of memories of good times and bad, echoes of laughter and tears; as much a part of the family as any one of them.

"Good heavens, what will happen to the rest of the livestock?" Alice asked.

"I do not think we will have to worry about that," said Benjamin, indicating with his eyes the group of scavengers already moving toward the house.

"Let's move out," said the captain, and they turned their backs on the farm and rode away in grim silence.

Chapter thirty-four

G uwaya, I know that you have considered the difficulties you are sure to face if you take that course of action," said John Carter.

Tom looked around the table at the resolute faces of the Ward family. Even little Sagi, plainly too young to understand the conversation, appeared to have a look of determination.

"As I have said, we discussed it and have decided that our only choice is to go into hiding. I know of places here in the mountains that the whites have never seen, even after all these many years of their settlements here. There is rough terrain that offers good hiding places because they are too rough to be used for farming."

John looked doubtful. "I hope you are making a wise decision. You will be hunted, and have to live off the land, with your mother and two small children."

"It is them I am thinking of. It is the only way to preserve their dignity. As you yourself have said, it would be honorable to fight, but suicidal. In my mind, going to ground is more honorable than giving up."

John nodded solemnly. He knew that once the Ward family had made their decision, it would be irrevocable. He would not be able to change their minds, and it was not his place to do so. Cherokee etiquette demanded noninterference and respect for the self-determination of others. Even if he believed someone was making a bad decision, it was not appropriate to belabor his concerns; he must accept their decision unless his opinion was sought. In his heart, John was not so sure it was a bad decision. Certainly extremely risky and dangerous, but was it really any more perilous than giving up the ancient homelands and being forced to move to unknown territory? He was torn between principle and self-preservation, as were many of his people.

Tom, however, was another matter, and John needed to make sure he understood the situation in which he was being placed. He excused himself to the Wards, and asked Tom to accompany him outside where they could speak privately.

"Tom, if Guwaya intends to take flight to avoid removal, the situation for everyone involved becomes much more complex. Living off the land with a family up in these mountains would be difficult enough, and with the additional pressure of pursuit from the militia, I do not much like his chances of success. Not to mention that you will be complicit in their illegal activities."

"Aren't they pretty much living off the land now?" Tom asked.

"They unquestionably possess the skills to live independently, but no, they currently are not living off the land entirely. Guwaya depends on supplies he gets from town, and they barter goods that they make and grow. If they are going to hide in a remote place, they will no longer have the resources of this farm or access to trade."

"Surely they would not expect to live in hiding permanently. I supposed they expect that if they hide out for a while, things will change and they'll be allowed back on their land. As I've told you, in my future that's not what happens, and I don't see it as very likely in any event."

"I agree. Once others get their hands on the land, it is certain that they will not give it up willingly. I believe that the best they can hope for is to hold out for a few weeks and try to join up with any others that may have taken the same course of action. A larger group will have a better chance at survival for a longer time. Then there may be an opportunity to find sanctuary as they continue to try to regain their lands. But as for you, it may be best if you return with me. This was not the situation I intended to put you in."

"You just said that with more people, their chances might be better. I haven't much experience at living entirely off the land and hiding out from a militia, but I can definitely lend them my support in other ways."

"I am sure you could, but if you choose to stay with them, you must understand that you could be putting your life at risk—much more than you have already."

"Guwaya is the only adult male in this family. I think that staying here to help him do what he believes is best for his family is worth the risk to my safety. In fact, I don't think my conscience will let me leave, knowing what they face and that I may be of some small service to them. My trivial contributions could mean the difference between life and death for them."

Tom gave no indication he was making a glib decision—he understood all that was at stake. John wondered if he had misjudged these people from the future, giving them less credit than they deserved. It was clear that they were inexperienced in the difficulties of everyday life, used to a much softer time, and were unaccustomed to the harshness of living in this world, but they also had demonstrated a doggedness to stand against injustice, both against themselves and others. If they truly represented the future, perhaps there was hope for the people after all.

"Your presence would certainly be useful to the Wards. I do not believe that your contributions would be trivial, and if we left them on their own my conscience would suffer as well. This is a fine family, and I would like to give them every opportunity to survive through whatever may happen. If you are certain that you understand the hazards you are likely to face, I will discuss some tentative plans with you and Guwaya. Obviously once you go into hiding you will be cut off from communication with me until I return."

"I'm about as sure as I can be about anything since meeting you back in that little valley," Tom said with a half-grin and shake of his head.

Back inside the cabin, Guwaya once again confirmed that he would be most appreciative of Tom's help. He explained his plan in more detail, and described the area he had chosen where he was sure his family would not be found by anyone intending them harm. He spoke to John and Tom of an isolated area where there were small caverns he was sure not many others knew of. John knew this part of the country was littered with caverns. He had explored many of them, but was not familiar with the place Guwaya was describing. The area he had picked was far from any roads, and it was not a place that John knew to be popular for hunting. Still, he could think of several problems with Guwaya's plan, and tactfully spoke about his concerns.

"I have come across many prospectors during my recent travels. You know that many have been conducting mining operations. The promise of our removal seems to have encouraged even more to head into the more remote areas to search for gold. In fact, when I first met Tom and his friends I thought that was what they were doing. You will have to keep a guard for the gold hunters who may come across your hiding place."

"There is only a single approach to the entrance to the caverns, so anyone coming could be seen well in advance," said Guwaya. "In exploring the cavern, I discovered a small rear exit which could be used to escape in an emergency. The exit is nearly impossible to see from the surface, and is not visible from the front entrance to the cave."

John was less worried about accidental discovery of their location than he was about the militia. "The Georgia government knows of your presence here. If they enforce removal, they will know that you have gone into hiding when they discover your abandoned home. If they send out militiamen to search for you they will be looking for areas like the one you have chosen."

"That was something I have considered," Guwaya said. "I have made it known to several merchants and traders with whom I occasionally do business that I am planning to relocate voluntarily, and have said that I intend to join with a group heading west. I realize that ruse will fool no one for long, nor protect me from search parties looking for others in hiding, but it may give me a slight advantage."

Guwaya told them he had already been provisioning his hideout, and he had made many trips to supply the cavern, being careful to take circuitous routes and avoid being observed. He said that there was fresh water nearby, and between his stockpile of supplies and whatever fresh game he could provide, he and his family could hold out for several months.

"Then what will you do?" asked Tom.

"My hope is that in time our leaders will prevail. If they are not successful preventing this madness entirely, they will surely not abandon those of us who have tried to remain close to our lands. If I run out of provisions before that, I hope we can find others who have taken the same course of action and join with them."

John Carter was still uneasy with Guwaya's plan, but saw no reason to disrespect him with further criticism. Frankly, as concerned as he was, he had no better alternative to offer him.

It was decided that all three men would go to Guwaya's cave in the morning, to bring additional supplies and disclose the location to John, who would be the only other person to know where they were.

The remainder of the evening was spent in more lighthearted conversation. John relayed other news of social events in the Cherokee community, informing them of council decisions, new farming ideas from the more progressive folks like Jimmy Deerinwater, elders who had passed on, and babies that had been born. Tom was at first confused when someone asked if the baby was "ballsticks," but it was explained to him that it was a customary way to refer to a male baby. He was aware of the Cherokee love of their stickball game, but he still thought the reference was amusing, and a little embarrassing.

There was, as always, more food, and the usual storytelling. Ahni told a story, speaking in Cherokee, about a place along the Tennessee

River known as "The Suck." John translated for him as she told the story, although Tom was enchanted by the silky-soft euphonious sounds of Ahni's voice speaking in Cherokee. It was the first time he had listened to the language being spoken other than a few short words at a time. He expected to hear harsh sounding words, but was surprised at the melodious sound her voice made as she put together each syllable, and it made him anxious to learn more Cherokee words.

Tom had heard of The Suck from friends who had kayaked the river and he thought he remembered it mentioned in an old Johnny Cash song. The Suck was a particularly dangerous place just south of Chattanooga, Tennessee, where the river currents created turbulent whirlpools. In the old days, according to Ahni's story, the whirlpools were intermittent, the maelstrom disappearing and reappearing at the most inconvenient times. She said the place was haunted, and travelers who tried to navigate that part of the river without taking the proper precautions could find themselves caught in the swirl of the whirlpool, which opened up to a room at the bottom of the river where the people who lived there would beckon the doomed travelers to come and join them.

The Wards prepared a place in the loft of the barn for John and Tom to spend the night, as the tiny cabin did not have much extra room. That was fine with both of them; it was a pleasant evening and the loft was well padded with sweet-smelling spring hay. As he lay down to sleep, Tom thought about the situation he was putting himself in by agreeing to stay with the Ward family. He knew what was coming, and wasn't at all convinced that history would play out any differently than the one he knew. He could understand why it was important for John and the other Cherokee to cling to the hope that things would work out for them, but he didn't believe it would do him any good to deny his own version of reality. Just being in 1838 was far enough from reality for his liking.

He had to admit that other than the time-travel ordeal, everything else about this place seemed more real to him than did much of his "normal" life. He could hear the soft nickering from the horses stabled below, and from where he was lying he had a view of the spectacular night sky through the open loft door. He could see a section of the glowing band of the Milky Way across the coal-black sky, and remembered the story Benjamin told of how it was formed by a giant dog spilling his stolen cornmeal as he ran away from the angry millers. Looking at the edge of the galaxy tonight with so many bright and clear stars, he could easily understand how that story was conceived. He thought about the strangely gruesome story Adam told, and the humorous animations of Alice's tale, and how they all became so close to Benjamin and his family in such a short time. He was surprised how much he had learned about his companions in the last several days. They had been together for years, and had taken plenty of trips together before, but this extraordinary adventure was providing them with not only an incredible insight to this period of history, but also some revelations about each other. He thought that once they returned to their own time, these experiences would probably bond them even more tightly, like the bond that forms between soldiers in battle. He wondered if they would ever get home to find out. He remembered the closeness of his own family, and it took a great effort to dispel the disquieting thought that he may never see them again. He was not going to let those thoughts cause him to panic; he would keep his mind focused on the situations he could deal with. He would draw strength from his knowledge of the great explorers, those men and women who had been first to enter new territories on land, sea, and space. They had chosen to put themselves at risk to open new horizons to the rest of their fellow men, and he would feel honored if he could even approach the bravery of those great persons. He only wished he had gotten to choose his path, rather than have it thrust upon him.

The next morning, Tom awoke feeling refreshed and anxious to begin doing his part for the Ward family. After enjoying a copious southern breakfast prepared by Woyi and Ahni, Tom, Guwaya, and John Carter began loading the supplies to bring to the cavern hideaway. The two extra men and horses would allow Guwaya to expedite the stocking of his hideout, although they would need to be especially cautious to avoid detection—three men with horses loaded with supplies would certainly draw questions if they happened to be seen.

Guwaya used a stick to draw a crude map in the dust, illustrating the route he would take to reach the cave, referencing several natural landmarks. They planned to travel together with Guwaya leading the way, so the directions were only a precaution if they happened to get separated. Guwaya explained that they would take an indirect route using lesser known trails to avoid happening upon another traveler. That prospect seemed unlikely to Tom; even the most direct route involved copious twists and turns due to the mountainous terrain. The area was so remote he could not imagine crossing the path of anyone by chance.

Leading the heavily loaded horses, they set off on an equestrian trail leading from the far side of the farm. The Ward's rustic mountain homestead was situated deep within the mountains of Georgia, and they didn't travel far before the trail turned into a steep mountain path. The narrow switchback snaked up the mountainside, a sheer rock face on one side and a steep drop-off on the other. Falling rocks, knocked loose by the horse's hooves, hollowly clacked as they tumbled down the slope.

The horses appeared to be undaunted by the precarious trails. They reminded Tom of the extreme mountain bike trails he had ridden in West Virginia. He didn't mind bicycling on steep, single-track trails, but horseback riding on such a steep trail where he had to depend on an animal's surefootedness rather than his own biking abilities made him uneasy. He was relieved to be walking on this trail rather than riding.

After crossing the first ridge, the trail became even more rugged. They were essentially following deer paths barely wide enough to accommodate the horses. Guwaya led them up scree littered slopes, across ridge tops, and down through ravines. He pointed out the landmarks he had indicated on his map as they passed each of them; a huge moss-covered boulder, a small creek, a uniquely twisted tree, and so on.

Tom wondered about the man's familiarity with these trails. What reason would he have had to be this deep in the mountain wilderness; hunting trips, perhaps? Then again, when he recalled some of the remote places he had ventured while growing up in Virginia—he probably could follow a path using some of the same sort of landmarks in his home stomping grounds, though not quite as deftly as Guwaya was able to.

It took them about three hours of fast-paced hiking, as fast-paced as the terrain allowed, to reach the caverns. They were standing at the edge of a precipice when Guwaya announced their arrival. From the cliff edge, Tom could see a broad panorama of the mountain range they had just hiked through, but saw neither a cave nor any place where there could be an entrance to one.

"It is easy enough to climb down to the entrance, but I brought along a ladder to make it easier for us to unload the supplies," Guwaya said as he unpacked a rope ladder and anchored it to a sturdy tree near the edge of the cliff.

Tom looked down over the edge. It was a drop of several hundred feet with nothing more than treetops below. The cliff was very steep, the rocks smooth and rounded with no obvious footholds for climbing. He closely examined the place where Guwaya's rope ladder dangled, about twenty feet below the cliff's edge. He could barely make out a tiny ledge that appeared to be nothing more than a ripple of rock on the cliff side.

Guwaya hoisted one of the smaller bundles onto his shoulder and headed down the ladder. "With three of us, we can relay the supplies to the cave. I will take this bundle, and you two can pass the rest down to me." When he reached the bottom of the ladder, he stepped effortlessly onto the tiny ledge, disappeared from view for a few moments, then reappeared and said, "I am ready when you are."

"That's certainly a well hidden entrance to his cave," said Tom.

"Most well hidden," John agreed. "It is a wonder that he found it." He stepped off the cliff and onto the ladder. "I will go halfway down to be the relay if you will unpack the supplies and hand them to me."

Tom nodded his agreement, and then began unpacking the supplies. He piled some of the items next to the cliff edge, then lay on his stomach at the top of the ladder and passed the bundles one at a time to John. It was only necessary for John to move a few rungs up and down the ladder as he relayed the bundles to Guwaya, who disappeared and reappeared from Tom's view as he took the supplies into the cave.

When the last bundle had been relayed, Tom led the horses several hundred yards from the cliff, into the woods where they could not be easily seen, and hobbled them so they could forage freely without wandering too far. He then returned to the ladder. Looking down, he saw John's head poking out from the side of the cliff. He gestured with a wave of his hand. "Come."

Tom was an experienced rock climber, and had no fear of heights or aversion to climbing down a rock face. He would have preferred to be equipped with some basic climbing gear, like a harness and safety rope, rather than a rope ladder tied to a tree. He set aside his safety concerns and climbed down the ladder.

Reaching the ledge, Tom could see that the foothold was merely a slight indentation in the rocky face of the cliff. Carefully stepping off the ladder, he took John Carter's offered hand and swung himself onto the cliff side to a wider ledge which had been hidden from view. From here he could see the opening to the cave, an oblong hole only about five feet high. The cave immediately angled sharply to the right, making it appear to be no more than a shallow depression in the rock. Once inside however, he could see that the cave opened up quickly to a large room-sized cavern expanding in all directions. A burning torch revealed the ceiling to be over ten feet high, and the cavern extended into the darkness beyond the reach of the torchlight. Guwaya had placed the supplies in a small alcove which was already extensively stocked with hanging joints of meat and an abundance of jugs and stacks of wooden casks, apparently containing food and drink. Another part of the cave had sleeping mats and a rustic table and chairs where he and John were seated. Tom sat down at the table and Guwaya filled a wooden cup with water from a jug for each of them.

"You appear to be well prepared for a long stay, Guwaya," Tom said, accepting the cup of water.

"And I feel better about the location," said John. "It is naturally well hidden, but not too inaccessible once you know the location. How did you find this place? I've hunted with you many times in this area and have even been to the cliff above, but I never knew the cave was here."

"I discovered it by accident during a hunting trip," Guwaya answered. "I sat at the top of this cliff taking in the beauty of the mountains, using my knife to repair a worn harness, when it slipped from my hands and tumbled over the cliff. I looked down and could see it landed on that tiny ledge. I climbed down to retrieve it and discovered this cavern. Had I not dropped the knife, I would have never had a reason to climb down here."

Tom thought that if it were him, he may have just left the knife rather than climb down the side of that steep cliff to retrieve it, but Guwaya had probably scrambled around on these mountains his entire life, so climbing down twenty feet without climbing gear would not trouble him.

"Won't it be difficult for your mother to get to the cave?" Tom asked. "And what about Sagi? Will he be safe staying here?"

"Everyone in my family has been here, more than once. Ahni is much more agile than she appears, and had no problem getting to the cave entrance, even without the ladder, which is good as I normally do not leave it in place. Sagi scrambles up and down the cliff with ease, not unusual for a youngster of his age."

Maybe not unusual for a Cherokee youngster, Tom thought, recalling how some parents were so protective of their youngsters they wouldn't let them get anywhere near the edge of a cliff.

"You said there was fresh water nearby?" said John.

"There is an underground spring that seeps into the cave. It has heavy mineral content, but is potable. And if you follow the cave to its end, it becomes very narrow, but eventually exits at the foot of the mountain. It is a tight passage, there are many jagged rocks and narrow places one must climb, but it is reachable in an emergency."

John nodded his approval.

"How did you manage to bring this table and chairs down here?" Tom asked.

Guwaya looked at him strangely, smiling at Tom as if he were a child asking a foolish question. "It wasn't a table and chairs when I brought it. I simply brought down the materials and assembled them here."

"Ah, of course," said Tom. "The nineteenth century version of IKEA furniture."

"IKEA?" John and Guwaya questioned.

"It's just a store that sells furniture you have to put together yourself."

"I already have to put together my furniture. Why would someone buy it if they still had to build it? It does not sound like a very good store to me," said Guwaya.

Tom remembered that they had not let Guwaya in on the time-travel thing, so he would have to be a little more cautious when he spoke.

"I will have to be leaving soon," John said, changing the subject. "I have much more travel ahead of me and will need to get started. I must go back to Red Clay to see if there is any more hopeful news."

Guwaya extinguished the lanterns, and the three men climbed back to the top of the cliff, where Guwaya rolled up the ladder and stashed it in a rock crevice. When they reached the horses, Guwaya and Tom said their farewells to John who rode off northward toward Red Clay.

"We can take a more direct route home," said Guwaya. "It is only necessary to take such a circuitous route when we are carrying supplies, to avoid explanations if someone were to see us. With the horses unburdened we can ride most of the way, and get home quickly."

Indeed, it was only about an hour before Tom began to recognize the landmarks that they had passed when they first left the cabin. It was good timing, Tom thought, since it was beginning to get dark. They bypassed the narrow, steep trails that they had followed before, but there were still several places that Tom thought would be a little too treacherous in the dark. He was also getting hungry and looking forward to another of Woyi's superb home-cooked meals.

Chapter thirty-five

om had plenty of opportunity to partake of Woyi's cooking over the next several days. He grew fond of the time spent with this close-knit family, and even began to enjoy the long, laborious days working side-by-side with Guwaya. Although many of their ways were foreign to him, within only a few days he began to understand the practicality of their traditions, and he began to notice similarities to his own family's customs. Observing the Ward's lifestyle helped him to understand how some of those traditions may have developed.

He especially enjoyed his time with little Sagi. The energy of the two-year old was boundless, and reminded him of his younger siblings when he was a child.

It had been nearly two weeks since John Carter brought Tom to the Ward farm. Most of his time had been spent working the farm, although he and Guwaya made two more treks to bring supplies to the cavern.

They were returning from the third trip, Tom anticipating another of Woyi's mouthwatering meals, when she suddenly appeared on the trail in front of them. Woyi ran toward them, *usdi* on her back and holding Sagi's hand, nearly dragging the boy along behind her.

"Wait, Guwaya!" she cried as she got closer.

Guwaya quickly dismounted and ran to his wife. "What is wrong? Why are you all the way out here?"

Woyi was wide-eyed and out-of-breath. "The men!" she said urgently. "They came to the house—they just came in. They took Ahni!"

"Who?" Guwaya's voice was fierce. "Who took my mother? Who were these men?"

Tom shuddered; the roundup of Cherokee families was beginning. So much for the theory that things might be different on this timeline, he thought. He said nothing, giving Guwaya a moment to reach the same conclusion. Tom lifted Sagi to his hip, comforting the young child who was sensing his parent's distress.

"It was the Georgia militia," Woyi said. Her voice quavered as she relayed the encounter. "I was out in the field with the children when they came, but when I saw them, I ran to the house. Ahni was watching for me and motioned for me to stay hidden. She pretended that she couldn't understand any English, so they had to bring in one of the men who spoke some Tsalagi. We hid close enough to hear what they were saying. He told Ahni that they came to take us all to the fort, where we must wait until they send us to the west.

"Ahni told them that we had already left for the western territory, like the story you planned, but they didn't believe her. They said we didn't go because all the animals were still here. She told them that that was why she was still here, to care for the animals and sell them, and send you the money. She told them you told her she was too old to go to the west, so you left her behind with the animals.

"The men seemed to believe her then. They laughed and said it was just like an Indian to run off and leave his old mother behind with the animals."

Guwaya bristled at that. He would never leave his mother behind, but he knew Ahni was clever to make up a story they would believe so Woyi and the children could escape.

Woyi went on. "They told her she would have to come with them. They would take her to a place where she would wait for removal to the west. Ahni protested; she told them she had to stay and take care of the animals or they would starve, but they told her to forget about the animals. They said they would belong to some other family now, a white family, and she had no choice but to come with them at once."

"Do you know where they took her," he asked. "How long ago did this happen?"

"It was about an hour ago, and I heard them say they were taking her to Fort Cummings. But I also heard the man in charge tell a couple of men to search the surrounding area in case we were really still there. I did not go back in the house; I ran here to warn you."

Guwaya nodded firmly. "That was the right thing to do." His hand rubbed the back of his neck as he considered what they should do next. "I must rescue Ahni, and there are still some things we could use at the house. I will go there first and try to sneak inside. You and Tom take the children and horses and go to the cave."

"Hold on, Guwaya," said Tom, placing a restraining hand on Guwaya's rock-hard shoulder. "Let me go to check out the cabin. You should stay with your family. Let me know what you need, and I'll get it from the cabin if I can."

"Thank you for the offer, Tom." Guwaya shook his head. But I cannot ask you to put yourself in such danger."

"It will be less dangerous for me than for you. If they see me, they won't know who I am. I can just say I was out hunting, got lost, and found my way to the cabin. They would have no reason not to believe me. I'll get your things if I can, and then we can take your family to the cave." Tom handed Sagi to him.

"You are right; you will probably have a better chance than I to make it to the cabin. But I cannot go to the cave—I must rescue my mother."

"You realize it will be extremely difficult to reach her if she has been taken to a fort. It will be well guarded, of course."

"I am not afraid of the militia," Guwaya said brusquely.

"I am not implying that you are. Did Ahni appear to be in imminent danger?" he asked Woyi.

"No. The men were rough, but they were not physically abusive. At least not that I observed," she answered.

"Then, Guwaya, don't you think it would be best to take advantage of the opportunity she gave you, at much risk to herself, to get everyone else to safety? Once there, we can consider a rescue plan."

Guwaya considered Tom's words, looking at his son who was clinging tightly to his shirt. "Once again you are right, Tom. I am letting my emotions cloud my judgment. I will return to the cave with my family and wait for you to join us. Can you find your way to the cabin and back again to the cave, even in the dark?"

"I can," Tom confirmed. "It's not that far to the cabin. I'll leave the horse with Woyi, and meet you back at the cave as soon as I can."

Guwaya told Tom which items he would like from the cabin, and where they were located. He wanted Tom to retrieve several weapons he had hidden and some gold coins he had been saving. Usually, he would not bother with money for a stay in the wilderness, but he thought under the circumstances a need for the coins may arise. There were other things he would have liked to have, but he did not want to make Tom carry more than necessary. He shook Tom's hand earnestly and urged him to use caution. He reminded Tom that the men may be watching the cabin. "At the least sign of danger, forget the things in the cabin and return to the cave."

Tom assured him he would be vigilant and headed down the trail.

He was within sight of the cabin in under a quarter of an hour. Approaching from the rear, he paused at the edge of the woods to observe the cabin. It was dusk, not quite dark. A blessing, he thought—dark enough to provide cover, but light enough to see his way. The insects and other night creatures had begun their nocturnal symphony, suppressing the sound of his approach. There was about a hundred yards of meadow between his position and the cabin, most of it covered in tall grass, waving deceptively serene in the evening breeze.

The cabin was still, but he could hear an intermittent plinking sound coming from the side of the cabin, blind to him in his current position. He edged his way to a better vantage point, keeping within the cover of the woods. He heard laughter, followed by two distinct voices. He could now see the two young men; neither looking barely more than twenty years old. They were sitting on stumps, tossing rocks at a wash basin they had propped up to make a target. Great luck, he thought, they were absorbed and making enough racket to cover up his approach. He realized he would have to move quickly, darkness was descending and soon there would not be enough light for the men to continue their rock tossing game.

Tom picked up a handful of black mud and rubbed it onto his face and forearms, darkening his white skin to dull any reflections from the fading light. He lowered himself onto his hands and knees and began creeping toward the opposite corner of the cabin, keeping his back below the level of the grass.

He stopped again when he reached the end of the tall grass. There was about another hundred feet to the cabin, but he would have to cross an area where Guwaya had scythed the grass short for a yard. He could still hear the stones clanking into the washbasin and the men's voices. They were not visible, which meant he wasn't visible to them as long as they kept their game going. Even so, the apprehension of crossing the open area caused his heart to pound. Taking a deep breath, he felt the adrenaline kick in as he rose to a crouching position and scampered swiftly across the yard. He reached the corner of the porch and ducked behind it for cover in case his approach had been heard. He froze in position, held his breath, and listened.

Another plink and more laughter. Tom willed himself to begin breathing again, slow and controlled, doing his best to calm his racing heart. He told himself that they were just teenagers, more interested in throwing rocks than watching for him. He also assumed they were armed, and knew that folks in this century were less likely to hesitate before resorting to violence. Still, he should be able to easily get into the cabin and retrieve

Guwaya's items without alerting them. If only they would keep playing their rock throwing game.

Tom silently vaulted onto the porch, stepping lightly as he moved toward the cabin's back door. He cringed and paused with each creak of the floorboards; even though there was no way the faint sounds could carry far enough to be heard. The door stood open; not unusual for a nineteenth century rural home, especially a Cherokee home where the doors were only closed during times of the most inclement weather. He paused once again just inside the cabin until he heard another stone being tossed, then made his way hastily to the bedroom where the weapons and money were stashed.

Crouching next to the bed, he looked underneath. A Kentucky longrifle had been secured beneath the mattress, tied to the ropes running between the bed frame supports. He untied the rifle, and laid it on the floor next to him, then reached back under the foot of the bed bringing out a buckskin game bag. He opened the bag, checking that it contained the items Guwaya said it did—powder, lead balls, and cleaning supplies for the weapons, and a small pouch heavy with coins. The final item he pulled from under the bed was a pistol, a muzzleloader pistol matched to the caliber of the rifle. He stood up, sticking the pistol into his belt, slung the strap of the bag over his shoulder, and picked up the rifle.

He breathed a little easier now that he had recovered the weapons. He couldn't hear the stone throwing from inside the cabin, and glancing out of the window showed it was quickly becoming dark. It would not be long before the two men would give up their game due to the fading light. He hefted the heavy longrifle, and swiftly strode to the door. All he needed to do was make his exit and sneak back across the exposed area around the cabin. Once he reached the woods, he would once again have adequate cover. Two steps away from the open door his exit path was suddenly blocked. The two men stood in the opening, obviously startled by his presence.

Their shocked faces quickly turned hostile. With eyes narrowing menacingly, one of the men spoke. "Who the hell are you?" he glared.

Chapter thirty-six

Adam caught up with Jimmy at the barn, where he was gathering the tools they needed for the morning chores.

"I got a little behind on the apple pruning," said Jimmy. "Too much time going to meetings and such. Most of the pruning should be done before the trees start to bud. With your help we can catch up pretty quick. The mature trees don't need as much care as they did when they were first planted. You helped Benjamin to prune peach trees, so it's the same idea with the apple trees. We just get rid of the deadwood and any overlapping branches."

"I always thought of apples as a cold weather fruit," said Adam. "I'm surprised that you can grow them in Georgia."

"They do pretty well here in northern Georgia because we have the cooler temperatures from the mountains. They aren't grown so much further south, though."

They carried the tools, lopping shears, saws, and a wooden crate to use as a step stool to the orchard and began pruning. Jimmy explained how when the trees were young he had to spread hay as mulch to keep down the weeds. Now that the trees were more mature he could just scythe around them once in a while. "It's still tiring work, especially when it gets really hot. Besides pruning, there's the harvesting and I have to fertilize in the fall. My small orchard is pretty easy to care for now, though. And I've never had a problem chasing down and catching any of the trees," he teased, chuckling as he gave Adam a friendly slap on his back.

"Very funny," replied Adam, remembering his embarrassing experience with catching sheep. He returned the conversation to apples. "Do you sell the apples at the market?"

"Usually we do. Depends on what else we have going. I mentioned that we also have tobacco and peanuts, and sometimes there is barely enough time to keep up with it all. If we have the extra time, Rebecca will make a few large batches of applesauce. Once the applesauce is put up, we can sell it during the off season. The applesauce is more profitable in years when apples are plentiful and the market price drops. Of course making and canning the applesauce costs us a little more, and takes more work, but we earn a little extra from our crop."

"That's what we would call value-add. It's a smart way to increase your profits by adding something extra to your product. You and Rebecca seem to be pretty savvy about farming, making sure you have the right amount of crops and livestock to make a living, and covering for all eventualities," Adam said.

"It is a balancing act sometimes. Even with all our planning we can still have bad years. That's one reason it would be devastating to be forced to move to another part of the country. We know this area, what to expect for climate, what crops will do well and which ones won't. Out west we would have to relearn a lot about farming in that part of the country."

"You'd still have your agricultural services ideas, though," Adam offered. "If you had to relocate, you could develop those ideas to generate revenue for your living."

"As excited as I get about developing technology, I'm not foolish enough to give up my familiar, reliable way of making a living. Those ideas are dreams, speculation that might eventually come to fruition. I wouldn't want to give up farming until I had first proven I could make a living from the farming services."

"Of course you're right," said Adam. "I didn't mean to suggest that relocating would be an easy thing for you to do." He thought about his own situation, where losing his job led to starting his own business. "It would certainly be a terrible loss if you had to give up your homeland. If that happens, you'll be forced to alter your lifestyle. It's possible that over time things might work out for the best. I mean, as far as making a living goes. Keep in mind I'm speaking from my own point of view, my future, where removal is a foregone conclusion."

"I cannot allow myself to believe that removal is inevitable," Jimmy declared. "But if it does happen, I hope for my family's sake I will still be able to provide for them. I believe such a disruptive upheaval would not be very conducive to starting a new enterprise."

From what Adam could remember about the Indian Removal, Jimmy was right. The turmoil would be tremendous. Even though they were initially greeted warmly, the arrival of so many new Cherokee emigrants in the Arkansas Territory eventually caused severe discord with the "Old Settlers," the Cherokee that were already there, and a civil war erupted.

Adam realized the situation Jimmy was facing was much more severe than his job loss. He didn't want to risk insulting him with an example of how things had worked out for him, and decided it was not a good topic of discussion. He changed the subject to something more pleasant for both of them—technology. Adam had no idea what the time-travel rules were, nor what might cause a paradox, but he felt the need to use his knowledge of the future to give him some sort of advantage. He saw no harm in giving Jimmy a few insights into the technological developments that were in store for him.

"In my version of history," Adam began, "mechanization had the most profound effect upon agriculture. I'm sure you've thought about the power of the locomotives. The country is currently in the process of laying railroad tracks across the country. You have certainly considered the advantage of the steam engine over horse power."

"I have," Jimmy answered, "and I've even attended some demonstrations of steam-powered engines on the farm. However, they have mostly proven to be too heavy, huge, and cumbersome to be used practically."

"At the moment, that's true. It's going to take another few decades of improvements in engine technology for them to become useful for agriculture. But, even though you can't accept that my timeline is unavoidable, you can surely see that technological advancement is inevitable. Invention will happen, and those on the forefront of the successful endeavors will prosper."

Jimmy nodded. "I will agree that the advancement of technology must occur. Short of a collapse of civilization, that much is unavoidable."

"There will be many labor-saving machines invented, such as your cotton gin that will revolutionize farming. Even before a replacement for the horse comes along, many practical apparatuses will be adopted. There was an inventor in my home state of Delaware, name of Oliver Evans, who used steam engines to power a grist mill. He built the first automatic flour mill."

"Sure, I've heard of Oliver Evans. He contributed much to the automation of agriculture with his inventions before he passed away. He also was working on a steam-powered vehicle, although with limited success."

"When you think about it, as the population grows and more inventions come about to produce crops more efficiently, the need for better ways to harvest, process, and store crops and grain will increase exponentially. It may be to your advantage," Adam continued, "to seek out and team up with an inventor whose ideas are compatible with yours. Attending a college or technical institute is a good way to meet an engineer like Oliver Evans. There is a man by the name of Cyrus McCormick, who I understand has just completed improvements on an innovative device his father worked on for years—a horse-drawn reaping machine. I'm willing to bet that his invention makes a significant contribution to agriculture. If you could hook up, uh, I mean meet, someone with mutual ideas of farm machine mechanization it would be to your benefit."

"I believe I have heard something of his machine. It is a good idea to attend a technical institution. Doing so would be difficult with so much to do on our farm, but you have encouraged me and I will discuss it with Rebecca. And maybe someday I will make Mr. McCormick's acquaintance."

Encouraging Jimmy to go to school, enticing him with Oliver Evans' inventions, and giving him Cyrus McCormick's name was about as close to creating a predestination time paradox that Adam was willing to risk. He was committed to doing what he could to lessen the suffering of his new friends. His principles demanded that he do something to give Jimmy a reasonable chance of success after he was relocated. It was quite possible, with his interest in agricultural technology, that Jimmy would find a way to attend a university anyway. Adam figured he wasn't meddling with destiny too much.

They were still working in the apple orchard when they heard the sound of horses thundering up the Deerinwater farm lane. Adam cast a quick glance at Jimmy, whose startled expression revealed he was not expecting visitors. Under normal circumstances, the Deerinwaters would welcome guests at any time. These days, strangers approaching his farm were a cause for alarm.

They could not see the lane from the orchard. They dropped their tools at the foot of the tree they were pruning and headed to the farmhouse at a run. Jimmy sprinted ahead, easily outpacing Adam and entering the farmhouse through the open back door. Before he reached the door, Adam could hear angry voices coming from the house. He felt an icy chill when he recognized one of the voices as belonging to Jeb Barnett, the head man of the Georgia militia unit that had accosted them.

He heard Jimmy shout "Get out of my house!" as he entered the farmhouse, just in time to see Jeb strike Jimmy's midsection with a vicious jab from the butt of his rifle. Jimmy expelled a great "oomph" as he dropped to the floor. Rebecca cried out and knelt to minister to Jimmy, who was clutching his abdomen and gasping for breath. Two other men that Adam recognized as some of Jeb's minions from the other day stood behind him, fully armed and smirking. Adam could see several other men standing with the horses outside the front door. Jeb drew back his rifle as if he was preparing to strike again.

"Learn him good, Jeb," said one of the minions.

"Keep away from him!" Adam cried as he placed himself protectively between Jeb and Jimmy.

"You're gonna be next, half-breed," Jeb snarled.

"Just tell us what you want," said Adam. He could hear his voice tremble in spite of his efforts to keep his fear from coming through. "There's no need for violence."

"I'll damn well be as violent as it takes!" Jeb grabbed Adam by a handful of shirt, and putting his face as close to his as he could, snarled, "What I want is you all outa here, right now! My orders are to git all the injuns livin' here to the fort right now, including you. Adam could smell Jeb's disgusting breath, a mixture of whiskey, tobacco, and gum disease, wafting in his face with each word. Jeb gave Adam a shake and pushed him back with a vicious heave. He raised his rifle once again, preparing to strike Adam.

"Don't hit him!" cried Rebecca. "We'll go to the fort, if you want. Just please don't hurt anyone else."

Jeb lowered the rifle and leered at Rebecca, as if seeing her for the first time.

"Since you asked so nice, little squaw, just for you I won't clobber him. Just remember that when I want a little somethin' from you," he said, slithering closer to Rebecca and giving her a depraved wink.

"Stay away from my wife, you miscreant!" Jimmy tried to yell. He was still on the floor, and his words sounded strained and breathless.

"Shut up," said Jeb, punctuating his words with a kick to Jimmy's lower back. "All three of you git outside, now!"

Adam and Rebecca helped Jimmy to his feet, supporting him on each side as they moved toward the front door.

"I can make it," Jimmy whispered. "It will be better if I try not to show weakness."

Adam glanced at Rebecca, who nodded. They eased away slowly from Jimmy until they were sure his own legs would support him, then all three went out the front door, followed by Jeb and his lackeys. Outside were four more men, two small horse-drawn carts, and three saddled horses. The three hesitated and immediately Jeb shoved them from behind.

"Git these injuns tied up and loaded in the carts," said Jeb.

Two of the men tightly bound Adam and Jimmy's wrists behind their back with short, coarse lengths of rope, and then began to do the same to Rebecca.

"Is there a need to tie my wife's hands?" Jimmy demanded. "Are you afraid she will overpower seven men?"

The man stopped tying Rebecca's hands and looked at Jeb, who scoffed and waved the man away. It was the first act of borderline decency Adam had seen from Jeb and was tempted to take advantage of it.

"Will you at least let them gather a few of their possessions?" he said to Jeb.

"Injuns don't believe in no possessions," he replied tersely. "No more 'n an animal does." He paused for a moment, as if considering Adam's request. "But I guess I'll let 'em gather up a few things."

He scratched at his scraggly beard as he lecherously appraised Rebecca, his eyes wandering the length of her body. Adam noticed the leering grin and worried that Jeb's sudden show of decency was only a ruse for a more sinister agenda.

"Zack, you and Joseph get these two loaded up and on their way to the fort," Jeb said, indicating Adam and Jimmy, "and me and the other boys will foller along later in the other cart with the little squaw here and some of their things. Drop 'em off and wait for us in town. We'll be along soon enough."

"I'm not leaving my wife behind," Jimmy said firmly.

"Ya ain't, huh? Zack, git these two loaded up. If they give ya any trouble, shoot 'em," Jeb said with a daring glare at Jimmy.

Zack grabbed Jimmy by the arm and attempted to load him into the horse cart. Jimmy twisted from his grasp and said, "I'm not leaving without my wife!"

In one swift motion, Jeb stepped up behind Jimmy, retrieved a lead filled sap from his pocket, and with a snap of his wrist brought the blackjack down on the back of Jimmy's head. Jimmy instantly dropped unconscious to the ground. Rebecca shrieked as he fell.

"Now load him up. And ya better hogtie him so he don't give ya no more trouble when he comes to."

Zack and one of the others picked up Jimmy and heaved him roughly into the cart, then tied his ankles looping the rope through his bound wrists.

Jeb turned to Adam, slapping the blackjack against the palm of his hand. "How you wanna go? Lights on or off?"

Adam did not reply, but glanced at Rebecca who was trying unsuccessfully to hold back her tears.

"Please go with Jimmy," she said.

"But Rebecca…" He looked at her with uncertainty.

"You must go. I will be fine."

"Yeah, she'll be just fine," said Jeb mockingly. "Now git in the cart afore I bust your head, too."

Adam reluctantly climbed into the cart, sitting on the floor next to Jimmy. He was extremely uneasy about leaving Rebecca with Jeb and his four thugs. He felt completely helpless, having no option other than to do as he was told or suffer Jeb's violence. He was no coward; he would willingly resist if he thought it would be of any use. A struggle against these armed thugs would be futile. If he were knocked unconscious, or worse, he would be of no use to anyone.

He looked at the unconscious body of Jimmy, prostrate on the floor of the cart, then into Rebecca's tearful eyes. "I'll do what I can for him. And I'll demand to speak to the colonel about this as soon as I get to the fort."

"You do that," Jeb snickered. "Git 'em outa here, Zack."

Zack and Joseph climbed into the seat of the cart and with a curt flick of the reins Zack put them in motion. Joseph, a heavyset, slovenly looking man, sat facing backwards, gun drawn, keeping watch on Adam and Jimmy.

Sitting low in the cart, Adam quickly lost sight of Rebecca. He knew it wasn't a very long ride to the fort at New Echota. He would speak to the colonel as soon as they arrived, and make him aware of the transgressions of Jeb. Surely a United States military officer would not condone this sort of thuggish behavior, and would send out a few soldiers to assure Rebecca's safety. He turned his attention to Jimmy, still unconscious and laying in a terribly contorted position. His legs, flailing with each bump in the road, were pulling against his arms and cinching the rope tighter with each bounce. He looked at Joseph and asked, "Is it really necessary to hogtie him that way? He's hardly a threat while he is unconscious."

"I'll untie him when we git to the fort," Joseph replied.

Adam shifted his position, putting his back toward Jimmy so he could use his hands to try and pull him into a more natural position.

"Don't be a-fussin' with him 'less ya wanna be hogtied too," snarled Joseph.

"I'm just trying to keep the ropes from cutting off his circulation. If he's crippled when we get to the fort, you'll have to carry him." The look on Joseph's plump face confirmed what Adam expected—the man didn't relish doing any more physical labor than absolutely necessary.

Joseph grunted and said, "Just don't try anything funny. I'd just as soon shoot ya both right now and save myself the trouble of foolin' with ya."

With some effort, Adam was able to move Jimmy enough to brace his feet against the side of the cart, giving him some relief from the strain of the rope pulling against his arms. Still, when he came to, Jimmy was going to be in plenty of pain, and extremely concerned for Rebecca if she had not yet made it to the fort.

He turned back to face Jimmy, looking him over. There was no blood as far as he could see. Adam knew that after sustaining such a brutal blow to the back of his head, Jimmy should be examined for signs of concussion. If his hands were free, he could at least inspect his pupils for disparity. Not much chance that his two guards would go along with that. A decent examination of serious head injury would have to wait until he was untied and Jimmy regained consciousness. If he was concussed, any further rough treatment could be deadly. The mental anxiety of being forced from his home and his worry about Rebecca could exacerbate a brain injury.

The ride to Fort Wool was mercifully short. Zack drove the cart unchallenged through the gates, receiving a curt nod from the guards, and proceeded to the large, newly constructed blockhouse.

"Two more for ya," said Zack to the soldier standing guard at the entrance to the blockhouse. "Some of that Deerinwater bunch."

"What the hell?" said the soldier. "This one's out cold and trussed up like a chicken, and the other 'n don't hardly look injun to me."

"He gave Jeb a bunch o' lip, so he had t' conk him one. That other 'n was with 'em. Half-breed, I guess."

"You're only supposed to round up the injuns, ya know. Not every dang half-breed in the county."

"He was with Deerinwater and they was on Jeb's list. I ain't about t' be arguin' with Jeb. Ya'll can sort 'em out here."

Adam was fairly certain he could get himself released. He would not be listed on the Georgia Cherokee census, and his physical appearance was more European than Native American. Not having any way to prove his identity might be a problem; then again, he doubted that anyone in this century carried proof of identity. Driver's licenses didn't exist yet and passports were uncommon. He might receive some questioning about his being in Georgia, for which he could probably find some credible explanation. For the moment he needed to remain in the fort. His priority was to determine Jimmy's condition and make sure he received medical attention if he needed it, and to speak to the fort commander about the treatment they had received from Jeb's gang, and to express his concern for Rebecca's safety. He needed to convince him to send someone after her if she didn't show up soon.

"I demand to speak with Colonel Lindsey immediately," he said to the soldier as he was pulled from the cart.

For a moment the soldier stared at him slack-jawed. Then he burst into uproarious laughter, joined by Zack and Joseph.

"Ya do, do ya?" he said through his guffaws. "Well, then, I best make sure he knows about yer demands. No doubts he'll want to change in t' his best dress uniform fer ya, an' order up some refreshments fer the two o' ya," he said with a wink to Zack and Joseph and more snorts of laughter.

Adam stared defiantly at the soldier. "For your own sake, you better make sure you tell him. I wouldn't want to be in your shoes when he finds out you incarcerated a non-Cherokee."

"I'm sure he'd be real upset about it," the soldier said with a smirk. "He'll be dealin' with ya soon enough." The soldier's expression changed just enough to reveal that Adam had instilled a little doubt, hopefully enough that he would bring it to the colonel's attention rather than risk a reprimand for his inaction.

Joseph was busy untying Jimmy's feet while Zack dumped a canteen of water onto his head. Jimmy stirred and let out a low moan. Zack and Joseph began pulling him from the cart, causing him to wince in pain as his cramped muscles protested the abuse.

"This man needs medical attention," Adam said severely. "He has been mistreated for no reason."

"Well, I could get him some medical attention," said the soldier, "but right now our veterinarian is tending to some sick pigs. And they're more important than this here injun," he said, getting more snorts and snickers from Zack and Joseph.

"I'm fine," said Jimmy, not very convincingly. "Where is Rebecca?"

"You should be checked by a doctor," said Adam, avoiding his question. "He gave you quite a knock on the head. It could be more serious than you realize."

"I ain't got time to be listenin' t' all this jabberin'," said the soldier, as he opened the gate to the stockade. "Get inside, then ya'll can chinwag all ya want," he said, shoving them both through the gate, causing Jimmy, still not fully in control of his balance, to go sprawling to the ground.

Adam crouched alongside Jimmy, awkwardly trying to help him to his feet—not an easy task as both still had their hands tied behind their back. Together they stumbled to a place against the rough-hewn timbers of the stockade wall, where they slunk to the dirt floor. For a few moments they said nothing, looking around at the other people inside the stockade. There were people of all ages; men and women both young and old, and perhaps a dozen children. Some were obviously families, sitting together on the ground. Others appeared to be lone individuals, sitting alone or leaning against the wall. They heard some low murmurings from parents attempting to console frightened children, along with an undercurrent of stifled weeping. Mostly the compound was eerily quiet. No one looked directly at them. Many sat staring at the ground, although Adam noticed a few unfriendly glances at him—certainly not the kindly Cherokee faces he had gotten used to. These were looks of distrust, even hostility. Not completely unexpected, he thought, given that he was obviously a member of the race who had subjected them to this indignity.

Adam could see the roof of the fort's blockhouse above the walls which provided barracks for the soldiers, and an attached parapet-like structure serving as a guardhouse overlooking the stockade. Inside the walls were two additional sheds which housed sleeping bunks for the detainees. Along the far wall was a shallow, open trench bordered on one side by a low rail; presumably the stockade toilet facility.

He turned his attention to Jimmy, looking into his pupils for signs of concussion and thankfully finding none. "How are you feeling?" he asked.

Jimmy did not respond. He looked at Adam as if he had just asked him the dumbest possible question.

"I mean physically. I'm only trying to make sure you haven't been seriously injured. How is your head? Are you feeling dizzy or nauseous?"

"It hurts. But I will be fine. I was a little dizzy but I am getting better."

"We can sit here for a while so you can rest a few minutes."

Jimmy shook his head. "What about Rebecca? Where is she?"

"She will be here soon. They are bringing her here with some of your possessions," Adam said, realizing as he spoke how naïve he sounded.

Jimmy put his head into his hands and looked at the ground.

"I wondered how long it would be before they brought you in, Deer-inwater," said a voice, startling Adam and Jimmy. The man had quietly approached before either had noticed.

"Jesse!" said Jimmy. "I see they have brought you here, too."

"We came in voluntarily about a week ago," Jesse replied. "They only started bringing folks in by force a couple days ago. You look like you have been beaten up. Where is Rebecca? Is she okay?" He glanced suspiciously at Adam, crouched beside Jimmy and began removing the rope binding his wrists.

"This is Adam, a friend of our family," Jimmy said, flexing his shoulders and rubbing his wrists, "who has been staying with us for a few days. I suspect I would have been beaten much worse if not for his and Rebecca's intervention. We were forcibly brought here and made to leave Rebecca behind with Jeb Barnett and his men. They are supposed to be bringing her and some of my things, but…"

"I understand. You have much cause for concern with those men, although this place does not offer much more safety." He motioned for Adam to turn and allow his wrists to be untied. When they were unbound, he offered his hand to Adam and said, "*Osiyo*, Adam."

"*Osiyo*, Jesse. Are you saying there have been people mistreated right here in the fort?"

"Some quite savagely. Many have been beaten. There have been several wives and daughters taken by the soldiers and…," he stopped, seeing the horror in Jimmy's widened eyes. "There have been incidents, but I have heard it is worse in the other, more remote forts."

"Then I must get to see Colonel Lindsey immediately and get a stop put to this. I'll have him send an escort for Rebecca."

"Lindsey heads the Georgia militia, and is not likely to find fault with Barnett and his men. You may find yourself thrown into his brig, or worse."

"There must be something I can do. Someone I can appeal to for justice. To make sure no harm comes to Rebecca."

"You could get released," Jesse told him. "You are obviously not Tsalagi. They have no reason to keep you. If you were free, you could go back to Jimmy's place and help Rebecca."

"He may be able to get released," said Jimmy, "but what good can a single, unarmed man be against those five thugs? He would be lucky not to be killed. The two of us were helpless against them before."

"But this time," said Adam, "they won't know I'm there. I can sneak back and at least see that she is not being mistreated. If she is, I'll find a way to get her away from them."

"I am extremely concerned about my wife, but you would be risking your life. I cannot allow you to endanger yourself to that degree." Jimmy lowered his head back into his hands and muttered to himself despondently.

Adam placed his hand on Jimmy's shoulder. "I don't see how you can prevent me," he said resolutely.

Chapter thirty-seven

al awoke with a moan. He was laying prostrate, sharp bits of gravel
grinding into his face, each effort to move greeted by an acute reminder
of his battle with the river rocks. His bruised and battered body declared
the rocks victorious; they had given him a thorough thrashing. Slowly and
gently rolling onto his back, he felt a sickening ache in his groin where
he suffered one rock's particularly vicious assault. Ignoring his protest-
ing shoulder muscles, he raised his hand to his face and began picking
out the rock fragments that were embedded in his cheeks and forehead.

The sound of the rushing river filled his ears as he conducted a more
thorough evaluation of his condition. He was hurting, bruised, and battered, but apparently he still had all his parts attached and no bones were
broken. Flinching abruptly, he recalled the calamitous rifle shots and the
wound that had been inflicted on Yonah. Rising judiciously to one knee,
he turned toward the Cherokee, who lay motionless on the shore next to
him. With great relief Sal detected the shallow rise and fall of the old man's
chest; at least he was still breathing. He carefully shifted Yonah's position
enough to inspect the gunshot wound. It was bleeding, but fortunately the
cold river water had slowed the flow significantly. He tried not to move
Yonah too much, fearing he would cause the bleeding to increase. He
cautiously performed a cursory examination which revealed the wound
was mostly superficial. It appeared that the rifle ball had been relatively
small, perhaps twenty caliber, and had passed through the flesh of Yonah's
upper arm without striking bone, or worse, severing an artery.

"Good thing those boys were hunting small game, Tonto," he said
quietly to the unconscious Cherokee. "A fifty caliber slug probably would
have taken a good chunk of your arm off."

He searched his pockets and found his soaking wet bandana. Rins-
ing it thoroughly in the river, he used it to cleanse and bind the wound.

Once he had the bandana in place to apply pressure, he gently rolled Yonah over onto his back, keeping his feet to the downhill side of the slight incline of the shore.

"Be a damn shame for you to wake up with all that gravel in your face, dude," said Sal, rubbing the indentations left in his own forehead. "Keeping your shoulder elevated will help slow the bleeding. Let's just hope you don't go into shock, and that you didn't crack your skull on that rock."

He agonizingly rose to his feet, wincing from the pain that shot through his body as he stretched. Having done all he could for Yonah, he scanned the landscape to get his bearings. He could hear the roar of the waterfall downriver, and began walking in the direction of the sound. In less than a hundred yards he was standing at the top of the falls, looking over the edge at the churning plunge pool more than eighty feet below. It was a magnificent view, but glancing back at the spot where they had come ashore, he shuddered at the thought of just how close they had come to tumbling into that churning chasm.

He inspected the rocky cliff below his feet, imagining the painful climb down. He had been expecting to portage around this knickpoint, but he hadn't counted on doing it with a damaged body. Fortunately for him it would be a while before Yonah was ready to make the descent. At least they didn't have to carry the canoe. Suddenly, the severity of that thought struck him. He had no idea how much further it was to Yonah's home, but walking was going to take a whole lot longer than a canoe ride.

Standing atop the rock he gazed into the flowing water, lost in thought, flexing the aching muscles of his arms. The events of the last few days had surpassed incredible. He remembered how eager he had been to complete the testing project, anxious to return to his familiar territory and activities. He chuckled as he thought about the excitement online role-playing games used to bring him. Even some of his more physical activities like biking, backpacking, even geocaching, which he previously considered demanding and exciting sports, seemed like childish play compared to his last few days. He realized that the experience of actual life and death situations and his first-hand involvement in the Cherokee struggle were affecting him much more strongly than anything else in his life ever had. It wasn't fear for his life or pity for the Indians. Yes, he felt those emotions, but he was feeling something much deeper, almost an epiphany, as if he were transforming from within. He had been made acutely aware that he took too much of his life for granted. He was now more motivated than ever to correct that. In these past few days his priorities had shifted. The things he previously considered important now seemed trivial, and things he considered inconsequential had become essential.

These atypical insights befuddled him; he had never before felt compelled to make his life count for something truly worthwhile. He was uncharacteristically concerned for the wellbeing of his friends. Anxious to reunite with them, not just for the comfort of their friendship, but to ensure they knew his true regard for them rather than the uncaring front he usually conveyed. Looking down at the treacherous climb and considering the potential perils he had yet to face, he wondered if he would get the chance.

From this viewpoint Sal could see the river slowly begin to flatten and calm beyond the falls, before winding out of view around the next bend. He was looking southward, downriver, and evening was coming on quickly. To his left, the bottom of the descending sun was nearly touching the tops of the western mountains, its deep orange-red glow reflecting on the misty splashes of the waterfall, creating a brilliant scarlet spray of aquatic fireworks. He turned away from the falls and walked back to shore where he had left Yonah.

"For a moment I thought you had gone over the falls," he heard Yonah's voice, slightly breathless with suppressed pain, "but then I realized it had to have been you who dressed my arm."

"Hey, dude, both of us nearly went over," said Sal, glancing over his shoulder to the top of the falls. "I'm happy you're awake. Your arm doesn't look too bad, but I was worried about the bash on the noggin you took when you smashed into that rock."

Yonah pursed his color-drained lips. "Is that what happened?" he said, rubbing the knot on his head with his uninjured arm. "They both hurt like hell, but I've been hurt worse."

"Yeah, well, you should lie still and get some rest, though."

"I intend to." He squinted at Sal. "You are not actually showing compassion for me, are you?"

"No more than I would for anyone, dude," Sal snapped. "I just don't want you to waste the effort I put into dragging your butt out of the river, that's all."

"It must have taken much effort," said Yonah sincerely, looking out at the swirling rapids. "You had to fight that strong current to get us both to safety. It would have been much easier to only save yourself. I have apparently underestimated you, and I apologize for that. You have saved my life, and I am greatly in your debt."

"You're welcome," said Sal, "but you're not in my debt, man. I couldn't very well let you go over the falls, could I? After all, I need you to find my way out of here." He gave Yonah a wry smile.

"Which we need to do very soon. I do not wish to encounter those men in my weakened condition," Yonah replied.

"I think it best if we just camp right here for the night," Sal said. "If you move around too much it could open up your wound and start it bleeding again. Anyway, I'm pretty worn out. We should be safe from those rednecks on this side of the river. They probably figure we went over the falls."

"I hope you are right, Squirrel-man. For now, you are in charge. If you wish to spend the night here, we must find something better than river rock to sleep on."

"You're telling me, dude," said Sal, touching the pits left on his face by the gravel. "The weather is clear and it looks like it's going to stay that way, so we won't need a shelter. I'll just gather up some leaves to make sleeping a little more comfortable. Only problem is that we might get kind of hungry since we lost all of our supplies."

"There is a river full of food right in front of you," said Yonah.

"I'm sure there's plenty of fish, but how do you propose I catch them? I don't think I'd have much luck trying to scoop them out with my hands."

"You could try it Indian-style."

"Indian-style, huh? I guess I could give that a try." He picked up a fairly straight branch and began removing the leaves. "I managed to hold on to my pocketknife, at least." He opened the blade and began to whittle the end of the branch into a point. "I'll walk upstream a bit and try to find a pool with some fish in it, and see if I can spear one."

"You could do that." Yonah tried not to show his amusement. "But that would be the hard way."

"What do you mean, dude?" said Sal. "I thought you said I should get some fish Indian-style?"

Yonah unbuttoned his shirt pocket and retrieved a small stick wrapped with a coil of string and a couple of hooks. "I did. But most Indians I know use a hook and line," he said with a lopsided grin. He held out the fishing line to Sal. "Lucky this stayed in my pocket."

"You're a real joker, Tonto, you know that? A regular Native American comedian." He grabbed the fishing line and tossed the branch aside.

Sal headed first to the woods, where he found plenty of dry leaves to use for bedding, then spent a few moments digging up worms to use for bait. He retrieved his branch-spear, to which he attached Yonah's hook

272

and line for a makeshift fishing rod. The fishing line was jute, spun from vegetable fiber. Monofilament was still an invention of the future.

He located a likely spot for fish along the river's edge. It wasn't long before he had a fish on, which he gently caressed to shore, careful not to break the delicate line. In less than an hour he returned with a couple of fish along with a few mussels he had pried from the river rocks.

Yonah nodded his approval at Sal's catch. "I agree that the shooters are probably no longer a threat, but it may be prudent to avoid making a fire. We should try not to draw any more unwanted attention. Besides, my flint and char-cloth is lost to the river."

"No problemo," said Sal. "An awesome helping of sushi is one of my favorite meals."

Sal cleaned and filleted the fish, and cracked open the mussels, letting the river wash away the waste, recalling Alice's chiding about attracting bears. That first night of camping seemed so long ago.

After they had eaten, he insisted that Yonah allow him to check and re-dress the gunshot wound. He gently removed the bandana, washing it in the river and dabbing the wound to remove some of the caked blood. So far, there was no sign of infection, but it was still a nasty, open wound that continued to bleed.

Yonah pointed to a clump of flowers growing at the edge of the forest. "Gather some leaves from those flat-looking flowers over there." Sal did as he was bid, plucking a handful of leaves from what looked like Queen Anne's Lace, and brought them back to Yonah.

"This is called Woundwort," Yonah said. "Some call it Yarrow. If you crush some of the leaves and mix it with some river water, it can be applied to the wound and will help stop the blood flow. It will also reduce the pain somewhat."

Sal mixed the leaves and water, crushing them into a paste using rocks from the river. He applied the green poultice as Yonah directed, and once again wrapped the wound with his bandana.

"I hope that helps, old man. At least enough so you can sleep. I'll check it again in the morning. For now, I think the best thing is for both of us to get some rest."

He heaped the leaves he had gathered earlier and fashioned a sleeping area for them. He helped Yonah into a comfortable position, and then situated himself for sleeping. "Not exactly a memory-foam mattress, but it's a hell of a lot more comfortable than those damn rocks," said Sal.

Even with the padding of the leaves, he could feel every rock poking into his bruised body. His muscles still ached, and the thought of spending the next few days, maybe even weeks, hiking through the mountains, weighed on his mind. He was exhausted, yet he knew he was in for a restless night. "Probably a lot worse for old Tonto," he thought, in a rare moment of compassion.

"I know you've got to be in a lot of pain, dude, but try to get some rest if you can." He looked over at Yonah, whose only answer was a snore, already soundly sleeping. "Man, that tough ol' bird probably enjoys sleeping on rocks," he muttered to himself.

Sal closed his eyes and tried to ignore his discomfort. He focused on the sound of the rushing rapids, letting it drown out Yonah's snoring, and eventually fell asleep.

In his dreams, he found himself back on the river, being accosted once again, this time by an entire army of guffawing yokels who stood on the banks of the river, drinking moonshine from brown jugs and bellowing foul invectives at him. He cursed them back with his usual vigor until he caught site of the weapon they were now leveling at him—a WW2 vintage Browning M2 .50 caliber machine gun. Probably could get those at the local Army surplus store, he dreamt.

He flattened himself in the canoe bottom as he heard the rat-tat-tat of the gun disintegrating the gunwale of the canoe, splinters of wood flying everywhere. He looked up to see Yonah sitting upright, impervious to the whizzing slugs flying around him. Yonah looked at him indifferently and said, "Must be squirrel season, white man."

He screamed as the machine gun ate away more and more of the canoe, until he finally awoke with a start. He looked around in panic, disoriented, still hearing the sound of the gun. His panic subsided when he realized the sound was a woodpecker, pecking out insects for his breakfast from a nearby tree. His relief quickly turned to embarrassment when he noticed Yonah, already awake, staring at him.

"Bad dream?" Yonah asked nonchalantly. "Not altogether unexpected after our misadventure yesterday. My own sleep was considerably restful and refreshing," he boasted.

"Just that damn woodpecker," said Sal, not bothering to elaborate. His heart was still racing from the nightmare. "Glad to hear you're feeling a little better. How is your head, dude? Do you have any dizziness?"

"It aches and I have a large lump. No dizziness. I have the hard head of a Cherokee warrior."

"That's for sure. What about the gunshot wound?"

Yonah had already removed the bandana and was tentatively probing his wound. "It is better, but too large to be left open. I think I will need to use some of our fishing line and one of the hooks to place a few stitches. It will be awkward for me to do it with one hand," he said with an inquiring look at Sal.

Sal shook himself fully awake and made his own examination of the wound. He could see that Yonah was right, it was going to take a few stitches to keep the gaping hole together so it could heal. "I'm not known for my sewing ability, but I'll give it my best shot."

Sal retrieved the fishing line and one of the hooks. He used a rock to grind off the barb and straightened it a little, leaving it slightly curved. He then threaded a short piece of the heavy fishing line through the eyelet. He washed it in river water, wishing he had a way to sterilize it. Sal was pretty sure antiseptic medicine hadn't been considered yet—he wasn't even sure if Lister had been born yet. Certainly no one had heard of using carbolic acid to sterilize a wound, although Yonah had probably been exposed to enough germs to be a lot more resistant to infection than he would be.

Sal wished he at least had a way to anesthetize the wound. He used cold river water to numb the area, but doubted it would help much once he began. He examined the area once again, visualizing the exact places he would make the stitches. He figured he would need at least three. That would mean six stabs to an obviously very painful wound, and then whatever fussing he would have to do to tie it off. He knew the Indian was a tough old dog, but he hoped this wasn't going to be more than he could take.

"This is going to hurt you more than it is me, dude."

Yonah simply turned his head and nodded.

He felt Yonah tense as he made the first stab with the hook, and felt him flinch again as he pulled the eyelet through the skin. He continued to work as tenderly as possible and as quickly as he dared. There was no sense in stopping to ask Yonah if he was okay or needed a break. The best he could do would be to work rapidly; thereby keeping Yonah's suffering to a minimum. Once again he passed the hook through the skin, gently pulling the line taught enough to hold the skin together. Yonah was silent, but tense, and the perspiration on his arm was making it difficult for Sal to hold onto. He hooked his left arm around Yonah's for a firmer grip, and continued with his stitching. Two more stitches to go.

He began the next stitch and heard Yonah's sharp intake of breath. "Sorry 'bout that."

"It is nothing," said Yonah. "Keep going."

Sal talked as he worked, helping to keep Yonah's mind on something besides the pain. "I'm worried about infection. That occurs because of dirt in the wound, so we'll have to keep it clean using the river water." He didn't think it would be a good idea to bring up the fact that the water was probably full of bacteria, not wanting to hear Yonah's reaction to being told it was full of tiny bugs too small to be seen. "It looks like that Yarrow stuff is already helping it to heal. It's a good thing you knew about it. Alice has some knowledge of medicinal plants, but I never got into it."

"Once you have stitched and bound the wound, you can apply more of the Yarrow poultice," said Yonah. "There are some other plants that will also help with healing, and I will look for willow bark to ease the pain. For now, the Yarrow, cold water, and sunlight will do."

"Your good night's rest also helped," Sal said as he pulled through the last stitch. "Hang on, I'm nearly done. I just need to tie off the end."

The wound had begun to bleed freely from the stitching, but at least Sal had managed to close up the hole somewhat. He rinsed his bandana again, washing away as much blood as he could before he applied more of the crushed Yarrow leaves.

"It's gonna leave an ugly scar," Sal said as he rewrapped the bandana around Yonah's arm, "but I think it will heal much more quickly now."

"*Wado*," said Yonah. "Once again I am in your debt."

"You're welcome, dude. I just hope you hold together long enough to get us out of here. It's going to be a pretty damn tough climb down that waterfall. And now we'll have to walk the rest of the way. Just how far is it to this mountaintop crib of yours?"

"Not so far, but it is very rugged country." Then with a wry smile he added, "Even for bears and squirrels. It would usually only take one full day of walking. We can follow the river for a short way, to the beginning of the canyon country, and then follow another trail that traverses less rugged terrain."

That news was a tremendous relief to Sal. The remoteness of the area led him to believe they were at least several days travel away from any-where. Hiking for a day or two, even in rough terrain, wouldn't be so bad.

Slowly getting to his feet, Yonah said, "We should begin right away. I know of a way down the waterfall that is not too strenuous, and once we are beyond this part of the river we can build a fire and prepare a proper meal."

"Sounds awesome to me, Tonto. Are you sure you can travel so soon?"

"I will be fine," he said confidently. "Let us go."

Yonah led the way to the top of the waterfall. He walked along the top of the rocks, away from the water, until he reached a trailhead that descended the mountain. The trail was rocky and narrow, with short, steep switchbacks, but was well used and it afforded them a much easier descent than Sal had anticipated. The river was a major transportation route, and Sal realized it should be no surprise that there was an established trail for portage past the waterfall. They were able to make their way down into the canyon with a minimum of climbing; only a few places on the trail required them to climb over some large boulders.

About half-way down they stopped, sitting on one of the boulders to catch their breath. Sal resisted asking Yonah how he was doing, knowing it would only aggravate the Indian if he excessively coddled him. He could see that the old man, who never usually revealed any signs of weariness, was breathing hard, and the bandana showed fresh blood seeping from the wound.

"We might have to find a way to immobilize your arm," Sal suggested. "It would be a shame to ruin my beautiful stitching job."

Yonah shrugged. "We will finish our descent first."

The remainder of the downward climb was less arduous. The switchbacks became wider and gentler. Near the end of the descent they scrambled over the talus pile at the bottom of the cliff, and made their way to the plunge pool at the base of the falls. The noise of the waterfall was much louder here, the crash of the cascading water echoing off of the canyon walls in a constant roar. They spotted the demolished canoe, rather what was left of it, lodged in between the rocks at the pool's edge.

The bow of the boat must have struck a rock full force at the bottom of the falls, shattering its frame. The scattered pieces looked like they had been hit by cannon fire, reminding Sal of his nightmare. They exchanged a silent glance, conveying a mutual thought—had they gone over the falls, their bodies would lie here amongst the devastation. Neither of them wanted to verbalize that thought.

They sorted through the wreckage hoping to recover some of their most useful items. They gathered some articles of clothing, drenched but otherwise intact, and a few odds and ends from Yonah's carry-sacks. Fortunately, the tin of flint and char-cloth survived undamaged, though the strips of cloth now looked like black globs of mud. Yonah shook the water from the tin and slipped it into his pocket. He picked up a small pouch and dumped its contents into his hand. He looked forlornly at his broken pipe and waterlogged tobacco, and then tossed them aside with a scowl. They found none of the *gahawista*; the parched corn had either floated away or been eaten by fish.

Yonah discovered his longbow farther down the river. The bowstring was missing, although the sinew cord would have been ruined by the water anyway. His quiver was nowhere in sight, but he found a few of the arrows and salvaged the surviving metal arrowheads. He would need to restring the bow and build some arrows, but finding the longbow meant they had some protection and an effective way of obtaining food.

"It is unfortunate the canoe struck the rocks as it did. I hoped it might be salvageable," Yonah said over the roar of the waterfall. "No matter—we will walk."

Moving away from the spray of the falls, Yonah stopped to remove the bandana and check his wound. "Your stitching has held fine, Squirrel-man. Our climb down the falls has started the bleeding again, however. I will have to be more careful."

Sal took the bandana from Yonah and rinsed it again in the river, then applied another layer of the Yarrow salve. Then he took one of the soaking wet shirts they recovered, wrung it out as best he could, and fashioned it into a sling.

"That oughta help keep your arm stable."

Yonah tied an additional loop in the cloth, slipped the sling around his arm and over his head, and then slid the longbow through the loop across his back. He made a few adjustments and when he was satisfied with the fit, nodded to Sal.

They continued walking, following the river southward as it descended into the canyon it had carved as it wound its way between the mountains. The canyon walls above the river became steeper, creating a spectacular hidden valley several hundred feet deep in some places. They climbed over several huge boulders along the river which had been chiseled by centuries of erosion, forming deep, watery grooves in the solid rock. Yonah became more relaxed and talkative as they progressed, sensing the nearness of his home quarter. He told Sal that he had taken many hunting trips into this canyon, and that there were numerous caves in the canyon walls which could be used for shelter. He suddenly left the path and headed for a patch of shrub-like plants, and began examining the reddish stems.

"Time to stop and pick some flowers, Tonto?" Sal watched him with interest. The old dude never did anything without good reason.

"This is Indian Hemp that I was hoping to find."

Sal didn't think it looked much like the hemp he was familiar with, and hoped the old man wasn't about to roll up a doobie from it. He made no comment, figuring the inscrutable Indian would explain more when he was ready, and not before.

"It is mid-morning, and this is a good place for a short stop," Yonah continued. "See if you can catch us a few more fish," he said as he began to pick some long stems of the Indian Hemp and pluck the leaves from them.

"Sure, no problemo. I'm an angler what knows all the angles," said Sal. "Hey you ain't gonna get buzzed on that stuff while I'm gone, are you, Tonto?"

Yonah looked at him quizzically, but did not reply.

Sal had been gone about three-quarters of an hour by the time he dug up some bait, found a good fishing hole, and caught a couple of fish. When he returned, Yonah had stripped fibers from the Indian Hemp and twisted them into a cord, which he was now using to string his longbow. He had also fashioned several arrows that he fitted with the salvaged arrowheads.

"I see you are becoming quite a good fisherman," said Yonah. "I will build a fire so we can eat them properly this time," he said, indicating the strips of char-cloth that had been laid out on a rock and allowed to dry in the sun. "This hemp cord is not as good as a sinew bowstring, but it will serve well enough." He inspected the bow and stretched the string approvingly. "I can provide meat for our next meal."

Once the fire was built, Sal cooked the fish while Yonah finished working on his bow. He put the final touches on his arrows by attaching some feathers for fletching and cutting a nock. He tested shooting a few arrows, awkwardly at first, trying not to move his injured arm any more than necessary. After a half-dozen shots, his aim improved and he was satisfied with the results. Setting the bow aside, he walked into the woods and returned after a few moments with a handful of bark. He then joined Sal next to the fire.

"This bark from the white birch tree can be boiled to make a mild pain-relieving potion," he told Sal. He crumpled some of the bark into his flint tin, added some river water, and set it on a rock next to the fire. "I will make enough for both of us. It will help relieve the pain of your overstressed muscles."

Sal thought that relieving all the pain his abused body was feeling would more likely require Percocet rather than tree bark, but he'd take whatever relief he could get.

By now the fish were ready, and both men devoured them with gusto. After the last few sparse meals of raw fish, the fire-roasted fish tasted exquisite. For dessert, they shared the analgesic birch-bark tonic, which Sal had to admit—it did relieve his sore and aching muscles considerably.

Nourished and revitalized they set off on the trail once again, walking at a brisk pace, yet somewhat slower than the first part of their journey.

Yonah said they should easily be able to reach the overland trail before dark, where they would depart the river taking a more direct route to his home.

"This canyon is awesome. I haven't seen many deep canyons like this in the southeast."

"The canyon becomes even deeper further south. However, we must climb out before reaching the deepest part. It is a very beautiful place, and an important area to the Cherokee. A few miles to the west is an important Cherokee town called Willstown. The whites built a fort there, commanded by Major Payne. A most appropriate name; he's been a real pain to us," he said with a wry smile.

"Sequoya lived there until he went to the western territory. Sequoya is the one who created the Cherokee syllabary so we could have a written language. Some of our legends say that our priests had a written language hundreds of years earlier. No one knows for sure, since we killed all the priests a long time ago when they began to think they were better than everyone else.

"Since then we have had only a spoken language. There wasn't much of a need for writing—our history is preserved in the stories that are told over and over again. Once Sequoya proved that his syllabary worked, everyone wanted to learn it. Now there is a higher percentage of Cherokee than whites who are literate. We even had a newspaper printed in English and Cherokee, the *Cherokee Phoenix*, which was printed in New Echota until the Georgia Guard destroyed the press. We hope that someday publication will be allowed to resume," he paused, not wishing to voice his further thoughts on that issue. He changed the subject.

"It is said that the Spanish explorer Hernando De Soto was the first white man to see this canyon about three hundred years ago. A very extraordinary man, though he caused much devastation among the Cherokee and many other tribes. He was strongly driven by an insatiable hunger for gold, the driving force of the so-called Conquistadors."

"From what I remember of my history, those Conquistador dudes really wreaked havoc on many peaceful civilizations."

"Wreak havoc they did, but those civilizations were hardly peaceful before the Conquistadors. The Incas were plagued by civil war, and capitalizing on their civil unrest was one of Francisco Pizarro's most effective strategies. Cortez formed alliances with the enemies of the Aztecs to defeat them. Both the Incas and Aztecs were aware of precious metals, and valued them highly. The Aztec society even permitted slaves, although it was not the same as the European version of slavery. Theirs was more of a form of punishment and not hereditary.

"The most devastating tragedy to those civilizations was the introduction of European diseases, such as smallpox, that annihilated much of their population. That was also the case here in North America. The smallpox brought here by De Soto reduced the Cherokee population by more than half."

The mention of De Soto sparked a memory for Sal. He seemed to remember a state park in Alabama, probably right in this area, which had been named in honor of De Soto. He wondered what Yonah's reaction would be to honoring the person who had decimated half the population of his nation by naming a part of their former homelands after him. While many would be insulted, he figured Yonah would be perversely amused by the irony.

By the time they reached the path out of the canyon, departing the river and climbing into the mountains, it was late afternoon. Even in the shadows of the canyon, the sun had warmed them nicely, drying out the articles they had salvaged from the river. The path switch-backed sharply up the steep canyon wall, bringing them to the crest of the ridge above the river. They paused at the top to take in the view of the towering mountain range to the west. Noticing Sal's look of dismay, Yonah assured him that they would not be climbing into the distant mountains.

"We will be traveling through the gap to the south. We still face a strenuous path. We will not need to climb much higher, but the trail is mountainous and we have several large creeks to cross. We should try to make another few miles before stopping for the night."

Sal assumed Yonah was feeling much better; Sal himself certainly was. Their pace had increased to become as brisk as it had been when they started out. The birch-bark tea had eased his pain greatly, the warming sun felt great, and he was finally completely dry after two days in damp clothing. The magnificent view from the top of the ridge recharged his spirit. He began to feel like his old brazen self, yet with a much deeper admiration of his traveling companion, and perhaps just a touch of humility.

"Lead on, Tonto," Sal replied, gesturing with a flourish.

Sal's hope of remaining dry for the remainder of the journey quickly faded when they reached the first creek crossing. It was not especially wide, but it was deep. They would need to wade waist-deep to reach the other side. He was pleased to hear Yonah suggest that they make an early camp and ford the creek in the morning.

"Better to keep dry for the night," Yonah said to Sal's agreement. "I will see if I can work my bow well enough to get us dinner. If we leave at first light, we will reach my home before midday."

They found a suitable spot close to the creek to spend the night. In the trees above their heads, Sal could hear rustling leaves followed by a screeching call, sounding like a cross between a bird and a cat. Yonah heard it also, motioned for him to be silent, and readied his bow. With more elegance than Sal would have thought possible having one arm bound by the sling, Yonah let loose an arrow, accurately finding its target. A squirrel, pierced through its mid-section by Yonah's arrow, fell at Sal's feet.

"Not a bad shot," said Sal approvingly. Actually, it was a superb shot, considering Yonah's wounded arm. Hitting a squirrel in a tree with a homemade bow and arrow was no simple feat. Sal offered no further praise. His admiration for Yonah had grown, but he was still Sal.

"The next squirrel will not be as easy," said Yonah, "now that they know we are here. You heard his warning call to the other squirrels."

Yonah picked up the squirrel, removing the arrow and mumbling a few words of thanks to the animal as he did. He handed the squirrel to Sal.

"I will see if I can get a few more," said Yonah. "Best you stay here so I don't shoot the squirrel-man instead of the squirrel."

Yonah left Sal with his flint and char-cloth. Sal had watched him enough to get the idea. He expertly started the fire, this time without causing himself injury. By the time the fire was going well enough for cooking, Yonah returned with another three squirrels. They cleaned the squirrels and cooked them over the fire on a stick, like "squirrel kabobs" as Sal called them. Yonah just grunted and wiped the grease from his chin.

"Awesome dinner, Tonto," Sal said, tossing the last of the squirrel bones into the fire, stretching and leaning back against a rock to get comfortable.

Yonah did the same. "Tell me, Squirrel-man, who is this Tonto you keep calling me?"

"Tonto?" Sal repeated, without the least bit of embarrassment. "Tonto was the 'faithful Indian companion' of a legendary western hero, The Lone Ranger."

"Hmmm; a companion to the Lone Ranger?" Yonah scratched his head. "I do not understand. If he was a lone ranger, why did he have a companion?"

"I guess he didn't want to get too lonely," Sal smirked. "I dunno, I guess he needed the skills of Tonto to track people and stuff so he could be a hero."

"What did he do that made him a hero?"

"He got into fights and beat up the bad guys after Tonto led him to them."

"Didn't Tonto fight? Was he a coward?" Yonah looked disgusted. "What tribe was he?"

"Naw, man, he wasn't a coward. Tonto was an awesome fighter, but he only fought when he had to help out the Lone Ranger. I don't know what tribe he was."

Yonah considered this for a moment. "It sounds to me like Tonto was the smart one. He did the tracking and let this Lone Ranger fellow do most of the fighting," he said. "He must have been Tsalagi."

"Yeah, well, I suppose you have a point, dude. But it was the Lone Ranger who was the hero. And I don't think he was Cherokee—the Lone Ranger and Tonto lived out west somewhere."

"He was probably only the hero to the white people," said Yonah. "I bet the Indians thought Tonto was the real hero. He probably just let the Lone Ranger believe himself to be the hero so he could use him to fight bad guys. I still think he could be a Cherokee. Maybe he was one of the Old Settlers that moved out west a while back."

"Whatever." Sal had a defeated look. "I probably shouldn't call you that, though, dude. I don't think the Native Americans who live in my time like the name very much."

"I do not mind. He seems to have been a very smart Indian traveling with a white man who thinks he's special. Sounds familiar to me," he said with a half-grin.

Chapter thirty-eight

The water was freezing cold. In spite of their discomfort, crossing the icy creek helped relieve their lingering muscle aches. Sal and Yonah were across the creek before sunrise, and by the time they reached the top of the next hill the rising sun had already begun to dry them. It was going to be a very warm day; a forewarning that the pleasant spring climate would soon turn into humid, sweltering summer days typical in the Deep South. Today they welcomed the warmth. They had a few more stream crossings to make and the bright sun would dry them quickly, sparing them the unpleasantness of walking in wet clothing.

It was barely past mid-day when they reached the top of the ridge, where they halted before making the final climb to Yonah's mountain. From the ridge they could once again see the river running through the deeply carved canyon far below. Yonah pointed at the river to their east, tracing its route in the air with his finger. He stopped when he was pointing at the place where the river divided.

"The tributary that divides off to the west flows along the southern side of my mountain. The creek continues to run through a deep canyon, hiding the approach to my cabin high on the mountaintop. It is the way we would have gone had we used the river. Coming from this direction, we need only to climb the northern side of the mountain," said Yonah.

"So we're coming through the back door, huh? I hope you didn't lose your house keys back there in the river," Sal quipped.

"There is only one door and it faces east. No lock. Someone may need to get in," Yonah said solemnly.

The climb was steep but not far. They emerged from the woods into a clearing at the very summit of the mountain. In the center of the clearing sat a tiny cabin, to Sal's eyes not much more than a large shed. The building measured no more than twelve feet wide by fifteen feet long. The walls were axe-cut trees, notched at the corners with mud plastered between them. A stone chimney overspread one side, tapering to a narrow flue jutting above the pine bark roof.

"Home, sweet home at last, eh Tonto? We probably oughta check out that arm of yours first thing. I don't suppose you have a Med-pack in there, do you, dude?"

"I have material for clean dressing and unguent, if that is what you mean," Yonah answered as they entered the cabin.

Both men froze as they stepped across the threshold. Inside the cabin was a shambles. Items of all kinds were strewn across the floor. The table that once sat in the middle of the room was pushed against the wall, and the two chairs were overturned. Containers that had once stood on a shelf near the hearth were upended, their contents dumped onto the floor. The cooking tools from the mantle had been scattered and blankets tossed down from the sleeping loft above.

"Someone has been here," said Yonah.

"No kidding! How can you tell, Tonto? Must be that keen Indian sense of yours. I just thought you were a terrible housekeeper. Maybe you oughta rethink that lock and key thing."

"I do not know why this was done. I have very little that anyone would want to steal."

It took them less than thirty minutes to put the tiny cabin back in order. Yonah said that only a few insignificant items were missing, mostly tools, a haunch of dried venison, and his animal traps were nowhere to be found.

Yonah pulled a loose stone from the hearth, and retrieved a metal box from a hole underneath. He opened the box and removed a pouch and a handful of coins. He inventoried the coins, and tossed them back into the box with a jingle.

"At least they didn't find my money. There isn't much, but I'll need it for supplies."

He opened the pouch and dumped the contents into his hand, revealing an ample pile of sizeable gold nuggets.

"Holy Jalapenos!" Sal's eyes bugged. "Dude, are those real gold nuggets?"

"I used to do a bit of gold panning before they made it illegal for the Cherokee. I figure these nuggets just might come in handy someday. They should be worth a good bit these days."

"I'd say so! They'd be worth a freakin' fortune in my time."

Yonah refilled the pouch and put the valuables back into their hiding place, then turned his attention to locating his medical supplies. They managed to find the salve and clean dressing for Yonah's arm. As he was tying the new bandage, Sal was startled by the sound of a loud, shrill whistle from outside. His first thought was that the intruders had returned.

"Calm yourself," Yonah said. "That was just my neighbor being polite, giving me a warning before he approaches my house."

"Your neighbor? Maybe he got an eyeball on whoever tore up your place."

"Perhaps, but not likely. Henri is my closest neighbor, but his cabin is several miles away." Yonah opened the cabin door and gave a brief wave to the man outside.

The man met Yonah at the door, leaning his rifle against the cabin and grasping Yonah's hand. He beamed a yellow-ivory smile, his mouthful of enormous teeth flashing through a dense, bushy blonde beard that hung in strands down the length of his chest and across his homespun flannel shirt.

"*Osiyo*, Yonah, *mon frère*. I'm happy to see you returned safely," he said in a thunderous voice, still shaking Yonah's hand as he entered the cabin.

He was as broad-shouldered as Yonah, and nearly a foot taller. The smile turned to an expression of concern when he noticed the bandage on Yonah's arm.

"You are injured!" he said, his deep, booming voice blasting against the cabin walls, reaching Sal's ears with the force of a cannon shot. The voice was an odd mixture of southern drawl with a substantial French accent.

"*Osiyo*, Henri. It is nothing," Yonah answered. "It would have been much more serious if not for my traveling companion, who pulled me from the river and saved me from certain death at Indian Falls, where we were shot at and lost our canoe. Henri Acres, please meet my new friend from up north. His name is *saloli*-man. I call him squirrel-man, because he may be small like a squirrel, but he is clever, quick, and has a plucky heart."

"Squirrel-man, eh?" Henri bawled, the smile once again radiating from his hirsute face. "*Mon Dieu, mon vieux!* I am so glad you didn't skin him and eat him afore he got a chance to save you." His deafening laughter at his own joke shook the timber walls of the cabin.

"*Bonjour*, Little Squirrel," he said, pumping Sal's arm. His massive head bobbed as he robustly shook Sal's hand, hair shaking like a dust mop in a windstorm. "I am pleased to meet the squirrel who saved a bear! *C'est bon*! A *tour de force!*" he said, setting off another explosion of laughter. "I am called Henri." He pronounced his name *on-ree*.

Sal was as stunned by the powerful handshake as he was by the unexpected praise from Yonah. Henri continued enthusiastically pumping his hand, which was completely enwrapped within the huge man's massive fist. He quaked from the energetic manhandling of his arm, sending tremors through his bones to his rattling teeth.

"Hey, I'm thrilled to meet you, too, dude," Sal replied, his voice trembling in time with the handshake. "But give me back my arm, will ya, big guy?" He tried to remove his hand from Henri's vise-like grip. "I might need it for something later."

"Oh, excusez-moi, Little Squirrel," he said solemnly, finally releasing Sal's hand. "I sometimes am too vigorous. I did not intend to hurt your little squirrel paw."

"No harm done, Goliath. And you can just call me Sal, okay?"

"I would like to hear more of your adventure," Henri said, "and how the little squirrel saved the big bear, but I am afraid I have to give you my news first, for your escapade may not yet be over."

"Would your news have anything to do with the condition I found my cabin in when I returned?" Yonah asked.

"*Zut alors*! Then they have already been here." He clucked and shook his wooly head. "Early this morning my home was also invaded by the miscreants. They arrived with the intention of driving me and my wife Meggie from our home."

"Surely they know you are white, and even though Meggie is full-blood, she is exempt from removal by her marriage to you," said Yonah.

"These scoundrels didn't care about any of that," he spat. "They were not soldiers, neither federal nor state militia. They were looking to get their hands on any property they could—steal it if they had to. By the grace of god, I had my muzzleloader primed and ready when they came. None of them were anxious to carry a musket ball home in his head. I suspected they would come this way next."

"They did," said Yonah. "Been here and gone. They only took a few things; not much else is worth taking except my small savings, which was well hidden and they did not find. Squirrel-man and I put the place back together in just a short time. I am appreciative of your coming to warn me, but it seems as though the danger has already passed."

"I am certain it has only begun," said Henri. "It is said that the soldiers have begun to round up all the Cherokee in Georgia. As soon as that is complete, Colonel Lindsay will begin the roundup here, and send the members of any Cherokee household to Fort Payne to await relocation.

"I believe the men who attempted to invade our homes are the forefront of many more to come—greedy, lawless men hoping to take advantage of the misfortune of others. Now that it is known that the government has begun to forcefully take the Cherokee from their homes, the scoundrels will descend upon them in droves to get first pickings from their property. I suggest that you sleep lightly tonight, and keep a weapon at the ready."

"We shall do that. Your words ring true to me, Henri Acres. I will be expecting thieves in the night. Those who come here looking for trouble will surely find it."

Henri nodded his approval. He began to speak further, but hesitated, glancing once at Sal then back again at Yonah.

"Yes, my friend?" questioned Yonah. "Is there something else you wish to tell me?"

"It may not be my place to ask," Henri replied, speaking hesitantly instead of his usual forthright manner, "but it is certain now that soon the soldiers will come for you if you do not report to the fort. Will you not try to avoid that confrontation?"

"I have no desire to leave my home," Yonah stated.

"But if it is forced upon you…"

"Death will also be forced upon me. Should I kill myself now to avoid facing it later?" Yonah said irritably.

"*Certainement pas*! Forgive me, *mon ami*. I should not have mentioned it. It's just that your sister is concerned, and frets for your wellbeing. We despise what is happening, and don't wish to add to your anxiety." He shook his great mop of a head and sighed. "*C'est la guerre!*"

Yonah sat down heavily and puffed out his cheeks. "No, I am not angry at you. It is understandable that my family is concerned, and has a right to ask about my intentions. I wish I had better words of comfort for you to take back to Meggie. I am holding out against hope that I may be able to remain on my own land somehow."

"What news did you learn on your trip to New Echota?" Henri asked. "We hoped you would learn something encouraging from the leaders in Red Clay and Washington City."

"Only that the change of the white government means nothing changes for us. John Ross is still speaking strongly against the false treaty of New Echota, but for the most part his words fall upon deaf ears. Much of my news is rendered moot now that you have told me the soldiers have been engaged. Once the whites have taken our land, I do not believe our leaders will be able to undo the treachery."

"*Je suis d'accord*," said Henri. "So far, I have only heard of military action in Georgia. Perhaps Ross can stop the madness before they begin here."

The room fell into silence. It was evident by the look on Yonah's face that he no longer believed the removal could be avoided, although he was still unwilling to speak the words aloud. Even Sal, who was never in doubt of what would occur, was stunned into silence by Yonah's sudden look of hopelessness.

Breaking the painful silence, Henri said, "I must be *en route*, Yonah. I do not wish to leave my Meggie by herself for too long. She is a strong woman who can take care of herself, but it would be best for me to be home before nightfall."

"Yes, of course. It would be best not to risk leaving her alone for too long." Yonah exhaled long and forcefully, ridding himself of his despondency in a lungful of breath. A faint glimmer of the sparkle reappeared in his eyes. "Tell my sister not to worry, all will be well. I will try to visit with her soon—perhaps I will even bring Squirrel-man. I know they would get along well, and I will try to convince him to take one of her clan-sisters for a wife."

"For a what--! Hold on there a minute, Tonto. I'm sure your sisters are real lookers, but I'm not really interested in, uh…" Sal stammered, cringing at the thought of life with a female Yonah, to the amusement of the other two men who began laughing again.

"Why Little Squirrel, you don't know what you would be missing! There is nothing better than a *tres beau* Cherokee *belle* to keep you warm through long winter nights," Henri said through tears of laughter.

"I would be happy to tell you of the many delightful qualities of a Cherokee wife, but I am afraid it must wait for another day. It has been a pleasure to meet you," Henri continued earnestly. He firmly placed his powerful paw on Sal's shoulder and shook his hand again with his other meaty fist. This time Henri remembered to let go after only a few jostling shakes. "I hope you do get a chance to visit with us. And again, *merci beaucoup* for saving our old black bear. *Au revoir!*"

"It's been a real whoop-de-do meeting you as well, Goliath. It'd be super cool to hop on over with Yonah for a visit one of these days," Sal said with some sincerity. He liked Henri, although he wasn't anxious to subject himself to the brunt of the two men's amusement again anytime soon.

Henri turned to Yonah and clutched him in a great hug. Yonah suppressed a grunt, not wanting to show the pain the embrace caused his wounded shoulder. He returned the hug with equal gusto.

As he exited the cabin, Henri stopped to retrieve his rifle and carry-sack. "Oh, I nearly forgot," he said, handing the sack to Yonah. "Meggie sent this food she prepared for you. Good thing, too, since the thieves took your provisions. There is more than enough for you both. *Bon appétit!*" He then slung his rifle over his shoulder and began walking back down along the mountain path, stopping only for a moment at the edge of the woods to turn and vigorously wave goodbye.

"Well, my friend," said Yonah as he plopped the carry sack down on the tiny table and began removing the contents. "Meggie has provided a feast for us, and she is an excellent cook. Shall we eat?"

"You bet, dude. Good cooking is one of the qualities of Cherokee women I already know about. Serve it up, Tonto; let's eat. I'm starving!"

Chapter thirty-nine

*I*t was a short ride that lasted an eternity. Staring blankly at the road ahead, none of them could bear to look back after their final glance at the farm. They rode along in silence except for an occasional sob from Sally, still tightly hugging her mother. Alice sat next to her, holding her tiny hand. She was too angry to think of any comforting words to say to the little girl. Everything that came to mind seemed trite and inconsequential.

The closer they got to New Echota, the more caravans of Cherokee families they saw. The procession of somber-faced families reminded Alice of movies she had seen of Jewish prisoners being herded into the concentration camps of Nazi Germany. The scene was surreal, incredible. While this was not her present, not even her century, it was her country. This inconceivable, racist transgression was happening in the United States of America. Alice loved her country and she considered herself patriotic, but this deplorable malfeasance was disgraceful and reprehensible.

When they reached the river, they joined the line of a half-dozen wagons queued up for the ferry crossing. The slaves running the ferry were now accompanied by a pair of soldiers, posted to keep order and expedite the normally lax operation. They barked out orders to the slaves, who mostly ignored them. The ferry workers moved at their usual dawdling speed, occasionally expressing their irritation with surreptitious glances of disdain. The wagon drivers paid the soldiers more heed, snapping to as they were gruffly waved forward onto the boat.

The Rogers' family and their escorts boarded the ferry without incident or conversation, other than a few terse commands barked by the soldiers. The ferry slaves exchanged a conspiratorial gesture with Isaac and Silvey, but no regard was given to any of the Cherokee families, as if they were no more significant than livestock being taken to market.

Even amongst the Cherokee there was barely any socialization. Hardly more than a curt nod was exchanged between longtime friends. The callous treatment embarrassed them. They felt like willing participants in a criminal act, even though the crime was being committed against them.

For months, Benjamin and Catherine held on to the hope that this day would never come. They were not alone in their belief; thousands of Cherokee families had remained on their ancestral homeland until they were forced to leave. In spite of their optimism, Benjamin and Catherine were practical people. They had done their best to prepare the children for the possibility of upheaval, discussing with them what might occur. Even so, like the death of a sick or elderly loved one, knowing that something tragic is likely to happen does not eliminate the emotions felt when it actually occurs.

Riding side-by-side, Benjamin could not see Billy's face. He could tell by the tension in the boy's grip that he had withdrawn into his anger ever since leaving the farm. Benjamin put aside his own urge to withdraw and spoke softly to him of whatever came to mind as they crossed the river. He commented on the pleasant weather, the flow of the water, their next hunting trip—anything other than the dreadfulness of what was happening to them. Slowly Billy began to respond, at first with grunts and monosyllabic replies, and eventually with complete sentences. They would all carry a permanent psychological scar from this traumatic experience, so Benjamin was relieved to see any sign of normal behavior from Billy. His priority would be to keep the family together, not just physically, but mentally, emotionally, and spiritually.

Most of his concern was for Sally. She was younger, and although the young typically recover quickly from disaster, she was the most attached to her home of them all. Living isolated in a rural area with no friends her own age close by, she filled her playtime with imaginary friends and places around the farm. Leaving it all behind would shatter her world. She had only recently begun to form a bond with Alice, accepting her almost like an older sister. Catherine had been wise to encourage the relationship, and Benjamin hoped that Alice's presence would help make this experience less traumatic for her.

After crossing the river they followed the dusty road to the rustic fort looming ahead. When they reached the timber bulwark, they halted at the blockhouse gate. "You will be quartered here until you can be transported to Ross's Landing," said Captain Martin. "Your wagon and goods will be stored until then."

The Rogers' family and their slaves relinquished the wagon and watched as their few remaining belongings were taken away. The blockhouse guard saluted Captain Martin, and then opened the gate without comment. The Captain escorted the family into the blockhouse courtyard. Silvey and Isaac joined a small group of black men and women, apparently the slaves of other families who had been incarcerated. The rest of the family proceeded to the central courtyard where a larger group of Cherokee were gathered.

"Alice!" Adam's voice echoed across the courtyard as he ran toward her.

"Adam! You're here too? What about Jimmy and Rebecca?"

"I'm relieved to see you guys are okay," Adam said as he embraced her. "*Osiyo*, Benjamin and Catherine. Hi, kids." He ruffled Billy's hair and winked at Sally. "Yes, I'm here with Jimmy Deerinwater. He's recovering from his injuries over there," he said, motioning to a less crowded part of the courtyard. "He was seriously roughed up by the scumbags who brought us here. They gave him a severe blow to his head. The main scumbag hasn't shown up here yet. He was supposed to be coming along behind us in a wagon with Rebecca and their possessions. Jimmy is extremely worried about her, and I am trying to see the colonel to demand my release so I can go find out what happened to her."

"Who was this man you are calling a scumbag?" asked Captain Martin. "Was this Deerinwater person resisting?"

Adam did not answer, but instead gave a questioning look to Alice.

"This is Captain Martin," she told him. "It was he who brought us here. Certainly not a pleasant experience," she smirked at the Captain, "though at least without the brutality you received. He did act professionally once Benjamin agreed not to resist."

"Jimmy didn't resist. He was beaten before he was even given an explanation for the intrusion into his home," Adam said. "When he protested leaving his wife behind, he was knocked unconscious and hogtied. The scumbag's name was Jeb Barnett."

Captain Martin's face grew dark with the mention of Jeb Barnett. "I know the man, and his actions do not surprise me. I understand the concern for the safety of your friend's wife."

"Exactly why I will demand to be released. I am not Cherokee, and neither is Alice for that matter. There is no justification for holding us," he said to Martin.

"I'm sorry, Benjamin," Adam continued, "I'm not trying to abandon you or Jimmy, but I think it is urgent that I go find out about Rebecca."

"I agree, Adam," said Benjamin. He felt more comfortable having Alice released now that Adam was with her. "Captain, these two people," he pointed with his chin to Adam and Alice, "are our friends who have been visiting with us. They are not Tsalagi. Can you not explain this to the colonel and allow them to go free?"

"They will not be held if they are not Cherokee. This would have come to light eventually as they will not appear on the Cherokee census, so I will arrange for their release. You should have told me you were not Cherokee back at the farm," he said to Alice.

"I wanted to stay with the children. Besides, I wouldn't like to think of staying behind with those thieves back at the farm."

"We would have given you safe escort somewhere. But what's done is done," he said with finality. Martin then turned to Adam. "It is not a good idea for you to put yourself in the way of Jeb Barnett. Our resources are stressed with this roundup, but I believe I can convince the colonel it is worth my going to assure the safety of the Deerinwater woman. He knows Jeb's temperament, and would not like to be embarrassed by his actions."

"That's more like it," said Adam. "And I'll go with you."

Captain Martin shook his head. "This is a military operation and will be handled by the military."

"You just said you were shorthanded. And I may not be military, but I am certainly more professional than that redneck you guys sent out to Jimmy's place."

"I must concede that point to you. I still believe it to be ill-advised, but I will speak to the colonel immediately and let you know his decision. Your accompanying me will be irrelevant if he does not agree that I should go." He turned and departed the blockhouse.

"I should tell Jimmy what's happening and see how he is doing," said Adam.

"Of course," said Benjamin. "We will all go with you. Perhaps it will bring some relief to him to know he is among friends."

They found Jimmy, head in his hands, sitting against the stockade wall. His friend, Jesse, was sitting next to him. They both looked up when the group approached. Jesse smiled at them, but Jimmy just stared blankly.

"Jesse was here at the fort when we arrived. Do you know him?" Adam asked the Rogers.

"Yes, Jesse is an old friend," said Benjamin.

Adam listened as Benjamin and Jesse exchanged greetings and some murmurings in Cherokee. He could not understand the words, but the tone was obvious—they were both vehemently expressing their anger at the treatment they had received. It was the first time Adam heard a cross word from Benjamin or Catherine. The expressions of anger instantly disappeared and Benjamin's voice once again became cordial as he introduced Alice.

Catherine knelt beside Jimmy and examined his injuries "I am certain you will feel much better once you know Rebecca is safe," Catherine said. "I have no medical supplies with me; what little we were able to bring is stored in our wagon," she said as she stroked his throbbing head.

"It is not important," Jimmy muttered.

Adam told Jimmy about his conversation with Captain Martin, and his plan to go with him to assure Rebecca's safety.

"Who is this Captain Martin? Do you trust this *yonega* soldier?" he asked Benjamin.

"I believe he may be the best one to deal with Jeb Barnett. Adam is well intended, but the captain will have the authority of his military rank. He took us from our home, but was not abusive. I cannot vouch for him any more than that."

Jimmy replied with a grunt. Adam started to say something to reassure him, but Benjamin signaled him not to speak. Jimmy was clearly distraught, and trying to calm him would be futile until Rebecca was safely at his side. Catherine continued to stroke his head, and spoke softly to him in Cherokee. Jimmy's responses, even to Catherine, were clipped and unlike his usual energetic tone.

Adam caught sight of Captain Martin reentering the blockhouse. "Here comes the captain. Maybe now I can get out of here and see that Rebecca is safe."

It was impossible to read anything from Captain Martin's face; his years of military leadership would not allow that. His pale blue eyes scanned the courtyard until they fixed upon Adam, and then he strode purposely toward him.

"Colonel Lindsey has made it clear that his utmost priority is the collection of all the Cherokee. He is not inclined to allow any other operations that will impede that progress, however..." he began.

"That's ridiculous!" Adam cried. "How can that take priority over the safety of this man's wife? Especially when he is the one who has put her in danger!"

"Her safety is not his concern. In fact, even your safety is not his concern. By the treaty of Hopewell, any white person entering Cherokee lands forfeits protection from the United States. But as I was saying," he raised his voice to stifle another outburst from Adam, "he has granted me a short time to go and assure that Mrs. Deerinwater is delivered here to this fort. He has also agreed to release the two of you," he nodded to Alice.

"Ma'am," he said to Alice, "where will you go when you are released? Do you have other friends, not Cherokee, with whom you can stay?"

"I'm afraid the only others I know here are Cherokee. I'd prefer to stay here with the Rogers."

"Then I suggest you do stay here until I return. At that time we can consider your options.

"As for you," he said to Adam, "I will take you with me to the Deerinwater farm under the condition that you understand that I am in command, and you are to follow my orders. I will not tolerate the reckless behavior of a civilian causing further complication of my duties. Agreed?"

"Agreed," Adam said, hoping he had not answered a little too readily. He had become very fond of Jimmy and Rebecca, and would do whatever he could to get them safely back together. He was not going to return without Rebecca, even if that meant breaking his agreement to follow the captain's orders.

"Then we will go immediately. Come with me and I will provide you with a mount. Be prepared for a fast ride." He touched the brim of his hat to the women, nodded to the others, and then advanced briskly toward the gate.

"I'll bring her to you, Jimmy," he promised, then jogged to catch up to Martin.

"Good luck and please be careful," Alice called after him. Adam responded with a thumbs-up as he followed the captain through the gate.

Alice thought about Captain Martin's warning. Adam might not realize the danger he could be putting himself in. "Is it true what the captain said, that whites have no right to protection when they are on Cherokee lands?"

"It is true that this is stated in the Treaty of Hopewell. Of course, that same treaty states many things. The purpose of the treaty back in 1785 was to guarantee the boundaries of the Cherokee Nation, and to set limits of further expansion by white settlers into our lands. You see for yourself how those terms are violated. To the white government, the treaties can change whenever they deem it to be advantageous to them. This happens so much that we call them 'talking leaves' because they blow away like leaves in the wind whenever abiding by them no longer suits the whites. So is it still a law the white man will honor? Only if it is convenient for them. More worrisome is that the whites are free to violate both their own laws and ours when they are on our land, without fear of repercussion from anyone."

"So people like Jeb Barnett and the thieves waiting to vandalize your farm can do whatever they like and get away unpunished?"

"That is the way the *yonegas* wish it to be," Jesse interjected. "My family has turned themselves in voluntarily to be relocated. It is not because we wanted to leave our homeland; it was because we could no longer endure the aggression of the whites. Nearly everything we own has been stolen and we have been abused in every way, just for staying on the land where our people have always lived. Your people will stop at nothing to get what they want," he said, glaring at Alice.

"I'm not about to justify what is being done," said Alice. "My goodness, it is despicable. I can only tell you that the government is under pressure to expand the country as more people emigrate here from other parts of the world, and they have decided their first priority is to continue that expansion. I certainly don't approve of removing people from their own lands, but in the past the fortune seekers simply enslaved or killed the native people. Good god, at least they aren't doing that."

"You think this is any better?" Jesse snapped. "Those fortune seekers as you call them at least were straightforward about it. They came with the intention of pillaging the land and made no bones about it. Making room for more settlers is just an excuse. The truth is that they want the gold that has been found here, and want to move us to someplace they think is worthless. They will give us promises and assurances that the new land will be ours forever, just as they did for this land, but it will only be valid until someone finds something else that they want. Then they will move us again. It would be more honest if they just killed us all! More honorable than making promises they have no intention of keeping!"

Alice didn't believe that Jesse really thought genocide was honorable, but she understood his point. Many treaties had been broken, and many more would be as greed overcame honor. She knew that as the country expanded west, genocide would occur. She could think of no response to Jesse's rage.

Benjamin sensed her discomfort and made an effort to change the subject. "We should deal with the immediate situation for now," he said. "Jesse, can you show us the accommodations while we are waiting for Adam's return?"

"Accommodations? Ha! Your horses are provided with better accommodations. Yes, I will show you."

They helped Jimmy to his feet and all followed Jesse to the crude barracks. The hastily constructed shelter was little more than a shed with a door-sized opening, without the door. Jesse paused at the opening, extended his hand, and said, "Welcome to your deluxe lodgings, ladies and gentlemen."

It was dark inside the barracks; the only light was coming through the door opening. There were no windows. While they waited for their eyes to adjust, they breathed in the musty air which smelled of freshly cut lumber and damp dirt, mixed with human sweat and the faint odor of sickness. Gradually the dirt floor and racks of wooden bed pallets came into focus. A bale of straw sat in one corner, soiled blankets in another. Straw was strewn about the floor. The bunks were stacked floor to ceiling, five high, and had only straw for padding. Several of the bunks were occupied, and they could hear labored breathing and an occasional cough from the motionless forms. There was not much more to see.

"Are we going to stay here, mommy?" Sally's soft voice broke the silence of their shock.

"Just for a little while, Sally."

"Many of those in here are sick and feeling too bad to do more than sleep. Unfortunately, that number is growing each day. Most prefer to sleep outside," said Jesse.

"Then that is what we shall do," Benjamin said. He pulled Catherine aside and spoke to her quietly so that Sally and Billy could not hear. "This place smells too much of sickness. I will go and try to find a better place for us in the courtyard. Take Alice and the children with you. Perhaps you can find a way to keep them from becoming despondent." Then to Jimmy he said, "Let us go look for a suitable place for our families. Your pregnant wife and my children need a clean place with fresh air."

Finding a clean place was difficult. Benjamin was able to claim a reasonably private area of the courtyard somewhat sheltered by one of the barracks that was large enough for them and the Deerinwaters. Jimmy was still downhearted, but with Benjamin's encouragement he became less miserable as he prepared a place to offer Rebecca some comfort when she arrived.

Alice and Catherine did their best to feign optimism, which helped brighten the mood of the two youngsters. They encouraged Billy and Sally to join in with some of the other children. The camaraderie distracted them from more serious matters, and before long they were in better spirits than the adults. The sound of their playing lightened everyone's depressed mood. Alice and Catherine were drawn in, joining a circle of children and other parents, inventing games and telling stories.

Sally pleaded with Alice to tell them all her Basil the Beaver story again. It was the last thing she felt like doing, but it was impossible to resist her charm. She gave in, further encouraged by the relief it brought to Catherine to see them smiling. Alice started the story hesitantly, but grew more confident as the children all began making the animal noises and laughing at the image of Basil's home getting full of the creatures that she painted with her words.

She finished the story with the usual clapping and cheering. Seeing the round, beaming faces of the children triggered an unexpected reaction from Alice. The color drained from her face, her eyes became moist, and she suddenly jumped up and ran from the group. Catherine followed her, not sure what had caused such an emotional display.

"What is wrong," Catherine asked, catching up to her. "Your story brought them happiness; just what they needed."

"Oh, my, I didn't want to spoil it for them," she sobbed, "but seeing their happy faces made me think about…"

"Think about what? Why did you become so sad?"

"I couldn't keep from thinking about how many of them are not going to make it through this horrible ordeal."

Chapter forty

R ebecca woke with a start, suppressing a gasp when she heard them still somewhere nearby. She dared not make a sound for fear of alerting them that she was conscious. The sound of their coarse voices sharply inflamed her senses, like ice water striking the exposed root of a tooth. She blocked out the memories of the attack that tried to push their way into her mind and focused on appraising her condition. She painfully flexed her abused muscles, biting her lip to suppress a cry when moving her leg sent an icicle of agony through her pelvis. Her head throbbed, and her hips and shoulders ached from restraint and maltreatment.

She lay naked, her clothes scattered in shredded rags around her. Her arms were bound at the wrists and tied with a length of rope to the headboard, securing them above her head. She ignored the disgusting dampness beneath her; rejecting the horrifying flashbacks which would once again cast her into a bottomless abyss of despair.

They did not take her easily. She had fought them with courageous vigor, calling on every drop of warrior's blood that ran through her veins. She was sure she had inflicted severe injury on one of the attackers, presenting him with a well-placed kick to the groin at an opportune moment. She exulted in his painful yelp; saw him fall to the floor, clutching his genitals. Even reducing their number by one, she was eventually overcome. The outcome was inevitable. They tied her arms to the bed and took their turns, each one heaving and grunting their animal lust as the other two held her legs. Once overpowered, she lay immobile, denying them any pleasure from her struggling. At least the one she kicked was unable to violate her; his molestation had been reduced to restraining her for the other two. He vented his frustration when they were through with a brutal blow to her head, knocking her unconscious. She knew he would extract his revenge even more savagely if she could not free herself before he returned.

There was little hope of that. Even if she could somehow untie her arms from the bed, she would not get far with a broken pelvis, dislocated hip, or whatever it was causing the intense pain at the uppermost joint of her leg. Escape was unlikely. When they returned, as she was certain they would, she resolved to find some way to inflict more pain. If she feigned submission, perhaps they would lower their guard enough for her to bite off an ear, or any other body part they were foolish enough to bring within range of her teeth.

As she plotted her attack, she was startled by the sound of additional voices. Had Jeb's other two henchmen returned? The muffled voices sounded heated, as if they were arguing over who would be next to take her. She despaired at the thought of having to endure the ravages of even more attackers. The desperation led her to one possible solution; an extreme measure, but one that would permanently deny them tormenting her further. If she could just slide herself close enough to the head rail to get the rope around her neck…

Chapter forty-one

*C*aptain Martin and Adam reigned in their galloping horses, raising a cloud of dust that billowed past them and onto the Deerinwater front porch, where Jeb and his two cronies sat watching them with apparent unconcern.

"What's the rush, Jimbo? Outhouse is 'round back, iffen ya need it real bad," said Jeb in a smarmy tone, winking at his two cohorts who rewarded him with snorts of laughter.

"You will address me as Captain Martin, sir," he said without a trace of amusement, his cold stare leveled at Jeb. "You were supposed to bring the Deerinwater woman and her possessions to the fort. Why have you not done so?"

"Well now, captain," he said with a smirk, intentionally mis-pronouncing the title as *cappy-tan*. "She ain't quite ready yet. We been makin' sure she gits all she needs afore she leaves."

"Undoubtedly you have been most helpful. Bring her to me immediately and we will escort her to the fort."

"Can't do that, cappy-tan. I'm a-feared she's tied up at the moment," Jeb said, inciting a chorus of snickers from the other two. "You just run along an' we'll bring her when she's ready."

"If you've harmed her I'll…," Adam threatened, before getting cut off by a hard look from Martin.

"You'll what, sonny-boy?" Jeb spat, his words dripping with malice. He said to Martin, "Leave this little mollycoddle here an' we'll change his nappy fer him. Should've fixed his wagon last time."

Captain Martin ignored the taunts to Adam. "You were ordered to enforce the relocation of these families, not to abuse them. And now I am ordering you to produce Rebecca Deerinwater to me, and then continue with the duties you have been assigned."

"I take my orders from Colonel Lindsey, not you. Don't be tryin' t' pull that regular army crap on me. Me and my men are contracted to the militia an' don't have to listen to your guff. 'Sides, I just done told ya we was helpin' her git ready an' we'll be the ones a-bringin' her to the fort. So you can just git on."

"You are performing duties for the Georgia militia, and are under the command of its officers. Now I am ordering you for the final time, bring forth Rebecca Deerinwater or I'll will fetch her myself and report your insubordination to Colonel Lindsey."

"An' I'm tellin' you for the last time, you ain't takin' nobody!" He planted himself firmly between Captain Martin and the doorway.

Martin stepped up to face Jeb, and then made a motion as if he was preparing to walk around him. Jeb shifted his position to once again block his path, and as he did Captain Martin, moving with cat-like speed, thrust his hip into Jeb's mid-section. He simultaneously grabbed Jeb's collar and deftly tossed the stunned man into the dirt behind him.

"Take your men and return to Fort Wool. I will deal with you further there," Captain Martin said.

Jeb jumped to his feet and shot a humiliated glance at his two men. "You'll pay for that!" he said.

"Do not make matters any worse for yourself. You already have a charge of insubordination to answer for," said Martin. He turned his back and walked toward the farmhouse door.

Adam wasn't about to be left standing alone with Jeb and his crew. As he followed the captain to the door, Jeb suddenly shoved past him, charging toward Captain Martin wielding a massive hunting knife.

"Captain, look out!" Adam yelled.

Captain Martin turned and drew his field officer's sword in a single, swift motion. Charging at full speed, Jeb drove the sword blade through his own body, unable to stop until he reached the eagle-pommel hilt. He stood impaled on the sword, still holding the hunting knife above his head, staring incomprehensibly at his intended victim. His mouth moved wordlessly as the gravity of what had just happened to him slowly dawned. The sword had entered his chest beneath the breastbone and exited his back, inflicting extensive damage along the way, not the least of which was severing his aorta. Blood from the high-pressure artery flooded his chest cavity, squeezing the pericardium so tightly his heart had no room to beat. Death was nearly instantaneous. Jeb's body dropped to the ground, sliding off Martin's sword as it did.

"Adam," said Captain Martin, wiping the blood from his sword and replacing it in its scabbard, "please see if you can find Mrs. Deerinwater."

Adam, shocked by the violence he had just witnessed, gawked at the dead man lying at his feet. Recovering his wits, he tore his eyes away from Jeb's body, nodded to Martin, and entered the house.

"Now," Martin said to the two other men, "you two will immediately report to Fort Wool. Any objections?"

"No, sir!" they replied. They ran for their horses, mounted them and rode off without another word.

Inside the house, Adam entered the bedroom and discovered Rebecca. She had pulled herself up far enough to get the rope around her neck, but was alive.

"My god!" he cried. He quickly took a blanket and covered her, wincing when he saw the bruises from the blows she had endured.

"Adam?" She looked at him, not sure if he was really there or a hallucination. "Is it you? Where are those men?" she asked in a quavering voice.

Adam heard the rasping sounds of her breathing, her neck constricted by the rope. "Yes, it's me. It's okay now. They won't be back to hurt you," he said. Gently lifting her head and taking the rope from around her neck, he began untying her. The left side of her face was already turning purple from the punch that had knocked her unconscious. She had been forced to fervently defend herself against impossible odds—because he had left her—choosing not to face those same odds. He choked back the overwhelming feelings of anger and guilt, and forced himself to focus on her immediate needs. He would deal with his conscience later.

"How badly are you hurt?"

"I do not know. My hip hurts a lot," she said, indicating her left side. "It feels like something is broken inside. Where is Jimmy? Is he safe? Can you take me to him?"

"Yes, of course. You'll be with him soon. He is at the fort. He is still shaken up, but mostly with worry about you. Do you think you will be able to ride?" If she had a broken hip or pelvis riding might be impossible.

"I can ride. I just need to go to Jimmy."

A sound from the next room caused Rebecca to gasp, her eyes growing wide with fear as she drew the blanket around her tightly and tried to coil into a defensive position.

"It's okay," said Adam calmingly. "It is just Captain Martin. He is the one who got me out of the fort and came with me to bring you to Jimmy."

Martin stepped into the room, momentarily losing his staunch military expression when he saw Rebecca.

"Damn their souls," he said. "Did they...?"

Rebecca averted her eyes and did not speak.

Adam answered for her. "I don't know the extent of the abuse, but she certainly has been molested. She thinks her hip may have been broken during the struggle. She is in a lot of pain on her left side. I never should have left her behind."

"Don't be a fool," Martin snapped. "Had you attempted to take them on unarmed, you would be lying where Jeb is now, and we would not be here to prevent further atrocities." He turned his attention to Rebecca. "Ma'am, if you will permit me, I must examine your hip to determine if you can be moved."

Rebecca hesitated, not sure that she could tolerate anyone touching her. She longed for the river, to swim in its cold, clear water until it washed away the disgust clinging to her, but her longing to be reunited with Jimmy was greater. She would endure whatever it would take to reach him. She nodded her reluctant permission.

He kept the blanket in place, but when he placed his hand on her hip she recoiled, from both pain and the foul memory his touch invoked. Rebecca clenched her teeth and endured the examination. She was grateful that he was swift, gentle, and considerate.

"I do not believe it is broken," he said after a cursory inspection. "The hip appears to be dislocated, and quite possibly some ligaments have been torn. I am sure it is very painful. It will be even more painful for her to travel. However, we may be able to pull the bone back into place and give her some relief. I am afraid that it is going to hurt very much for a few moments, but at least riding will be more bearable. I will have to pull..."

"I am familiar with the procedure," Rebecca said. "Just get it over with so I can go to my husband."

Captain Martin had encountered victims of sexual attacks in the past, and he was not surprised by her curt reply. It was better for her to express her anger than repress it. Her physical injuries would heal long before the psychological ones did. It also did not help that he represented the people who were forcing her from her home.

He instructed Adam to stand behind the bed and showed him how to hold her while he repositioned the ball and socket of her hip. "You will have to hold tightly, Adam. It takes quite a bit of force to pop the joint back into position. Are you ready, Mrs. Deerinwater?"

She took a deep breath and nodded.

Captain Martin placed one hand on her ankle and the other behind her knee, checked that Adam had a firm grip, and pulled. Rebecca pressed her lips so tightly together they turned white, but she did not cry out. With great relief, she felt the hip joint pop back into place and Captain Martin gradually released the pressure on her leg. She was even more relieved to have their hands off of her.

"That should help to relieve some of your discomfort," Captain Martin said. "Take a few moments to—compose yourself, and then we will go to the fort. We can use the wagon so you will not have to travel on horseback. I will go and prepare our mounts; come as soon as you are ready." He grabbed a few blankets and then turned and left the room.

"I'm so sorry this happened, Rebecca," Adam began. "I should have…"

"Adam," Rebecca interrupted, "you should have done exactly as you did. You have nothing to be sorry for. Captain Martin was right. The best you could do was to allow yourself to be taken to the fort and come back with help, just as you did, and I thank you for that. But now I need to get to Jimmy."

"Yes, of course. We'll go as soon as you are ready." Adam knew he would never be free of the guilt he felt for not being able to prevent the attack, but her words gave him some reassurance that he had done the right thing.

He helped her to a sitting position, and brought her a pitcher of water and some clothing from the armoire. He told her to let him know when she was ready and he would help her to the horses, and then left the room.

Agonizing as it was, Rebecca washed and dressed quickly. The pain prevented her from putting any weight on her leg, so she would need Adam's help to walk. When she finished she called him back into the room.

Adam sensed her unease at his touch and did his best to give her only enough support to walk without holding on any more than necessary, though he kept himself ready to catch her if she stumbled. They slowly made their way through the door.

Captain Martin stood holding the horses. Rebecca gasped when she saw Jeb's body and he said, "I apologize, ma'am. I should have used one of the blankets to cover him."

"I would rather you did not soil my blankets with that filth. Where are the other two?"

"I sent them ahead to the fort. I did that before I knew what they had done to you. They may not show up, fearing punishment when I report what has happened here. Even if they do, I'm afraid I cannot promise you they will suffer the appropriate consequences. They may only face charges of insubordination and dereliction of duty."

"You mean it doesn't matter what they did to me because I am just an Indian."

"Mrs. Deerinwater, if it were up to me…," he nodded toward Jeb's body, letting his earlier actions speak for him. "I will strongly recommend a severe punishment for their offenses, but I know, as do you, that it is not likely. It would be dishonest for me to lead you to believe otherwise."

Rebecca thought to herself that it was much easier to tell others they should expect unfair treatment than it was to suffer it yourself. At least he was being honest. He had dealt with Jeb, and she gave him credit for that.

Captain Martin had placed a nest of blankets in the wagon, tethered Adam's horse to the rear, and then they gently helped Rebecca aboard. He briefly instructed Adam how to drive the wagon. "We will go slowly, and I will ride alongside you," he assured them.

Martin led them at a slow but steady pace—doing his best to avoid any jostling that might cause Rebecca more anxiety than he thought she could handle. Rebecca rode soundlessly in the wagon behind Adam. All she had to do was hang on, but Martin knew riding in a bouncing wagon in her condition must be agonizing. He rode next to Adam, glancing often at her, checking for any indication that she could not tolerate further travel. Her face was a mask of pain, but she did not cry out or ask to slow the pace.

At last they reached the ferry and the river was mercifully calm. Rebecca remained in the wagon as it would be more painful for her to get in and out than just to endure the jolts and bounces of the ferry crossing. She brightened markedly once they landed and the stalwart walls of the fort on the hill above New Echota came into view.

They rode directly to the fort's stables where they helped Rebecca from the wagon and handed off the horses to the stablemen. They each took an arm as they helped her walk to the stockade. The ride had sapped her strength, obliging her to tolerate the discomfort of their touch. She blocked out everything else and fixated on finding Jimmy.

Once inside the gates of the stockade, they immediately encountered Benjamin. His look of relief turned to alarm, then ill-concealed anger when he saw Rebecca's condition. He said nothing, asked no questions, but took the captain's place at her side.

"Jimmy," Rebecca said to him. She could not find the energy to say more.

"He is over here, waiting for you, Rebecca," he said, walking her toward the area where he had left the others.

"I must report to the colonel," said Captain Martin. "I will find you later, Adam." He turned and departed without another word.

They found Jimmy where Benjamin had left him, sitting, back against the wall with his eyes closed. He opened his eyes as they approached, momentarily looking at Rebecca as if he wasn't sure if she were really there or part of his dream. Realizing he was truly awake, he jumped to his feet and ran to her, circling her in his arms and taking her from Adam and Benjamin. They stood locked in a silent embrace, neither one having the strength to stand on their own. Together they looked as if nothing could tear them apart. Adam watched in awe, marveling at the power of their love for each other, and hoping it would be powerful enough to heal them both.

He felt Benjamin tug at his arm, leading him aside. "For the moment, they only need each other," Benjamin said. "We should find Catherine and Alice to let them know you have returned with Rebecca. Catherine can attend to her later."

Neither Jimmy nor Rebecca noticed them leaving, oblivious to everything except each other. For the moment, even the pain of their injuries could not penetrate the fortress of love surrounding them, insulating them from all intrusions, shielding them like a suit of armor. They whispered to each other in the voices that lovers use, using words that bypassed the ear and traveled straight to the heart.

Gradually the relentless tugging of reality, like a child clamoring for the attention of his parents, pulled them from their reverie. Jimmy was aware that Rebecca had been abused; her bruised face made that obvious, though he did not know the extent of her maltreatment. He gently eased his embrace as they both sunk to the ground, keeping her cradled in his arms. Jimmy would not ask her about her ordeal. He held her firmly, caressing her head, knowing she would eventually reveal to him the horrible details. They kept no secrets from each other, and he silently prayed he could endure the horrors she would tell him.

Rebecca was less patient. She questioned him thoroughly about his injuries, and would not speak of herself before he repeatedly assured her that he was recovering well and would be fine now that he was with her again. She suddenly became silent, and Jimmy knew she would begin telling him things he dreaded to hear. He steeled himself, resolving to listen to her without interruption, wanting to give her the loving response she needed. He did not want his anger at the attackers to deprive her of that. Very soon after she began to speak he knew he was not prepared to keep his resolution.

She apologized to him. Tearfully, she told him how sorry she was that she had not been able to fight off her attackers. She tried, even managed to injure one of them, but inevitably succumbed to their attack. She hoped he could forgive her for not fighting harder.

It was too much for Jimmy to bear. His own eyes flooded with tears as he hushed her, shaking his head and placing his fingers on her trembling lips. He could barely speak, but managed to choke out enough words to tell her she had nothing to be sorry for, that he could never put any blame on her for the heinous torment she had suffered.

"But you must let me finish," she whispered, her head nestled against his chest.

Jimmy remained silent, watching their tears mingle as they fell down his body. He felt her hand on his chin, gently guiding his head to look into her eyes. Her fingers brushed the purple-black bruise circling her neck. He saw the rope burn and assumed it was one more outrage she had suffered during her struggle.

"This is what I am most sorry for," she continued. "When I believed they would return to attack me again, I lost all hope. I believed I could not go through more, and I tried to use the rope they tied me with to end my suffering—by taking my life. It was not until I began to tighten the rope around my neck that I realized I could not go through with it. Not because I was afraid to die. I longed for that. It was because of you and our unborn child. I realized I had no right to take his life or to take him from you, to leave you alone, deprived of both your wife and child. I am so ashamed of attempting such a selfish and cowardly thing."

Jimmy vehemently shook his head and forced himself to speak. "You must not feel any shame for anything that you did or anything that was inflicted upon you. Who could not have felt as you did. What matters most is that now we are together again. Had you not returned, I do not know if I would have wanted to go on..."

"Jimmy, no! Do not say such things!" she said horrified. Her tears began again.

Jimmy immediately regretted his words. He struggled to find a way to express himself without causing her more anguish.

"What I mean to say is that I am the one who must live with shame. Not because of what they did to you," he added quickly. "I should have found a way to protect you, instead of letting myself be so easily incapacitated, leaving you to be tortured by those animals."

"That is just not so, Jimmy. Do you think it would have been better for me if they had killed you? I will return your own words to you— what matters most is that we are together again. Adam also expressed unfounded feelings of guilt..."

"Adam!" Jimmy interrupted. "I was foolish to trust him! He should have never let them keep you behind. Just another white who only cares for himself!"

"You are wrong, husband," she admonished. "Think before you speak. He was as powerless to stop them as we were. What would you have had him do differently? Would I be here now if not for him? He is not beholden to us, yet he risked his own safety to ride back with the captain to confront my attackers. And play a part in the killing of their ringleader."

"That should have been my prerogative. But, yes," he agreed, "they acted honorably, and I am grateful for their efforts to rescue you. I still do not think I can completely trust a white man again."

"You cannot condemn an entire race because of the actions of a few."

"It is the white government that is inflicting this upon us. They are the representatives of them all, are they not?"

"Yes, but that does not mean they are all in agreement. You know there have been many whites who have argued in our favor."

Jimmy could not understand how she could defend them after what she had been through. He knew she was wise, and perhaps it was his anger shaping his thoughts. He was not ready to concede, but he did not want to argue with her. He grunted noncommittally and pulled her more tightly to him. "You should try to get some rest now," he told her.

Chapter forty-two

*A*lice and Catherine were relieved by the news of Adam's safe return. They listened in horror as Adam told them how Captain Martin defended himself against Jeb, and of the horrors Rebecca had suffered. They praised him for his bravery, and thanked him for bringing Rebecca back to Jimmy. Adam insisted that it was Captain Martin who deserved their praise, not him. He still felt guilty for leaving Rebecca behind in the first place.

It took firm persuasion from Benjamin to convince Catherine not to immediately seek out Rebecca. "Give them some time together, wife. That is the best medicine for them both right now. Adam has told you her hip has been reset. She will need you more later on." His orders given, he tempered his strictness with a few words of praise. "You did well seeking out the other children for Billy and Sally. The distraction seems to have lifted their mood," he said, pointing with his chin to the group of children.

"They are in much better spirits now," Catherine agreed. "Alice enlivened them all with one of her funny stories." Benjamin smiled and nodded his approval at Alice.

"Some of those children look ill, though," said Alice. "I hope the stress of being here is not making the little ones sick. Gracious, the conditions here are very unhealthy!"

"Not very hygienic from what I have seen," said Adam. "I noticed the toilet facilities are no more than an open pit. This whole place has an ungodly stench."

"They are saying we will not have to be here for long," said Benjamin. "Jesse Weaver told me the plan was for us to be sent to Ross's Landing, and take a river boat from there to the western territory. I hope that happens soon; the weather is becoming quite warm."

Adam and Alice shared a concerned look, remembering from their history how the hot weather devastated the first group sent to the western territory. It was so bad that John Ross convinced the government to delay the removals and let the subsequent groups be led by him in cooler weather. It was a well-meaning but misguided capitulation that resulted in more time spent within the horrible stockades and then dealing with extremely cold weather in a weakened condition. In either case their friends faced a perilous ordeal.

Their attention was drawn to a ripple of movement through the crowd. Captain Martin had returned to the stockade, the people becoming silent and pulling back from him as he passed. He was oblivious to the scornful looks he was getting from the incarcerated Cherokees, focusing his attention on his objective, which apparently was Adam.

"Adam," he began, after giving a quick tip of his hat to Alice. "How is Mrs. Deerinwater?"

"About as well as can be expected, I guess. She is with her husband. How about her other two attackers? Locked up, I hope."

"As I expected, they did not return to the fort." Clearly it was not a subject he wanted to discuss inside the stockade. "I spoke with the colonel about you and Alice, and of course he agreed that you are both free to leave."

"I don't think either of us cares to abandon our friends," he said, getting a nod from Alice. "Besides, we are a long way from home, and really have nowhere locally we can go for now."

"I understand your situation. To remedy that, my wife and I would like to extend the hospitality of our home to you both. We have a house close by, outside of the fort boundaries. You are welcome to stay until you can make arrangements for transportation home."

"That's kind of you, but I don't think we could consider staying with you while our friends are being held here in this place."

"Certainly not," said Alice in agreement. "These people have been very kind to us, and we are not going to desert them."

"I encourage you to reconsider," Captain Martin said sincerely.

Benjamin interjected before they could reply. "Adam, Alice… if I may suggest… perhaps you should take advantage of this man's offer. I understand your reluctance, but there is no need to subject yourselves further to this place if there is another option."

"Yes," said Catherine. "It would make sense to go if you can. No one would stay here if they were not forced to," she said, emphasizing her words with a glare at the captain.

"You would be free to come and go as you please," said Captain Martin, not rising to Catherine's bait. "So there is no need to feel you are abandoning your friends. I must report each morning, and you could return each day with me if you like."

Adam and Alice exchanged a tentative look, still not convinced that accepting the captain's hospitality was entirely proper. As honorable as he may be, he still represented those who had forced their friends from their homes.

Benjamin sensed their hesitation and offered some additional points for them to consider. "This stockade is becoming quite crowded. If you choose to stay with this man, it will make more room for those who have no choice but to stay. You should also consider that there is likely to be some that hold animosity toward all whites—forcing someone from their home and incarcerating them just because they are Cherokee can cause those types of feelings in people who would normally not have them. Therefore, your safety here, especially at night, may be at risk. That is a difficult thing for me to say, but it is true. You are both always welcome to be with us, and I believe especially beneficial for our children, but staying through the night would only needlessly endanger you. I strongly encourage you to accept this man's accommodations. Visit us here each day if you wish."

Adam noted Alice's determined look, and was well aware how stubborn she could be once her mind was made up. He recognized the astuteness in what Benjamin said—that there was likely to be animosity toward them. Adam felt obligated to persuade her to accept the relative safety of Captain Martin's home. He'd seen the outcome of the ruthless attack on Rebecca. The last thing he wanted was for Alice to be subjected to such violence; he still felt responsible for getting her into this dangerous situation. He knew she would not allow herself to be terrorized, but he hoped her stubbornness could be penetrated by a sensible argument.

"Alice," he began, "Benjamin has a good point. I don't think now is the time to stop taking his advice. Maybe we should stay with Captain Martin. There is little we can do here at night, and our presence just might infuriate many of those who are being kept here. It could even bring trouble for the Rogers' if they are seen to be protecting us. I know you wouldn't want that any more than I would."

"Yes, you're right, I most certainly wouldn't want that." She gave a hard stare to Captain Martin as she considered. "Alright, I will agree as long as staying with them isn't going to offend Benjamin and Catherine."

Both Benjamin and Catherine shook their head adamantly.

"But first," Alice insisted, "I have to talk to Sally and Billy to let them know, and reassure them that I'll be back to see them in the morning."

"Sure," said Adam. "And I'll tell Jimmy and Rebecca."

Captain Martin was visibly relieved that they had finally agreed. He was hoping he would not have to tell them that they had no choice. Colonel Lindsay had made it clear to him that because they were not Cherokee they were to be released immediately and would not be allowed to spend nights in the stockade. It would certainly be asking for trouble; all civilians who were not incarcerated or in the employ of the military must leave at sunset.

"That will be fine," the captain said. "I have some additional duties to perform, so talk to your friends and I will meet you at the gate in thirty minutes." He politely excused himself, turned smartly, and left the stockade.

Alice spent the next thirty minutes with the children. Both Sally and Billy easily accepted that she would be spending the night elsewhere. To them, it seemed completely practical, and they were delighted to hear she would be back to spend time with them again tomorrow.

Catherine insisted on going with Adam to attend to Rebecca. Benjamin did not complain—he had done his part by giving them some time alone. Rebecca's injuries should also be looked after, and he believed it would be beneficial for her to have another woman to talk to.

Rebecca was genuinely pleased to know that the captain offered his home to Adam and Alice. She expressed her gratitude to Adam once again for him coming to her rescue. Adam replied to her with more words of outrage of what had been done to her. He began to tell her he hoped she would soon be feeling better, but Catherine shooed him away so she could examine Rebecca's injuries.

Jimmy reacted coolly, not speaking much or seeming to care what Adam had to say. Adam assumed he was preoccupied with concern for his wife, and the anger at what had happened to her. He would have liked to say something to console Jimmy, but his better judgment told him it was probably best to remain silent. If it were his wife who had been attacked, he could not imagine anything that anyone could say that would make him feel better. He told Jimmy he would see him tomorrow, but received only a grumble in reply.

When Adam and Alice arrived at the gate, they found Captain Martin waiting. "It has been a long day for all of us," he said to them, "and I will be glad to put it behind me. My home is within walking distance, so if you are ready..."

"Lead the way," said Adam.

Alice waved goodbye to Sally and Billy through the closing gates, following despondently behind the two men.

Chapter forty-three

The hand that clamped forcefully over Sal's mouth smelled of fish and damp dirt.

Drowsy from the huge meal Henri Acres brought them, Sal and Yonah fell asleep quickly and soundly. Yonah had prepared a sleeping mat for Sal next to the unlit fireplace, and then retired to his own sleeping area in the cabin loft. The last thing Sal remembered was lying down on the mat. He slept soundly until the rude awakening.

He was staring into the rheumy eyes of some middle-aged hooligan, breathing the stench of his clammy, foul smelling hand. He had the feeling this was not going to be one of his better days.

The rube crouched closer, putting his face next to Sal's ear and muttered, "Don't ya dare move, princess!"

The stink of the man's hand was overwhelmed by his putrid breath. Sal realized there were a lot of twenty-first century amenities that one could do without, but oral hygiene wasn't one of them. The only thing that kept him from attempting to respond to the "princess" remark was the thought of opening his mouth and getting a taste of the rancid smelling hand. That and the fact that in the man's other hand was an enormous, bone-handled hunting knife.

Sal worked to clear the sleep from his mind and evaluate his situation. There were bright rays of sunlight streaming through the cabin window indicating it was already early morning. He heard the footsteps of at least one other person inside the cabin. He glanced up at the loft. It was empty. Yonah was nowhere in sight.

Sal's thoughts were interrupted by more foul-smelling invectives. "Now lookee here, princess. I'm a gonna take my hand away so you can answer a few questions. If'n ya holler, I'll gut ya with this here knife." The rube flashed the knife in Sal's face. "You understand?" he asked as he slid his hand down from Sal's mouth and took a grip around his neck.

"Up yours, fish-breath," said Sal fiercely. "Get your stinking hands off of me!" Following directions wasn't one of Sal's strong suits.

The man tightened his grip on Sal's neck, throttling him before he could speak again. He flipped the hunting knife in his other hand, grabbing the blade and sharply flicking the heavy haft down on Sal's forehead with a sickening thump. It struck Sal right between the eyes, the pain so intense it blurred his vision. He tasted that stomach-turning metallic tang caused by a sharp blow to the nose. Sal was blinded by a dazzling starburst, as if someone had set off a camera flash in his eyes, and felt a warm stinging in his right eye as the blood from his forehead trickled into it. He choked on the blood from his bleeding nose running down the back of his throat.

"You smart-mouth me again, princess, and I'll drive this knife right into your brainpan. Now, first thing I wanna know is, are you the only one here?"

The grip of the man's hand around his neck prevented him from speaking, but it loosened enough that he could nod affirmatively. Better, he thought, not to tell them about Yonah.

"If yer lyin', yer dyin'. I know this ain't your place. Where's that injun what lives here?" He loosened his grip on Sal's neck slightly.

Sal's mind raced to form a credible response. He coughed, and said hoarsely, "Gone hunting."

"Huntin', huh?" He stood, pulling Sal up to his feet by his neck. "And just who might you be, princess?"

The sudden shift to a vertical position caused Sal's forehead to throb intensely. The blood was still flowing, as head wounds do, and Sal had to blink to keep it out of his eyes. He felt the point of the blade dig into his side, just below his rib cage. He put aside a wisecrack about who he might be and sputtered, "Watching the place for him."

The answer amused the rube greatly. He opened his toothless, smelly cavern of a mouth and brayed like a mule. Sal assumed it was laughter.

"Watchin' the place? You doin' a hell of a job, princess!" he said between bellows of laughter.

Sal heard a voice from behind say, "Knock off the clownin' and get him to tell you where the old man keeps the gold. Then we can cut his throat an' git outa here."

"Shut up, dumbass!" said the man holding Sal. "He ain't gonna tell us nuthin' if'n he thinks we're gonna kill him anyway." He looked into Sal's eyes fiercely and tightened the grip around his neck. "Lookee here now, princess, we know that ol' man's got gold hid here somewhere. You tell me where it is, and I'll try to keep dumbass here from killin' ya."

"There ain't no gold here," Sal whispered huskily.

The blow struck him with enough force that it would have lifted him from his feet had he not been held in place by the hand around his throat. His spine felt as if someone had swung a baseball bat into the small of his back. After the initial intense pain, his legs went completely numb. When the grip on his neck was released, he sunk to the floor as if his bones had turned to jelly.

The second man, standing over him with a wooden cudgel, smiled at him and said, "Wanna try that answer again, princess?"

"Don't… have… any… gold," Sal spoke slowly, not able to catch his breath. He clenched his eyes shut and tried to shield his head with his arms, anticipating another blow.

"Git him outside," said the man with the cudgel. "He'll tell us once you start a choppin' off a little of him at a time."

They each grabbed an arm and dragged him to the door, then tossed him through it. He landed hard in the dirt. Sal let out a low moan, followed by a yelp of pain as each of the men gave him a kick. They brusquely pulled him to his feet. The man who struck him with the cudgel held him upright while the man with the knife grabbed his left hand, placing the blade tightly against Sal's index finger.

"You're gonna tell me where that gold is, or I'm gonna start by cuttin' yer fingers off. Then I'm gonna move on to more important parts. Last chance to keep your finger, princess. Where's the gold?"

Sal blinked away enough of the blood to look into the man's eyes. He knew they would kill him whether he told them or not, so his choice was to either suffer through their torture, or give in to what they wanted and hope they killed him quickly. Unfortunately for Sal, he was never one to give in.

"Screw you, hillbilly," croaked Sal, spitting a mouthful of thick, bloody saliva into the man's face.

A momentary look of disbelief crossed the man's face as he wiped away the bloody sputum with his shirt sleeve. He stared into Sal's eyes with rage and hatred. "That just cost you yer whole hand." He tightened his grip on Sal's hand and repositioned the knife, pressing it into the flesh of his wrist.

Sal clenched his teeth and with incredible resolve, resisted pleading for his life. He defiantly locked eyes with his attacker. "There ain't no freakin' gold!" he insisted. He felt the pressure of the knife on his wrist increase.

"You'll tell me one way or t'other!" He pressed down even harder on the knife. Blood began to flow from Sal's wrist.

Suddenly, the man's eyes turned glassy and blank. He dropped the knife and clutched at a wooden shaft which had abruptly burst from his neck. His mouth moved as if he were trying to speak, looking like a fish gasping for air. Instead of words, he emitted a wet, gargling sound as blood erupted from his mouth. Still clutching the arrow, he dropped heavily to the ground, exposing the arrowhead piercing through the back of his neck. His legs twitched reflexively for a moment before all movement ceased.

The other man stared in horror at his fallen cohort. A sudden movement drew his attention to Yonah, standing no more than twenty yards away, who had just released a second arrow. The man was still holding Sal, depriving Yonah of a clear shot. Sal heard the arrow hiss as it flew past, narrowly missing the man's head and then burying itself into the cabin wall beyond. The man let out a shriek of fear, released Sal, and hightailed to the safety of the woods. Yonah quickly loosed a third arrow, which grazed the man as he dove for cover. Sal heard his scream as he disappeared into the trees.

Yonah ignored the fleeing man and turned his attention to Sal, who had fallen to the ground when the man released him. "Are you hurt badly, my friend?" Yonah asked, examining Sal's forehead, still bleeding freely where he had been struck with the knife handle.

"My head hurts, my back is killing me, and my legs are tingling like they're on fire," he answered through the blood running from his nose and across his lips. He wiped his sleeve across his face and looked at the dead man lying next to him, arrow protruding from his neck. "But I'm in a lot better shape than that dude. That was pretty awesome shooting, Tonto."

"Not that awesome. I was aiming for his heart."

"Hey, you got him anyway, and I'm damn glad you did. That moron was going to cut my hand off!

"You won't call me princess anymore, will you, stink-breath." Sal gave the body a half-hearted kick and was rewarded with a spasm of pain in his back. "Too bad you missed the other one." He paused a moment to consider. "Hey, man! You missed your mark on the first dude, and then you shot at the other one while he was still holding me. Holy crap, you could have shot me!"

Yonah shrugged. "They were going to kill you anyway. I think my arrow would have been a better way to die than getting chopped into pieces."

"How considerate; you're a regular Dr. Kevorkian. Thanks ever so much, dude," Sal said sarcastically.

"You are welcome," Yonah replied, his expression offering no indication that he was being facetious. "But I also regret I did not get the other man. Now we must get you well enough to travel and leave here hurriedly."

"Leave? Why? I bet that dude is still running. You're not worried about him coming back, are you?"

"He will not return right away, but he may report what happened here to the militia. They will come to arrest me for killing this man. After they have taken me away, he may return to continue his search."

"You killed him in defense of me and your home! No way they can arrest you for that, man. And you've got me for a witness."

"This is a white man," Yonah said, indicating the body. "I am red. That is all that will be seen. They will arrest me for his murder."

"Not if I can help it, Tonto. I ain't gonna stand by and let them hang your ass for saving my life."

"There is not much you can do to prevent it. You have proven your bravery, Squirrel-man, but even you cannot take on the entire military."

Sal's face was a mask of frustration. He was not used to situations where he could not get his way. "In that case Tonto," he winced painfully as he struggled to get to his feet, "I better get cleaned up so we can make tracks."

"Easy, my friend," Yonah said, putting his arm around Sal and helping him to the cabin. "We should assess the damage before you move too much. The tingling in your legs is probably a good sign, but we must hope that the blow to your back did not cause any permanent damage."

Sal washed the blood from his face and wrist, and then let Yonah apply some of his homemade salve to retard further bleeding. His nose had stopped bleeding, and Sal rinsed his mouth with salt water to get rid of the bad taste. Yonah gave him some analgesic herbs, examined his back, and ordered Sal to move his legs into various positions.

"There appears to be no broken bones, and you are getting the use of your legs back quickly. I am afraid, though, that you will be in much pain for a few days. Your back is already bruising nastily. The herbs will help reduce your soreness. You have a nasty gash on your forehead and both of your eyes are blackening, so you will be quite ugly for a while."

"You ain't no beauty queen either, Tonto, even without getting beaten up."

"That is true, Squirrel-man," Yonah laughed. "We make quite a pair."

Then Yonah became quite solemn. He placed his hand upon Sal's shoulder and spoke earnestly. "I must tell you," he said, "you have once again shown courageousness in the face of life-threatening danger, and you have my great respect. I have now seen your bravery with my own eyes. But I must ask—why didn't you just tell them where the gold was hidden? Surely my small fortune is not worth sacrificing your life."

"Hey man, it's the principle. I'll be damned if some redneck is going to push me around—especially one who calls me princess. But now I've got a question for you, Tonto. How the hell did you get outside from up there," nodding his head toward the loft, "without going through the door?"

"Surely you know that all us Indians have magical powers? I simply transformed myself into a bird and flew out the window."

"Turned yourself into a bird, huh? I think you turned into a bull, old man, because the crap's getting deep in here."

"It seems your wisdom is emerging along with your bravery," Yonah grinned. "In fact, the truth is much less mysterious. I simply had risen earlier, and gone out to greet the sunrise. When I returned I heard the thieves accosting you, and waited for an opportune time to act."

Yonah reexamined Sal's injuries. "If you think you can travel, we should be going now. We will first go to Henri Acres place, and let them know what has occurred."

Sal flexed his legs and nodded in the affirmative. "Yeah, I think I can make it to old Henry Pym's place if it ain't too far," he said, unconcerned that Yonah would not understand his reference to the comic book character.

They each put together a carry sack, including the medical supplies, the leftover food Henri had brought, and some other odds and ends. Yonah carried his bow, which he had restrung with a spare piece of sinew, and a quiver of arrows. He also had his hunting knife and a small hatchet tucked into his belt. Yonah then went to the fireplace, removed the stone, and retrieved the bag containing his gold and the handful of coins. "I will bring this along, since you paid such a high price and nearly gave up your life for it. It may prove to be very useful later." He dropped the gold into his carry sack.

When they were ready to go, Yonah took a moment to give his cabin a final look. He sighed but did not speak. It was likely to be the last time he would see the place.

Exiting the cabin, Sal prodded the dead man and said, "What should we do with him?"

"Did you want to take his scalp?" Yonah asked.

"His scalp! No way, dude! I meant, should we bury him?"

"I know what you meant, Squirrel-man. We will let his own people attend to him. They are likely to be here soon enough."

Henri's cabin was a few miles of climbing up and down switchback trails, which proved quite painful for Sal. He was relieved when they finally ascended the last rise and saw the cabin. Yonah gave a sharp whistle as they approached, but Henri Acres was already coming through the door when they entered the clearing.

"*Osiyo!*" Henri roared, jogging out to greet them. "I am delighted you came for a visit! I did not expect to see you again so soon! *Bienvenue, mes amis!*" he said, placing his brawny hand on Yonah's shoulder. He was startled when he caught sight of Sal's battered face. "*Sacrebleu!* What happened to the Little Squirrel? He is looking more like the raccoon than the squirrel." Both of Sal's eyes had blackened.

"Look here, Goliath," Sal snapped, "I'm in no mood..."

"As you predicted, Henri," Yonah interrupted, "we were visited by thieves this morning. They caught Squirrel-man unawares and tortured him, attempting to force him to disclose the hiding place of my valuables. He was most brave, and revealed nothing to them, even when they threatened his life."

"*Quelle horreur!* They abused you most dreadfully." He winced at Sal's battered face. "How did you escape them?"

Sal glanced at Yonah. He wasn't sure how much he should reveal to Henri.

"That is why we are here," Yonah answered without reservation. "I caught them inflicting their malice upon him when I returned from my morning walk. It was necessary to take dire action."

"Yonah, *mon vieil ami.* Surely you did not..."

"I am afraid so. I placed an arrow through the man's windpipe. He is dead. There was no choice; he was about to inflict a mortal wound to Squirrel-man. Unfortunately his cohort escaped."

"*Mon dieu,* this is most distressing. They will surely be after you for this. We must conceive a plan to keep you from their grasp until we can be assured of your fair treatment. Let us go inside quickly, and not remain here exposed. Meggie will be pleased to see you, in spite of the circumstances."

"I do not believe there is any immediate danger, Henri. The other man was well frightened, and will spend some time washing out his britches before he considers telling anyone about what happened to his partner. He may eventually realize that it would be to his advantage to do so. As far as my getting fair treatment, that is not likely no matter what steps I take."

While they were walking toward Henri's cabin, a woman appeared at the open door. She had the same obsidian-black, piercing eyes as Yonah, and her wizened face was just as wrinkled. Her straight, raven hair was parted in the middle, pulled back tightly, and folded into a chignon. It was a contrast to her brother's thick, white hair. She stood in the doorway, hands on her hips, staring admonishingly at Yonah.

"So," she said in mock anger, "you have finally come for a visit with your sister. Is my cooking so bad you can only tolerate it once each season?"

"Meggie, *'siyo*. I am sorry I have not come to visit sooner. You know you are the best cook in the entire wolf clan. *Wado* for the food you sent yesterday. It was delicious and much appreciated."

The solicitation and compliment was clearly a practiced ritual between the siblings, nevertheless, the praise of her cooking transformed her grimace into a smile.

"Had I known you were coming, I could have prepared an evening meal more fitting for guests. As it is, you will have to settle for a less elegant repast. I do have *gahnohayna* if you will come in and allow me to serve you," she said as she turned and reentered the cabin.

She poured each of the men a bowl of the thick hominy drink, and said, "Henri has told me of your encounter, and I see you are still carrying your arm in a sling. He also told me of your heroic companion, little *saloli*," she said, nodding to Sal, "who rescued you on the river. He did not tell me he had also been seriously injured." She regarded Sal's assaulted face with compassion.

"Squirrel-man, this is my sister, Meggie, as I am sure you have already surmised."

"*Osiyo*, ma'am. It's a pleasure to meet you. Please just call me Sal."

Meggie did her best to remember her manners and not stare at Sal. She found it difficult not to look at his grotesque injuries. "*Osiyo*, Sal. Thank you for your valor saving my brother from the waterfall."

"Squirrel-man sustained the injuries you see only today. We had an encounter with some would-be thieves, quite possibly the same hooligans who attempted to cause you and Henri some mischief."

"His poor face looks like it was kicked by a cow. Could you do nothing to prevent their brutality to him?"

"They came upon him while he was sleeping, after I had gone to greet the morning," Yonah said, then hesitated before continuing. "I was forced to deal with them most severely upon my return."

Prompted by the questioning look from Meggie, Yonah continued with the details of the encounter. Meggie listened quietly until he revealed he had fatally wounded Sal's attacker, when she was unable to suppress a gasp of horror. Sadness filled her eyes. Her reaction made Sal realize just how much of a sacrifice Yonah had made by killing the white man. He had most likely given up his home and contact with his family for the foreseeable future; and quite possibly had traded his own life for Sal's.

They sat quietly, sipping the *gahnohayna*. The tiny cabin was filled with the heartbreak of the brother and sister, knowing that their separation was inevitable. Sal so strongly felt the ache between them that it nearly overcame the pain of his own physical injuries.

What will you do?" Meggie asked meekly, foreknowing his reply and dreading it.

"Perhaps I will head to the western territory. It is where they wanted me to go anyway." Yonah kept his voice neutral, trying not to add to the gloomy mood. "You know that it is quite likely I would have been forced to go anyway. I can travel alone to avoid the white authorities, and ensconce myself until the trouble subsides. But let us not talk about it any further at present. We should enjoy each other's company today."

"*D'accord*, I agree!" said Henri. His booming declaration of agreement reverberated inside the cabin, causing Sal to flinch. "Little Squirrel, if you are feeling well enough, I would be most pleased to provide an *excursion grande* of Acres' acres and allow the brother and sister a few moments together."

"Sure, Goliath. I think I can handle a little looksee around the place. Lead the way, dude." Sal followed him outside.

Henri sucked in a great breath of fresh air, his body seeming to expand as it was released from the confines of the cabin. The cabin and property were nearly identical to Yonah's, situated on a mountaintop with a view of the river far below, which Henri indicated to Sal with a broad sweep of his massive arm.

"Many years ago, *mon père*, who was a trapper and trader from Canada, used that river to trade with the Cherokee. His father before him was also a trapper. The Tsalagi resisted contact with the whites for many years, except for a few French traders they believed trustworthy.

Back then the game was plentiful, and one could make a living from the land. It is no more; the bounty of the land has long been overused. As a young man, I accompanied my father on many of his trips here to the south. When I met Meggie on one of those trips—for me it was *coup de foudre*—love at first sight. We were married soon after. That was when I settled here.

"With strong ties of three generations, I have a deep regard for this Indian land. Now I cannot imagine living anywhere else. Meggie and Yonah's bond to this land go back hundreds, perhaps even thousands of years. Giving this up will be *tres* difficult for Yonah, Little Squirrel."

"Yeah, man, I do understand how difficult it's gonna be. He and a whole heap of Cherokees are about to be put through a butt load of suffering and loss. I made some good friends in the short time I've been here, and it pisses me off to see them mistreated like this."

"*C'est la vie, mon ami*. It is heartbreaking. I share your anger, but anger will do no good. The people will do what they will do."

"Yeah, dude, I guess you're right. But now, because of me, Yonah has gotta live like an outlaw. I hate to think what will happen if they catch the old dude, and it's all my fault."

Henri's immense eyes widened. "*Sottises*, Little Squirrel. Nonsense, you are not to blame; he acted to save your life. Were you not willing to suffer abuse to protect him? What would you have him do? You do not understand Yonah very well if you believe he could stand impassive while a friend's life is endangered!"

Sal acknowledged him with a grunt. He had been with Yonah long enough to know that what Henri said was true. He also knew that there would have been no reason for Yonah to shoot the man if he hadn't allowed himself to be captured.

Henri sensed that Sal was still feeling guilty about Yonah, and the pain he was feeling from his beating was evident. In spite of Henri's rough, mountain-man appearance, his heart was as big as the rest of him. He felt compassion for Sal, and wished there was something he could do to help him feel better. He suddenly brightened as a solution came to mind.

"Come with me, Little Squirrel. Between your look of pain, your blackened eyes, and your dour mood, you are not going to enjoy my little tour. I have just thought of something that may help you feel better."

He led Sal past a stable and corral. Several horses nickered and ran to the fence when they saw Henri, who whispered soothingly in French to them as he passed. He continued walking toward a large storage shed, breaking into a French song. Sal's French wasn't good enough to make out all the words, but he could make out enough of the bawdry lyrics to realize Henri's song wasn't exactly *Frere Jacques.*

Henri pulled opened the shed door, continuing to sing and motioned for Sal to enter. They picked their way through, stepping over heaps of feed sacks and farm implements until they reached a dusty old cabinet buried behind a mishmash of items at the very back of the building. Henri began moving things away from the cabinet, slinging them to the tune of his song until he made enough room to open the creaky cabinet door. Great clouds of dust rose from his efforts, setting off a sneezing and coughing fit from Sal.

"Good god!" Sal coughed, waving the dust from his face. "What the heck are you up to, Goliath? You got the family heirlooms hidden in there or what?"

"Je suis désolé, mon *petit ami,*" he apologized. "No heirlooms; only this." He held up a brown, dust-covered jug for Sal to see. "This was given to me by an old trader friend passing through long ago. It is what we call calvados. In this country they call it applejack. I have kept it here in case there was ever a, uh, medicinal need."

He wiped the dust from the neck of the jug, pulled the cork, handed the jug to Sal and said, "A drink or two of this will help ease your pain."

Applejack is produced by distilling hard cider. If done properly, the final product can be as strong as eighty-proof liquor. Henri's calvados had aged while stored in the cabinet, increasing the alcohol content considerably.

Sal took a sniff of the open jug. It had the smell of strong liquor, but with a sweet, pleasant apple overtone. He figured Henri was right; a good, stiff drink would probably help ease his pain. He took a swig.

"Sweet suffering superman!" he whispered hoarsely. The calvados tasted more like pure grain alcohol than apples. The burning in his throat took his breath away and made his eyes water.

"Oh ho!" said Henri. "Maybe the drink has become too strong? I should have sampled it first."

Sal handed the jug back to him. "Be my guest, dude," he said, recovering slightly from the unexpected assault on his throat.

"Perhaps just a drop," Henri said, accepting the jug and taking a long pull. "*Mais oui,* it has aged well."

"Aged? I think it's gone senile. You could remove paint with that stuff, man!"

"It is a taste one must grow accustomed to. I myself have all but given up strong alcohol, but I hoped a small imbibe might lessen your pain."

Sal had to admit that his pain was beginning to dull as the warmth of the drink spread through his body. "You know, I think it might be helping a little after all."

Henri grinned broadly and passed the jug back to Sal. "*C'est grand!* Perhaps a bit more, then?"

Sal took another drink, this time a little more tentatively, and found that the second swallow went down much more smoothly. He was able to detect the sweet undertone of apples that the beverage had retained. Sal seldom drank hard liquor, despite an outward show of the wild lifestyle he tended to present. He occasionally enjoyed a glass of wine with dinner or a cold beer on a hot day, eschewing drinking just for the sake of drinking. It wasn't that he had anything against sensible drinking; he'd done plenty of partying when he was younger. More recently though, his career and other activities filled his life and he had gradually become estranged from the party crowd. It wasn't really a conscious decision; just something that happened as he grew older.

"Not quite as rough the second time," Sal said and passed the jug back. "Why do you keep it buried out here in the shed, Goliath? Hiding it from the missus?"

"Not so much of the hiding, Little Squirrel. The strong spirits have been most harmful to many of the Tsalagi people. To some of my French-Canadian friends, the wine and spirits are *douceur de vivre* and they could not imagine doing without it. For myself—*prenez-le ou laissez-le*—I can take it or leave it as you say," he said. He took another swig, wiped his sleeve across his bearded mouth, and continued. "Some of the Cherokee seem to have something in them that makes them like it too much. Both Meggie and Yonah have seen many of their kinsmen's lives ruined by the drink, and because of this they have developed strong feelings against any form of alcoholic drink. It is for this reason I do not keep it in the house; to respect their wishes. I think they would not approve even of medicinal use," he said sheepishly, "so it may be wise to not speak of it to them."

"Mum's the word, big guy," Sal winked. The third gulp began to deaden the ache in his back and replace it with a warm glow. "Hey, I wouldn't want to disrespect them either, you know. I feel the way you do; I can take it or leave it. I've also seen folks whose lives have been devastated by drinking too. Back in Jersey, I had a bud who was killed in an accident while he was drunk, so I can understand why someone who had to put up with a family member with a drinking problem might have strong feelings against alcohol."

Agreeing that they understood Yonah and Meggie's feelings about alcoholic drink, they continued to pass the jug between them, certain that because they could not be seen, they were doing nothing offensive. Sal's pain faded a little with each drink, and Henri's social etiquette demanded he not let Sal drink alone.

"Say, Goliath," said Sal, slurring slightly, but feeling much better. "What was that tune you were singing on the way here? It was kind of catchy."

"Tune? Oh, *oui*. It was *Chevaliers de la Table Ronde*. Just an old song we used to sing when good friends got together. I still remember most of the words." He began to sing, his huge barrel-chest producing a rich baritone.

"*Chevaliers de la table ronde, Goutons voir si le vin est bon. Goutons voir si le vin est bon. Goutons voir, oui oui oui. Goutons voir, non non non. Goutons voir si le vin est bon.*"

Sal understood enough French to recognize that the song was about the Knights of the Round Table, but not much more than that. His pain had been significantly dulled by the calvados, and despite their conversation moments ago about alcoholic drink, the pair continued to pass the jug of applejack between them. The song seemed to have endless verses, and Henri sang them heartily. Between the buzz from the applejack and the hooking melody of the song, it wasn't long before Sal joined in, singing the "*oui, oui, oui*," and the "*non, non, non*" lines of every verse. The singing stopped abruptly when the door swung open and a man stepped into the shed.

"*Qu'est-ce que c'est? Qui vive?*" Henri whispered, then "John Carter!" he boomed. "*Osiyo, mon ami.* I did not hear you coming," he said more timidly. Sal stood holding the jug of applejack, for the moment too startled to speak.

"*Osiyo*, Henri," John replied. "I am not surprised you did not hear me. Such caterwauling! I whistled to announce my presence, but it was drowned out by the braying. I even watered and placed my horse in your corral and still you did not hear me."

"*Je suis désolé.* I was giving the little Squirrel-man here a tour, and we were distracted by song."

"I believe you two were more distracted by the jug Sal is holding. Is that the same jug you have been hiding out here for so many years? *Osiyo*, Sal Lolliman. What has happened to your face? Do not tell me Yonah has done this to you."

"Yonah? No way, dude," Sal replied, recovering from the shock of John's sudden appearance. He hiccupped and handed the jug to Henri, who gently placed it back into the cabinet. "Good seeing you again, Squanto. It's a long story, but among other things I was attacked this morning by some thieves who snuck up on me. I probably wouldn't even be here if not for Yonah saving my butt."

"Snuck up on you, you say. I would think that would make you want to be more vigilant rather than dulling your senses with applejack. Suppose I was another attacker? Both of you would have been caught unawares."

Embarrassed by John's admonishment, Sal and Henri offered their poor excuse that they were partaking of the applejack only as a pain reliever for Sal. John Carter snorted and made no further comment, but his expression made it clear that he did not find their explanation satisfactory. He was more concerned about their lack of vigilance than their partaking of drink.

"You are right, *mon ami*," Henri conceded. "It has been a difficult day and we have yet to tell you all that has occurred. We have no good excuse for not being more watchful. Yonah and Meggie are at the cabin saying their farewells, and the situation calls for us to be on guard. We have been *négligents*."

"Farewells?" John said. "What has taken place?"

Henri and Sal brought John up to date, beginning with the shooting on the river, and ending with the attack at Yonah's cabin this morning. John followed the story intently, stone-faced as usual, until they got to the part about Yonah killing the white man. At this, John's cool expression turned apprehensive.

"I have been dreading that something of this nature would happen. A killing even in self-defense will only add fuel to an already inflammatory state of affairs."

"Yonah is planning to take a circuitous route to the western territory," said Henri, "hoping to avoid retribution here. He believes he may be treated more fairly if he can delay his capture."

John Carter rubbed his chin as he considered Yonah's quandary. "I was on my way to Yonah's place to bring him news of Guwaya. There may be an alternative for him to consider. I will go and speak to him now. You two should first take a walk to clear your heads of applejack, and then we will all have a sober discussion to make our plans. I will not mention the drinking to Yonah and Meggie."

Henri nodded gratefully. John's sudden appearance had already startled most of the intoxicating effects of the applejack from them. Nevertheless, he and Sal took the long river path while John headed directly to the cabin. By the time they completed their walk, Henri and Sal were quite clear-headed. At Henri's cabin, they found John listening to Yonah retell his story. Apparently true to his word, John had not mentioned the applejack.

While they spoke, Meggie prepared an herb and willow potion for Sal. The pain relief from the applejack was short-lived, and now he had a headache in addition to his other aches. He hoped Meggie's willow potion would prove to be more long-lasting than the applejack.

John proceeded to tell them of Guwaya's decision to move his family to the caves. He expressed his concern about the plan, but admitted that the place was well hidden and well stocked, and that Guwaya had worked hard to prepare the cave for his family. He stopped short of suggesting that Yonah change his plans, merely planting the seed of the idea and letting it germinate. It didn't take long to show signs of life.

Yonah scratched the back of his neck as he contemplated John Carter's news. "Perhaps they would not mind if I joined them," he said. "Guwaya has always been a good friend, and I may be of some use to him. It will be a long journey, and I am likely to be captured along the way, although no more likely than if I followed my original plan."

"It will not be such a long journey on horseback, *mon ami*," said Henri. "I will provide you with a horse. And one for the little Squirrel-man if he is also to accompany you."

"You bet, Goliath. I've come this far with the old bear," said Sal. "Can't hardly desert him now."

"*Wado*, brother-in-law. And to you, Squirrel-man; your company will be most welcome," said Yonah.

"I am returning there as well," said John, "So the three of us will ride together. I suggest we leave at first light. I might have suggested leaving immediately, but I am certain Meggie will not allow you to depart without being well-fed." No one would object to a delay if it involved partaking in one of Meggie's delicious meals.

"You are right, John Carter," said Meggie. "I will not miss what may be my last chance to cook for my brother. You and he will need a good meal to travel on, and the little squirrel could also stand to be fattened up a bit."

Chapter forty-four

*E*r, howdy, boys," Tom said in his best southern drawl. He'd gotten plenty of chance to practice it when he first moved north. On more than one occasion he had been treated to a bad impersonation of Gomer Pyle by some bonehead wise-ass whose entire knowledge of the south came from watching re-runs of *The Andy Griffith Show.* It used to annoy him, but he learned that if he put on his own good ol' boy act it baffled them; not knowing whether he was putting them on or not.

This time it was no joke. His life just might depend on how convincing he could sound to these two men; and whether they were gullible enough to swallow the king-sized helping of baloney he was about to feed them.

"Howdy, hell!" said the taller of the two young men, who was blocking Tom's exit through Guwaya's cabin door. Tom surmised that this man was the leader of the two. He had a slightly more intelligent look about him, though neither appeared to be Mensa candidates. The shorter man just stared at him, slack-jawed and dim-witted, but there was a wild meanness in his look that conveyed danger.

"I'll ask you agin," he said, moving closer to Tom, "who the hell are you and what the hell are you doin' in here?"

"Give me a chance, boys!" Tom gave them a toothy gee-whiz grin. "That's a helluva lot of hell fer me to git through all at once." He stalled to steady his nerves and focus his racing mind. He already had his back-story prepared, but had been hoping he wasn't going to need it.

"Well, you best be gettin' through it right quick like, afore I put somethin' else through ya," he said, placing his hand on a pistol stuck in his belt.

"Easy now, fellas." Tom leaned back and held up the open palm of his free hand. "No need to be gettin' yourself all riled up." He had weapons of his own; unfortunately both were muzzleloaders and not prepared to fire. He figured that was probably the case with the other man's pistol, but he couldn't be sure. He knew Samuel Colt was working on his patent for the revolver about this time, although he was pretty sure pre-made ammunition hadn't become commonplace much before the time of the Civil War. Still, he wasn't going to gamble his life upon it.

"Name's Tom," he said with a toothy grin. He offered his hand to them in a gesture of friendship. Neither of them took him up on the handshake. He withdrew his hand, looked at his palm with a shrug, and then wiped it on his shirt as if their refusal to shake was due to some nonexistent grunge.

"I was just out doin' me some huntin' an' came across this here cabin. Thought I'd be neighborly and stop fer a visit. This here your place, boys? Sure is right homey."

"Knock off the hogwash, cornball," the taller man said. "You expect us to believe you came in here to be neighborly? We know what yer up to."

Tom's heart sank. Maybe these guys weren't as stupid as they looked. He kept the disappointment out of his eyes and stuck with his act.

"Honest, fellas," he said. "I sure as heck wasn't up to nothin'. Jus' hopin' to make yer acquaintance. Maybe get a cup o' coffee, that's all."

"Cup o' coffee my hairy ass. Ya' ain't out here this far from nowhere lookin' fer new friends. Ya' know'd this here's an injun cabin, and you be a-scavengin' it. We be with the militia roundin' up them critters an' takin' 'em to the fort, so we git first dibs on everythin' in here."

So that was it, thought Tom. No honor among thieves. It was going to be tough to convince them he was just a hunter who stumbled upon a cabin. The Cherokee removal had been anticipated by the white settlers for years, and the land already auctioned off. Anyone local who had their eyes on Cherokee property would have been waiting for their opportunity to rummage the abandoned properties before they could be claimed. He had no choice now, though, except to stick to his story.

"You fellas got me all wrong," Tom said. "I ain't stealin' nothin'. I come out huntin' 'round here all the time."

"All the time, huh? Then how come you ain't seen this farm before?"

Oops, Tom thought. Lying didn't come easily to him, and he struggled to recover. "Well, I ain't been to this here exact spot afore, but I've done quite a bit a huntin' in this general area," he stammered.

"Yeah?" said the tall man. "So if you been a-huntin', where be your game? I think what ya been a-huntin' is right here in this cabin."

Another hole in his story, Tom thought. As plentiful as the game was in the surrounding woods, he was going to have a hard time convincing them he hadn't killed anything.

"I left my kill over yonder," he said, pointing with his chin toward the woods. "But I just ain't been too lucky, I guess." His story was beginning to sound bogus even to himself.

"That be the first thing you said that was right—yer luck jus' ran out. Ain't no way ye left fresh meat out there in the woods fer some critter to run off with. Now, I'm gonna tell ye what's gonna happen. First, I'm a-gonna take a look at what all yer carryin', an' then me an' Shorty here are gonna give ya a whoppin' to remember us by."

Tom tensed for an attack. He could take care of himself pretty well against a single attacker, but he wasn't foolish enough to believe he had much of a chance against two men at once. He made a final attempt to talk his way out of the situation.

"No need fer any of that, boys. I can see I jus' got myself into yer business, so I'll jus' be goin' along ..."

"You ain't a-goin' nowhere, cornpone. We're jus' about t' have us some fun."

He reached out to grab Tom by the arm, but stopped abruptly when a voice suddenly called from outside the cabin. The voice sounded strangely familiar to Tom.

"Tom! Hey, boy! Whatcha doin' in there? I ain't a-standin' out here all day waitin' fer ya," cried the voice.

Tom had no idea who could be calling to him. He was happy for the diversion, though for the moment too confused to take advantage of it. His confusion turned to outright shock when he glimpsed the face that peered around the door.

"Let's git goin'," said Sal as he stepped into the cabin. "It's too dark for any more huntin' anyhow." He feigned shock at seeing the two men. "Oh, 'scuse me, fellers."

Sal gave Tom a clandestine wink. "Whadda ye know, Tom. I guess ye was right, there was somebody home after all. Just like you t' be in here a-jawin' and leave me out in the woods holdin' these here squirrels."

Sal nodded to the two men. "Pleased t'make yer acquaintance, boys." No one offered to shake hands. "Sorry to interrupt yer little tea party, fellas, but me an' ol' Tom here need to git. We got a long walk back to th' camp, an' it's gettin' dark," Sal continued. "Ol' Tom here's always forgittin' the time when he's makin' new friends. He's jus' a friendly sort, I guess."

"Ya mean you two was really up here huntin'?" asked the tall one.

Sal gave the man a wry look and held up two freshly killed squirrels by the tail. "What'd ye think we was doin', ye nitwit? Pannin' fer gold?" he said sarcastically.

The locals were taken back, not sure now what exactly to believe about Tom and Sal. The tall man was still skeptical, but much less inclined to violence now that the odds were no longer in his favor. He managed to compose himself enough to put some of the authority back in his voice, and said, "You two hicks go on an git outta here. We be part of an official military operation at this here cabin, an' you two fools are just in the way."

"Don't git yer panties in a wad, Jethro," said Sal. "That be fine with us. Like I said, we need t' be a-goin' anyway. Come on, Tom, let's leave these fellas to their oh-fficial military operation," he said with a smirk. "They ain't got no compunction t'be shootin' the breeze with ye anyhow."

"Eh, sure, okay," said Tom, still shocked by Sal's arrival and at the same time trying to contain his amusement at Sal's impersonation. He sounded like a cross between Jed Clampett and Ernest T. Bass. Tom stepped between the two locals, tipped his hat to them, and walked out the door with Sal. If either of them had looked back, they would have seen the two locals staring after them in open-mouthed bewilderment.

As soon as they were out of earshot of the cabin, Sal heard Tom ask, "What the heck are you doing here?" from the side of his mouth.

"Ain't ye glad t' see yer ol' huntin' buddy?" Sal replied, still in character.

"More than ever," Tom replied. "But you can knock off the *Dukes of Hazzard* routine now. You sound ridiculous."

"Not too ridiculous to get your butt out of a jam, dude. And you look pretty goofy with that dirt smeared all over your face. I'm just glad they were too stupid not to notice I didn't have a hunting rifle."

"The squirrels were a good detractor. You took a heck of a risk coming in there unarmed. Speaking of faces, what the heck happened to yours? Are those black-eyes for real? You look like you were kicked in the head."

"Yeah, well, they ain't part of the act. It's a long and painful story that I'd rather forget about for a while."

Tom gave him a sidelong glance and dropped the subject. He made a half-hearted attempt to wipe some of the dirt from his face. "How did you know about the story I was telling them?"

"We were outside listening to you, man. Almost had me believing you for a minute or two."

"We?" asked Tom.

"Yeah, my posse." He nodded toward the two men standing just off the trail in front of them, just barely visible in the deepening twilight. "They're why I wasn't too worried about coming in unarmed."

"John Carter! And Yonah!" Tom smiled as the two new arrivals clapped him on the shoulder. "But how did you …?"

Actually, we were on our way here, to Guwaya's cabin," said John Carter, "when we ran into him and his family on the trail. He told us what had happened—about Ahni being taken and what you were planning to do. Guwaya took our horses and continued on to his hideaway, while the three of us hiked here to see if you required our assistance. When we approached the cabin and heard voices, Yonah crept close enough to hear what was going on. That is how Sal knew about your fabrication. We came up with a plan to send in Sal to back up your story if need be."

"It's a most fortunate thing that you did," said Tom. "I'm quite sure I was just about to have my head handed to me."

"No way, dude. There was never any chance of that," said Sal. "Not with us three dudes out here. We thought it would be better if I went in to back you up so you could skip out peacefully and not take a chance on blowing Guwaya's cover.

"Old Tonto here quickly bagged a couple squirrels for props," Sal continued. "Let me tell you—you don't want to get in front of the business end of this old dude's bow and arrow."

"Great idea," said Tom. "I think the squirrels are what convinced them. I don't know if they knew what to think about Sal's performance."

"Hey man, if you can't dazzle them with brilliance, baffle 'em with bullshit," Sal gloated.

"So," said Yonah, "the Squirrel-man with the squirrels saved the day."

They laughed at that, even Sal, who held up the squirrels by their tails and shook them in triumph.

"We should put more distance between ourselves and the cabin," said John. "The others will be returning soon and may not be as gullible as those two. Let us make haste; we will be in full darkness before we reach Guwaya's cave."

With that, they set off for the cavern, filling in Tom on the events of the last several weeks along the way. Yonah explained how Sal received his injuries, in spite of Sal's earlier reluctance to speak of it. Tom noticed that Sal didn't mind too much; Yonah generously embellished the story with Sal's acts of bravery. The relationship between Sal and Yonah had certainly turned out a lot different than Tom expected.

The telling also refreshed their memory of the desperate situation they faced. As they walked in the twilight, the joviality of the reunion and small coup faded into a more somber mood, like a night fog settling onto a mountaintop, obscuring the stunning views with dismal gray shadows.

Chapter forty-five

My home is just over yonder," said Captain Martin, indicating a large, handsome house at the end of the street. The entire street, in fact, was lined with a dozen or so stately homes, contrasting with the rustic look of the other parts of town Adam and Alice had seen.

Captain Martin's house was an elegant, attractively landscaped two-story residence, charmingly adorned by a copious wrap-around front porch. The porch flowed from the sides of a set of wide, sturdy steps, leading to the substantial walnut double doors of the main entrance. A sturdy railing with close-set balusters and generous support columns defined the front edge of the porch. Intricate lattice work was strategically draped above the railing, tastefully screening the view from the street and providing filtered shade on hot summer days. To the left of the entryway, the porch blossomed to a semi-circular pathway around a turret which formed the left front corner of the house. The right side of the porch led to a *porte-cochere*, through which a carriage could pass and allow visitors to disembark while sparing them exposure to the elements. Five gleaming windows on the second floor sparkled in the brilliant orange glow of the setting sun above the porch. The house was hardly a mansion, although it was amply proportioned and had the curbside appeal of a lavish southern plantation house.

"Quite a place," said Adam. "Military pay must be pretty good these days."

"I am afraid the pay is quite modest," Captain Martin answered, not appearing to take offense at Adam's remark. "This house does not belong to me. It was provided to us when I was transferred here. Most of these homes were owned by the prosperous Cherokees who lived here. Many of the owners sold them to private buyers when they relocated west, but a few, like this one, were purchased by the military for officer housing."

As they ascended the porch steps, the front door swung open revealing a young woman wearing a floor-length summer dress. The puffy lower sleeves and narrow waistline of the deep royal blue day gown rose to a wide, modest neckline, where it delineated the alabaster complexion of her shoulders. Loose coils of auburn hair framed her unpretentious face, which glowed with a healthful radiance. Her countenance was generally unremarkable except for her deep, azure-blue eyes, so strikingly captivating that one instantly fixated upon them. The effect gave her a classic and intelligent look, the way one might expect a Romantic poet of the Georgian Era to appear.

Captain Martin sprinted up the porch steps, embraced the woman and tenderly kissed her on the cheek. "Constance," he said, "these are our guests I spoke to you about, Adam Hill and Alice Delvecci."

"Welcome," said Constance, only momentarily making eye contact with Adam and Alice before shyly looking downward, aware that her striking eyes could be unsettling to some people at first. "Please come in. I hope you will be most comfortable here."

Her demure smile implied that whatever profound thoughts she held would not be hastily imparted, being thoroughly pondered and tested for flaws before they would be spoken, as if speaking them aloud certified them as fact. To her, prattle was not only ill-mannered, it was intolerable.

They entered the house through a well-appointed entryway, the most prominent feature of which was the ornately carved walnut staircase leading to the second floor. Surrounding the staircase were several closed doors, also of carved walnut, and an open doorway partially obscured behind the staircase which led to the kitchen area. The floor was made from wide planks of hard, yellow Georgia pine, and every corner and door frame was trimmed with intricately carved walnut, from the foot-high baseboards to the crown molding lining the ceiling fifteen feet above them.

Constance opened the closest door and said, "Would you care to sit with us in the parlor?" She gestured for them to enter the room.

The parlor was tastefully appointed. Less ornate than the entryway, it had the inviting, comfortable atmosphere of a practical, yet elegant, living area. The bulk of the furnishings in the sitting area were English imports, complimented with a few sturdy American made pieces, most notably a writing desk and a card playing table.

Constance cast them a graceful smile. She sat in a maroon French country wing chair, and said, "Please," indicating that they should take seats wherever they felt comfortable. Captain Martin stood resting his hand on a mahogany armchair. He glanced at Alice, waiting for her to sit first as his manners dictated. She and Adam took a seat on the small sofa facing their hosts.

"You have a very beautiful home," Alice said to Constance.

"Thank you, but I am afraid I cannot take credit for it. The house was provided for us."

"Yes, Captain Martin told us that, but it has been decorated wonderfully."

"Nearly everything you see was provided with the house. We are fortunate to have been offered it. I suppose it was part of the military's enticement to make this distasteful assignment more palatable to James."

Captain Martin's face showed a slight hint of disapproval at her remark. He said nothing and the look disappeared almost instantly, but not before it was noticed by Adam and Alice.

Alice decided not to question Constance's comment for the moment. "Goodness, it's quite a large house for only two people. Do you have children?"

"Yes, we have two daughters, Emily and Sarah." She indicated a portrait of two small girls hanging above the fireplace mantle. "They came with us when we first moved here, but we recently sent them back home to school."

"Aren't they lovely!" said Alice, to Constance's obvious delight. Captain Martin allowed his pride to show, for once not attempting to mask his feelings. "Where is home for you?"

"James and I are from Tennessee, near Jonesborough. We both have large families there. It is quite a beautiful area. Have you ever been there?"

"Yes, both Adam and I have visited there. I agree, it is very beautiful with lots of surrounding mountains." She didn't mention that they had been in Jonesborough while hiking the Appalachian Trail, since it wouldn't exist for about a hundred years. "You must miss your daughters, though. Will they be returning from school soon?"

"Well, I am not certain," she said. "I guess it depends on how things develop here in Georgia." This time is was her turn to send a meaningful glance to Captain Martin.

"We sent them home to school not only for their education," said the captain. "Our decision was also based on the events occurring here."

"Because you were concerned for their safety?" asked Alice.

"Partly. Most of all we wanted to spare them exposure to the unchristian actions being taken here." The captain's frank remark was followed by a conspicuous pause. It wasn't the sort of remark either Adam or Alice expected to hear from him.

"Are you talking about the violence, like what happened to Rebecca? Or the Indian removal in general?" Adam asked.

"No decent man would condone what was done to Mrs. Deerinwater. Unfortunately, that type of violence is part of the world we live in, and we could not realistically expect to completely shelter our children from it. We can counter it by teaching them proper behavior and giving good examples. What we were not willing to do was to have them witness the unchristian actions of our government against an entire race of people."

Until now, he had shown them nothing but a complete dedication to his duty, revealing no hint of his personal feelings about it. He had shown compassion of course, exhibited during Rebecca's rescue, but this last statement exposed a personal conflict between duty and his true feelings.

"Forgive me," said Adam, "but I have to ask. If you feel that way then why …"

"Why am I partaking in it? Because I am a soldier with a sworn duty."

Alice wasn't about to let him off so easy. "A sworn duty? What about the duty to the Christian beliefs you claim to have? How can you justify being part of this atrocity? Good lord, do you think it exonerates you just because you sent your children away, to where they don't have to witness what you're doing?"

"Alice," said Adam, "take it easy. If you remember, Captain Martin saved Rebecca's life today. Mine too, probably."

"It is quite alright, Adam," Captain Martin said. "Alice's questions are none that I have not heard before." His eyes shifted momentarily to Constance. "None that I have not asked myself, for that matter. As for the matter of my daughters, I fully intend to tell them about the events here, as well as the part I played in them. The reason for sending them away was not to hide that from them, but to spare them from living through it. When they are older, they can make their own judgment about my actions.

"I hope they will understand that as a soldier I have a duty to obey the orders of my superiors. My choice was to resign my commission or stay on and carry out those orders as honorably as possible. Since the removal will occur regardless of my decision, I chose the latter. I also had to consider my duty to support my family. General Wool decided to resign his commission rather than carry out this removal, but I have not had the luxury of a general's salary to fall back upon. Not even those of a captain for that long for that matter."

He anticipated Alice's response. "No, getting paid for a job does not justify it, yet it must be a consideration since my family depends upon my income to survive. My decision was not an easy one, and not without the risk that in hindsight I may wish I had chosen differently. But that," he said in an even voice and unyielding eyes, "is only between myself, my family, and my creator."

"How long have you been stationed here in Georgia?" Adam hoped he could prevent the conversation from turning into a heated debate.

"Only for about three years. I was offered the commission by General Wool himself, who knew of my service in the United States Army. I was stationed in Tennessee and only a lieutenant there, so a promotion to the rank of captain in the Georgia Guard represented a significant financial increase for us. At the time the mission was to help keep order and prevent unrest in the area. To be honest, I expected the Cherokee nation would be voluntarily relocating to the western territory, and never imagined a forced removal would be carried out."

"Apparently neither did the Cherokee," Alice said brusquely.

"I suppose we were all a little too naive. It was hard to understand how Old Hickory could let down the people who fought so valiantly for him. To be fair to President Jackson, I think he honestly believes that this is the best course of action for them. He believes they will never be able to withstand the encroachment of white settlers on their lands, and moving west is their only option."

"And the only way the Georgians can get their greedy hand on the gold beneath their lands," said Alice.

"Yes, there is that. There are surely greedy motivations as well," said the captain. "But it is not true of everyone."

Constance came to her husband's defense. "There are many of us, non-Cherokee that is, who do not agree with this forced relocation. Many prominent figures have spoken out against it as I am sure you are aware. One senator from your own part of the country—James mentioned you are from Delaware—Senator Theodore Frelinghuysen, spoke extensively denouncing the bill in Congress. Senators Sprague of Maine and Edward Everett of Massachusetts also rose to support Frelinghuysen's position. A number of missionaries have even spent time in prison for their support of the Cherokee."

"Yet the removal proceeds in spite of those efforts," said Alice.

"Yes, it does," Constance said. "Our nation is currently experiencing unprecedented growth, and many feel that it is not only their right but their duty to expand the country and claim its resources with no regard for any prior claims, especially by those they consider uncivilized. I fear that future generations will not look kindly upon that attitude."

"I'm sure you're right about that," Alice agreed.

Constance continued. "My point is that not everyone is in accordance with that attitude. The Cherokee people have many friends among the whites, who are outraged by the idea of removal. While we may show support for the Cherokee by continuing to speak against removal, it is clearly going forth, regardless of the outrage being expressed. Is it not also supportive for James to do his part to see that this inevitable removal, as unchristian as it may be, is at least carried out with a modicum of respect and compassion?"

It was obviously a rhetorical question. Alice was by nature a fighter, especially when it came to standing up against the unjust treatment of others. But Constance's words gave her pause to consider. Was there a point at which it would be better to set aside the protestations, accept the inevitable, and do what you could to make the best of a bad situation? Certainly the Cherokee people did not believe so; it would be much easier for them to give in and accept removal. She understood that the vast majority of them had made a formidable sacrifice to express their indignation through peaceful resistance, by refusing to give up their homeland until they were forced to do so. But what of the whites who had stood on the side of the rights of the Cherokee nation? What would she do if she were a soldier facing this situation; quit or do as Captain Martin had done? The answer was no longer as clear to her as she first thought it to be.

"There is also the fact that the United States is facing a number of internal disputes," Captain Martin added. "The rights of the individual states are in jeopardy because of the need for a strong central government. The issue of slavery has been a bone of contention between the northern and southern states, and is the cause of a great rift between them. I believe that men must be level-headed enough to work out all of these issues, lest we run the risk of destroying our own country."

"That's not exactly the attitude I would expect from a military man," said Alice. "Don't you believe that some things are worth fighting for?"

"Of course I do," he answered. "But are you suggesting we fight against our own citizens? Do you understand how devastating that would be to our country?"

Indeed she did. Unfortunately, she thought, so would he in a little more than twenty years. She hoped he'd be retired from military life by then. "I certainly wasn't suggesting a civil war. I was just surprised that a military man would be against that option."

"I think you will find most military men, and their families, consider going to war a last resort. After all, I believe we are the ones who must do the fighting and have the most to lose."

"And I believe," said Constance, "that I have been a poor hostess who has not offered my guests any refreshments. Alice, if you would not mind putting aside this heavy discussion for now and lending me a hand, I have some cool drinks and pastries we can serve. I am sorry to impose, but we have no servants…"

"Of course, I'd be happy to help," Alice replied, following her to the kitchen.

The conversation became more lighthearted when they returned to the parlor with tea and a tray full of baked goods. When Constance heard Adam and Alice intended to return to the fort each day, she expressed a desire to come along with them when she was able, and volunteered to provide supplies that might be needed on days when her household chores kept her at home. Adam and Alice readily agreed. If Captain Martin had any objections, he kept them to himself for the moment.

After finishing the tea and cakes, Constance showed her guests to their rooms. Alice was taken to a very feminine room containing two beds, which was apparently the Martin girls' bedroom when they were at home. The room was as tastefully decorated as the rest of the house and invitingly comfortable. Several dolls sat on a shelf between the beds, patiently waiting for their mistresses' return.

Adam was shown to a more neutrally decorated bedroom; a room that served as the Martin's guest room. Both rooms had brightly colored pitchers of fresh water and a washing bowl, along with a chamber pot for nighttime toilet use.

"I am sure you would both like to freshen up," Constance said, "and I have taken the liberty of placing clean clothing in each of your rooms. I believe you are both slightly taller than James and myself, but I think what I brought should fit adequately. Please make yourselves at home, and let me know if there is anything else that you need."

They thanked her for her hospitality and headed off to their respective rooms. On his way, Adam thought amusingly that Constance's motives may be more than just hospitality. Both he and Alice were still in the same torn and grubby clothes they had been wearing while laboring on the farms, and they both probably smelled as rough as they looked.

Constance would no doubt appreciate having them cleaned up and in fresh clothing while they were in her beautiful home.

Chapter forty-six

*G*uwaya watched the four men approaching from his lookout atop the ridge, recognizing them and standing in the moonlight to make his presence known. By the time they were close enough to converse, the rest of Guwaya's family had joined him on the ridge.

"I sent you to fetch a few items, Tom Woody, and you return with a posse of warriors," he said with a wide grin.

"Thanks to the warriors," said Tom, "I was able to recover these." He handed the weapons and coin pouch to Guwaya. "Without them, I may not have gotten back at all!"

There had been no time for pleasantries at their first meeting, when Guwaya told them of Tom's mission to the cabin. Now there was less urgency and they exchanged proper greetings. Guwaya and Yonah were clearly old friends, and John introduced Sal as Saloli-man, something Sal had begun to accept as unavoidable and no longer bothered to correct. Guwaya welcomed Sal, expressing his gratitude for the assistance he gave Tom. He presented Woyi and Sagi, though he did not mention the infant who was strapped in his usual spot on Woyi's back. Tom wondered how Ahni would have reacted to Sal's squirrel-man name; he was certain she would have been quite amused.

Greetings complete, Tom relayed the events at the cabin. Sal interjected details, embellishing his contributions only slightly less than usual. The Ward family listened to them both with polite silence, careful not to interrupt before the tale was complete. At the conclusion of the story, Guwaya and Woyi praised their courageousness.

Little Sagi, not as intimidated by Sal as he had been initially by Tom, regarded him meticulously, giving special attention to the two squirrels Sal still carried.

"Hello there, little dude," said Sal, picking the boy up and hoisting him to shoulder level. "*Osiyo*, I mean."

"'*Siyo*, Saloli-man," the youngster replied in a soft voice, drawing a chuckle from those close enough to hear. He was still gawking at the two squirrels Sal was holding.

"These are a gift for your mother," Sal said handing the squirrels to Woyi.

"Wado," said Woyi, gratefully accepting them. "What are you doing, Sagi?" she said to the boy. He had clambered onto Sal's shoulders and was hanging over examining Sal's back, wiggling so much Sal had to hold tightly to his legs to keep him from tumbling to the ground.

"I am looking for Saloli-man's tail!" he answered matter-of-factly, getting a big laugh from everyone.

"Hey, little dude, I don't have a tail," Sal chuckled. He lifted the squirming boy above his head and gave him a gentle jostle.

"You don't?" the boy said wide-eyed.

"Of course not. Your name means onion, doesn't it?"

"Yes!" Sagi answered, surprised that Sal knew the meaning of his name, forgetting that his mother had mentioned it only moments ago.

"Well, I don't see any onions growing out of your ears," Sal said to the giggling boy as he turned him back and forth, pretending to examine each of his ears.

John Carter observed that Guwaya and Tom had made some clever modifications to the cave site. From the ridge atop the cave they had installed a permanent attached rope ladder, just below the edge of the cliff, anchored securely into the rocks. It was not visible to anyone standing on the ridge without peering directly over the edge. The rope ladder was rolled and stored in a small niche in the cliff face, and they had attached a set of twisted vines to it, allowing it to be unfurled from either top or bottom. There were vine loops serving as pulleys so the ladder could be rolled back into its niche simply by pulling on the vine, like opening and closing a window blind. Once stored, anyone looking at the cliff face even in full daylight would see nothing more than a few dangling vines. John was impressed; Guwaya's cleverness together with Tom's engineering skills had undoubtedly created the ingenious retrofit.

Guwaya led the group to a copse of trees where he and Tom had rolled some rocks and logs to make a comfortable sitting area. This was where the family intended to spend most of their time, using the cave mostly for storage, sleeping, and for cover in times of inclement weather. Woyi excused herself, saying she would prepare some food for them, and headed down the ladder with Sal's squirrels. She left Sagi with Sal, with whom the boy seemed to have bonded. He still stole the occasional glance at Sal's posterior, not completely convinced that he wasn't hiding a tail somewhere.

John noticed there was a fire pit in their sitting area that did not appear to have been used for some time. He asked Guwaya if they were planning to use it to prepare meals.

"The occasional fire would likely be attributed to a hunter's campfire, but keeping a fire up here would attract unwanted attention," Guwaya answered. "It was a problem that caused me much concern until Tom Woody constructed our cave stove."

"Cave stove?" John asked.

"Yes. Tom found a cranny inside our cave with a fissure through which we could feel air movement. We built a small fire inside the cranny and watched as the smoke was drawn into the fissure. After some searching, we discovered the smoke dispersing through several small cracks within boulder piles on the other side of this ridge." He paused and allowed Tom to continue.

"Once I knew there was a natural flue for the smoke to exit and not give away our location," said Tom, "I constructed a cooking stove inside the cranny, using rocks and some iron plates Guwaya had in his barn. It has a pot crane to hold heavy kettles over the fire, and even a compartment for baking. We can build a good size cooking fire in it and have all the smoke routed out the other side of the mountain. We've only made a few small meals so far, since we haven't been here full time until today, so whatever Woyi is cooking up for you all will be its first full inaugural meal."

"Awesome, I'm starving! I hope she's got more than just those two squirrels to cook up," said Sal.

"Don't worry. The cave's larder is stocked with enough to last the Ward family for months, even if they entertain guests with appetites like yours," said Tom.

Guwaya turned the discussion to more serious matters, specifically the need to rescue his mother from her captivity. Sitting in the purple darkness of the copse they considered their options while enjoying the delicious entrees Woyi brought up from the cave.

"We can be assured that the compound will be well guarded," said Yonah. "We must find a way to communicate to her whatever plan we devise. She needs to be aware of our efforts, and be prepared to escape. Perhaps we can get a message to her."

"As far as I know," said John Carter, "none of us has ever been inside of Fort Cummings." He scanned their faces and received nods of agreement from everyone. "Lack of knowledge of the stockade layout will compound our difficulties. We may be able to discretely breech the stockade wall, but selecting an appropriate spot from the exterior may be impossible."

They considered, and quickly dismissed, having someone voluntarily turn himself in to get a look at the inside of the fort. "That would still leave us with the problem of communicating with our man on the inside," John Carter pointed out. "What we need is for someone to get in and back out again."

They pondered the problem, silently ruminating as they finished off the remains of the meal. Tom, just about to take a bite of biscuit, stopped midway to his mouth and thoughtfully stared at it. "Isn't it true that the military used to, uh, I mean they allow traders to enter the stockades," he asked, "to bring in supplies—food and stuff—to sell to the Cherokees being held there?"

"That is true," John answered. "They even allowed the sellers of whiskey to sell their poison there, a practice they finally agreed to prohibit when it proved to cause them much trouble."

"In that case," said Tom, "why couldn't I enter the fort as a trader, of something other than whiskey of course, to speak with Ahni and do some reconnaissance? That would seem to solve most of our problems."

"It may do just that," said Yonah. "As a trader, you could enter and exit the fort with impunity. You will certainly not be mistaken for an Indian. You do understand that there is still an element of risk, don't you? If it is discovered that you are not really a trader, you are likely to be detained and questioned, possibly even imprisoned. And you would be on your own in there."

"He might be taking a risk," said Sal, "but he won't be on his own. You ain't a-gonna leave your ol' hunting buddy behind," he said to Tom in his countrified accent. "I'll be right there with you, dude."

"Hold on," said Tom. "It would be less conspicuous for just one of us ..."

"You hold on," Sal interrupted adamantly. "I'm a heck of a lot less conspicuous as a trader than you. Remember when we had those extra concert tickets to sell? You'd still be standing in the stadium parking lot holding them if it weren't for me scalping them for us. You know Ahni, and she will recognize and trust you, so you can get the message to her. While you're doing that, I can hawk knickknacks and scope out the stockade at the same time."

Tom had to admit, Sal probably would play the part of a vendor better than he. "Okay, I suppose you're right," he agreed reluctantly. "Just go easy on the Gomer Pyle vernacular."

"Gaawlee! No sweat, Barney," Sal quipped.

"Then we have a plan," said Guwaya. His face turned somber as he regarded Sal. "Just one question, Saloli-man; did you really scalp someone?" The others gazed skeptically at Sal and Tom, anxious to hear his reply.

"Sal would be more likely to bite someone's head off than to scalp them," answered Tom. Seeing their astonished stares, he clarified. "Not literally! Let me explain about ticket scalpers..."

Chapter forty-seven

As usual, Captain Martin left home before sunrise, reporting for duty just as dawn was breaking over the southern end of the Chattahoochee Mountains. He paused briefly before passing through the gate to savor the serenity of the view, giving himself a moment to complete the transition from civilian to army officer. The rising sun was ruby red, illuminating the flat-bottomed lenticular clouds, stacked like pancakes over the mountaintops. The deep scarlet was reflected in the river below turning it into a flowing ribbon of crimson. Combined with the ruddy Georgia soil, it appeared as if the entire valley was drenched in blood. Martin hoped it was not an omen of the days to come.

Just about the time Captain Martin was receiving his orders of the day, his wife and their two guests were making plans of their own to visit the fort.

"I think it is important for us to be there," said Alice, "even if for no other reason than for a show of support."

"I'm not saying we shouldn't go," Adam said. "I'm just not sure how useful it will be. How much good will our show of support do at this point? How is our being there going to help the situation?" Adam was concerned that their presence in the fort could be misinterpreted. It could appear that they were flaunting their freedom to the Cherokees.

Alice did not agree. "You go to visit a friend when he's in the hospital, don't you? Even though there isn't much you can do for them, your visit lets them know you care. On top of losing just about everything they own, these families have gone from a busy life full of farming chores to sitting idle inside that filthy stockade. We can at least help relieve their boredom."

"Indeed," said Constance. "We can also take the opportunity today to examine the situation and determine other ways to be of service. Perhaps that will mean bringing in food and other supplies or running an errand for someone. I have no doubt we can be useful in many ways."

Adam nodded, acquiescing to their argument, although he couldn't completely shake the feeling that they should do something more important. He could not imagine that there wasn't a more significant purpose other than to relieve someone's boredom after having been transported into this situation across decades of time. Adam was tempted to mention this, but then discarded the thought when he considered the likely outcome of telling Constance they were time-travelers. They would at the very least lose their elegant accommodations, if not find themselves relocated to one of the fort's brigs. Unable to come up with a better plan, he agreed to accompany them to the fort.

The sun was a full hand-span above the mountain peaks by the time Adam, Alice, and Constance arrived at the fort. Captain Martin had already left to continue his part in the Cherokee roundup. All three latecomers were granted entry through the main gate, and on into the inner stockade without challenge or comment, although the guard at the stockade gate shared a sneer with his companion as they passed. Whether his scorn was directed at Adam because of their confrontation the previous day, or at Constance, who had not made any attempt to hide her feelings about the Indian Removal, was not clear; nor did it matter. All three ignored the soldier completely, irritating him more than if they had reacted.

They heard Benjamin call out to Adam as they entered the jam-packed stockade courtyard and shouldered their way in his direction. Adam introduced Constance, whom Benjamin eyed suspiciously but greeted cordially. Constance cordially returned his greeting without pretension or aloofness. Benjamin appeared much his usual self, revealing only a hint of weariness from his night of incarceration.

"Is your family doing okay this morning? How are Rebecca and Jimmy?" asked Alice.

"As well as can be expected. Rebecca of course is feeling pain from her ordeal, but she is much better than yesterday. Even Jimmy seems more himself today; the improvement in Rebecca's condition has also improved his demeanor. Catherine spent the night with her, and has told me that although Rebecca's sleep was fitful, she was able to get some much needed rest. This morning Catherine is looking after Sally, who woke up feeling sickly, probably due to yesterday's unsettling events. Billy is with his mother, and they found a quiet, shady place for Sally to rest."

In spite of Benjamin's assurances that Sally would soon be fine, Alice insisted on going to check on her immediately. She took off in the direction Benjamin indicated with Constance in tow. Adam and Benjamin maneuvered through the crowded courtyard to where Jimmy and Rebecca were camped. Reaching them, Adam was relieved to see both of them offer him a faint smile in greeting. It did indeed appear that some of the warmth and cheerfulness he was accustomed to from the Deerinwater couple was beginning to return. Their resilience was remarkable; it was amazing that so much healing had occurred in only a single night. Regardless, Adam thought it best to measure his words carefully. It had only been a day since the horrific ordeal and even a slight careless remark could be misunderstood.

"How are you feeling, Rebecca?" Adam asked.

"Like I was thrown from a horse and trampled, but much better than I would have been if not for you. Thank you for coming to my rescue."

"I think Captain Martin is the one you should thank," Adam said humbly. "If not for him ..."

"If not for you," said Jimmy, "he would not even have gone to her rescue."

After his evening with the Martins' Adam was certain that wasn't true. He thought it best not to contradict Jimmy. "I only did what anyone would have done. If only I could have prevented this terrible attack completely."

"That was not within your power," said Rebecca. "It is irrational to wish you had accomplished something beyond your brave and selfless actions. Be content to know we are appreciative of what you did. There is no doubt we are all the better for having you as a friend." She took Adam in her arms and kissed him on the cheek. Adam felt himself flush at the show of affection. Not knowing how to respond to her compliment, he grinned foolishly.

Jimmy took his hand and shook it, breaking the spell of Rebecca's kiss. "Adam, I know that I said some unkind things to you in anger. That was thoughtless of me, especially since you had just risked your life to rescue my wife. I should never have allowed myself to place blame upon you for the actions of those others. I hope you can forgive me."

"As far as I'm concerned, there is nothing to forgive. You had been beaten, your property was stolen, and your wife was attacked and brutalized. Fortunately for me, I've never had the experience of such a horrific assault against a loved one. Your reaction was certainly understandable, I know it wasn't personal."

"It is too easy to use that as an excuse," said Jimmy earnestly. "Having those incongruous thoughts about a good friend because of actions by members of his race shamed me. I acted no better than those who are bigoted against my own people. I am appreciative of your forgiveness."

Jimmy's expression suddenly turned grim. "But while I do not hold an entire race accountable for the actions of a few, I will hold malice in my heart for those contemptible individuals who committed the transgression against my wife. I pray for the chance to mete out retribution."

The hatred in his voice startled Adam. Jimmy had every right to feel entitled to revenge, but Adam hoped he could control his rage enough to avoid bringing even more trouble on himself. Their friendship having just been reinstated, Adam chose his words carefully before speaking.

"I don't doubt that I would feel the same if a member of my family had been attacked," said Adam. "Where I come from, it is a crime to take the law into your own hands; law enforcement and the courts must determine and impose the penalties for criminals. I believe those laws also exist here—not that I have much hope that you can expect justice from what I have seen. Still, I hope you will keep in mind your duty to your family."

Jimmy misunderstood Adam's meaning. "That is exactly what is in my mind," he retorted. "Have I not just told you that?"

"Yes, I heard your commitment to vengeance. You must also remember your obligation to your family's future."

"What about their future?"

"They will need you to be part of it. I hope you'll not be so narrow sighted in extracting your revenge that you put yourself in jeopardy of being taken away from them. Your child is going to need you with him, not locked away in a jail cell. "

"I see what you are getting at," said Jimmy. "But what child wants a coward for a father?"

"Coward?" Adam shook his head. "Who is braver, the man who satisfies his own need for vengeance, or one who swallows his pride for the benefit of his family? What would you advise your own child to do if the roles were reversed?"

Jimmy ran his fingers through his hair, stealing a glance at Rebecca as he pondered Adam's words. "You make a strong argument. That's some pretty wise counsel from a white man."

Adam smiled, relieved that Jimmy was receptive to reason. "It's not so much wisdom as common sense, Jimmy. I'm sure you'll be a wonderful father, and I'd hate to see you do anything to mess that up."

"I will remember your common sense advice, Adam. I will still look for an opportunity to settle the score, and I will keep in mind that the white government's laws may work against me. In times not so long ago, our law, blood law, would support my seeking retribution and my honor would demand it. I believe that law is still held true in the hearts of righteous men. That must be true even in your future world. It is unnatural to depend upon others to right the wrongs committed against one's family."

"You may be right about that, Jimmy. I can't deny your right to defend your honor. However unlikely, I hope that the law, or perhaps fate, will provide a justice that will satisfy you. I believe your sharp mind and wit will provide you with a rewarding life. Sometimes success can be the best revenge against those who would try to destroy your dreams."

Benjamin, who had been listening silently throughout the exchange, caught their attention with a shuffle of his feet. "Jimmy can find some comfort in knowing he has many brothers who will not allow his wound to fester," he said with a meaningful glance at Jimmy. "We respect the laws of the whites, even when we are not given the benefit of them. Fortunately, he has another avenue for pursuit of justice. It is true that in the past honor would have demanded that Jimmy impose his own justice, but the Cherokee Nation has adopted a set of laws very much like the legal system of the whites. Because the transgression against his family occurred within the Cherokee Nation, this is one time being a Cherokee is to his advantage. It may take time for us to recover from this upheaval, but the crimes will not be forgotten."

Benjamin's reminder of the Cherokee legal system seemed to provide some relief to Jimmy, slightly softening the hardened glare in his eyes. Adam remembered that there had been many attempts to define and clarify the legal jurisdiction of crimes committed within the boundaries of a sovereign nation inside the United States, and in fact were still being argued in his own time.

When Adam looked at Rebecca, the monumental effort she was putting into her smile, unable to completely hide her pain, incensed his own wrath. He wanted Jimmy and Rebecca to know that despite his plea to Jimmy for non-violence, he also was galled by the criminal actions against them. "I hope you will also both remember," he said, "that although I may not have any influence over the white law enforcement, I will support you however I can within the law to see you find justice. While that may not be much, I give you my word that I also will not forget the injuries inflicted on my good friends."

"Certainly we know that, Adam," said Rebecca. "We know you as a true friend, and that assuages our spirits. I believe that the human heart has only so much room for love and hate—both cannot reside in the same place within us. Your friendship and love will help to displace the bad feelings in our hearts, and speed our healing process greatly."

Imposing justice through the Cherokee Nation may be just as futile as through the white courts. But if it gave Jimmy hope, it might possibly keep him from taking the law into his own hands, at least for now. He had a good chance to get his life back on track and begin to rebuild it in the western territory, if he could set aside his anger and desire for revenge, and focus on his prospects. He would need to rediscover the enthusiasm he had shown Adam when they first met.

Adam recalled his earlier conversation with Alice, questioning the value of their presence at the fort, and came to the conclusion that she was right. It would be beneficial to engage Jimmy in conversations about the things he loved; his growing family foremost, as well as agriculture, farm modernization, and automation. He could offer him insights to the future better than anyone else, and keep his entrepreneurial dreams alive. For the moment, it was enough that they could rebuild their friendship.

No one spoke for several moments. Adam was unused to verbalizing such strong emotions and was a little uncomfortable speaking about such personal feelings. Conversations in his modern world were subdued, and he had become accustomed to keeping his feelings repressed. He was glad Jimmy and Rebecca did not have such inhibitions, and it was a relief to know he still had Jimmy's friendship. The openness of their emotions increased his fondness for them; he felt as close to them as he did to the members of his own family. Still, he was relieved when Jimmy shifted the conversation to a less emotional tone.

"I believe what will assuage my spirit most of all would be a decent meal. The provisions here are lacking."

"Leave it to Jimmy to relate everything to his stomach. Nothing can affect his appetite for long!" said Rebecca, getting a chuckle from them all.

"I agree with him though," said Benjamin. "The vittles we get here are far from what us farm boys with healthy appetites are used to. And a good meal will help you both recover. Catherine is planning to put together something for us. If anyone can turn meager rations into a banquet, she can."

"I should go and help her," said Rebecca, stifling a groan as she moved to rise.

"No," said Benjamin. "She gave strict orders that you were to remain at rest." Rebecca settled back with a frustrated sigh, even though the pain of her aching muscles was obvious. "Don't worry; she has plenty of help with Billy, Alice, and Constance. I will go to her as well and see how Sally is doing. We will all return shortly, with nourishment for everyone," he said over his shoulder as he strode off.

"Constance?" asked Jimmy.

"Constance is the wife of Captain Martin. She wanted to come here with us and offer assistance to those who may need it," replied Adam.

"And to spy for the military?" Jimmy scowled.

"That's not very likely. She has a dim view of what's going on, and she truly wishes to be supportive of the families who have been brought here. Besides, why would she need to spy for them? You are under their roof—not much you could do that the military isn't going to know about."

"Of course you are right, Adam. It is difficult for me not to let my ill feelings about what is being done to us cloud my judgment of individuals."

"Understandably," said Adam. In truth, Adam thought Jimmy's effort to restrain his anger was immense. He made an attempt to pacify Jimmy's mood with a lighthearted comment. "She will at least be able to bring in some better food. That alone should warrant you giving her a chance," he grinned.

"Indeed, it does," he agreed, returning Adam's smile.

Chapter forty-eight

From their well-concealed surveillance point, Guwaya, Yonah, Tom, and Sal were in perfect position to observe any comings and goings through the main gate of Fort Cummings. John Carter had agreed to remain behind at Guwaya's cave, conceding that it was best for at least one adult male to stay with the rest of the family, despite Woyi's insistence that it was an unnecessary precaution.

They had traveled in darkness, arriving before dawn and quietly placing themselves at a wooded spot about a hundred yards from the gate. Low-lying clouds had settled into the valley during the night, providing additional cover. Upon their arrival the fort was dark and silent, giving no indication of the multitude of families incarcerated within. As the rising sun warmed the earth, the fog gradually dispersed and their view of the still-sleeping fort improved, even though as yet there was little to see. The four men battled drowsiness, lulled by the soft twittering of early morning birds. At sunrise they were startled to alertness by the blare of a bugle sounding reveille, calling the sleeping troops to morning roll call as the flag was jerkily raised over the fort. The morning's activity steadily increased after the call to colors concluded, as visitors and traders began arriving at the fort's open gate.

"They do not seem to be challenging the traders," whispered Guwaya. "No one has been refused admittance, or even questioned very much before they are allowed to enter."

"They are likely to be more concerned with the people who are leaving than those who are entering," said Yonah. "There must be a secondary gate within the fort for entrance to the stockade. It would be helpful if we knew what occurred there."

"The rear wall of the fort is still in the long shadows of morning," said Guwaya. "I will make my way there to see if I can hear what is going on inside." He crept stealthily to the rear of the fort, moving as quietly as mist through the trees, until he disappeared from view.

Yonah whispered a warning to Tom and Sal. "Fort Cummings is manned by the Georgia Guard and local volunteers under the command of Captain Sam Farriss. Many of the traders will be recognized as local merchants. Some will even be neighbors of the soldiers. As strangers, you two can expect more scrutiny."

"Our story will be that we are new settlers who only recently came to the area," said Tom. "If questioned, we'll say that we usually keep to ourselves and have been busy with the clearing of fields and construction of our farm buildings. But we couldn't resist taking a break to do some trading and take advantage of the higher prices we can get from the Indians. That should be believable, since most of our goods are from Guwaya's food supply, things from his own farm."

Yonah snorted in agreement. "They will certainly believe you want to take advantage of their prisoners."

The traders they observed carried a variety of goods, some with wagonloads of supplies and others carrying only a small sack. It appeared that many of them were just as Tom described; local farmers who were bringing their goods and produce to sell to the fort's detainees. The opportunity to turn their labor into cash was too tempting to ignore. Many had the same idea, and they arrived in droves. If the traders were expecting to sell at inflated prices, the number of competing merchants should help to keep their prices reasonably fair.

A gentle rustle of leaves came from the bushes next to Tom. He was stunned to see Guwaya squatting next to him, having returned as soundlessly as he left.

"It is as we expected," said Guwaya. "There is an inner stockade where the people are being held. I was able to speak to a Tsalagi man within the stockade, who told me that the inner gate is guarded, but it also remains open to allow access for the many traders. The soldiers are not challenging any of them, except those who have brought whiskey to sell. Those are being turned away for fear that the intoxicating drink may lead to an unmanageable situation inside the stockade. All others are freely admitted.

"The man did not know Ahni. He said there were over four hundred people being held here and most keep to themselves. Understandably, as the man himself sounded intensely depressed.

"I confided to him that someone would be entering the fort as a trader to get a message to my mother. He said that he would do what he could to locate Ahni and help you find her."

"We better hope the dude's trustworthy, then," said Sal. "How do you know you weren't talking to one of the guards?"

"Not likely," Guwaya answered, "as we were speaking in Tsalagi."

"Your most difficult task will be finding Ahni," said Yonah. "Having someone on the inside will be most beneficial, especially one who can speak Tsalagi. Ahni herself only speaks a little bit of English, so this man will help you to communicate with her. Guwaya, how will he recognize our messengers?"

"I have described them to him and he will watch for them. His name is Jason Springwater."

"What does he look like?" asked Sal.

"I could not see him through the fort wall, but I am certain he looks like an Indian."

"Real helpful, dude. That narrows it down to only four hundred possibilities. How did you describe us? A couple of white guys?"

"A couple of white guys, one with a cantankerous attitude," Guwaya answered wryly. "He will recognize you by the red smudges on your faces."

"What red smudges?" asked Sal.

Instead of answering, Guwaya grabbed a handful of bright red clay from the ground and deftly smeared it across Sal's forehead.

"Hey, what the heck!" cried Sal, vainly attempting to wipe the sticky red dirt from his face. A sharp pain reminded him of the gash on his forehead he had sustained from fish-breath's knife handle.

"It will make you to look like a true Georgia dirt farmer," said Guwaya. "And it will help to hide your wounds from the soldiers, who may ask you to explain them. You need some more on your cheeks," he said, reaching to smear some more dirt on Sal's face.

Sal dodged the second helping, blocking his face with his arms. "Back off, dude. I'll do my own makeup if you don't mind."

"There's that cantankerous attitude you mentioned," laughed Tom. "I'll do my own as well, thank you."

Once they were all in agreement that the smears of red were adequate, Yonah insisted they go over their plan again. "Remember," Yonah said, "all you need to do is make contact with Ahni and let her know it is our intention to free her. Make a few mental notes of the layout of the stockade and get out. No heroics. Once you are safely back here with us we can make further plans on how to proceed."

Satisfied that they were as ready as they could be, he gave them a final stern warning to take no unnecessary chances and to keep their dialogues with the militia men amicable. He directed the latter warning directly to Sal, who responded with a shrug and a wide-eyed look of innocence.

Without further comment, Sal and Tom gathered their sacks of trade items, nodded to Yonah and Guwaya, and made their way back through the woods to a bend in the road leading to the main gate. It would appear to anyone watching that they had just arrived. The number of people on the road had already begun to dwindle; the most ambitious traders had arrived early.

The two soldiers standing guard scrutinized them as they approached the gate, causing Tom a twinge of nervousness. The guards hardly looked like soldiers; in their civilian clothes they appeared more like bouncers collecting the cover charge at a night club, if not for the weapons they held. Tom overheard one of the men remark "Lookee at these two bumpkins" to the other, who responded with a snort. Tom instinctively glanced at Sal, searching for any sign of Sal's usual temper. Sal appeared not to have taken any notice of the comment.

"We came to sell a few goods," said Tom to the two guards.

"You and everyone else in the county," the man answered. "Except most of the rest of 'em are already here." To Tom's great relief, he motioned with a flick of his head that they should enter the fort. They strutted forward without hesitation, passing through the gate and out of the view of Yonah and Guwaya who were watching them from the woods.

"So far, so good," said Tom.

"Easy-peazy. There's the inner gate just ahead," Sal replied, motioning toward the guarded entry of the stockade.

"I was relieved you didn't react to that guy's comment."

"Hey, I figured if I look like a bumpkin to Homer and Jethro back there, all the better. The red mud must be working."

The inside of the fort was stark. There were sets of crude stairs leading to the tops of the rifle towers at each corner of the fort, two or three open doors leading into small rooms that looked like officer's quarters or offices, and a larger structure that appeared to serve as barracks for the rest of the soldiers. There was another small but heavily fortified building with a closed door used as the arsenal, clearly the most secured area of the fort. Several other closed doors gave access to various storage areas for food and livery supplies. A few horses were tethered to hitching rails, presumably only those currently required for duty as the rest were housed in the stables.

The stockade appeared to be a recent addition to the fort. An opening had been freshly cut through the upright logs forming the fort walls, and a heavy, rough-hewn log gate had been installed. The gate was smaller than the main entrance, barely large enough to allow a wagon to pass through. Two uniformed guards stood at the gate, implying that the commander had decided to place his regular, full-time soldiers at this point instead of the volunteers he stationed at the main gate. As Tom and Sal reached the stockade, one of the soldiers stepped in front of them, blocking their way.

"All parcels must be inspected for contraband before entering the stockade, sir," said the soldier. Evidently he had orders to be polite to the traders.

"Okay, no problem, Corporal Agarn," said Sal. "What sort of contraband you looking for?" He held out his sack of goods for inspection. Tom did likewise without comment.

"Whiskey and weapons," the soldier replied stiffly. "And I'm a sergeant, not a corporal."

"Don't got neither of those, Sarge," Sal replied with what he hoped was a farm-boy grin. "We just want to sell a little of our produce."

"That's what most folks are here for, but we still have to check. You know how these injuns get with a little whiskey in 'em."

"Makes 'em pretty stupid, I guess," Sal grinned. "Good thing they got you F-Troop boys here to protect 'em."

"Damn right," he answered.

Satisfied that they were harmless, the soldier motioned them through the gate.

Entering, Sal whispered, "Like I said, dude, easy-peazy."

Tom was relieved they didn't need to resort to their cover story, but entrance was granted easily, almost too easily, which gave him an uncomfortable feeling.

"I expected them to challenge us a bit more," he said. "And knock off the F-Troop comments!"

"Hey, man, they're probably just pissed about pulling vegetable duty," Sal answered. "You know they'd rather be doing something besides looking through bags of veggies. They seem like they don't care because they don't. So what if I mention F-Troop? You don't think they watch the reruns, do you?"

The stockade was crowded and noisy. Tom and Sal shouldered their way through the crowd; clusters of traders and their customers were randomly scattered throughout the courtyard and had stopped to offer their goods wherever they pleased. People were everywhere, sorting through the merchandise and loudly negotiating prices. It was not going to be easy to locate Ahni or casually conduct surveillance without being observed. Fortunately, the profusion of activity gave them plenty of cover; with all the turmoil, it was likely no one would pay them any heed.

Peering over the heads of the crowd, they could see that only the gated stockade wall was constructed from the same upright logs as the rest of the fort. Where it had been expanded the stockade had been made from smaller logs, bound together with rope. While still a substantial barricade, it appeared to be less sturdy and somewhat more vulnerable than the older wall.

"If there's a weak spot," whispered Tom, "it'll be in that new section of wall."

"You get over and take a closer look. I better start hawking some veggies." Sal took a handful of produce from his sack, held them over his head, and began crying, "Vegetables here! Get your nice, fresh vegetables! Best prices in Cherokee land!"

Tom made his way to the rear wall, noticing several large gaps between the logs, large enough to see through from several paces away. It must have been through one of these gaps that Guwaya had his conversation with Jason Springwater, their inside contact. He walked along parallel to the wall, peering across the top and mentally noting the placement of the larger gaps by their distance from the corners.

While none of the gaps were large enough to allow slipping in a contraband item, like a firearm or a whiskey jug, they were easily wide enough to hold a conversation or pass a note through.

Turning back toward the main fort, Tom observed the guards posted in the fort's four rifle towers. They did not appear to be paying much attention to the goings on in the stockade, although their position high above the wall afforded them an excellent view of the entire interior of the compound. In the daylight at least, any suspicious activity would be quickly spotted. Any attempt they made to get Ahni out of the fort would have to be a nighttime operation.

Not wanting to linger too long, Tom made his way back in to where he had left Sal selling vegetables. He spotted him engaged in conversation with a prospective customer, a smallish Cherokee man about the same stature as Sal, although much more broad-shouldered.

"Dude, I told you I don't have any dang strawberries," he heard Sal saying to the man, sounding slightly agitated.

"But I have some for you. You want these strawberries," the man replied. Tom noted the man's exasperated look.

"Look, man, I told you I don't want any...," Sal began.

"Wait, Sal," said Tom. "We probably could use some strawberries," he said to the man, giving Sal a quick wink and silently mouthing "Ahni" to him.

"What? What the heck do we want with...? Oh, yeah, maybe we do."

"Please come with me and I'll show you what I have," said the man, greatly relieved that Sal had finally caught on.

They followed the man, who strode unhesitatingly to a less hectic area of the compound, until they reached a group of men who nodded knowingly to their guide. The men stood aside to allow them to pass, and then closed ranks to provide a reasonably private area between themselves and the wall of the fort.

The man turned and addressed Tom and Sal. "I am Jason Springwater. You are looking for strawberries?"

"Yes, we are," Tom answered. "Our friend Guwaya is very interested in strawberries. My name is Tom, and this is Sal."

"*'Siyo*, Tom and Sal. Ah, yes; Guwaya said to expect you. I was afraid I had the wrong red dirt farmers for a moment." He motioned to Sal.

"Well excuse me, Chief Waterboy. My black ops tradecraft is a little rusty," Sal quipped.

"Sal hasn't met Ahni, and neither of us speaks Tsalagi," Tom interjected.

"I see," Jason said. "It is not a problem. Guwaya is fortunate to have such good friends who are willing to jeopardize their own safety for his mother's sake. We can talk quietly in English. My friends here," he motioned to the men surrounding them, "will warn us if the soldiers approach.

"I have been able to locate Ahni, and I told her that I have spoken with Guwaya. She is quite relieved to know that he is safe. I am afraid, though, that Ahni herself is very ill. She has been taken to one of the bunkhouses where she can rest. At least as much as that is possible in that stifling place. I will take you to her, and will act as a translator for you, as her English is limited. I will have one of my friends stand guard at the door so you can talk freely with her. Not that any of the soldiers would go in there without good reason."

"We only need to speak with her for a moment," said Tom. "Just long enough to give her a message from Guwaya. But the message is, uh, not for everyone's ears. Will we be able to speak with her in private?"

"As I said, it is not very likely that there will be any soldiers present, however, the bunkhouse is small and crowded, and so a private conversation may not be possible. Perhaps it would be better to tell your message to me now, and I can relay it to Ahni in Cherokee."

"That's probably a good idea. At least that will prevent any English-only listeners from overhearing. We need to tell her that Guwaya is going to try and find a way to get her out of this place and take her to, uh, somewhere safe. He wants her to know this so that she can be prepared to leave quickly. From what I was able to see of this compound, it's likely she will have to leave in the night."

"I will give her the message. However, I must tell you that Guwaya's plan may be much more difficult than he thinks."

"That doesn't bother us a bit, Chief Waterboy," said Sal. "We're not afraid of a few difficulties."

"I was not implying that you were afraid, *ugineli*," said Jason. "Getting a person out of here is not easy, but it can be done. I know of a few who have already successfully escaped, even without the help of someone on the outside. The difficulty I refer to is Ahni's health. I believe her illness has made her much too frail for an escape attempt. You may assess her condition for yourselves, of course. Let us go now and speak with her."

Jason spoke a few Tsalagi words to one of his friends, who accompanied them as they walked to the bunkhouse. The bunkhouse was newly constructed; a lean-to looking more like it was built to accommodate livestock than people. It was an unpainted structure with a single door and no windows. The roof was hardly more than six feet at its highest point. Jason's friend, acting as lookout, leaned against the bunkhouse and began smoking his pipe while the other men went inside. Tom had to duck to get through the door.

Inside, the smell of human stench was overwhelming. With limited airflow, the stinking, tepid air had no place to escape, making the temperature inside the bunkhouse at least twenty degrees warmer than outside. Once their eyes became adjusted to the dark interior, Tom and Sal could see the bunks had been built from rough-cut wood and stacked three-high, floor to ceiling. The floor was littered with filthy straw, used in the bunks instead of a mattress, the only cushioning between the occupants and the hard planks. There were a few piles of soggy blankets on the floor, soiled and discarded.

Ahni was lying in one of the middle bunks of the rack adjacent to the door. Her eyes were closed and her breathing shallow. To Tom, she looked much older, the wrinkles on her aged face deeper and more prominent than he remembered. Her skin was as pale as the blond wood bunk she was lying upon.

"I helped her move to this bunk," said Jason. "She gets a little more fresh air here being closer to the door."

"That was very thoughtful," said Tom. "Guwaya will appreciate your kindness to his mother."

On hearing Tom's voice, Ahni's eyes flew open and darted back and forth, searching for him. He moved to her line of vision and smiled, then gently brushed a strand of her thin, gray hair from her face that had stuck to her skin with perspiration.

"*Osiyo, elisi.*" During his stay with the Wards, Tom had taken to calling Ahni *elisi*, which Guwaya told him meant grandmother, a term of respect for an elder woman.

"'*Siyo, tawodi,*" she whispered. She managed a twinkle of amusement in her rheumy eyes at calling him *tawodi*, the Tsalagi word for hawk and Ahni's pet name for him.

Although they only shared a few words of each other's language, Tom and Ahni had developed a fondness for each other. Tom figured he amused her by his unfamiliarity with things she considered commonplace. She was quick-witted, and could usually understand the gist of their conversations even when Guwaya wasn't available to translate.

There were only a few other people in the bunkhouse, lying in bunks, and not likely to be interested in their conversation. Still, Tom thought it best not to speak of any escape plans in English, lest they be overheard by a guard through the thin walls. "Please tell her that I am sorry she is not feeling well, and pass along Guwaya's message," he told Jason.

Jason softly spoke a few words of Tsalagi, and relayed Ahni's appreciation for his concern back to Tom. He then spoke for a much longer time, delivering the message of Guwaya's plan. Ahni's face knotted into a stern expression as she shook her head and interrupted Jason with a sudden outburst of Tsalagi. Interrupting someone was very untypical of a Cherokee, and something Tom had never heard Ahni do before. Neither Tom nor Sal could understand their words, but the tone of their conversation implied that Jason was asking questions and Ahni was answering in terse, confident replies. Finally, the long exchange came to an end. Jason nodded to Ahni resignedly. He sighed, and turned to answer Tom's questioning look.

"She forbids Guwaya to make a rescue attempt," Jason said.

Sal motioned as if getting ready to speak, but halted when Tom gestured for him to wait. He did not want Sal to say anything argumentative. Tom understood the significance of Ahni's words; in a matriarchal society, as the elder female of Guwaya's family, her word was law.

"Did she tell you her reasons?" Tom asked.

"She did. She said that she is very sick, and wants Guwaya to give his attention to the rest of the family. She believes that an escape attempt would endanger the others, and she does not want Guwaya to risk capture, leaving her family without an adult male. As you could probably tell from her outburst, she is most resolute."

"Her recovery would be quicker if she could get out of this place," Tom said.

"I have made that point to her. It was then she told me that the camp physician diagnosed her with camp fever. As you may know, her chance of recovery from that is... not very good, even if she escapes this fort."

"Camp fever? You mean typhus!" Tom took Ahni's hand and looked at her in disbelief. She nodded to him, unemotional, but confirming the dreadful diagnosis.

"Damn, man. I know typhus is serious," said Sal, "but it's curable, ain't it?"

"It is with antibiotics," Tom answered.

Sal frowned. "Which they didn't have in 1838; I forgot about that. We take stuff like penicillin for granted. Holy crap," he exclaimed. "Is there nothing that can be done for her?"

"The military is not overly concerned about curing an old Indian woman," said Jason. "In any case, there is not much to be done other than providing her with a place to rest, which they have done. Our Tsalagi healers have had some success using special plants, but that requires a knowledgeable gatherer who has the freedom to collect them. Even with treatment, at Ahni's age, recovery is unlikely."

"Dude, we can't just leave her here to..." Typical of Sal, he expressed the sympathy he felt for Ahni with anger. "The old lady deserves to spend her last days somewhere better than this stinking shed. Can't you dudes convince her to change her mind?"

Ahni, either understanding enough of Tom and Sal's questions or guessing their meaning, tightened her grip on Tom's hand and began speaking in Tsalagi. Her leathery hand felt warm and dry against his skin as she spoke to him with gentle resolve. The three men let her speak without interruption until she completed all she had to say. Tom and Sal looked to Jason for a translation.

"Ahni said that she is appreciative of your concern for her well-being and knows how difficult it is for you, who have had very little teaching in the Tsalagi ways, to understand her decision. She explains that she is simply joining with those who have already gone to the west before her.

She also asks that you carry her message back to Guwaya. Ahni says that most times she allows Guwaya to have his way, but this time she insists he must respect her wishes. She said to tell Guwaya that he is to give his full attention to Woyi and the children, protecting them from harm while they are in hiding and returning to their land when the time is right. She says that his children are his future, not her. He is not to make an attempt to remove her from this place; this is where she will spend the last of her days. That is her decision, and she will speak no more of it."

Once again Sal looked as if he were about to argue, but Tom spoke up first. "Please tell her that we understand her traditions enough to respect her authority, and will sadly relay her message to Guwaya. Also tell her that it has been a privilege to spend time with her, and thank her for the kindness she has shown to me during my stay at her home. Tell her that I very much enjoyed our time together, and I will pray for her recovery. When she is better I will return, hopefully to hear she has reconsidered."

Jason translated Tom's statement into Tsalagi and the old woman responded in kind, her words followed with a slight smile and a shrug.

"Ahni says you are most welcome, and that knowing you has been interesting and enjoyable. She said she appreciates your prayers, but she is certain that she will depart for the West from here.

"If there is nothing further," Jason continued hesitantly, "I suggest that we leave this place before drawing suspicion."

"Yes, of course," Tom answered. He choked back the sadness he felt, not wanting to embarrass Ahni with what she would consider a show of weakness. He hardened his face and gave her a final, solemn nod, then slowly released her hand.

Sal handed his bag of produce to Jason. "I'll leave this stuff for Ahni. The fresh veggies will be good for her."

The three men exited the barracks and were joined by Jason's friend as they walked toward the gate. "I believe it would be best for us to take our leave here," Jason said. "I am glad I was able to be of assistance to you and Guwaya. I wish the outcome were better. I do not envy the message you must deliver to him."

"I ain't really looking forward to it either, Chief Waterboy," said Sal. "Thanks for your help with Ahni, though. I know going out west ain't your choice, but I hope you get there safely." Jason accepted Sal's good wishes with a nod.

"I'm not sure how Guwaya will react to Ahni's message," said Tom. "It's possible he may want to contact you about her…"

"I am at his disposal if he should wish it; contact me as before through the stockade wall. Farewell and good peace to you both, Tom and Sal."

Tom and Sal departed the fort without incident, easily merging into the procession of exiting vendors, relieved to be leaving the fort but dreading the news they carried to Guwaya.

Chapter forty-nine

A dam and Alice were shocked at how rapidly the Cherokees in Fort Wool had deteriorated. Deprived of access to adequate facilities for proper hygiene and to their own supplies for even a change of clothing, combined with the crowded stockade and the anxiety of the forceful removal from their homes, their usual tidiness had become displaced by a rough and shabby appearance.

The deplorable conditions began to adversely affect their health as well as their appearance. The provisions distributed by the military barely met the minimum nutritional requirements for survival. The additional food Constance, Adam, and Alice brought in was never enough, since it was shared with as many people as possible. Many who became sick worsened, as their weakened state put them at risk of contracting one of the many illnesses running rampant in the fort. The warming weather added to the misery by providing the multitude of viruses and bacteria with an ideal breeding environment.

Sally's health degraded swiftly. She became listless and generally nonresponsive to Catherine's attention, refusing to eat or take the crude remedies her mother could produce from her limited supplies. The little girl was somewhat more responsive to Alice, brightening visibly when she was around. Alice spent every day with her, tirelessly adlibbing stories about Basil the Beaver while holding her hand and shooing the flies from her perspiration-soaked face. To Catherine's relief, Sally more willingly accepted food and medicine whenever Alice was around.

Constance was also worried about Sally's declining health. It pleased her to know Sally was benefitting from the food she was bringing and was determined to do something more. Normally Constance would not consider using her husband's position to get special treatment. In this case, however, she believed the seriousness of Sally's illness compelled her to take advantage of her status with the fort's physician. Already overworked and none too happy about tending to the health of the stockade full of Indians, the doctor was at first reluctant to pay any heed to Constance's request to examine Sally. He roughly dismissed her, claiming he could hardly keep up with the seriously ill adults and had no time for a child's complaints. Her persistence, and a subtle reminder of her husband's rank, eventually persuaded the grumpy doctor to give Sally a brief, cursory examination.

The doctor emitted a few professional hums and murmurs, his demeanor relaxing as he realized the urgency of Sally's condition. He provided Catherine with a bottle of elixir he claimed would help alleviate her symptoms. "Plenty of rest and fresh air along with the medicine should do the trick," he prescribed.

Slowly, thanks to the doctor's prescription and Alice's attentions, Sally's health began to show signs of improvement. Catherine and Alice shared a look of cautious optimism when the youngster improved enough to emit a tiny giggle, as brief and diminutive as it was, in response to one of Alice's stories.

Initially Constance had been guardedly tolerated by the Cherokees. Eventually her gentle and caring personality, the food she brought, and her intercession with the doctor, softened the Indians taciturn manners. Her charity was offered with respectful kindness rather than pity, treating each person with politeness and quickly catching on to the cultural mores that eluded many other well-meaning whites. The Cherokees rewarded her with their typical warmth and friendliness.

She was also gaining favor among the soldiers. There were still those who resented her interference, voicing their disdain with loud conversations about "Indian lovers," which Constance simply ignored; a remarkable accomplishment considering their volume. Abusive guards were not the majority, but certainly the most vocal. She instead gave her attention to the soldiers who showed respect and compassion for their Cherokee charges, rewarding them with choice bits of the vittles she brought. This sparked a competition among several of the men, each trying to perform acts of kindness that might win them one of Constance's pies or cakes. Even those not participating in the competition refrained from chiding their peers in hopes of receiving a share of the reward.

True to her station as a respectable southern woman and officer's wife, she kept her feelings about the Indian removal to herself. This became increasingly difficult for her to do; as she became more personally involved with the Cherokee families, the more her disapproval of the unjust policy developed. The experience was giving her insight into the inner conflict her beloved husband was dealing with.

Captain Martin was undaunted in the performance of his duty, yet he was increasingly conflicted by his personal objections to the forced removal. This was not the first time he had to put aside personal feelings in deference to duty; wartime actions sometimes demanded that. He had sworn an oath of allegiance as a military officer, something he did not take lightly and would not disavow. Still, the pride he had once felt from serving his country now felt tainted. He could find no honor in displacing an entire nation of indigenous people.

Each day he spent ushering people to the fort increased the burden on his conscience. Today he had received new orders; he would be escorting a group of Cherokees to Ross's Landing. The change in duties was bittersweet, thankful not to be removing families from their homes, but dreading the difficult and sorrowful exodus he was to lead. There was little time to dwell upon his new distasteful assignment. He was to inform the Cherokees that they would be departing at sunrise.

Most of the detainees accepted the news with dispirited indifference. Departing the cramped, unhealthy fort and escaping the hostilities of the abusive guards would be a relief. The reality of being force-marched away from their homeland—a reality many had refused to accept until now—was terrifying.

For Benjamin and Catherine, the news was devastating. Sally had scarcely shown the barest signs of recovery and was in no condition for an arduous journey. Benjamin protested loudly to the guards, so vociferously that he was on the verge of receiving a thrashing had Captain Martin not interceded. He took Benjamin aside, calming him slightly by sincerely listening to his objections. While sympathetic to Benjamin's concern for his daughter, there was little he could do. His orders were clear; they would leave at sunrise for Ross's Landing, heedless of any objections, complaints, gripes, or illnesses.

Benjamin's wrath was slightly eased with the news that their wagon and goods would be returned, and if Benjamin could make room, Sally could ride in it. Captain Martin also suggested Benjamin request the fort physician reexamine Sally.

"I have already done that," said Benjamin. "A waste of time! Not but a few days ago, he prescribed plenty of rest. Today he says the exercise will do her good!"

"I see," said Captain Martin, making a mental note to have a word with the good doctor. "Perhaps he believes her to be recovering well enough to change his treatment recommendations."

"Sally can barely stand, let alone exercise!" Benjamin said, his ire rising.

"I do understand your concern," Martin said sympathetically. "Unfortunately there is no alternative. Even if she were allowed to stay, the rest of the family could not, and I am quite sure you would not want to leave her behind on her own. As I have said, she will be able to ride in your wagon to Ross's Landing, and she will at least be with her family. You are aware that the conditions here are not very healthful, so a change of environment may be beneficial."

Benjamin responded with a hard stare, not nearly convinced. Martin sensed his skepticism and could hardly blame the man. He would feel the same way if it was his own daughter, but the decision had been made by his superiors and was out of his hands.

"I truly wish I could give your daughter a few more days before making the trip, but it is just not possible. You will have to make her as comfortable as possible in your wagon." He turned and strode off before Benjamin became enraged once again, knowing it would not be constructive to debate the issue further. He would only tolerate so much; he had his orders-- regardless of how desperate the pleading or how guilty his conscience made him feel.

He was unable to put the matter to rest entirely, however. Returning home that evening he found Constance, Adam, and Alice waiting for him at the door, determined to question him about the wisdom of sending a sick child on such a strenuous trip. All speaking at once, they bombarded him with their demands. Captain Martin held up his hands, signaling for calm. He invited them into the parlor where they could sit and converse privately. The conversation was not one he wanted to have in public, within earshot of anyone walking along the street.

Once they were seated comfortably in the parlor, he listened to their complaints. They told him nothing he hadn't already considered, including Alice's biting remark that Sally probably wouldn't be sick in the first place if she had not been incarcerated. He tried to remain unemotional as he addressed them.

"It matters not if I agree with you. As I told Mr. Rogers, the decision is not mine. My orders are to escort the group to Ross's Landing, and have been told explicitly that no exceptions will be made. I also explained to him that his wagon would be returned and he should make room for his daughter to ride in it."

"I understand that you must obey orders," said Constance. "But that little child is so ill and frail. I cannot help but be concerned for her."

"I am concerned for her as well," he answered, "as I am for the many others who must make this journey. There are others who are also sick, elderly, and even lame. All I can do is to try and get as many safely to Ross's Landing as I can."

"I know you will do your best, James." Constance saw through her husband's veneer of professionalism, sensing the anguish he was attempting to hide. She changed the subject hoping to spare him any further pleading from Adam and Alice. "I should be used to the assignments that take you away from home, but I will miss you and pray for your swift, safe return, and for the safe passage of the poor souls you will be leading away from their homeland. At least this time I will have the company of our visitors while you are gone," she said, smiling at her guests.

"I'm afraid," Adam replied sheepishly, "that Alice and I have decided to go along to Ross's Landing."

Constance's chin dropped. "Oh, my; you mustn't do that. It is quite far, and you are not accustomed to traveling long distances on foot."

Alice took her hand. "Constance, we didn't make the decision lightly. We want to help our friends, and Sally has responded positively to my attention. Adam and I felt that my being there would be good for her. Your husband's hands may be tied, but ours are not."

"I'm sure she would like you with her, and your selflessness is admirable; but I don't think you two realize how perilous that journey could be. Besides, it is a military operation and I don't think you would be allowed to go. Isn't that right, James?"

Captain Martin didn't give her the answer she was hoping for. "Actually," he said, "although it is a military operation, traveling to Ross's Landing on public roads is not restricted. They are free to do as they wish. The military has no authority to prevent them from doing so." He knew Constance would like their company while he was gone, but he felt their presence probably would be beneficial to the little girl. And they both seemed plenty healthy enough to make the trip without too much exertion. "Of course, they will not be given free passage on the river. They will either pay their own steamboat fare or return with me."

"That is understood," said Adam. "We'll have to make that decision when we reach Ross's Landing."

Constance had grown fond of her guests and was not anxious to see them leave, especially if they could be putting themselves in harm's way. She could, however, understand their reason for wanting to go, and respected them for it. "I suppose you are right, James; it is their decision. I still think it is rash, but if you are determined, I will pray for safe travel for you both."

"I'm sure we'll be fine," Alice said. "We appreciate your gracious hospitality, inviting us into your home as you did. As Adam said, we'll decide about going on further west later. We have our other two traveling companions to consider."

"Of course you are both welcome in our home when you return," said the Captain. "When the time comes, Constance and I will assist with your travel arrangements back to your own homes in the east."

Adam wished they really could help with those travel arrangements. He appreciated the sentiment and thanked them for their generosity.

Captain Martin stood, sighed heavily, and suggested, "Sunrise comes early, and tomorrow will be a long day. I advise we all turn in early tonight and get a good night's sleep."

They avoided any further discussion of Sally and tomorrow's journey for the rest of the evening.

Chapter fifty

I must enter the fort to speak with her," said Guwaya.

They were the first words he had spoken since Tom and Sal had returned, informing him of Ahni's condition and her decision not to allow a rescue attempt. They candidly reported the bleak facts, unsullied by any wisecracks from Sal. Guwaya had simply nodded and walked off away, then squatted with his shoulder propped against a tree. He remained that way for over an hour, staring into the depths of the forest. Yonah assured Tom and Sal that Guwaya would let them know how to proceed when he was ready. He bid them to remain silent and patient in the meantime.

"I'm not sure it would be a good idea for you to be seen inside the fort," said Tom.

Guwaya was adamant. "I may not be able to enter through the gate as you did, but perhaps I can find a way to enter clandestinely. You have said the rear wall is not well reinforced. Maybe I can get in somehow. In any case, I cannot simply accept her refusal second hand. I must hear it from her directly, and have a chance to make an appeal. Furthermore, if she is as ill as you have said, it may be my last opportunity to…." He cast his eyes toward the ground, keeping his face stony in an effort to control a show of emotions.

Yonah, who had been quietly sitting and smoking during Guwaya's musings, tapped out his pipe and purposely cleared his throat, indicating his intent to speak. "Guwaya, certainly you would want to see your mother when she is in ill health. But for you to enter the fort during daylight, whether through the gate or otherwise, is reckless. You would not be likely to convince Ahni to reconsider her decision by acting rashly. Nightfall will be upon us soon enough; would it not be wise to contact Jason Springwater under cover of darkness first? He could also inform

Ahni of your intentions, so that she is not taken unawares in her frail condition."

Guwaya tugged at his braids, pondering Yonah's suggestion. "Perhaps it would be better to give her some time to prepare. And Springwater may be helpful finding an obscure weak point in the wall. Yes, I will accept your recommendation, Yonah."

"In that case," said Yonah, "let us reposition ourselves closer to the rear of the fort while we have some remaining daylight. The sun is setting quickly."

The four men made their way around the perimeter of the fort, keeping well hidden from the watchtowers, until they found a spot from which they could see the entire length of the rear wall. There they would wait for enough darkness for Guwaya to make his approach. With little else they could do until then, they talked quietly, Tom and Sal giving Guwaya as good a verbal description of the inside of the fort as they could. Eventually the discussion returned to Ahni.

"I do not discount the seriousness of camp fever at Ahni's age, yet I feel she may be refusing to escape the fort for fear she will jeopardize our family. I must try to convince her that this is not the case." Guwaya glanced at Yonah, expecting him to sanction his decision.

To Guwaya's chagrin, Yonah challenged him instead. "Are you certain that is the case? What of Ahni's welfare? Would subjecting her to an arduous escape be more for her benefit, or yours? You may feel it is your obligation to return her to your family, but it will not be easy for her. She has lived a long life, most of it in service to her family. She has earned the right to a peaceful passing if that is her choice."

Guwaya's eyes momentarily flashed with irritation, and then softened as he considered the truth of Yonah's words. "I am fortunate you are here to enlighten me. Of course you are right; I must keep in mind what is best for Ahni. Still, I wish to attempt to visit her and assess her condition for myself. At least then I will have the opportunity to say a final farewell if that is what is to be."

"I would want the same," said Yonah. "You must do so, however, only if there is minimal risk of your capture. That event would not only be disastrous for you, but for your family and Ahni. Your plan to contact Springwater is sound. Use his knowledge of the fort to get inside if it can be accomplished discretely."

At that moment their attention was drawn to the sound of a bugle playing taps, indicating the day's end and ordering lights out for the fort. "It is time," said Guwaya. Without further words, he stood and began creeping stealthily toward the fort wall. The darkness covered his movements, leaving the remaining three with little more than an occasional glimpse of his silhouette until his shadow reached the wall, where it remained motionless. Guwaya had made contact with someone, hopefully the correct someone who would notify Jason Springwater and not alert the guards. They strained their eyes to watch, but the dim moonlight revealed no more than vague shadows. It was impossible to determine any more about what Guwaya was doing.

"One thing's got me puzzled," said Sal, oblivious to the tension. "When we were talking to Ahni, she said that she was going west to meet the others who had gone before her. Did she mean that she expected to recover and be sent to the western territory?"

Yonah shook his head and explained. "To the west lies the Ghost Land, Tsusginai, the place of death. She meant that she expected to die."

Sal was rarely uncomfortable or at a loss for words. Right now he was both. He ran his fingers through his hair and looked to Tom for help with an appropriate response, but Tom offered none. The three men returned to watching the shadows in silence until Guwaya made his way back to their hiding place.

He reported his conversation. "Jason tells me it is possible to enter the fort unobserved, through a hole some of the men have dug under the wall. He indicated the place to me, and said that I must return in four hours, when the guards will be their least attentive and the patrols are fewer. I can then make my way to the barracks where Ahni is quartered, speak with her, and make my exit before sunrise. If Ahni is willing and able, she could exit the fort through the hole with me."

"It would be wondrous if she is recovered and you can accomplish her escape. I will pray for that triumph," Yonah said sincerely, although not without a trace of doubt in his voice. "I suggest we use the hours until then to get some rest. We shall take turns keeping watch while the others sleep. I will take the last watch to be sure and wake you at the proper time." He marked the position of the moon, showing Tom and Sal the distance it would move as each hour passed.

Tom took the first watch, followed by Sal, then Yonah, who insisted that Guwaya rest undisturbed as he would need all his alertness to enter the fort. They all woke when Yonah alerted Guwaya that the time had come.

"If all goes well, I will return to this place well before sunrise. If Ahni is with me, we can be clear of the fort before the vendors start to arrive." Guwaya accepted their final words of caution and made his way back to the appointed place in the fort wall, the others watching as before. This time he was even less visible; clouds had formed during the night, dimming the moonlight. He disappeared from view and it was impossible to tell if he had entered the fort.

"I can't imagine how Ahni would have the strength to come back with Guwaya," said Tom. "She was extremely weak when we saw her."

Yonah nodded curtly, then raised his eyebrows and said, "Nevertheless, we should be prepared for her. While we wait Guwaya's return, let us fashion a travois for her."

"Fashion a travo-what?" Sal asked.

"A travois is like a v-shaped stretcher," Tom answered for Yonah. "One end is narrow so it can be dragged by a single person. Do you think a travois will work on such hilly terrain, Yonah?"

"It will be good enough to help her part of the way, depending on her condition, and will be much easier on us to pull rather than carry. We may need to refashion it as a stretcher for part of the way." Yonah was very doubtful that Ahni would agree to leave, but he would stay positive for Guwaya's sake. Assembling the travois would also give the two white men something to do while they waited.

"We will need two long green poles of the same length and some strong vines to form a web between them. Tom, if you are familiar with a travois you know what we need. We must be quiet in our work; even though we are far enough from the fort, be cautious that the sound of our labors does not become too loud. Sounds can carry far on such a still night, and we do not want to endanger Guwaya by alerting the guards."

Tom and Sal were able to find two sturdy saplings that had been recently cut, probably left over from the construction of the stockade. They lugged them back to Yonah, who was busily stripping leaves from the vines he had gathered. They were in the process of wrapping the vines around the poles when they were startled by Guwaya's voice. He had returned much sooner than they expected.

"That will not be necessary," he said, indicating the travois, his voice very low and somber.

"That was a quick trip, dude," said Sal. "How is she doing? Wouldn't she come with you?"

"It was not necessary to enter the fort," he mumbled.

"Why the heck not?" Sal asked.

Tom and Yonah exchanged an unhappy glance. Tom placed a restraining hand on Sal's shoulder and shook his head, halting any further questions.

"Springwater informed me that my mother passed away in the night," Guwaya replied.

"It is a great loss to you, Guwaya. You will suffer, but hers has mercifully ended," said Yonah. "I am sorry you did not get a chance to speak with her a final time."

Tom and Sal also offered their condolences. Guwaya made no reply for several moments, and then abruptly said, "We should depart while there is still darkness. My family awaits our return." Not waiting for a reply, he began a fast-paced walk in the direction of the cave.

The others followed in silence, leaving the unassembled travois behind.

Chapter fifty-one

*A*fter Benjamin and Isaac rearranged the wagon, Catherine and Alice prepared a snug niche for Sally to lie behind the seat. There would be room for two on the seat, one to drive the wagon and another to tend Sally. The others would walk alongside.

The preparations for departure were hasty. It was just barely after sunrise when the soldiers began hustling the Indians through the gate, beginning their march to Ross's Landing. The officers did their best to keep order amidst chaos, not tolerating any deviation from their schedule. While the majority of the soldiers conducted themselves professionally, there were incidents of callousness by some of the lower ranks and mercenaries. For now, the worst behavior was tempered by the belief that justice, as far as the white Georgians were concerned, was finally being carried out. The bulk of the abuse today was limited to shoving and needlessly harsh commands to prod the Cherokees along.

In fact, many of the Cherokee themselves were gratified to be leaving the stench of the crowded stockade behind. The number of captives held in the fort had grown to over five hundred people, with only the bare minimum of facilities for half that number. In those conditions they had become filthy, tattered, unhealthy, and ill-tempered. Even with the long, difficult march ahead, the thought of leaving Fort Wool was liberating.

The Rogers would be among those relieved to be leaving, if not for their unease about subjecting Sally to the journey before she had had a chance to fully recover. Still pale, her color had only just begun to return. She was still too weak to walk or stand on her own. Benjamin did his best to keep his anxiety concealed, smiling as he carried her to the wagon and passed her to Catherine. He reassured her that he would be near, walking next to the wagon if she needed him. His voiced cracked when he saw her respond with a feeble smile. Catherine would take the first turn riding with her, sitting next to Isaac who was driving the wagon.

Benjamin was just about to give Isaac the order to move out when he felt the sudden jolt of a soldier shove him from behind. "Git goin'," he heard the soldier command. Benjamin scowled, but resisted the urge to retort. Instead, he nodded to Isaac, setting the Rogers family, along with Adam and Alice, into motion as they joined the long procession of people shuffling through the fort's gate.

Constance had also arrived at the fort early, bringing with her fresh, clean blankets for Sally's bedding, and some jars of broth that the sick youngster could tolerate better than solid food. She had grudgingly given up trying to persuade Adam and Alice to reconsider their decision. This morning she contented herself with farewells to them and the Cherokees she had come to know. She reminded them all that they would be in her prayers.

The early morning fresh air and surrounding mountain views was uplifting, in spite of the gloomy circumstances. Those who had retained their good health appreciated the openness after having been confined in the stifling fort for many weeks. Billy, who had been downcast the last several days, livened considerably and asked his father's permission to join a group of his friends. Benjamin agreed, happy to see his son regaining some of his lost vigor. If only Sally would respond in kind, he thought.

The initial gratification of their release from confinement was regrettably short-lived. After only about five miles of the more than fifty mile march, weariness began to set in, especially among the elders, and the monotonous trek lent itself to silent contemplation of the loss of their homelands. Most trudged along in silence.

There had been no rain for several weeks and the climate had been hotter than usual. The trail was dusty and the passing of so many feet raised a cloud of dust, covering all but those in the very front with a layer of fine, red dirt. Many of the smaller creeks had gone dry, creeks that they had intended to use to replenish water supplies. There would be plenty of water when they reached the river at Ross's Landing, but it would be a long, dry walk getting there.

In fact, Ross's Landing was merely the beginning of their exodus. The site was part of the Cherokee Nation, a thriving river port that was once known as the "Old French Store." It had been owned by John Ross, where he operated a trading post, warehouse, wharf, and ferry service. It would now serve as one of two main embarkation points for larger groups of Indians being evicted to the western Indian Territory. The second embarkation point was at the Cherokee Agency near Rattlesnake Springs, Tennessee.

Once they reached Ross's Landing, the Cherokees would be loaded onto riverboats, where the next leg of their journey would take them southwest via the Tennessee River to the Mississippi, then finally to the Arkansas River and Fort Smith, located at the border of Indian Territory. Captain Martin would only accompany the detachment as far as Ross's Landing, where he would return to Fort Wool to lead additional groups along the same route. He was to continue this duty until no Cherokee remained in Georgia.

Adam was troubled by his recollection about the timeline of the Trail of Tears. He had read that these first groups, who were led along what became known as the water route, suffered some of the most tragic consequences. Casualties were so high due to sickness caused by the extreme heat and lack of clean drinking water that the removal was postponed until cooler weather. The result of that decision caused weeks of detention at Ross's Landing in even more crowded conditions. An alternative land route was selected, which meant much greater distances had to be traversed on foot, and the cooler weather quickly turned to freezing temperatures. He would feel no less distress for his friends if they were part of the latter group.

He walked along with Jimmy and Rebecca, more toward the front of the line than the Rogers family. Having been ejected from their home in the manner they were, leaving nearly all of their possessions behind, they had little to carry. He spoke with Jimmy about farming technology, and although Jimmy only half-heartedly participated in the conversation, it served to keep their minds from more dreadful thoughts.

Rebecca seemed to have essentially recovered from her ordeal, or at least she was hiding her discomfort well. Adam presumed this was mostly for Jimmy's benefit, noticing that she still flinched any time one of the soldiers raised his voice or approached too closely.

By mid-day, the weariness of walking through the clouds of dust began to take its toll. The goal of fifteen miles per day was aggressive considering the conditions and the mountainous terrain, particularly for the elderly and small children. The procession halted frequently, though only for moments as the soldiers would not tolerate longer delays. Any group pausing for one reason or another would be passed by and badgered by the soldiers until they were underway once again.

Suddenly, an event occurred that caused both Cherokee and soldiers to come to an abrupt halt. A single, tremendous wave of thunder rumbled over them from behind, shaking the earth as it rolled from east to west, as if the land itself was making known its disapproval of the mistreatment of its ancient caretakers. The sky remained clear, the sun bright, with no sign of an approaching storm; just a final resounding grumble of outrage. All stood in silence, looking at the sky until it passed, then once again continued the trek that would lead the Cherokee away from their primordial homeland forever.

The procession moved slowly enough that Catherine, Alice, and Silvey could climb in and out of the wagon as it moved along, taking turns looking after Sally. The women regularly wiped the dirt from Sally's face to relieve her from the irritation, and moistened a cloth for her to breathe through, trying to prevent the great clouds of dust from congesting her lungs. In spite of their efforts, Sally's breathing became labored, causing her fits of coughing. Aware of her distress, Benjamin led the wagon to the side of the road, away from the worst of the billowing dirt clouds.

"Move along; no stopping!" one of the soldiers yelled at Benjamin.

"My daughter is ill and cannot breathe in all this dust," Benjamin said.

"We can't stop every time someone coughs," he said tersely. The soldier looked into the wagon at Sally, who was coughing and hacking, trying to catch her breath. He flinched when he saw her pallid face. "Only for a moment," he conceded. "We must keep going. The dust will be worse further to the rear."

Another soldier approached him as he was walking away. "What's the holdup here?"

"They are stopping to get the little girl out of the dust. I told them they could stop only for a moment. She looks pretty poorly."

"So what? Ya feel sorry for 'em? One less to deal with, I say. It ain't like they're human or anything."

The first soldier shook his head in disbelief at the man's callousness, but made no reply to him. "Get going as quickly as you can," he said to Benjamin. He grabbed the other soldier by the arm, leading him away.

Benjamin and Isaac used a blanket to rig up a tent-like covering in the wagon to cover Sally. It would make it more difficult for the women to tend to her, but it might keep some of the dust away. They had barely finished when the next pair of soldiers came along, yelling at them to get moving. Sally's hacking had eased for the moment, so Benjamin obliged the soldiers by pulling the wagon back in line.

The tent helped a little, although much of the fine, red dust still managed to find its way around the sides and onto Sally. The soldier had been right, the dust was even worse toward the rear.

The march continued until late evening, when the officers passed word down the line to stop for the night. It was barely dusk, but they had arrived at some open pastureland that would serve as a good place to camp. They needed the remaining light for the Cherokees to prepare their evening meals from the rations they brought. Tents were made available, but most of the Indians were too hot and too tired to need them. Many simply collapsed on the ground, some not even possessing the energy to eat.

Sally was in dire shape. She rasped with every breath, and her fever was once again elevated. Silvey warmed some of Constance's broth over their campfire, which Catherine hoped would sooth her raw throat. Sally would take in very little, most of which she could not swallow without setting off another coughing fit. She became frustrated with the effort, and even Alice could not persuade her to continue eating. She was exhausted, sleeping very little during her ride. The bumping and jostling of the wagon had kept her awake even when she wasn't choking on dust.

Jimmy, Rebecca, and Adam made their camp along with the Rogers family. Rebecca made a strong, sweet-smelling tea from the bark of a cherry tree, which she said would sooth Sally's throat and ease her coughing, helping her get to sleep. As she encouraged her to sip the soothing brew, Alice told Sally's favorite story, *Basil, the Builder Beaver*, which she never seemed to tire of hearing. Alice had barely gotten halfway through the story before the girl fell asleep, soon followed by the rest of the group.

The sound of reveille woke them at sunrise. With barely enough time for morning routines or a quick breakfast, the Cherokees were once again jostled into line to continue their march. The livestock were given adequate care, considered more important than the Indians, especially to the Georgia Militia who were finally ridding themselves of the primary obstacle to procuring the valuable Cherokee lands.

Sally continued to sleep as Benjamin tenderly carried her to her place in the wagon. She had slept fitfully during the night, her fever elevated though she seemed slightly cooler this morning. Catherine gently washed her face once again, and situated her into a comfortable position, careful not to wake her. Her breathing was still labored and shallow.

The forced march commenced, absent of any elation the freedom from the fort had given them. Having no other choice, they shuffled on, muscles aching from the previous day of walking and the night spent on the hard, damp ground. The morning dew that had been keeping the dust to a minimum burned off quickly as the rising sun, bright and hot, assured another scorching, dusty day. By mid-morning, the billowing red dust clouds enveloped everything.

Sally drifted in and out of an uneasy sleep for most of the morning. When she finally became fully awake, she was struck by a violent fit of coughing and hacking as her lungs tried to clear themselves of the thick mucus and dust. Catherine held her as she hung over the side of the wagon spitting out globs of phlegm. Sally reeled from the effort, slipping and banging her head against the side of the bouncing wagon. Her mother gripped her tightly, preventing her from falling under the turning wagon wheels, but the blow had rendered the girl unconscious. Catherine screamed at Benjamin, who was driving the wagon, to stop as she clung to the limp girl. He immediately reined the horses, bringing the wagon to a halt, and helped Catherine pull Sally back to safety.

Benjamin looked at his daughter, who was unconscious, covered in dirt-caked mucus, and bleeding from the gash on her forehead. He slammed his fist on the wooden seat and said, "That's it! We go no further." He had stopped the wagon in the center of the road, causing all who followed behind to detour around him.

A redheaded sergeant rode up to investigate the cause of the congestion. "What's all the shenanigans here, laddie, holdin' everything up? You'll be gettin' this wagon moving!" the sergeant said in a heavy Irish accent.

Benjamin scowled. "I will not! My daughter is sick and now injured and I must stop to care for her."

"Ye cannot stop here, ye dosser. Care for her if ye must, but keep your wagon moving!"

"No! The dust is too much for her. She needs to rest and breathe air free of all this dirt."

"I said get yer arse up the yard now, afore I deal you a sockdolager to knock ye to motion!" the short-tempered Irishman commanded forcefully, clenching his fists.

Benjamin was not intimidated. He folded his arms across his chest and stared at the soldier, daring the man to force him to move.

The sergeant unholstered his pistol and leveled it at Benjamin. "I told ye to get this wagon movin'. I will not tell ye again."

Benjamin continued to stare obstinately at the man, clearly intending to ignore his order. A small crowd of Cherokees had gathered around the wagon, witnessing the exchange. A few grumbled in protest, but most remained silent, waiting to see what would happen next.

"I will not endanger my child's life further. Shoot me if you will, but we are stopping here until she recovers."

"I've had about all the effrontery I'm gonna take from ye," the soldier said, aiming his pistol truculently at Benjamin's head.

"At ease, sergeant!" a voice commanded. Captain Martin had ridden up behind him to investigate the gathering crowd.

"Sir," the sergeant said lowering his pistol but keeping it pointed at Benjamin. "This here coffer refuses to move. His wagon is blocking the road and he will not obey me orders."

"Holster that weapon, sergeant." Captain Martin recognized Benjamin and asked, "What is wrong, Benjamin? Is your daughter worsening?"

"She is. The dust from the trail is severely impairing her breathing, and she has fallen and hit her head. I will not go on until she can be tended to."

The Captain looked into the wagon at Sally and said, "I see, but you cannot block the road. Please pull over to the side so the others can pass." He looked at the sergeant and said, "That will be all sergeant. Back to your duties."

He shook his redheaded mop in disbelief. "But I ..."

"I said that will be all," Martin commanded. He placed his hand on the hilt of his sword.

"Yes, sir!" The sergeant jerked his horse's reins, whipping around and galloping off.

"The rest of you move along," Martin said to the crowd of Cherokees. Benjamin moved the wagon to the side of the road as the crowd dispersed.

"For heaven's sake, we must get her out of all this dust for a while," Alice told Captain Martin. "Her fever is back, and she can hardly breathe."

"I can allow them some time to tend to her, but they must be back on the move before the line passes."

"That is impossible," said Benjamin. "She cannot travel in all this dust."

"And the blow to her head may have given her a concussion," said Alice. "Moving her too much could kill her, you fool!"

Catherine gasped at Alice's statement. "Captain, please! You must not put my daughter's life in more jeopardy."

Captain Martin was at a loss for words, not at all pleased with Alice for frightening the girl's mother, perhaps needlessly. His charge was to bring this group to Ross's Landing, and he could not disobey his orders, yet he felt sympathy for the Rogers.

"Captain," said Benjamin, "please let us stay here until we are sure Sally is able to travel. We can follow later, perhaps by tomorrow, well behind the line and out of the dust. I give you my word I will continue on to Ross's Landing as soon as Sally is recovered."

"I cannot simply take your word for that! If you were to run off, I could face court-martial for dereliction of my duties!"

"If Benjamin gives you his word," said Adam, "you can be certain he'll keep it. If I know him at all, I know that."

Captain Martin stared at him with incredulity. These people expected him to trust them not to run off if he gave them a chance? They must think him a fool. Still, if he ordered them on and something happened to the little girl… He looked at Benjamin and detected not a hint of deception, only the pleading face of a loving parent, and thought of his own daughters. He could hardly believe what he was considering.

"He'd better. I will allow you to camp here and tend to her, but you must be on your way before I return with the next group. Otherwise, you will travel once again in their dust. If you attempt to run off, the military will find you and I cannot be accountable for the consequences."

"Wado, Captain Martin," said Benjamin. "I have given you my word, and will not break it."

"And I have the word of you others as well?" Captain Martin asked Jimmy and Rebecca. They nodded in agreement, as did the two slaves. He accepted their promise, wheeled his horse, and galloped off. He was certain he had just destroyed his career.

Chapter fifty-two

*B*enjamin made camp in a shady clearing well away from the well-traveled road, adjacent to a much smaller and less used trail coming down from the mountains to the west. The small glen was quiet and protected from the elements with a nearby stream for fresh water. It was a good place to make their camp while Sally recovered. The distraught father carried her from the wagon and gently laid her on a bed of soft leaves and blankets. Catherine bandaged her forehead and kept her cool with a damp cloth while Rebecca scoured the area for plants she could use for medications. Sally had not recovered consciousness since hitting her head on the wagon. She was breathing easier, but her fever had become even higher.

Jimmy and Billy had gone off hunting fresh meat for their dinner, and the two slaves busied themselves with gathering firewood and other chores, leaving Alice and Adam the opportunity to speak privately.

"With everything else that's been going on," said Alice, "we haven't had a chance to think about our own problems. Have you thought any more about how we can get home?"

"I've thought about it almost constantly," said Adam. "I haven't had any other ideas, though, other than hoping we'd be led to a solution that would take us back."

"You haven't mentioned the LANav for a while. Is that thing even still working?"

"I've kept it out of sight for obvious reasons, but yes, it's still working. I've checked it from time to time when I had the chance. For a while it showed four separate points on the display when I set it to 'show current location'. One was always at my location, so I assumed the other three dots were you, Sal, and Tom. I confirmed that when we met up at the fort; the four dots became three. Some time back, the three points became only two—one at our location and another that has moved around quite a bit. I assume that must mean that Tom and Sal are together now."

"Oh, dear! Or it could mean that..." Alice didn't finish her thought.

"That something happened to one of them? Yes, I thought about that too. Not something I want to consider without knowing for sure. Anyway, the second dot has been moving steadily toward us. If it is either Tom or Sal, or hopefully both, we'll all be together soon." Adam pulled out the LANav and held it up to show Alice the two flashing dots on the display. As she watched, the two green dots moved slightly closer together. "It's kind of incredible that it can track all of our current locations."

"You find that kind of incredible?" She looked at him wide-eyed. "The damn thing sent us back in time! After that, I'm not going to be surprised by anything it can do!"

"Yeah, point taken. Guess that was just the geek in me talking. Anyway, from the speed the dots are converging, they should be here sometime tomorrow. It will be good to see them both, and hopefully they've had a less eventful time than we have."

"Hopefully-- if it's even them. With Sal, though, I've a feeling their time won't have been less eventful."

"You're probably right about that," Adam replied with half a grin.

Jimmy and Billy returned from their hunt with several squirrels and a couple of rabbits. Alice helped Silvey with the preparation of the food, leaving Catherine and Rebecca free to tend to Sally. Rebecca had managed to find a number of suitable plants to concoct several herbal remedies. She applied a topical salve to the wound on her forehead, but could not administer any of her internal remedies while the girl was unresponsive.

Suddenly, while Catherine was cradling her daughter's head, she jolted awake and began to vomit. When the spasm finally passed, she lolled her head and asked, "Where am I? What happened?"

"Shh," her mother said. "You hit your head on the wagon and we have stopped here to camp. Just rest now."

"The wagon? Why were we in the wagon? Oh, my head is ringing and I'm going to be sick again." She vomited violently again. When she calmed, she fell back into a semi-stupor, mumbling incoherently.

Rebecca rushed to her side and examined her, finding one of her pupils to be grossly dilated. "The blow may have been more serious than we thought," Rebecca said. "Her head could be bleeding inside. We must try to keep her calm."

Rebecca was able to administer a few sips of her herbal tea, which she said would help to settle her stomach and quiet her, although each time Sally moved, she quivered and retched. Catherine was beside herself with anxiety for her child. Benjamin did his best to withhold a show of emotion for Catherine's sake, lovingly hugging his wife, trying to provide comfort. Alice took her place next to Rebecca, stroking Sally's head and speaking softly to her.

"Your voice seems to calm her even more than my tea," said Rebecca. "Keeping her still is imperative; you should keep talking to her."

Alice kept her vigil, speaking tenderly, telling her Basil the Beaver stories and anything else she could think of. No one felt like eating, but they passed around a few morsels while everyone sat in a tight circle around Sally, all listening to Alice's soothing whispers. They sat like that for hours, as the night descended upon them. Catherine and Benjamin embraced, their free hands upon Sally, while Rebecca nursed her with sips of herbal tea when she was able to take it in.

It was nearly midnight when Sally abruptly called out for her mother. Alice stopped speaking, and Catherine answered, "I am right here, *ayoli.*"

Sally looked up at her mother and father and said, "I was down at the river with Basil, mommy. He told me to tell you and daddy to be forgiving, like the way he forgave the animals that wanted to live in his home." Then her eyes closed, and she shuddered.

Rebecca moved to her side and placed her hand on the little girl's tiny neck and gasped. "I'm so sorry," she said to Catherine and Benjamin. "I'm afraid she…"

"No!" cried Catherine. "Eee! That cannot be! You are wrong! She is just sleeping!"

Rebecca looked at Benjamin and shook her head. With tears flowing down his face, he tightly embraced his shuddering wife. Billy moved forward, entwined his arm with Catherine, his eyes locked in disbelief on Sally's motionless body. He tried to say something to comfort his mother, but choked on his tears and could not speak.

Benjamin struggled with a flood of thoughts and emotions, anger second only to his overwhelming grief. He had always been a peaceful man with gentle ways, living as he taught his children, loving his fellow man and selflessly forgiving those who caused him pain. His daughter's last words echoed in his head, asking him to be forgiving. He would do anything his daughter asked, but for this, there could be no forgiveness. He could only resolve to display no visible sign; he would harbor his outrage within. Hatred for those who had stolen the life of his precious child had permanently etched a vein of blackness upon his heart.

Neither Alice nor Adam had ever experienced a death first hand, let alone the death of a child. The sorrow and loss Alice felt was intense. Sally had found her way into her heart, and Alice had begun to imagine her as the daughter she would like to have someday. Always having been focused on her career, she had not given much thought to parenthood. Sally had touched her in a way that made her realize she had maternal instincts after all.

Rebecca, though outwardly stoic, was also profoundly affected. Her empathy for the Rogers' loss was intensified by thoughts of the child she carried, when faced with the possibility of losing her baby during the attack. Her heart went out to Catherine and Benjamin, understanding the devastation they would have to bear.

The night's silence was broken only by the faint sound of mournful weeping. Suddenly, a startling, ear-piercing screech of an owl echoed through the camp. Catherine gasped, the color drained from her face as she searched the branches of the trees above her in overt panic.

"Quickly! We must gather closely around Sally," Benjamin whispered urgently. "She is still vulnerable."

The group closed ranks, forming a tighter circle around the little girl's body. They built four small fires, one at the head, another at the foot, and one at each side of Sally. Rebecca began speaking in Tsalagi, the others joining in, reciting the undulating words in harmony with her. Although he was not able to understand the words, Adam surmised that it was a prayer. He sat closely around Sally with the others, keeping his head bowed reverently, expressing his sorrow for Sally and her family in the only way he knew how, in respectful silence. At the end of the prayer, Jimmy leaned near him and offered an explanation.

"The time of death is very crucial in Cherokee tradition," he said. "For several hours before and after death, the dead or dying person is at his most vulnerable to evil forces who will try to invade the body. That is why it is necessary for all of us to gather close to Sally and pray; to keep them at bay. It is not important for you to pray in Tsalagi. Christian prayer, or even just your loving thoughts, will work equally well."

"I understand," Adam answered. "But why did the screeching bird frighten Catherine so much?"

"The bird was an owl," he said, as if that explained everything. Seeing Adam's uncomprehending look, he continued. "One of the most evil spirits, or witches if you will, is a Raven Mocker. A Raven Mocker feeds on the dead and dying, stealing their souls to add time to their own miserable lives. They often take the form of an owl or raven when stalking their victim. Our prayers and presence will help keep any lurking witches away from Sally."

Adam had always been pragmatic and not particularly religious. He was skeptical of most things that had no empirical evidence to support them, and was not superstitious. Of course he didn't believe in time travel either until recently. He was astute enough to understand that it was not only the grieving that was important to Sally's family, honoring the ancient traditions of their ancestors was equally comforting. He wasn't sure about witches, but he bowed his head and prayed that the malevolent spirits of anguish and bereavement would soon be cast from the hearts of Sally's family and friends.

The praying continued until dawn, when the gathering light of morning urged the need for burial preparations. Silvey and Catherine went to the stream, and Silvey returned with a bucket of water, which she gave to Rebecca. Rebecca removed Sally's clothing and reverently washed her body clean of impurities, using the water to which she had added crushed lavender flowers. After washing, she wrapped Sally in a clean, white blanket.

Catherine returned from the stream, where she had raggedly cut her long hair short with Benjamin's hunting knife; a tradition among Cherokee women in mourning.

Benjamin took the other men with him to find a suitable burial place. He selected a tiny clearing several yards from the smaller trail they discovered earlier. Jimmy used his knife to fashion three locust wood digging sticks, and after clearing away the groundcover they took turns digging the grave. The dry ground was rocky and hard, and the digging was slow.

With the digging halted while Jimmy and Isaac used their knives to hack away at a stubborn root, Benjamin abruptly motioned for them to cease. He put his finger to his lips, and then cupped his hand to his ear, signaling them to keep silent and listen. All four men now attentive, they could hear the faint sound of movement along the trail, heading toward them. They gently crept out of the clearing and into the brush where they had a view of the trail, the knives and digging sticks now held as weapons. The trail was empty as far as they could see. In the stillness of the morning the sounds traveled a great distance, giving them ample warning. It was evident a large group was approaching.

Benjamin whispered, "We must go and warn the others. It is best we all stay out of site until they pass." As he spoke, he caught site of a single person on the trail, well in advance of the others. "Look!" he hissed, pointing with his chin. "They have someone walking ahead on point, and he is carrying a long rifle." The other men looked to where Benjamin indicated, seeing a single figure walking down the small path, rifle slung over his shoulder. "We have no choice but to subdue him. He is far enough ahead that we can silence him and make it back to camp to warn the women." He tightened his grip on the digging stick, barely breathing, keeping his eyes on the figure coming down the trail.

All four men crouched with their weapons, understanding that they would need to quietly overwhelm the approaching man before he had a chance to prepare his rifle to fire or shout a warning to the others following behind him. As he got closer, they tensed, preparing to leap upon their prey, when Jimmy whispered, "Wait! He is Tsalagi! I could swear he looks like..."

"Guwaya!" Benjamin said as he stepped out onto the trail.

Guwaya stopped in his tracks, hastily grabbing at his rifle. He stared wide-eyed at Benjamin as if he were an apparition, and then gasped as Jimmy, Adam, and Isaac appeared on the trail behind Benjamin. "Yoh!" he shouted in surprise. Recovering and lowering his weapon, he said, "My brothers; you gave me a start. I nearly shot you! How is it all of you come to be here?"

"And we nearly beaned you with our digging sticks. We are camped just ahead," Benjamin said, skirting the question. He embraced Guwaya, then pushed him to arm's length and asked, "Who is it that follows you? I must warn the others if there is danger."

"No danger from them," Guwaya said, smiling at Benjamin's concern. "My family follows, accompanied by a small tribe of friends; John Carter, Yonah, and two white men—proven friends—named Sal and Tom Woody. They are not far behind. We travel east to North Carolina, to escape removal by the Georgians." The wound from the loss of his mother was still raw, and Guwaya sensed a similar sadness in the others. Courtesy restrained him from probing the cause. Instead he looked at Adam and said, "I do not know you, but Tom Woody spoke of his friend who went to stay with Jimmy Deerinwater. Perhaps you are he?"

"I am," Adam answered. "My name is Adam Hill." He shook hands with Guwaya. "I'll be happy to see Tom and Sal again. We were worried about them. My other, uh, traveling companion, Alice, is back at our camp."

"There has been much apprehension among us all. Certainly providence has brought us together. It will be good to see everyone." Guwaya risked some probing, "Were you out on a hunt?"

"No," said Benjamin. "We were…" He stopped, unable to speak the words, not wanting to hear himself say he was digging a grave for his daughter. He shook his head and looked at the ground.

Jimmy interceded for him. "I will walk with you back to your family, and we can apprise each other of what has passed along the way."

"Very well. Let us go quickly, they will soon be upon us," Guwaya said. They walked back up the trail, leaving the others to return to their somber task.

By the time they returned, everyone in Guwaya's party was aware of the Rogers' tragedy. Jimmy led them to the gravesite, where they embraced Benjamin and expressed condolences.

Adam greeted Tom and Sal, greatly relieved to see them both alive and well. Sal's face still bore the bruises and battering from the attack, which Adam was certain had a captivating explanation. He chose to withhold his curiosity for a more appropriate time.

The bittersweet reunion continued back at the camp, where they all gathered except for Isaac, Tom, and Sal, who remained behind to finish the grave. Catherine and Benjamin welcomed the arrival of Guwaya's group; having many friends and family present at her funeral was a tribute to Sally. Yonah's presence was particularly appreciated; Benjamin asked him to conduct the service, a responsibility customarily given to an elder.

Tom and Sal soon appeared and informed the family that their task was complete. They shared a quick embrace with Alice, postponing the elation of the reunion in respect for the Rogers' grief. Alice was still quite distraught; sharing the details of their adventures would have to wait.

Yonah announced that it was time to commence the service. He reverently lifted the tiny girl's body onto his shoulders, leading the procession to the gravesite. Once again Adam heard the group begin praying as they slowly walked to the grave, most of the prayers in the Cherokee language, in addition to a few Christian prayers, such as *The Lord's Prayer*, which were spoken in English. Upon reaching the site, Yonah gently lowered Sally's body into the hole, placing her face up, with her head toward the west, knees flexed and feet flat against the bottom side of the grave. When he was satisfied with her position, he retrieved a single eagle feather from his carry-sack which he ceremoniously placed on Sally's chest. Climbing out of the hole, he built a small fire next to the grave, and waved the smoke in all four directions. He then stood, lifted his arms toward the sky and, in a deep, resonating voice, recited his own prayer in Tsalagi, and then repeated it in English.

"Life is but the flash of a firefly in the night, like the breath of a deer in the wintertime. It is the little shadow which runs across the grass and loses itself in the sunset. All things share the same breath; the beast, the tree, the man, the air shares its spirit with all the life it supports. The Great Spirit is in all things. He is in the air we breathe. The Great Spirit is our Father and the earth is our Mother. That which we put into the ground she returns to us. Do not stand at this child's grave and weep, she is not there. She is the winds that blow, the snow on the mountain's rim, the sand at the water's edge, the star that shines at night."

When the prayer was finished, Yonah nodded to Jimmy who began to refill the grave. Adam and Isaac stayed behind to help Jimmy while the others returned to the camp, praying as they walked. Yonah also remained behind, chanting at the head of the gravesite. When the grave was finally filled, Yonah crouched on his haunches, pulling his tobacco bag and pipe from his sack, which he lit using an ember from the fire. He continued to chant, blowing the smoke from his pipe as he moved his head in each direction.

Jimmy nodded toward the trail, indicating that it was time for Adam and Isaac to follow him back to the camp. "Yonah will remain here throughout the night," he said to Adam. "It is his duty to guard over Sally until her spirit has safely left on her journey to the western land of the dead."

The camp was quiet; sympathetic whispers, expressions of condolences passed between one family who lost a child and another that lost a mother. Adam, Alice, Tom, and Sal spoke quietly, relieved that the four of them were still relatively unscathed, although too affected by the sadness of the others to celebrate a joyful reunion. The camp made a half-hearted attempt at an evening meal, and as twilight turned into sleepless night, the muted sound of weeping and prayer pierced the blackness around them.

Chapter fifty-three

The morning sky was cloudless and brilliant blue, providing a seamless canvas for the picturesque glen and surrounding mountaintops, painted with the feathery brushes of vivid green trees gloriously lustrous in the radiant sunlight. Dewdrops clinging to spider webs sparkled like crystals as they were struck by the sunbeams. The beauty of their surroundings were felt more than noticed, in the way Mother Earth unobtrusively soothes the souls of her lamenting children.

Yonah had arrived shortly after sunrise, and was speaking in hushed tones to Benjamin and Catherine, assuring them that he had safely guarded their daughter's spirit as she set off on her westward journey of the dead. He had not slept or eaten since well before the burial service, yet seemed fully awake and alert.

After the morning routines had been attended to, John Carter stood at the center of the camp and asked for their attention. He raised both hands, palms outward, and spoke. "Though we have had little time to mourn the loss of our loved ones, the urgency of our situation demands that we discuss these pressing matters while we bear grief in our hearts. Our camp here is close to the Federal Road that leads to Ross's Landing, and it will not be long before the military passes by. Those who have chosen to evade removal should not be here when they do."

He continued, telling them that Guwaya's family and Yonah had made the decision to travel to North Carolina. He went on to explain that a man, a Tsalagi named Tsali who had been accused of a crime and was in hiding there, had made a bargain to give himself up in exchange for the right of other Cherokee to remain in the state. The story had been repeated often enough to be accepted as true. They felt going there would be a propitious option, promising enough to leave the safety of Guwaya's well-stocked cave. They would go to North Carolina, bringing only the supplies that the four horses could carry. He told Benjamin and Jimmy that their families were welcome to join them.

"I wish you well," said Benjamin, "but I will continue to Ross's Landing and on to the Western Territory."

"You do not wish to join us in North Carolina?" Guwaya asked.

"What I wish makes no difference," he answered. "I gave my word that I would continue on."

"How many times have they broken their word to us? The whites have demonstrated many times their words have no honor," Guwaya said.

"That is true of them, but I am Tsalagi. Even though I loathe their deplorable actions and the unforgivable heartbreak they have caused, my word is my word, and I do not give it unless I intend to keep it. What sort of example would it set for my family, or my daughter's spirit, if I did not honor the bargains I made?"

Guwaya grumbled and shuffled his feet, kicking up dust. Benjamin was right; a Tsalagi was honorable, even if others were not. He was ashamed that he had to be reminded of that. He looked at Jimmy. "And you?"

"I made the same bargain and will continue to Ross's Landing. Anyway, with Rebecca's pregnancy, hiding out in the mountains of North Carolina would not be good."

Adam doubted that being force-marched for a thousand miles would be any better for Rebecca. He glanced at his team and was going to ask them how they wanted to proceed, but John Carter spoke first.

"Adam, I recommend you and your friend come with us to North Carolina. The planned route from Ross's Landing continues on several legs of riverboat travel, and the military will not provide for your passage. You would also be heading in the wrong direction of your homes back in the east."

"That's true, but I wouldn't want to abandon Jimmy and Rebecca, nor Benjamin's family." Alice nodded in agreement.

"You should go with John Carter," said Jimmy. "There is no reason for you to go to Ross's Landing; you will be stranded there after we leave. With no way to pay the steamboat fare, your only choice would be to return to New Echota. Rebecca and I appreciate the things you have done for us, but the time has come for us to part."

"Alice," Benjamin said, "You have indeed become like part of our family, and we will keep you with us in our hearts, but you should do as John Carter says."

Adam glanced at his three companions. Tom and Sal looked non-committal; they would go along with his decision. Alice's face was puffy and her eyes red from crying, and she had become tearful once again. The decision was his to make. He still didn't like the idea of leaving the Rogers and Wards, nor did he want to split his group up again. Ross's Landing was only a dozen miles or so further, and John and Jimmy were right, once they got there, they'd be stranded. They had no money to pay for riverboat passage. Going with Carter's group seemed to make sense. He peeked at the LANav. The display indicated a single point for their present location, and a new anomaly point, clearly in the direction of North Carolina.

"My advisors appear to be unanimous," Adam said. "Looks like we're going to North Carolina."

"Then we are settled," said John Carter. "Let us make the most of our time. We should break camp and leave within the hour."

Packing up the camp took them very little time. They spent the better part of their hour on farewells, each group wishing the other well and promises of prayer for their safety. Adam and Jimmy spoke again of Jimmy's ideas about agricultural technology; Adam insistent that Jimmy promise to continue to pursue his dreams when he reached the western territory. Rebecca thanked Adam profusely once again for the part he played in her rescue.

"We will miss you, Adam, and think of you every time we have to catch sheep," Rebecca said with a sly grin. She hugged him tightly and kissed him on the cheek.

Adam reddened, embarrassed by the kiss. Even in worn-out clothing and grime from the trail, Rebecca was still one of the most beautiful women he knew.

Alice helped Catherine and Silvey load the Rogers' belongings into the wagon, while Benjamin and Isaac hitched up the horses. Billy sat off by himself, quiet and depressed, as he had been since Sally's death the previous night. Finished with the loading, Alice went and sat next to him.

"I miss her too, dear," Alice told him.

"It's not just that I miss her." Billy's voice quavered as he spoke. "I keep thinking about all the things I said I'd do for her and never did. I remember the times I lost my temper with her, and the times I made fun of her for being silly or not being able to do something as well as I could. I wish I had spent more time with her and done more of the things she asked of me." Tears streaked his face. He wiped at them, embarrassed at showing emotion in front of Alice.

"Sally loved you very much," she told him, trying to withhold her own emotions. "She told me several times how much you always did for her, like teaching her how to hunt birds, and taking her with you even when you would have rather gone by yourself. When we lose someone, it is normal to think about all the things we should have done, but you know, I think Sally would want you to remember the good times you had together."

"I know she would, but I can't help thinking about the other things."

"Of course you can't. In time though, those thoughts will be replaced with fonder memories. It will happen quicker for you than for your mother and father, because you are younger. They are going to need your help to live with their heartbreak. Helping them is something you can still do for Sally."

Billy picked up a pebble and tossed it into the woods, mulling over Alice's words. "I guess you're right; I'll try."

"I'm sure if you try, you will succeed." They both stood, and Alice gave the young man a hug. "Thank you for making me feel welcome in your home, and for teaching me how to hunt birds with a blowgun."

"That was fun. Thanks for all the stories you told us. They were, uh, ..."

"Cool?"

Billy looked perplexed. "Your stories were cool? What do you mean?"

"It's just something we say where I come from. When we think something is exciting or interesting, we say it's cool."

"I like it. Cool."

"Please be careful on your journey, Billy dear," Alice said in a more solemn tone. "It will be very long and difficult."

"I know, and I will be cautious. Besides, once we get out there, there will be many new things to discover. I think some of them will even be cool."

Alice thought that she could see a faint twinkle in his red eyes. "I'm sure they will be, honey," she said, smiling, amazed that he could see anything positive in what he was being put through. "I'm very sure."

When the packing was complete and all were ready, John Carter called the group together once again. "It is time for our brief reunion to come to an end. Sadness, such that we have never known, envelops us; yet we must not let it overcome us. Although we have chosen different paths, the choices we make would not be necessary if not for the greed and avarice of the Georgians. I, like yourselves, am connected to this land in my very soul. Our people have lived and hunted here for generations, and our claim to title predates the *Yonegas* by centuries. This land was given to our ancestors by god himself. Despite the legitimacy of our claim, we are vastly outnumbered and overpowered. They have caused undue suffering to us and our children, and I am certain beyond all doubt that we can no longer remain here. We will never forget our homeland, but we must leave the lands we love behind. We will keep that love in our hearts, whether we go westward or escape to the remote mountains of North Carolina. We will also remember the greed and maltreatment. We will remember, but we will not allow those dark feelings to subjugate us, for that is not the way of the Tsalagi. The Principal People will endure. Let us go now on our separate paths. I wish you all a safe journey."

After a few more hugs and handshakes, the two parties set off, Benjamin's family and the Deerinwaters taking the Federal Road to Ross's Landing, and the others taking the smaller trail eastward. The latter group resumed their previous formation, sending a scout ahead who would double back at regular intervals to assure the main body of travelers that the trail ahead was clear. They also appointed a trailer, a person who would follow along behind making sure that they were not approached from the rear.

John Carter cautioned them to travel quietly, reminding them that Benjamin had heard their approach even before their advanced scout reached him. "The militia will be searching for absconders, particularly this close to the Federal Road." He considered dividing the group, reasoning that smaller groups could travel more quietly with less chance of discovery. All except Adam's group were skilled hunters, used to moving stealthily through the forest, so there were advantages to keeping the group together; a large group was safer for the women and children, and communication was much simpler if it became necessary to take evasive action to avoid a militia patrol.

John and Guwaya had planned a route that would take them back to the Cohutta mountain area, keeping to less traveled hunting and wildlife trails as much as possible. It would be impossible to avoid all of the known roads, since they were limited by the numerous creeks and rivers which had to be crossed wherever they could be safely forded. Their biggest obstacle was the Conasauga River which formed the boundary between Whitfield and Murray counties. If they could keep up a good pace, they could reach his preferred river crossing just before nightfall and ford the river while they still had enough light to pick their way across.

They halted in the foothills just before reaching the Conasauga. It was darker than John would have liked for a safe crossing, but the weather had been dry and the water level was down. He and Yonah scouted the area around the river while the others waited in a secluded part of the foothills. Once they determined there was no one else around, they signaled the others to join them at the riverbank.

John Carter addressed the group, raising his voice enough to be heard over the sound of the rushing river. "We will cross now, and make our way to the foothills on the other side. Once across, it is only a short hike to a hunting camp where it should be safe to spend the night. Tomorrow we will have the rugged mountains to deal with, which will mean traveling slower, but they will give us good cover as we make our way north."

Guwaya led the way. He had crossed this river often on more enjoyable occasions while tracking game, and knew there were easier places to cross, but those places were more likely to be watched by the militia. If everyone followed his lead and tread carefully, they should reach the other side without incident, even with the dwindling light. He carried his boy, Sagi, atop his shoulders. Woyi followed close behind carrying the bundled baby. Yonah came next; he was also familiar with this ford, and led the way for Adam and his team. John Carter would bring up the rear, leading the string of pack horses.

Proceeding single file across the river, they reached a point where they were nearly waist deep. Guwaya passed word along that this was the deepest spot, but the river bottom would be fairly flat and sandy until they reached shallower water.

Alice, trying to watch her footing in the faint light, failed to notice a log floating down the river heading toward her. Sal, right behind her, saw the log and shouted a warning, then lunged ahead to shove her out of its path. He struck the center of her back with both hands, propelling her safely out of the way. Caught unaware by the blow from behind, she plunged face first into the water. Sal tried to use his momentum to dive past the careening log, but lost his footing in the sand, and caught a glancing blow to his midsection as the log floated past. He emitted an "oomph" as the air was knocked from his lungs, and disappeared underwater.

Tom caught Alice by the arm, pulling her to the surface. Drenched, with hair dripping, she turned and sputtered a shriek, "Sal, you jerk! What the heck did you do that for?" before realizing he was nowhere to be seen. As she stood looking for Sal, another unseen blow from behind once again sent her sprawling into the river. This time it was Yonah, diving past her to the spot where Sal had vanished. Tom caught her arm again and helped her to her feet, just in time to see Sal emerge from the river with Yonah holding him up, his arms around Sal's waist. Yonah gave Sal a squeeze to clear the water from his lungs, causing Sal to emit a stream of water into Alice's face.

Alice's eyes flashed in anger. "That does it!" she said. She balled her fist and threw a punch at Sal, hitting him squarely on the nose. The blow would have knocked him back into the river if he hadn't been supported by Yonah. Alice stood her ground, glaring at Sal through her dripping wet hair, daring him to retaliate.

Sal was far too dazed to consider a counterattack. He gasped for air and felt his nose, checking for damage, then looked at Yonah in disbelief. Yonah shrugged, and with a lopsided grin said, "You certainly have a way with women, Squirrel-man," producing laughter from everyone who had gathered around them; everyone except for Sal and Alice who continued to glower at each other.

John Carter stepped between them and flashed a grin. "I hate to interrupt the games of two young lovers," he said, causing Alice and Sal to break their stare at each other and cast it on him. "But if you are done with your frolic, I must remind you we are in the middle of a river and should be on our way." He gestured toward the shore where Guwaya already stood waiting, and winked at Yonah. Tom walked alongside of Alice, explaining to her about the log; that Sal was only trying to prevent her from being hit, and what had happened to him. Her anger vanished as it was replaced by embarrassment, ashamed that she had acted so foolishly rash. Obviously she would apologize profusely to Sal and thank him for putting himself at risk for her. She also agonized over the interminable chastising she'd receive from him, probably for the rest of her life. She supposed she deserved it; she had socked him pretty hard.

Yonah determined Sal was steady enough to make his own way and released his grip. He plodded through the river between Sal and Alice, like an attentive parent separating two misbehaving children. He could not help chuckling as he walked.

"I'm glad you're amused, Tonto. She could have broken my nose!" Sal sneered sarcastically.

"I believe she could have. She must be of stout warrior stock. Good thing she likes you and did not put all of her strength into that punch. I am glad you were not severely injured." He kept facing forward so that Sal could not see the immense look of amusement on his face.

"She's the one who could have been injured! It's a good thing you were holding me, dude!"

"Indeed. If I was not, her blow would have put you in the river again."

"No way, man. I would have clobbered her good if she wasn't a girl!"

"I am not so sure, Squirrel-man. She is a most robust woman, smart and attractive as well. Perhaps you should consider her for a wife. I believe she would give you fine, strong children, and could protect you against aggressors. Your poor face cannot take much more abuse."

"Say what?" Sal exploded. "I don't need anyone to protect me, Tonto, and she's the last person I'd pick for a wife!"

Yonah laughed so hard he nearly stumbled. "You are right, Squirrel-man. Best for her to have someone who can handle such a strong woman, he said through his guffaws. "We will find you a meek Cherokee woman from my sister's clan."

Sal grumbled something like "goofy old Indian," fully aggravated by the goading. At least it distracted him from the dull ache in his side and his throbbing nose.

Chapter fifty-four

The site for their camp was ideal; a glade nestled within an atoll-like bowl, encircled by enormous peaks on all sides. They were in the foothills of the Cohutta Mountains, an immense, looming range directly to the east that stretched endlessly before them. The little niche, as Guwaya had promised, was secreted well enough that they risked a small campfire. A welcome comfort since they were still wet from the river crossing.

They carried enough food from last night's camp, so there was no need for a hunting party. Yonah, Guwaya, and John Carter scouted a wide perimeter around the camp just to be sure no one else was in the area. A schedule for nighttime sentry duty was agreed upon; one person to stay awake while the others slept. They preferred to avoid contact with any others, at least until they reached the Georgia border. Their watchfulness increased since last night's reunion with Benjamin. They were fortunate that it had been a friendly encounter; they could have just as easily stumbled into a militia camp. It was a reminder not to allow their caution to become lax and to keep alert to the gravity of their situation.

After making camp, Alice sheepishly confronted Sal, apologizing for the misunderstanding in the river and for punching him in the nose. She expected a verbal attack and was willing to tolerate some of his abuse as a penalty for her transgression. Sal's response was so unexpected and out of character she was awestruck.

"I'm just glad you didn't get clobbered by that log," Sal replied. "You're okay, aren't you, Alice?" He gave her no indication of sarcasm, no trace of a smirk, showing genuine concern and waiting earnestly for her reply.

"Uh, yeah, I'm fine," she said. He's just trying to get me off-guard, she thought as she steeled herself for the expected outburst. When none came, she said, "I'm really sorry about your nose, Sal. I hope it doesn't hurt too much." She figured she'd play along; give him whatever opening he was waiting for and get it over with. Once again she was dumbfounded by his response.

"My nose? Oh, that. It's fine. I hardly felt a thing; nothing to worry about. Well, I'm glad you're okay. Have a good night!" He smiled and winked at her, then turned and walked away.

Wow, she thought, as she stood watching his retreating back. She wasn't prepared at all for that kind of reaction; he actually seemed sincere. Was it possible that this experience had changed Sal for the better? She put that idea out of her mind as quickly as it had entered. Selflessness and gallantry were not on her list of Sal's qualities. She pondered his motives. "He must be really planning something nasty. Well I've got news for Sal; there's only so much I'm willing to put up with from him." She shook her head and walked to her own sleeping area, trying to imagine what sort of deviousness he could be up to. She didn't notice Yonah standing in the shadows, feigning disinterest, smiling, smugly pleased with his coup.

At dawn, Tom, who had been assigned the last sentry duty of the night, roused those who were not already awakened by the chirping birds. Several flocks had also selected the glade as a safe and pleasant place to spend the night, and they filled the canopy above the sleeping travelers. Had they known, they could have dispensed with sentry duty; the birds would have given them ample warning if anyone approached. As dawn became morning, the volume of their screeching crescendo intensified.

"Man, what a racket," Sal grumbled. "Sounds like a headbanger concert!"

Yonah raised his hands to the sky and gazed at the treetops. "They are celebrating the morning, Squirrel-man. They are telling you to join them in rejoicing. Spread your wings and shout." He placed his hands on the small of his back, stretched to ease the kinks that had crept in during his own morning ritual, and let out a loud whoop. "They are also telling us we are quite alone. Otherwise they would have scattered."

"Yeah, whatever, Tonto. I just wish they would celebrate a little more quietly. I could have used a few more zees." Sal yawned and did his own stretching, forgoing the whoop.

Morning rituals concluded, they set off again, leaving the birds in sole possession of the glade. The tiny trail ascending into the mountains was extremely brutal. This part of the Cherokee Nation was completely uninhabited. Very few people, neither Cherokee nor whites made their homes in this part of the mountains, being much too rugged for farm or homestead. Huge boulders and massive stands of old-growth forest dominated the landscape. Wild grapes and shaggy poison ivy vines, some as thick as a man's arm, stretched between the trees, draped across their path.

The density of the foliage and the steep crags made their leading and trailing scouts ineffective, so they settled for traveling in a single group, counting on the remoteness of the area for protection. They took frequent breaks from the grueling hike. At each pause they sent a pair of men, armed with Guwaya's long rifle, to higher ground to try and glimpse the next leg of their journey.

The only one of the time-travelers familiar with a flintlock was Tom. Guwaya gave the others a brief lesson in how to load and fire the weapon, limiting each of the three to a single shot. Not that he was concerned with the noise; it would not be unusual to hear shots fired by hunters in this part of the forest. He carried only a limited supply of shot and powder and had to ration it judiciously. The lesson would not make them proficient at shooting the unwieldy rifle, but they would at least be familiar enough with it to use in an emergency.

They progressed slowly for the next several days through the arduous mountain trails. Their circuitous route was dictated mostly by topography. John Carter, Guwaya, and Yonah knew the area well, consulting each other at trail junctions about which route would keep them moving in a generally northwest direction, avoiding the areas where they might encounter hunters or prospectors. To the team, the terrain seemed prehistoric and monotonous. The massive trees, rocky outcrops, and thick undergrowth were unchanging, mile after mile, the only deviation being whether they were climbing or descending. It was always one or the other; flat ground was nonexistent in the depths of this wilderness.

On their fourth day of travel since entering the forest, they stopped for a mid-day break next to a cold, pristine brook, where Adam spotted a few likely fishing holes. He offered to attempt to catch a few fish while the others sat on the abundant granite boulders, cooling their hot, tired feet in the stream.

Sal and Yonah climbed up the adjacent hilltop, following their routine of scouting the trail ahead. Sal carried Guwaya's flintlock, using it as a walking stick to make his way up the rocky slope, while Yonah walked effortlessly alongside, his longbow slung across his back. Reaching the top, Sal's view was seemingly identical to every other time he had done this—nothing but vast stretches of wilderness in all directions.

Yonah pointed in the distance to a thin, greenish-brown crease winding through the trees. "That is the Toccoa River. We must cross it, and then follow one of its tributaries to the border of North Carolina. Only a few days walk."

"Sweet! Now that's some good news, dude. My dogs have had enough walking to last a lifetime." Sal looked toward the river, trying to gauge its distance.

"You still have much walking ahead, Squirrel-man. Even upon reaching North Carolina, we must try to locate a safe haven where we can remain unseen until we have assurances that we will not be molested."

Sal wasn't about to let that dampen his spirits. He was elated just to have a goal in sight after so many days trudging through the mountains. "I hope this 'safe haven' has a soft bed and a hot bath. And a nearby pizza joint would be most awesome."

"You are most peculiar, Squirrel-man. If not for our circumstances, what place could be better than these magnificent mountains and all the bounty they provide? Do you not yet understand the reasons for our unwillingness to leave our lands?"

"Yeah, I do, Tonto. It sure beats the hell out of a traffic jam on the turnpike. Chill out, will you? Nothing wrong with wanting a little comfort once in a while, is there? It's an awesome place, but there's nothing here but a whole lot of nothing."

Yonah grumbled disapprovingly. In his opinion, these white folks from the future had already had enough comfort to last several lifetimes. "Where you see nothing, I see much. Generations ago, my people filled these lands. If circumstances permitted, I could show you spiritual places, ancient carvings designating meeting places of my ancestors, and streams with countless fish traps built centuries ago. There was a time when everything needed to live was provided by these mountains."

"Yeah, dude, sounds great, but I still…" Sal was abruptly cut short when Yonah suddenly lashed out, clasping his rough hand over Sal's mouth as he pushed them both to the ground. Sal struggled ineffectively against Yonah's bear-like grip until he realized the old man was pointing at a group of men making their way along the trail. He went motionless, his indignation forgotten, replaced by a sense of urgency as he watched the men moving toward the others who were resting by the stream below and unaware of their approach.

When Yonah was sure Sal comprehended the danger, he released his grip. "We must remain quiet," he whispered to Sal. "They will be upon them in a moment."

"Why don't we shout a warning, or try to head them off?" Sal asked in hushed desperation.

"No. There are at least five armed men, and they are between us and the others. Shouting a warning will only alert them to our presence. Guwaya has his pistol, but he can do little against so many. It is better we remain unknown to them. We both have weapons, and must quietly make our way down from this mountaintop to where we can use them effectively."

Sal looked uncertainly at the flintlock. He'd had his lesson, but until now had not seriously considered that he might actually have to use it against another human being.

Yonah noticed Sal's hesitation and scowled at him. "Squirrel-man! We are needed!" Yonah's harsh whisper was punctuated by a woman's scream from below—the men had reached the others. Sal shoved all other feelings aside, tightened his grip on the flintlock and followed Yonah down the mountain.

Chapter fifty-five

*A*dam dropped the fish at the sound of Woyi's scream. He knew she was about fifty yards downstream, just out of sight, washing clothing and bathing her two children. His first thought was that she or one of the children had fallen, slipping on one of the slick rocks that lined the creek. He dashed toward her, hoping no one had suffered a serious injury.

He was shocked by the sight of a shabbily dressed militiaman roughly clutching Woyi by a fistful of hair. Guwaya, having more accurately assessed the reason for her scream, arrived at the same moment with his pistol drawn. He was instantly clubbed from behind by a second man, sending him to the ground and the pistol flying toward Adam's feet. The attackers had anticipated that the scream would bring rescuers to Woyi's aid and were prepared to neutralize them. Adam stooped to retrieve the pistol, freezing when he felt a hard jab in his ribs.

"Not so fast, chum," Adam heard whispered in his ear by the bearded man behind him. The man held a short-barreled Brown Bess tightly against Adam's mid-section. He used his foot to scoot the pistol away from Adam, picked it up, and jammed it into his belt. He smiled at Adam, flashing a shiny gold front tooth, gleaming like a beacon amidst a mouthful of dingy yellow teeth. Using the barrel of his gun, Goldtooth shoved Adam toward Guwaya, who was slowly rising to his feet and trying to shake off the pain of the blow to his head.

"Release my wife," Guwaya said to the man holding Woyi. Woyi stood with the baby strapped to her back and a frightened Sagi clutching her leg.

"Shut up," said Goldtooth. He waved the gun back and forth, alternately pointing it at Guwaya and Adam. "How many more of you critters are out here?" When no answer came forthright, the man who had clubbed Guwaya forcefully prodded Adam in the back with his cudgel.

Guwaya answered before Adam could respond. "There are no others."

"Now why don't I believe you?" said Goldtooth. "Maybe a couple more screams will bring 'em out." He jutted his chin and the man holding Woyi gave a sharp tug to her hair, causing her to cry out in pain.

"Leave her be!" said Guwaya, locking eyes with Goldtooth. "What sort of coward are you to molest a harmless woman with her young children?" Woyi's eyes pleaded with her husband to not antagonize the men.

"The sort that knows how to handle a lyin' injun. An' you best hope I don't show you just how friendly I can be to yer little squaw there." He flashed another evil smile, malevolence glinting from the golden tooth.

Guwaya tensed, the huge muscles in his arms and legs bulging, like a panther tensed to leap upon its prey. He and Goldtooth stood eye to eye with pure hatred silently passing between them.

Their standoff was broken by the sound of others approaching; two more armed men led John Carter into the clearing and shoved him toward Guwaya and Adam.

"No more, huh?" Goldtooth sneered at Guwaya. "This'll bring us a good bounty from the regulars at the fort. I told you all it'd be good huntin' up here."

"Ye think there's any more of 'em?" one of the other men asked.

"Naw; that one's bellowing would've brought 'em out by now if they was here. Get 'em all together there and tie 'em up good an' tight. Just their hands so we can march 'em in."

The man holding Woyi released her hair and said, "You heard him; git over there." He brought out a length of rope and began tying them up, one by one, while the other men kept their weapons leveled at the group.

As they were securing their prisoners, a sixth man entered the clearing, pushing Alice roughly by the scruff of her neck and holding a pistol tightly against her back. "I found me the gran' prize!" he announced, beaming lustfully.

"You keep it in yer drawers," said Goldtooth. He strutted over to Alice and grabbed a fistful of her hair, desirously rubbing it between his fingers. "'Sides, if anyone's gonna taste this sweetmeat it's gonna be me."

Adam strained against his bindings, stilled only when John Carter gave him a barely perceptible shake of his head. He looked at John frantically, feeling the *déjà vu* of his helplessness during Rebecca's attack. John's eyes did nothing to reassure him.

Alice jerked her head away in disgust and received a painful yank of her hair for her effort. She raised her hand to strike at Goldtooth's face. He was quicker, catching her wrist and twisting it with a painful wrench. "Get some rope on this one," he said. "I like 'em spry but I don't want her scratchin' my eyes out. I'll tame her quick enough." He rubbed his groin as he leered at Alice.

Her captor started to protest, but Goldtooth exerted his dominance over the man with a hard stare. "Don't worry, you all 'll get your turns. We'll get paid just as much for 'em even if we all have a little fun first."

John Carter spoke up. "You should release these two," he said, nodding at Alice and Adam. "They are obviously not Cherokee and will bring you no bounty."

"I ain't so sure. You injuns don't always look like injuns. And it wouldn't be polite not to show this here cutie some of our warm hospitality." He winked at Alice, whose hands were now tied behind her back. Goldtooth tore open the front of her shirt, grabbed her breast and began kneading it painfully in his meaty paw. She attempted to twist away from his assailment, but was still being held by her captor. She writhed in disgust, and spit into his face as he groped her.

Goldtooth released his grip on Alice and backhanded her across the face, splitting her lip. He used his sleeve to wipe the spittle dribbling down his cheek, and then stuck out his bulbous yellow tongue, making a show of running it over his lips and across the gold tooth. He thrust his hips backwards and forwards, the bulge in his groin plainly revealing his arousal, and then let out a thundering guffaw.

"Leave her alone, you piece of garbage!" Adam shouted.

Goldtooth turned his smile toward Adam. "Oh, it'll be a long time before she's alone, me chum. And when we're done with her, a few o' the boys might give you a go. Then we'll see who's a piece of garbage!"

"Let these two go," John Carter repeated. "In return, the rest of us will give you no trouble." Guwaya snapped his head toward him, not inclined to enter into such a bargain. He glanced at Alice, blood dripping from her lip onto her torn shirt, and reluctantly nodded his agreement to John Carter.

"Well, that's mighty nice of you to offer," said Goldtooth, "but I don't see how ya'll would give us much trouble. Tell ya what, how 'bout you all just sit there quiet like whilst we have our fun with these two, an' maybe we won't start in on that other squaw." He jerked his thumb toward Woyi. "Make sure they're tied up tight," he directed his men. "An' if they keep squawkin', stuff something in their mouths and gag 'em. Make yerselves comfortable, boys. I might be a while." He grabbed Alice by a handful of hair and hauled her off into the woods.

"No!" Adam yelled. He continued to plead, curse, and rage against the departing Goldtooth until one of the other men punched him in the face, rendering him unconscious.

Chapter fifty-six

*A*t first, Tom thought Woyi's scream might be the cry of an animal. He had wandered far from the camp, searching for the chickweed and wood sorrel plants Alice said he was sure to find in the damp, shady spots on the east side of the mountain. The sound of her scream distorted as it reverberated against the trees and rocks before reaching their ears. He thought it was most likely only a bird, but he decided to head back to the camp just to be certain. Anyway, he had already collected enough wild plants to compliment the fish that Adam offered to provide for their meal.

Tom enjoyed the solitude, and had readily agreed to go in search of the wild plants Alice had specified while she gathered others that grew near the brook. He knew she would never admit it, but she was obviously making an effort to appease Sal with a special meal, still feeling guilty about the altercation at the river. Or perhaps she was trying to head off a reprisal by Sal. Whatever the case, he didn't mind getting off on his own for a while, and everyone would benefit from one of Alice's appetizing meals.

Before he was halfway back to camp, a sharp whistle caught his attention. The whistle came from Yonah, who was just reaching the bottom of the trail coming down from the mountain. He signaled Tom into the cover of the bushes, urgently putting his finger to his lips to command his silence. A moment later he saw Sal, who was easing down the mountain behind Yonah, clutching the rifle as if it were his most precious possession.

Yonah told Tom that he spotted him heading toward the camp and had hurried to intercept him before he unknowingly stumbled into danger. Tom's jaw clenched as he gave Yonah his full attention while he relayed what he and Sal had observed from the mountaintop. Tom's serene mood from his walk evaporated.

"It is good we caught you before you got any closer. They have already captured the remainder of our party and have been searching for others. We must act quickly and cautiously to free them."

"Sal and I could try our hillbilly hunter routine again," Tom offered.

"I fear that ruse will not work against these men," said Yonah. "They are anticipating a bounty for their captives, and are not about to give up their prize. More than likely they will assume you are after the same, and will not hesitate to eliminate competition. I believe that violence is the only thing that will deter these villains."

Tom and Sal weighed Yonah's words, comprehending the gravity of his statement, but neither offered a less severe course of action. Yonah told them they must silently creep to the place where the captives were being held, observe the positions of everyone, and formulate a plan of attack. "We must catch them by surprise. Our numbers are unequal, and they are better armed. We should expect that each one will at least carry a firearm, and perhaps a knife."

Their own cache of weapons consisted of Sal's rifle and Yonah's bow. Additionally, Yonah had his hunting knife, and Tom carried a digging stick he had been using to harvest the plants. To Sal's relief, Tom swapped his digging stick for Guwaya's rifle, him being more proficient with it than Sal. His relief vanished when Yonah handed him his hunting knife.

With the weapons distributed, Yonah led them quietly through the woods. Before they were in sight of the others they heard Adam's desperate yelling. They followed the sound of his voice, arriving just in time to see one of the men punch Adam in the face, abruptly silencing him. Yonah cast an anxious glance at Tom and Sal, hoping neither would react rashly to the violence against their friend and spoil their advantage of surprise. To their credit, both of them looked on in horror at the bleeding, unconscious Adam, but kept their wits and held their positions.

Yonah gathered them into a huddle and whispered. "They no longer appear to be searching for more of us; that is to our advantage. I did not see Alice, or the sixth man. It may be that she was not captured, or she escaped her captors and one is in pursuit. Adam may have been yelling a warning to her, and that is why they silenced him. We must know the final man's position and prevent his interference after we begin our attack."

"I'll try to find him, Tonto," said Sal. "Adam's yelling was coming from that direction," he indicated with his chin. "That's where I'll look."

Yonah nodded agreement. "Proceed with caution, Squirrel-man. When you locate him, return and report to me. Tom and I will prepare for an optimum attack, but I will remain in this spot until you return."

Yonah was encouraged by the change in Sal's demeanor. The act of violence against Adam had removed Sal's reluctance to the use of deadly force. He hoped he would retain his pluck. Bloodshed was likely, and they could not afford hesitation when the time came.

Once Sal set off on his mission, Yonah conveyed his plan of attack to Tom. He directed him to a position opposite his own, with the men and hostages between them, where Tom would silently wait for the signal to attack.

Sal had no difficulty finding Alice and Goldtooth's trail. He could hear Alice's cries and curses, punctuated by gruff rebuffs from Goldtooth. Evidently she had not escaped, and Sal dreaded the meaning of her being taken to a secluded spot away from the others. He kept back far enough to prevent his presence from being detected, but closed the gap when he heard a dull, vicious slap causing Alice to momentarily go silent. Closing in, he paused at a point where he could observe Alice and her attacker. What he saw confirmed his fears. The brute of a man had thrown Alice to the ground, and was ripping at her clothing as well as his own—his intentions plain. The assault renewed Alice's screams. She flailed uselessly against his advances, her bloodied face contorted in desperation. Her defense was formidable, but she was crushingly overpowered and no match for her brawny assailant.

Sal did not hesitate. He lunged toward the unsuspecting Goldtooth with knife drawn, clearing the distance between them in less than a single beat of his racing heart. Goldtooth however, surprisingly nimble for his bulk and in spite of his preoccupation with Alice, reacted quickly enough to Sal's charge to partially twist his huge frame in the direction of the attack. He managed to parry the knife thrust, receiving a deep gash in his forearm for the effort, but saving himself from a potentially fatal injury. While still atop Alice, using his weight to keep her pinned to the ground, he grabbed the wrist of Sal's knife hand in one burly fist and dealt him a hammering blow to the jaw with the other. Sal's head jerked backwards from the force of the blow, presenting Goldtooth the opportunity to seize him by the neck. Goldtooth kept Sal's knife arm pinned uselessly to the ground as he applied pressure to his throat, cutting off Sal's air supply. He was helpless in Goldtooth's unbreakable grasp, Alice still somewhere next to him under the weight of the man's prodigious body. Unable to move, or even cry out for help, his fear was overshadowed by frustrating humiliation. Not only had he botched Alice's rescue, his own life would be lost in the feeble attempt. He believed he had just faced the most significant, and probably final, test of his life, and failed miserably. As darkness enveloped Sal's oxygen starved brain, a looming object growing in size behind Goldtooth's head captured his attention.

Sal's attack had given Alice a precious moment free from Goldtooth's attention, which she used prudently, clawing about the ground around her for something to use as a weapon, until at last her hand closed upon a softball-sized rock. Using all of her remaining strength, she wind-milled her arm, bringing the rock down on Goldtooth's head with a satisfying thud. His thick skull prevented him from losing consciousness, but it momentarily rendered him senseless, and caused him to loosen his grip on Sal's throat. Sal gulped in the revitalizing air, returning him to his senses and renewing his confidence. He knew he would only have a moment before Goldtooth shook off the blow and resumed his assault. In a single, swift movement, Sal wrenched his arm holding the knife free from Goldtooth's grasp, and plunged it deeply into the center of the man's chest. Goldtooth went still, his eyes staring at the knife protruding from his chest in disbelief. To Sal's amazement, Goldtooth peered at him and smiled evilly, flashing the gold tooth one final time. Slowly his smile faded, then his eyes fluttered and he fell backwards onto Alice, dead. Sal jumped to his feet and lugged the hulking body off of Alice, hearing her gasp for breath as he relieved her of the crushing weight. He sunk back to his knees in exhaustion, staring in shock at Goldtooth's lifeless form.

For several moments Sal and Alice remained motionless, with only the sound of their heaving breath disturbing the silence surrounding them. Regaining her strength, Alice pulled her tattered clothes back into place as best she could, and placed her hand on Sal's shoulder, who was still staring at Goldtooth's body. "Thank you," she murmured.

"I killed him," Sal replied without looking up.

"He would have killed both of us if you hadn't. You had no choice."

"I hate this place. Why the hell are we even here? We can't help any of these people. I just want to go home."

"So do I, but we're here and have to deal with it. You were wonderful, Sal. You saved my life, and from an even worse fate at his hands. He and his friends would have…" Her tears began to flow as the horror of the attack overwhelmed her.

Sal looked at her battered and bruising face, her tears running red with the blood from her wounds. "Of course, Alice. I'm sorry you had to go through that." He retrieved Goldtooth's huge flannel shirt from the ground and draped it over her shoulders. The long shirt hung to her knees, covering her better than her ripped clothing. She continued weeping, hugging Sal tightly. Feeling her tremble, he returned her embrace to calm her. "It's okay now, Alice. It's over."

"I'm glad you killed him," she sobbed. "He deserved it."

Sal bent over Goldtooth and pulled the knife from his chest, releasing a flood of fresh blood. He wiped the blade on Goldtooth's pant leg, and stuck it into his belt. "We should go now if you can. Yonah is waiting for us. We still have to deal with the rest of them and release the others. We have to be quiet."

Alice nodded and tried to suppress her tears. When she was composed, Sal took her hand and led her back through the woods.

Chapter fifty-seven

They were positioned in a deadly pincer at opposite sides of the unaware bounty hunters. Yonah promised Tom an unmistakable signal when the attack was to begin. He instructed him to watch for his arrow to be loosed into one of their targets, and then fire the rifle into the group as they moved away from the hostages in search of the archer. The gunfire would instill panic in the remaining men, causing them to run for cover. When they did, they would close the pincer and carry on the attack.

"Just do not shoot me," Yonah warned Tom. "I am not yet fully healed from the last musket ball."

When Sal arrived, he told Yonah he had discovered Alice being brutalized and recommended that she sit out the attack in the relative safety of cover. Yonah agreed, but Alice refused. Even though she was still shaking from the shock of her own ordeal, she insisted on taking part. Sal and Yonah conceded and assigned her to a position between them and Tom, where she would wait with her digging stick to catch any of the scoundrels that tried to escape in that direction.

"And Alice's attacker?" Yonah asked Sal after Alice was beyond earshot.

"He won't be a problem," Sal stated flatly.

Yonah arched an eyebrow, got nothing in return from Sal other than a hard stare, and then nodded in understanding. He sensed the change in Sal; as if he had begun a transformation from reckless young buck to seasoned stag. The old Indian made no comforting comment, wise enough to know that words would do Sal no good. Taking a life for the first time was an arduous journey, a journey Sal had to make alone. Yonah was confident Sal had the mettle to endure it.

"Then let us end the captivity of our friends at once." Yonah selected his target, the man who was standing next to Adam. He nocked an arrow and sent it flying toward its target with a soft twang of the bow string. The arrow pierced the center of his target's chest with a thud. The man emitted a short gasp as the tip of the missile plunged through his heart before exiting his back.

For a moment, Adam thought the splash of blood against his face was rainfall, until he saw the projectile sticking out of the man's back. He watched in shock as the man fell hard at his feet, and then dropped behind the man's body, using it for cover from the unknown archer.

The bounty hunters rapidly went on the offensive, brandishing their weapons as they searched for the source of the attack. "It came from that-a-way," one of them shouted, leading a charge toward Yonah and Sal.

Yonah fired another arrow into the group, hitting a second man, though his weaving charge spared him from instant death. He aimed his pistol and shot at Yonah, and then dropped the weapon and fell to his knees as he clutched at the arrow shaft protruding from his mid-section.

The pistol shot struck Yonah in the chest, the force of the blast causing him to fall backward at Sal's feet. Armed only with the hunting knife, Sal raced to position himself between Yonah and the oncoming men, crouching to a defensive position in front of his wounded comrade.

On cue, Tom fired his rifle. He aimed low, remembering Yonah's warning. The shot struck one of the charging men in the backside, blasting off a sizeable chunk of flesh, but apparently not striking bone. The wounded man leaped into the air, clutching at his bloodied behind, and darted into the woods shrieking and whooping as he bounded away.

The remaining two men acted as Yonah had predicted. The sound of Tom's rifle halted their charge toward Sal. Fearing they were now outnumbered and outgunned, they bolted for the woods, following in the footsteps of the man Tom shot. As they flew past Alice, she rushed after them, brandishing the digging stick. She delivered a sound whack to the trailing man who yelped and accelerated his pace, making no attempt to retaliate; escape was his only goal.

Alice ceased her pursuit, watching to make sure they kept running. Once the men were out of sight, she returned to help Tom cut the bonds to free their friends. The freed hostages vociferously thanked and praised them for their successful rescue, laughing at the speed with which the men had fled. Their celebration was cut short by Sal's cry for help.

Rushing to the sound of his voice, they found Sal hunkered over Yonah, using both hands attempting to stem the flow of blood from the bullet wound in his chest.

"Oh, my god! Someone help him," Alice pleaded.

Woyi knelt on the ground beside him, examining the wound as best she could through the blood flowing around Sal's fingers, gasping as she heard the sucking sound when Yonah inhaled. The bullet had punctured his lungs; the wound was undeniably fatal.

Yonah looked up at John Carter and said, "The man who shot me…" He was worried that the injured man might launch an attack from behind.

"He is dead," replied Carter.

Yonah nodded. "Even so, it seems he will have his revenge." Bloody foam seeped from his lips as he spoke. He fumbled with his hands, reaching for his carry sack. Sal opened the sack and placed it where the old man could reach inside. He pulled out a small bundle, and indicated for Guwaya to come closer. It was the bag containing the gold nuggets he had carried from his home. He placed the bag in Guwaya's hand and said, "Please take this for your family. It is not a fortune, but it should be enough to provide your family with shelter and sustenance once you are settled."

Guwaya closed his hand on the bag and choked a simple reply. "Wado, Gvnigeyona."

Yonah turned to Sal, who still crouched next to him. Sal's eyes were red-rimmed from the strain of holding back his tears; Yonah would not approve of such a show of weakness. "I am afraid the squirrel must go on without the bear, my friend." He reached into his carry sack once again and pulled out the tin box of flint and char-cloth. He passed the box to Sal and spoke slowly and haltingly. "You should keep this. It may help you to remember to keep the fire of your spirit burning strong, but to dampen the heat of your temper, Salvador Lolliman."

It was the first time Sal had heard the man speak his full name. He was surprised that he even remembered it. At this moment it seemed especially significant, and Sal's emotions overwhelmed him. Tears streamed down his face as he took the tin from Yonah's hand. "Thank you, Gvnigeyona. Wado; I will try to remember."

"And I will remember our time together as I await the arrival of Squirrel-man in the Land of the Dead. Many years away, I pray, but inevitable nonetheless. Then we will journey together once again, and I will be proud to call you my friend."

The old man gave a final shudder, and the light faded from his eyes. Sal reached forward and pulled Yonah's eyelids closed. He hung his head in silence, feeling Yonah's warmth leave the world, as if someone had poured water on a campfire, dousing the flames and leaving behind nothing except the darkness and chill of the night.

They buried Yonah on top of the mountain. It was no small effort to carry him up the steep grade and to excavate the grave from the rocky mountain soil, but they all agreed it was the most suitable choice for his final resting place. He had lived on a mountaintop, and the view of the river below was reminiscent of the view from his home. They laid his body in the grave and piled the stones that they had unearthed, marking the site with a cairn.

John Carter spoke a few words over the grave. "Yonah's life can serve as an example to us all. He did not fear death. He knew that fear of death was to fear life, inhibiting a man from reaching his full potential. He did not hesitate when called upon to make the supreme sacrifice for his friends; for though he loved life, he loved his friends even more. We will honor your sacrifice by living on, striving to live as you did, committing our total being to each endeavor."

After a reverent pause, John Carter continued. "Gvnigeyona has not left us. He will watch over us from above through the stars that shine in the night sky, as they are windows between our worlds, and whisper his guidance to us in our dreams until we once again join with him in the Land of Ghosts. Until we meet again, my dauntless friend."

Alice gently placed the flowers they had gathered on top of the cairn, and they stood in a silent circle around the grave, listening to the sound of the wind as it whistled through the sparse trees on the mountaintop. Finally the silence was broken when Guwaya said, "We must go and bury the other two men. It would not be proper to leave their bodies unattended, no matter how despicable they were in life."

"Yes, but one of us must remain here with Yonah," said John Carter.

"I will stay," said Sal. "I've come this far with him; I should finish the journey."

"I agree," said John Carter. "The rest of us will attend to the bodies, and then return here to camp for the night. Yonah's ghost will be on his way by morning, and we can once again be on ours."

Sal watched the others make their way down the mountain until they were out of sight, and then sat on a rock next to the grave, remembering the time he spent with Yonah. Even though they had been together only a few weeks, he felt like he had known Yonah much longer. He thought about Henri Acres and Yonah's sister Meggie, wondering how long it would be before someone could get word to them of Yonah's death. He remembered how sad and worried she had been when they left. He didn't really believe in ghosts, but he hoped that the belief could provide some comfort to Meggie.

His thoughts were interrupted by a shuffling sound coming from the brush behind him. Turning toward the sound, he found himself looking into the eyes of a huge black bear. He froze at the sight, his mind racing. He knew better than to try and run, too frightened to do anything other than remain motionless and pray that the bear would not attack. The bear approached even closer and made a deep grunting sound, like the cough of an asthmatic old man. It pawed at the ground, the huge claws gouging the dirt and raising a cloud of dust. Sal heard a chattering noise and shifted his eyes enough to see a tiny squirrel, foraging at the edge of the woods. After a final look at Sal, the bear turned, and slowly walked toward the squirrel, both disappearing down the mountain side toward the river. With a great sigh of relief, Sal looked at the deep grooves made by the bear's claws. He shook his head, and thought that perhaps he was going to have to reconsider his belief in ghosts.

Chapter fifty-eight

They reached the Toccoa River by mid-day. Reconsidering their tactics, they decided to travel in a single group; the forest was simply too dense and the mountains too rugged for a forward scout to give them any practical advantage. Relying upon their ears rather than their eyes, they walked as silently as possible and stopped frequently to listen for the sound of movement in the woods around them. Sound carried far in the mountains, and they were more likely to hear any roving militiamen and bounty hunters before they saw them.

Silence came easily, especially to the four time-travelers. The events of the previous day inundated their thoughts; the brutality of the bounty hunters and the violence of their counterattack played in an infinite loop in their minds. Foremost in the minds of the entire group was the loss of Yonah. He was the stout backbone of their group. His presence had bolstered their confidence in times of uncertainty and reinforced their resolve with his steadfast determination. Yonah's absence today was very noticeable. Today, even little Sagi walked with less self-assurance.

The Toccoa was wide and slow moving, although fording it would still be a dangerous undertaking. In the river they were more exposed than in the woods and the sounds of its flowing waters prevented their hearing anyone else approaching. John Carter had led them to a place where the river made a sharp bend to the north, where its path narrowed and the current slowed even further. The water depth was only calf deep, so they were able to slosh through uneventfully and quickly return to the cover of the trees.

Once across, they veered away from the main river and followed a much smaller branch that flowed from the northeast, keeping it within site but far enough away not to interfere with their listening. Guwaya told them that some called the tributary Wolf Creek, and it would lead them into North Carolina. They were no longer following a trail, and the terrain was no less rugged. There was no choice other than to follow the path of the creek, which wound its way through the valleys and ravines between the mountains. The route spared them from steep climbs, although the vegetation was thick and lush, most of it bristling with thorns. The moist soil near the creek was ideal for multiflora rose, blackberries, thistle, barberry, and a variety of spiny brambles. By the time they began to run out of daylight and called a halt to their trek, no one had been spared ripped clothing and painful abrasions from the prickling underbrush.

"Now I know how a porcupine feels," said Adam, plucking a few thorns from his ankle.

"Tomorrow the going will be less painful. Ahead is an old hunter's trail going northward, so it will no longer be necessary to follow the creek," said Guwaya.

"That's a relief," said Adam. "I don't think I could handle much more of those brambles."

"And I have more good news," said John Carter. "We entered North Carolina a few miles back."

"We made it? That's great news!" said Adam.

"We are in North Carolina, but by no means safe," John Carter answered. "The trail Guwaya mentioned is very remote, and not too well known. However, we must cross the Unicoi Turnpike to reach our destination."

"The Unicorn Turnpike? What's that, some kind of fantasyland freeway?" asked Sal.

"The Unicoi Turnpike. And it is no longer free," corrected John Carter, misinterpreting Sal. "Long ago it was a trading trail, called the Wachesa Trail, used by many Indian traders to traverse the Unicoi Mountains. It passed through the ancient Cherokee town of Great Tellico, once the largest of our cities that exists no more. It is now used as a main thoroughfare for settlers and many toll collectors are in place along the road. They now call it the Unicoi Turnpike, and it is in use by the military for a Cherokee removal path from Fort Butler here in North Carolina to Fort Cass in Tennessee. We will have to use great caution when we reach it, for it is likely to be in heavy use."

Guwaya cleared his throat and spoke. "Our destination is to the north of that road, in the depths of the Unicoi Mountains. The remoteness of the mountains will offer many places to seclude ourselves, and it is there that we are likely to encounter other Tsalagi families attempting to avoid removal. The land has many caves and deep gorges, some so deep the sun does not reach the bottom until mid-day. It is my hope we can remain there undiscovered, in a place I have selected, until North Carolina grants us permission to remain on some portion of our lands."

They prepared a simple evening meal, their appetites depressed by thoughts of their fallen comrade, in spite of the strenuous day slogging through the brambles. Alice and Woyi prepared an herbal salve to ease the discomfort from the skin abrasions, which Alice also used on the lacerations Goldtooth had given her.

Sal made no mention of Yonah, although he was clearly distraught. His expression had been stonily grim as he fought his way through the briars, and he remained somber throughout the evening. He felt not only the sadness of the loss, but anger that Yonah had been unjustly deprived of a single, selfless desire, to be left alone and allowed to live in peace on his own land. He struggled unsuccessfully to fulfill Yonah's last words of advice to him, to keep his temper in check. While he couldn't prevent the anger, he would at least keep it to himself.

As distressing as his grief for Yonah was, dealing with his memories of his battle with Goldtooth was worse. When those thoughts came, they felt more like memories of a dream than something he had actually done. Thanks to his volatile temper he'd been in plenty of tiffs. He gave out a fair number of thrashings and received even more, but taking a man's life was never something he considered himself capable of doing. Yes, it was self-defense and yes, the man probably deserved it. Still, as vile as he was, he most certainly had a family, a family who had done Sal no harm, and his death would cause them pain. Sal tried to relax and feel the soothing relief of the salve as he worked it into the abrasions. He applied some to the red welt around his neck left behind by Goldtooth's strangling clutch, and the strong medicinal smell of the salve caused the memories to come rushing back—the metallic odor of blood gushing over his hand as he plunged the knife into the man's chest. He wondered how long that memory would haunt him.

The next day, walking on the tiny hunting trail proved to be much easier going. They no longer had nearly as many of the prickly vines to contend with, and they traveled much faster even though the trail was considerably steeper. It took them only a few hours to reach the road—the Unicoi Turnpike.

The group paused under cover several yards from the road. John Carter explained that at times it was heavily used, and there were many inns, taverns, mills, and other businesses along its path. There were also several toll bridges where the road crossed and re-crossed the river. The particular stretch he and Guwaya had led them to, he said, was unpopulated. It was wider and better maintained than the Federal Road; the roadbed was still dirt, but constructed of a compressed, sandy material, and appeared to be regularly graded. There were wagon wheel tracks and hoof prints, indicating heavy use, but the road was only mildly rutted, and thankfully unoccupied at the moment.

Hearing no human voices or hoof beats, not a sound to disturb the silent remoteness around them, they proceeded to cross the road. Sal kicked a rock and scoffed as they walked across the deserted road. "Some turnpike. Looks like the road to nowhere."

John Carter stopped in the middle and waved his arm. "It may not look it, but the road is heavily used at times. To the east is Fort Butler," he said, pointing to his right. "It was built two years ago in preparation for our removal. The site on which it is built we call *Tlanusi-yi*, the Leech place, because of the giant red and white striped leech that lives there. We have been hoping the *Tlanusi* would rise up and suck the fort into the depths of the river, but he hasn't done so yet.

"This road continues westward through the gap to Fort Cass," he continued, now pointing to his left. "It is the road the Cherokee will follow as they are marched from their lands. We are fortunate that the road is not occupied today, as the military would be on guard for Cherokees who try to escape.

"To the north the land becomes even more remote, as Guwaya has already described. Once we are well clear of this road, our chance of remaining undetected is greatly improved."

"That's all very interesting," said Adam, "and great to hear that we have almost reached our goal, but don't you think it would be a good idea to get out of the middle of the road before the military comes along?"

"We would hear anyone coming long before they reach us," said John Carter. "But yes, we should be on our way and get back into the cover of the forest. We still have many miles to travel before we reach the place Guwaya has selected to camp." He nodded to Guwaya who led the way back into the trees.

It was nearly dark when Guwaya announced they had reached the camp. The darkness came more from the shadows of the surrounding mountains than from the lateness of the hour. Adam now understood just how accurate the Cherokee description of the place, the Land of the Noon Day Sun, was. They had passed through one tiny gulley after the next; ascending the peaks into the sunlight, then back down into the gloomy valleys. Each ravine was so completely surrounded by mountains that the sun only reached the depths when it was at its highest. The flora alternated between light-loving plants on the peaks to shadow dwellers in the depths of the dreary glens. As rugged and inaccessible as it was, it was an outdoorsman's paradise; as beautiful as it was unique.

Besides being miles away from the Unicoi Turnpike, Adam could see nothing particularly distinguishing about the place that would make it appeal to Guwaya as a haven for their camp. The glen they were in appeared to be identical to the dozens of others they had passed through. Whatever Guwaya's reasons were for picking it, everyone was relieved they were finally here. The days of hiking up and down the steep mountainsides had been exhausting, and they were grateful for a place to build a fire, prepare the evening meal, and settle in for the night.

After they had eaten, Guwaya rose from his place by the fire and walked to an outcrop of rock. He placed his hand on one of the protruding boulders and said, "This is the reason I selected this place." The others looked at him questioningly. The rock looked no different than the thousands of others they had walked over, under, and around for the past few weeks. Guwaya winked at John Carter, who was apparently the only other one aware of the secret of his mysterious rock.

"Let me guess," said Sal. "It's some magical Cherokee rock that's going to open up to another world where we can hide." Guwaya just smiled at his sarcasm and continued to pat the rock.

John Carter laughed and said, "You are not far from the truth, Squirrel-man. Guwaya told me of this place he had found many years ago. I have since used it more than once during my travels, when I needed a place where my presence would not be detected. Best show them, Guwaya, before they think we have both taken leave of our senses."

Guwaya jerked his head, indicating for the others to follow him around the side of his rock. Examining the outcrop from the side, they could see a horizontal fissure running down its length. Barely two feet wide, the dark crack blended in so well that if not for the cool air flowing from it, the opening would appear to be no more than a shadow. Guwaya reached deeply into the crack and retrieved a firebrand, which he set alight in the campfire. He then squeezed himself into the crack.

His voice echoed from the flickering crevice. "Come in, everyone." One by one the group pressed through the opening. Once inside, they stood gawking at the immensity of the chamber. "This cavern goes on for a long way," Guwaya said. "Further than I cared to venture."

"You seem to have a knack for finding caverns," said Tom.

Guwaya shrugged. "One tends to look for places to weather a storm when on long hunting trips away from home."

They explored the cavern for a short distance and located several branches leading to chambers even larger than the one they entered. The cave they were in was part of an immense system of subterranean caverns.

"I strongly urge you to forego the exploration of the depths of the cavern for now," said John Carter. "It is extremely easy to become lost, especially if our torch goes out. The darkness in the deeper chambers is ominous. There will be plenty of time to explore if we are to remain here.

"I know of one other entrance to the cavern, equally secluded, which would serve as an escape route if needed. Given its size, there are undoubtedly other openings. The cavern will serve well as a hideout. It is unfortunate that so many of the supplies Guwaya stocked had to be left behind, but we have brought enough for a while and the surrounding mountains have plenty of game."

They spent the night in the clearing outside the cave. In the morning, they made additional torches and gathered material for bedding, spending the better part of the day making the cavern comfortable. John Carter showed them the path through the cavern to the second opening, which led through nearly half a mile of the twisting cave, the path branching several times along the way. The route was inconspicuously marked with grooves cut into the rock at each intersection, making it possible for one who knew the way to follow the path in darkness, but nearly impossible for one who did not. The second entrance was an oval hole, just large enough for an adult to squeeze through, leading into a sinkhole, a sunken depression about fifteen feet deep. After an easy climb to the surface they would then be on the opposite side of the mountain from the other entrance.

Returning to camp, they considered their situation. The cavern was an excellent choice for the family to hide while the Cherokee roundup was ongoing. It was secluded and well hidden, and the second exit would prevent them from being trapped in the unlikely case they were discovered. The disadvantage to being so well isolated was lack of contact with the rest of the world. They had heard the rumors that North Carolina would allow them to stay, but they had no confirmation of it. They would have to establish some means of communication to know when it was safe to come out of hiding. It would be to their advantage to locate any other families who were hiding in the area to share information.

John Carter told the group he would go on a scouting mission to seek out other families that might be hiding in the area. He said he would travel in the direction of Fort Butler, where he was most likely to find reliable sources of information. Adam and his team offered to go with him.

"You may find it useful to have us along to make contact with the non-Cherokee folks you find," said Adam. "We could find out if they are friendly or hostile before you expose yourself to them. We could pretend to be new settlers in the area. It'll also give Guwaya and Woyi a chance to get situated in their temporary home."

Agreeing to Adam's suggestion, John Carter said they would leave at first light.

Chapter fifty-nine

*J*ohn Carter and the team followed the ridgeline on the south side of the Unicoi Mountains. It was encouraging that they had not seen any signs of bounty hunters or militia. At least for the moment, it appeared the military was not deploying bands of hunters to search the mountains for ensconced Indians, perhaps an indication that they were becoming less zealous at those efforts, expecting that the families remaining would be allowed to stay.

By noontime they had made contact with two groups of Cherokee, a single family of five and a multi-family group of twenty, both of whom had established hideouts in the mountain range's many caverns. They learned from them that there were at least a dozen other groups of Tsalagi refugees who had fled to the mountains. All of the families had heard the story of Tsali's bargain with the military, and they confirmed the rumor that North Carolina would consider allowing them to stay, but no one was sure when it would happen. They planned to stay in hiding until receiving assurance that they would not be subject to removal.

The local Cherokees were aware of several white families who were sympathetic with their cause, and they agreed with John Carter that they would need to remain in contact with them. They told John Carter that there was a white-owned farm to the west and that the family living there had a connection to the military—one of the farmer's sons was an Army officer at Fort Butler. The family was well-known to the local Cherokees and had been good friends with some of them. The family had expressed strong disagreement with the removal policy in the past, but no one had been in touch with them since the removal began. If the family was willing, they could be a good source of information for the isolated Indians.

"We'll go talk to them first," said Tom, "and see how they react. With a son who's an officer at the fort, they'd be likely to know about any policy changes, but we should make sure they wouldn't feel obligated to report you."

The farm was nestled in a tiny valley in the foothills. John Carter and the team paused at the crest of an overlooking hilltop, where John would watch as the team made contact. If the team got a positive response, they would signal John to join them at the farm.

Adam led the way as the team made their way over the rolling landscape, the farmhouse appearing and disappearing from view as they crested each hill. At the top of the final hill, he stopped abruptly, nearly causing Sal to crash into him.

"Hey, dude! What's the big idea?" Sal bawled at Adam.

Adam had gone pale. "Look," he said, pointing ahead.

Sal, Alice, and Tom nervously looked in the direction of Adam's gesture, fearing he had spotted a detachment of militia. There was no threat, but what they saw was certainly disconcerting and completely unexpected. The farmhouse was gone, replaced by a black line of highway and a modern service station. They peered in disbelief as cars sped along the road.

"My god, we're back," said Alice.

"Apparently so," said Tom, looking down at the road as if it were an illusion.

"But what about…" said Adam. He didn't need to complete the thought. All four turned and looked back at the hilltop where they had left John Carter. The hilltop was deserted.

"What the heck?" Sal said. "Now what do we do?"

The only answer he received was blank stares. The shock of the twenty-first century panorama suddenly appearing left them spellbound. Adam pulled out the LANav and looked at the screen, expecting some suggestion of what had just occurred, but the display showed only a single blinking light indicating their present location. He almost dropped it when it emitted an electronic ringing sound.

Recovering from the shock, Adam remembered the sat-phone capabilities of the LANav. The display indicated an incoming call, and a soft key appeared labeled "ANSWER." He touched the button and placed the LANav to his ear.

"Hello?"

"Adam? Thank goodness I finally reached you. It's Edward Odan."

"Uh, hi," Adam said. "It's Dr. Odan," he whispered in answer to the others questioning stares. "How are you?"

"I'm much better now that I've reached you. I expected to hear from you before you began backpacking, you see. Are you and your team okay?"

"Okay? Sure, we're doing okay, I guess."

Adam realized he sounded foolish. The facts were, they were hardly okay. They had been beaten and battered, and probably were now on the verge of shock from the sudden time transition.

He needed to inform Odan about the experience they had just been through, and wondered how he was going to do that without sounding incompetent, if not mentally ill. He pulled himself together and attempted a more professional tone.

"Actually, okay may be inaccurate. We've had a most unique experience with your device that I need to brief you on. I believe it would be best to do that in person rather than over the phone. It will take us a while to get back to our vehicle, but we should get together as quickly as possible."

"That's quite fine, Adam. I will get together with your entire team right away. The most important thing is that you are all safe. I see that your three engineers are with you."

"You see? How…" Adam wasn't aware that the LANav had video, although that would hardly be amazing considering its other capabilities.

"No mystery, Adam," Odan said with a hint of dry, Bostonian amusement. "Look down at the road below you, if you please."

Adam did as he was asked, and saw the SUV that had pulled off onto the shoulder of the road. A man standing next to it, holding another LANav, was waving at him.

"Why don't you and your team come on down and we can have our meeting right now," Adam heard through the earpiece.

Adam pointed out the man and vehicle to Tom, Alice, and Sal and said, "Looks like our ride is here."

He had no answers for the team's questions as they headed down to the road. "I'm more concerned about how we're going to tell him what happened to us without him driving us to the nearest insane asylum."

"The dude's going to think we've spent the last few weeks tripping on acid," said Sal.

"I wish we had some time together to put together a reasonable sounding explanation," said Adam.

"A reasonable sounding explanation?" Tom shrieked. "How could we possibly give him a reasonable sounding explanation when we can't even give ourselves one?"

"Good point," said Adam. "Something tells me that he might not be as surprised as we think, though. Anyway, we're about to find out," he said as they approached the vehicle. He extended his hand to Odan. "Dr. Odan, it's nice to finally meet you in person. How did you know we'd be here?"

"I was able to track you on my LANav, you see. Your path has been interesting, to say the least, for the past few days since we last spoke. Goodness, you covered quite a bit of territory."

"The past few *days*? You mean *weeks*, but more importantly, we need to tell you about our experience since then, and I hope you can keep an open mind while we do."

"Not to worry; that will not be a problem. I'm anxious to hear your report, but why don't we get off the side of the road and you can talk while I drive."

They piled into the SUV, seeing their own gear and realizing that they were in the vehicle they left at Fort Mountain Park. "Fortunately the SUV was rented in my name, you see, so they let me have a spare key," Odan explained. He pulled the gearshift lever into drive, and accelerated onto the highway.

"Well, Dr. Odan, I guess the good news is your LANav is a pretty

awesome navigational device," Adam said, handing his LANav to Odan.

Chapter sixty

*O*dan listened without interruption as Adam relayed the events of the last several weeks, his only response an occasional nod or "Mm-hmm." He remained poker-faced, keeping his eyes on the road, showing no sign of disbelief or astonishment at the story.

Adam stuck to the facts. He described how they had first met John Carter at the location of the first beacon and explained how they had gradually come to accept that they had been transported to 1838. He described the landscape and the events that occurred concerning the Cherokee removal. He did not reveal the personal relationships they had formed with the people or try to describe the tragedies and abuses they had witnessed. He didn't believe those to be pertinent to his description of the LANav's function, and he believed that speaking of them would only stir his and the rest of the team's emotions and sidetrack his report. Tom, Sal, and Alice remained silent for the most part, only responding when Adam asked them for help to confirm a particular fact or timeline. Needless to say, they had all ceased taking written testing notes after meeting John Carter.

Odan's emotionless responses and seemingly casual acceptance of the report began to annoy Adam. "I can't tell if you simply don't believe any of this or what! Why do I get the feeling you're not surprised by what happened?"

Adam's sudden outburst startled Odan. He gave Adam a sheepish look and said, "Well, you see, we did in fact have some suspicions that…"

"What? Don't tell me that you *knew* what would happen to us! We faced great personal danger at times, not to mention the shock of…"

"Oh, goodness no! We certainly did not know the device would actually transport you back in time! Our suspicions were only that the anomalies may be related to events of some historical significance. In fact, none of our hypotheses suggested that you would actually be transported back in time. My dear Adam, I would never have knowingly sent you into such a dangerous situation!"

"Well, Dr. Odan, I think you need to come clean with us. After what we've been through, we at least deserve that much. Exactly what sort of 'hypotheses' *did* you come up with?"

"Yes, of course. You are most correct. I agree that you deserve some honest answers. Firstly, I must say that I don't believe I have been dishonest with you—don't mistake my subdued reaction to your report as evidence that I intentionally misled you. I was simply controlling my responses to allow you to continue uninterrupted, you see. As a scientist, I'm usually not prone to, uh, outbursts of emotion. Believe me; I am, in fact, very excited by your report. Incidentally, the length of time you were out of contact was only several days, not weeks. Had you been missing longer, there would have been rescue teams searching for you. Not that I doubt your account of the time, of course. To me, you see, it indicates a difference between the time frequencies; apparently a day in the present is not equal to a day in the past."

"Okay, but I suspect you knew more than you told me. I remember you telling me that knowledge of American history was something that we might need. At the time, I didn't see the connection, but now…"

"You remember that I told you we detected several anomalies?"

"Yes, you told me you suspected they were ripples caused by a disparity between earth-time and space-time."

"Most correct. What we determined, in fact, was that at the site of each beacon, some major historical event occurred. I left that out before, not wanting to influence your findings. I did not want you making assumptions about what you found at the beacon site, you see. If you knew they were related to a particular historical event, you would look for evidence of that; which is one of the reasons we wanted someone who was not connected with our project and had no pre-conceived ideas about the nature of the anomalies."

"I guess that sounds reasonable. So the historical event at our beacon site was the Cherokee Removal of 1838. What were you expecting us to find there?"

"We honestly had no idea. As I said, there were several hypotheses. One was that the ripple was just an echo of the event, a sort of ghost, if you will, and no visible artifact existed. Another was that the site would reveal some previously unfound archeological evidence to be studied. My goodness, being transported back to the time of the event was too farfetched to suggest, although I'm sure it crossed the minds of some of our more imaginative engineers."

"Well, now what? Now that you know the LANav's capability to transport people back in time, I suppose you can consider the device a huge success."

"On the contrary. The enormity of the discovery is astounding, of course, but it is a disaster as a commercial enterprise. A device with such power could never be made available as a consumer product, you see. We have no idea what effect a visit to the past may have on our current timeline. Changing something that already occurred could be more devastating than nuclear weapons!"

"We considered the possibility of time-paradoxes. In our situation we were more concerned with our immediate survival than changing history."

"That's because you weren't prepared to suddenly find yourself transported back in time, you see. If someone went back with the intention of making a change, well, who knows what the outcome might be. As you can imagine, this will require years of careful scientific study. And the discovery will have to be kept in the utmost secrecy, of course. We will not even be able to announce our findings for fear that someone else will make reckless or unethical use of the technology! My goodness, your adventure was history making, but none of us can go public about it, at least for now."

"That's something I hadn't considered. But my question is still valid—now what? Do you intend to turn this over to the government? I'm not sure that's a good idea either."

"Nor am I. At the moment I don't have an answer for you. Private research may be the best alternative, but the type of funding required for such long term analysis may be out of reach for anyone except the government. And I have my current investors to consider, of course. In fact, with this revelation my only choice may be to report that the project was a complete failure, and likely ruin my reputation by doing so.

"If I may, I suggest the four of you accompany me back to Boston. I will put together a small core of key engineers that can be depended upon to remain discreet, and they will want to talk to you folks as the pioneers of this technology. Together we can discuss the options and determine how to proceed, you see. I believe if you are willing, there will be long-term involvement in this project for your team."

"I don't think any of us would object to a meeting in Boston," Adam said, getting nods of agreement from his team. "We need to take care of a few matters down here first, though." That statement brought quizzical glances from the others. "Our departure from 1838 was abrupt, and while it may not be important to the technical nature of your device, we were all intensely involved with people's lives while we were there. I believe we'd all like to do some research of our own, of a more personal nature, to see if we can determine what became of them."

"I certainly understand," said Odan. "If you please, you can drop me off at the Atlanta airport, and meet me in Boston tomorrow. Will that give you enough time to complete your research, my friend?"

"A day of searching historical records should tell us what we need to know."

"Wonderful. I'll make the flight arrangements, call you with the details, and see you there tomorrow. I, ahem, trust you will keep all this confidential?"

"You can depend on it. Who'd believe us anyway?"

After depositing Odan at the airport Adam made a quick stop to change clothing. Their luggage with spare clothes was in the SUV, and showers could wait until they checked into a hotel. They still looked rugged from hiking through the brambles, and everyone except Tom bore battle scars, but at least they had clean clothing.

Adam headed to the Georgia Institute of Technology. Dr. Odan told them that Georgia Tech had one of the best research libraries in Atlanta, and provided them with an associate's name to use as a contact. At the library, the mention of Dr. Odan's name got them priority assistance from a seasoned library research director without a second glance at their scratched and bruised faces. They explained the type of materials they were looking for, and the director led them to the appropriate areas, pointed out a conference table and computer kiosk they could use, and gave them a priority logon. He provided his telephone extension, told them not to hesitate if they needed anything, and left them to work undisturbed.

They began with a search of the Dawes Rolls. Although the Dawes Rolls began in 1898, the rolls seemed the most likely place to begin looking for the family names they intended to research. The Dawes Rolls are lists of individuals who were confirmed members of the so-called "Five Civilized Tribes," the Cherokee, Creek, Choctaw, Chickasaw and Seminole, created as an inducement to those tribes to give up their sovereignty in exchange for allotments of land. The rolls were highly disputed; many fraudulent applicants, tempted by the promise of free land, had been disqualified, and many legitimate Cherokee were either unable to provide the required documentation or refused to apply.

The team discovered the rolls contained many individuals with the names Carter, Rogers, Ward, and Deerinwater, as all four names were pervasive among the Cherokee. Since the rolls were compiled more than fifty years after the removal, the team focused on the names of the children they knew, Billy and Sagi. Even at that, the task was problematic. Billy was a common name, and could be listed as Billy, Bill, William, or Will. There were fewer entries for the name Sagi, but they found the spellings of names were highly variable and could be spelled phonetically.

They turned to older records, circa 1800 census lists of Cherokee families, online genealogical databases, even military muster lists, hoping they could find references to the names they knew and trace them forward. The more sources they discovered, the more daunting the task became.

Adam suggested they take a different approach. "We should make a list of the things we know to be factual, where they were at the time we left, and combine that with the events in our historical records. For example, we know that Guwaya's family was in North Carolina, and we have learned that the state did finally allow some Cherokee to remain. Those people became the Eastern Band of Cherokee. Let's assume his family was one of them, so we can narrow our search for his family to the records pertaining to the Eastern Band. We don't know for sure if John Carter intended to stay, but we can look for clues for him in those records as well.

"We also know that Jimmy and Rebecca went along with Benjamin's family to Ross's Landing. We can assume they at least got that far and search the records for their names on the steamboat logs. We can also look for records from Fort Smith, the final outpost they would have reached before entering Indian Territory.

"It's still an overwhelming task, but we can divide it up to make it a little bit easier. We could research the family we were assigned to…" Adam wished there were a way to grab the words from the air and pull them back. He cursed himself for being so thoughtless, seeing the look of pain on Sal's face as if he had struck him. "I'm sorry, Sal, I didn't mean to…"

Sal reached into his pocket and retrieved the tin flint box Yonah had given him. He gave the box a gentle shake, grateful that it had been transported along with him. He shoved it back into his pocket.

"I know, dude. It's okay. I'll look for records of John Carter. You may not realize it yet, but we actually lost them all today." It was a surprisingly astute and somber realization coming from Sal; everyone they had been with just this morning was now dead for many years.

With silent recollections of their friends and renewed focus, they continued their research. Tom was the first to make a significant discovery.

"There was something called the Mullay Roll, compiled in 1848, that recorded the Cherokees who remained in North Carolina after removal. It appears as if there was a Ward family among the original members of the Eastern Band. The head of household is listed as '*Kuwaya.*' I looked up the word in the Cherokee language dictionary, and it's one of the spellings for a word meaning 'huckleberry' which is what Guwaya told me his name meant. He had a family of four, wife Woyi, and two male children, unnamed. That has to be them! I think from this, we could trace their descendants using the later rolls."

"Great find!" said Adam. "It would be interesting to trace their lineage, but what would you say to a descendant? 'Hi, I knew your great, great, grandfather's family back in 1838? I'm not as old as I look!'"

"No," Tom chuckled. "I wasn't thinking of making contact. Now that I know they survived, I'd just like to know how they lived, you know, and what became of the two boys."

"I do know. I'd really like to know what became of Jimmy and Rebecca. Jimmy has, er, I mean had such an active and brilliant mind. I'm sure he would have done well for himself if he ever got the chance."

"Oh, dear, no luck finding them in the records so far?" Alice asked.

"A lot of references to Deerinwater, but that was a common name. I haven't found anything to confirm his particular family. How about you? Find anything on the Benjamin Rogers family?"

"Actually, yes, I think so. Rogers was also a common name, so I'm having the same problem as you. But there is something called the Drennen Roll from 1852 that lists the Cherokees who came to Indian Territory on the Trail of Tears. It mentions a Benjamin Rogers and son, Billie, and two slaves, but says 'wife deceased'. Oh, my. If that's our Benjamin Rogers, it means that…" Alice didn't finish her thought.

Adam finished it for her. "It means she didn't make it. The Cherokee lost nearly one-third of the population on the Trail of Tears. Three of the handful of people we met died, and the long exodus to the west had hardly begun. Not talking about it doesn't make it any less horrible."

"No, it doesn't. I can't help thinking about poor Benjamin though, losing Catherine. His heart was already broken when Sally…" Alice's eyes reddened and her tears flowed at the mention of Sally. "Sorry. I know they're all gone now, but Sally's death really got to me."

"Of course it did," Adam said. "You don't need to apologize for showing emotion about losing a friend, especially when the friend was a young child. She was a charming little girl, and you got really close to her. Sally was obviously taken with you as well. No surprise there, you can be pretty charming yourself, you know." Adam's compliment was rewarded with the smile he hoped for. "You know, I wonder if part of the reason we were taken back there was to stir our emotions. We read about these types of injustices that occurred long ago and somehow they don't seem quite real—more like a story. Not quite the same as living through it. Maybe we need to be reminded once in a while that these things happened to real people."

"Hey, look at this," said Sal. "I think I've found something on John Carter. There are a few John Carters listed on the Mullay Rolls, but here's one who became active in the tribal government. This dude worked as a liaison to the U.S. government, helping to negotiate terms for allotments and making sure they received payments they were promised. That certainly sounds like our Squanto!"

Sal poked at the book with his finger. "And there's some stuff here saying that he claimed to have seen the future, and knew without a doubt that the relations between whites and Tsalagi would improve. You think he was talking about us, man?"

"Could be," said Adam. "It would be nice to know we had some positive effect while we were there."

"It also says that he eventually moved to West Virginia and had a large family there. His ancestors still live there and in the Charlottesville, Virginia area. Hey, ain't that your old stomping ground, Tom? You got some Carters in your family tree?"

"It's quite possible," said Tom. "I have attempted some genealogical research on our family, but with little success. It seems as if some of my ancestors were very guarded about their backgrounds. I will endeavor to perform a more exhaustive search someday."

"Yeah, dude, you should do that. Maybe you'll find out ol' Squanto was your great, great, granduncle!" Sal teased.

"That would be most interesting—and flattering to have an ancestor who was a statesman," Tom said.

"Here's something else that's interesting," said Adam.

"Did you find something about Jimmy and Rebecca?" Alice asked.

"I'm not sure. There were so many references to the Deerinwater name that I started doing online searches for each one. I traced one name to a guy who posted a bunch of his ancestor's letters. There are a few letters from a Jimmy Deerinwater, written to his wife Rebecca, while he was attending a mechanical engineering school in Canada. This must be him! It's good to see he got to further his education. He mentions in each of the letters how much he misses the children, so I guess they did raise a family."

"You already knew that," said Alice.

"How would I have known? Rebecca was pregnant but she hadn't had the baby before we left."

"No, dear, but you said an ancestor published the letters." Alice regarded him with a "duh" look.

"Oh, yeah. Good point," he said, ignoring her scoff. "Now this is fascinating; the letter mentions he has a friend at school named Robert Dunbar, with whom he spends hours discussing the inventions of Oliver Evans. Dunbar was the engineer who helped Joseph Dart to invent the grain elevator. I was the one who told Jimmy about Oliver Evans!"

"Oh, get real," Sal scoffed. "You think that you mentioning Oliver Evans to Jimmy led to the invention of the grain elevator?"

"Well… I suppose it would have happened anyway. But it is an interesting coincidence."

"Yeah, dude, well I wouldn't go submitting my name to Who's Who just yet."

Adam just shook his head at Sal. "At least I'm pretty sure from this that Jimmy and Rebecca survived the journey. And since Dunbar worked on a lot of projects in Buffalo, New York and along the Erie Canal, maybe Jimmy worked on a few with him. I wonder if he ever got to meet Cyrus McCormick?"

"Now that's a good possibility," said Alice. "If he was as bright as you say, Dunbar would most likely have kept in touch with him, and McCormick's company was probably looking for good engineers."

"Speaking of bright people," Tom segued to another subject, "what about Dr. Odan? We agreed to meet him in Boston for a discussion, but what's the long-term plan?"

Adam knew they needed to have a conversation eventually. They had uncovered as much as they could for now about their surviving friends, so it was as good a time as any. "It sounded to me like he hoped to find private funding to continue research on the LANav. And I think he wanted us to be part of it."

"Doing what, exactly?" asked Tom.

"Field testing, I would imagine."

"Field testing a time machine?" said Alice. "My goodness, are we qualified for that?"

Now it was Adam's turn to look at her incredulously. "We have more experience than anyone else in the world, don't we?"

"Good point," she said, imitating his earlier response.

"The question is," said Adam, "is it something we would consider?"

"It would certainly be a unique career path," said Tom. "Yes, I'm pretty sure I'd be willing to be part of a history-making project." Alice nodded her agreement, and the three looked at Sal for his input.

"Are you for real?" he grimaced. "You're asking me if I want to be a professional time-traveler? Put my life in danger by following some cockamamie gizmo to who knows where or even *when*, and might not ever bring us back? Are you asking if I want to play some bizarre game of geocaching through time with you dudes?"

"Yeah," Adam smiled. "That's what we're asking."

Sal's scowl transformed into a sly, beaming grin. "Sure, man, why not? Just call me a Timecacher."

Glossary

A-gi-'yo-si—I am hungry
Ahni—Strawberry
Alisdayvdi—Food
Anetsa—Cherokee ball game
Ani-sahoni—Blue Holly clan
Ani-tsisqua—Bird clan
Ani-yunwiya—Cherokee People, Tsalagi
Asduda—Shut up, hush
Chooja—Boy
Dagul-ku—American white-fronted goose
Dayunisi—Water beetle
Dodadagohvi—Until we see each other again, speaking to one person
Donadagohvi—Until we see each other again, speaking to a group
Elisi—Grandmother
Gahawista—Parched corn
Gah-no-hay-na—Hominy mush drink often served to visitors
Gili(s)—Dog(s)
Gili-utsun-yi—Milky Way (where the dog ran)
Guque—Quail
Guwaya—Huckleberry
Guwisguwi—John Ross, great bird
Gv-li (Guh-tlee)—Raccoon
Gvnigeyona (Ga-na-gay-yoh-nah)—Black bear
Hi-tsalagi-s—Are you Cherokee?
Ja-yo-si-ha-s—Are you hungry?
Junaluska—A Cherokee chief, means "He tries, but fails"
Ka-ma-ma—Butterfly
Kanona—Mortar used for pounding corn
Nihina / Ni-na—And you?

Osda / Osdi—Good
Osda sunalei—Good Morning
Osiyo —Hello
Sagi—Onion
Saloli—Squirrel
Siyo—Shortened version of osiyo (hello)
Soquili—Horse
Tawodi—Hawk
Tlanusi—Leech
Tla utso-a-se-di—No trouble
Tohigwu / T'o-si-gwu / Tdo`hi quu—I am fine
To-hi-tsu—How are you?
Tsalagi—Cherokee People
Tsi`tsa-ne-lv—I rode with him
Tsilugi—Welcome
Tsiyu Gunsini—Dragging Canoe, Cherokee war chief
Tso-la-nv—Window
Tso-lu—Tobacco
Tsusginai—Place of death
Tugawesti—Blow gun
Ugineli—My friend
Unehlanahi—Sun god
Usdi—Baby
Utsanati—Rattlesnake
Wado—Thank you
Wisgi—Whiskey
Woyi—Pigeon
Yansa—Buffalo
Yonega / Yoneg—White person

About the Author

As an Information Technology executive, Glenn R. Petrucci was sometimes criticized for his intimidating demeanor and for lacking a "sense of urgency." He attributes his critics' erroneous allegations to their diminished capacity to appreciate cynicism or comprehend the humor of hardware failures. Over the course of his career he has produced countless white papers, product test plans, user guides, quality analysis reports, and strategic planning documents, many of which surely should have been classified as fiction. He has also written several short stories which were actually intended to be fictional works. Timecachers, his first full-length novel, is the result of the encouragement by friends and family to continue writing.

Glenn has resided in many of these United States and has enjoyed discovering the treasures of each of them, hiking through the Southwestern deserts, biking in the mountains of the South, and touring the Northeast's historical sites. In addition to writing, his more sedentary activities include reading a good story, watching classic movies, and indulging in a glass of cheap red wine. Still a geek at heart, he enjoys keeping up with the latest consumer technology developments, scoffing at most of them as needless and trivial but buying them anyway. He is devoted to his wife and best friend, Kathy.

Made in the USA
San Bernardino, CA
28 September 2016